"The Balkan wars ended one of the longest periods of peace in European history. My company, Bavarian TV, reported extensively from the Bosnian War about unimaginable atrocities and victims of unspeakable violence. This war had an unerasable impact on the collective consciousness of Europeans and others around the world. Joel Levinson's debut novel, *The Reluctant Hunter*, demonstrates a deep understanding of that conflict. But his novel is much more than a brilliant account of historical facts. It transcends the limits of time and place to convey the truth about human nature at its best and at its worst. Jusuf Pasalic is an unforgettable character. His coming of age unfolds in the chaos of war among 'brothers' and reaches its culminating point in the most crucial decision a human being could possibly face…and the unfathomable guilt it carries with it. And yet *The Reluctant Hunter* is not only about despair and darkness, but also about survival, hope, friendship, and the healing power of love. Levinson's symbols are beautiful and his writing style is very much his own, which is something significant to say about a debut novel. I hope *The Reluctant Hunter* finds the large audience it deserves."

—**CLAUDIA MATHE is a news-editor at BR/ARD, the public broadcasting authority in Bavaria, Germany. She also has an MA in American Literature.**

"The writing is fast-paced and full of energy. There's something refreshing about Jusuf's character that takes the edge off of reading about such a dark and disturbing chapter in history. *The Reluctant Hunter* took me on a dark, disturbing, and powerful journey and when I finished, I felt like I was leaving a part of myself behind the now-worn manuscript pages. The fact that Levinson's writing could reach me this deeply says a lot about his ability as a writer. I absolutely LOVE Dado. His character is so interesting and colorful. Dado may very well be my favorite character in the book."
—**ALEXIS BARAD, author, editorial consultant, former Associate Publisher at PlayBac Publishing, USA.**

"The use of poetic devices in Joel Levinson's novel is reminiscent of Hemingway and Remarque, while the content and style are comparable to works by James Jones, Norman Mailer and Jerzy Kosinski. Levinson's approach (unusually modern) and language (bold and personal) are fresh and original. The stark images, abundant but perfectly justified, evoke the black-and-white World War II films made in the 1950s by the directors of the Polish School, Andrzej Wajda in particular. *The Reluctant Hunter* should be read by high school students (preferably as required reading), in order to destroy the false and over-romanticized preconceptions of war created by a plethora of action movies and computer games."
—**HENRYK HOFFMANN, author; Chair of the World Languages Department, Perkiomen Preparatory School, Pennsburg, PA; MA in English Philology**

THE RELUCTANT HUNTER
A NOVEL

JOEL LEVINSON

iUniverse, Inc.
Bloomington

The Reluctant Hunter

Copyright © 2012 Joel Levinson

All rights reserved. No part of this book may be used or reproduced by any means, graphic, electronic, or mechanical, including photocopying, recording, taping or by any information storage retrieval system without the written permission of the publisher except in the case of brief quotations embodied in critical articles and reviews.

This is a work of fiction. All of the characters, names, incidents, organizations, and dialogue in this novel are either the products of the author's imagination or are used fictitiously.

iUniverse books may be ordered through booksellers or by contacting:

iUniverse
1663 Liberty Drive
Bloomington, IN 47403
www.iuniverse.com
1-800-Authors (1-800-288-4677)

Because of the dynamic nature of the Internet, any Web addresses or links contained in this book may have changed since publication and may no longer be valid. The views expressed in this work are solely those of the author and do not necessarily reflect the views of the publisher, and the publisher hereby disclaims any responsibility for them.

Design of hardbound and paperback covers, map, and pronunciation guide by Amanda Lippert Design

ISBN: 978-1-4759-3898-2 (sc)
ISBN: 978-1-4759-3900-2 (hc)
ISBN: 978-1-4759-3899-9 (e)

Printed in the United States of America

iUniverse rev. date: 9/4/2012

Dedication

This book is dedicated to my indefatigable home editor, Janet Thomas, my supportive adult children Aaron and Julie Levinson, my dear Bosnian friends Azra Hromadzic and Amra Sabic-El-Rayess, and to our 'adopted' Bosnian daughter, Aida Pasalic—three brilliant and spirited young women who were lucky enough to have escaped a war nearing its end but a war which had already turned their country into a nightmare.

Amra, Aida, and Azra, were sitting around my dining room table one evening, sixteen years ago, and mentioned in several brief sentences what a man from their town had to do during the conflict presumably in the interest of love and devotion. Those circumstances were so heart-shattering, so stupefying, that I was compelled to start writing the very next morning what I thought would be a short story. I have borrowed for this novel a few of my Bosnian friends' names and the names of some of their friends and relatives, but bear in mind that there is absolutely no connection between the names I borrowed and the characters I created in *The Reluctant Hunter*.

I feel I would not serve the broad ideal of justice if I did not also dedicate this book to a man I never met and whose name I never knew. He became for me and presumably will become for you *The Reluctant Hunter*. If the young man whose tragic circumstances ignited my writing in the first place is still alive, it should be known by all that the reluctant hunter I brought to life in this novel is a totally fictionalized character. I hope I have brought understanding to what this nameless man went through and to what those in Bosnia on all sides of the conflict had to endure in a war that, like most, should never have begun. Perhaps your reading of *The Reluctant Hunter* will explain why.

*This map was prepared specifically for the contents of this novel. The size of the dots do not correspond to the actual size of cities, but reflect more on the importance of the city, town, or hamlet to the story.

*The Grmec Mountain range extends quite a distance north and south of the triangle marker.

*The light gray line separating the Republika Srpska and the Federation of Bosnia and Herzegovina is an approximation. The current relationship of a city, town, or hamlet to that demarcation is therefore not reliable, nor is it critical in understanding the story line of *The Reluctant Hunter*.

CHAPTER ONE

URGENT POUNDING AT THE front door startled him. Jusuf squeezed out from behind the refrigerator, paint roller in hand, and dashed into the living room, intent on getting to the front door before another knock wakened his mother from her afternoon nap. He pictured her eyelids fluttering, her right hand jerking away from her Qur'an and against her thigh, as it often did when a strange sound startled her as she dozed.

Jusuf hoped it was Sasha, his high school buddy, beckoning him to join a soon-to-start game of soccer. Already Jusuf felt himself dashing across the field and kicking the ball with certain accuracy. But Sasha always knocked with a gentle, musical beat, and after so many years, he knew this was Ismeta's naptime.

The last thud rattled the door on its old hinges, sounding more like it came from a ramrod than a row of knuckles. As he turned the knob, he half-expected to see Sasha's halo of blond curls and his familiar green sweatshirt. Instead, there stood a behemoth of a man silhouetted against the distant range of snow-covered mountains that surrounded his town of Kljuc. The sight of camouflage fatigues unnerved Jusuf, and when the soldier shifted his grip on his black Kalashnikov assault rifle, Jusuf's attention shifted to the gold and red patch on his sleeve, and he knew immediately that the recruit was with the Yugoslavian People's Army. Jusuf stepped back but quickly tried to conceal his unease.

The soldier hocked a gob of straw-colored spit on the stone stoop.

1

When he belched, Jusuf caught a whiff of plum brandy and, oddly enough, peanuts. The soldier wiped a slick of saliva from his sausage-thick lower lip and then cleaned the back of his hand on the seat of his pants. "Are you Jusuf Pasalic?"

Jusuf considered using a false name but feared the consequences. "Yes, I'm Pasalic." He tried to force a calm voice on top of his racing heart. "Is there a problem … some trouble in the neighborhood?"

The soldier sucked peanut mud from his teeth before he barked the question, "You have any weapons in the house?"

Jusuf was distracted by the man's huge pumpkin head with its spiky crown of copper hair. The color reminded Jusuf of the warm, butter and paprika, *zaprska* sauce his mother had poured over last night's stew. "What? I'm sorry. What did you say?"

"Didn't you hear me, Turk? Guns! You have any guns in the house? Are all you fucking Muslims deaf?"

Jusuf stared intently at the soldier in an effort to make sure his eyes didn't inadvertently rise in the direction of the attic where his father's dust-covered hunting rifles stood in a rack next to the attic dormer.

"No, we don't." Lying about the guns was easy. Revisiting his dark thoughts about those weapons was something else.

As the soldier barged across the threshold, Jusuf half-expected him to stomp upstairs and head directly for the homemade gun rack.

"Are you telling me you have no guns in the house at all?"

"Well … we used to have a few guns."

"Used to? What do you mean, used to? When?"

"We sold them about five years ago when my father died. Needed the money. My dad didn't make much. He was just a—"

"I don't need your goddamn life history. And who's the *we*?"

"My mom and me." Jusuf instantly regretted mentioning her. He hoped she wouldn't awaken and come down the stairs, particularly if she was still wearing her headscarf.

"She home?"

"No. She's out … shopping." This lie was also easy because Ismeta loved to shop, even though she rarely had money to buy anything other than food and occasionally a gift to herself of a new pair of Italian leather gloves.

"You know anyone in the neighborhood with guns?" It sounded, given the soldier's obvious impatience, as if he had asked these same questions many times earlier in the day.

"No, I don't. A few people around here used to hunt with my father, but that was years ago."

The soldier glared. Jusuf blinked and scratched the finger-wide strip of brown beard that ran from his lower lip to the end of his strong chin. The soldier looked down into Jusuf's small, dark brown eyes before turning and squinting past Jusuf into the bright, half-painted kitchen, his head cocked to the side like a dimwitted but curious bird.

"Who's back there? You said your mother was out!"

"No one. It's my music. I was painting the—"

The soldier shoved Jusuf's thin frame against a chair and barreled into the kitchen, leaving a trail of white boot prints tracked from a puddle of paint that had dribbled from Jusuf's roller. There were three pots on the cast iron wood-burning stove and a half-eaten sandwich on a plate next to an open can of beer buzzing with two circling flies. Jusuf followed the soldier into the kitchen and stood near the sunny window. As the soldier looked around, Jusuf, by habit, inserted his index finger in the flowerpot closest to him to test the soil for dryness. He pinched back a leggy, near-leafless offshoot. The soldier swiped a pack of cigarettes off the counter, left the night before by one of Jusuf's friends, and slipped it in the patch pocket of his jacket.

"Damn," Jusuf muttered, mostly to himself.

"What did you say, you little shit?" As the soldier swung around, his freshly pressed fatigues snapped like tent canvas in a gust of wind.

"The paint. On the floor. You're … I … I mean, we're making a mess of the place."

"Drop that roller and follow me, you goddamn *jebem ti mater*." The soldier walked out the front door, assuming Jusuf was just behind him.

"Now, goddamnit!" the soldier barked. "You think I'm on holiday? Get your fucking ass in the street or I'll put a bullet up your nose."

Jusuf tried to carefully set the sopping paint roller onto his college brochures fanned out on the coffee table, but the roller dropped, sending paint splattering across the couch and over the large crocheted doily draped across its back. "Damn!" He snatched his leather vest from the back of a worn corduroy-covered chair and reached for his keys on the hook next to the framed but faded photograph of Marshal Tito.

"Hey, Turk, you won't need that stuff where you're going! Now let's get out of here. I got another field to plow before the sun goes down."

The soldier walked out ahead of Jusuf, spitting another gob of peanut saliva on the pavement. As Jusuf stepped outside, he noticed a three-legged dog hobble an arc into the garden of his neighbor, Suljo Begovic. Jusuf hoped he'd see Suljo smoking one of his beloved cigars on his front porch. His father's beer-drinking partner from years ago and now Jusuf's good friend, Suljo was a lawyer who spoke deliberately and was not readily intimidated. Jusuf was certain Suljo would have spoken up for him, but neither Suljo nor either of his two sons was in sight. At the bottom of the steps, Jusuf turned to see if his mother had awakened and might be peering through the curtains of her bedroom window. He was relieved not to see her but was now concerned that no one was witnessing his arrest, or whatever it was that was happening to him.

The soldier spun on his heels. "Just a minute, Shorty." Jusuf was surprised the soldier knew his nickname but grew alarmed that the soldier had changed his mind and was now going to search the house. Maybe the gun rack had been visible through the dormer window. Or had he noticed Jusuf looking up at the bedroom window?

"You probably thought the party was free. But it's going to cost you. You're gonna need three hundred deutschemarks."

"What are you talking about? What party?"

When the soldier guffawed, Jusuf again smelled the *slivovitz*, its pungent, plum aroma rising from the soldier's gullet on the surge of another belch. "They got Madonna and Michael Jackson in town. But it's gonna cost you."

"Madonna! No way Madonna's playing out here in Kljuc, in the sticks. Sarajevo, maybe, but—"

"Is that a wallet in your pants? I know it's not your cock 'cause you Turks never had much to speak of down there."

Jusuf wanted to punch the guy and might have if the soldier's finger was not hooked around the trigger. "Yeah, it's my wallet, but I don't have three hundred deutschemarks." When he sensed that the soldier was growing increasingly impatient, Jusuf figured he better tone down his air of defiance.

"How much you got there, smartass?"

"About a hundred and fifty."

"You Muslim shits always lie. Let's see the fucking wallet."

Jusuf didn't move.

"Now, goddamnit!" The soldier pointed his rifle at Jusuf's groin as Jusuf reluctantly tugged the wallet out of his jeans. Before Jusuf could open it to reveal the few deutschemarks stashed inside, the soldier snatched it and tossed it in the air, apparently gauging its heft. Seeing there were several bills stuffed inside, he dropped the wallet into the pocket of his fatigue jacket, alongside the cigarette pack.

"Hey, I need that stuff!" Jusuf instantly regretted the remark. The soldier raised his gun barrel and brought it to within an inch of Jusuf's cheek. A trace of heat from the late afternoon sun still radiated from the black steel. The soldier slowly rubbed Jusuf's cheek with the barrel before pressing the muzzle against Jusuf's lips. Jusuf's heart thumped an errant beat, and for a moment, he feared he would faint.

"What did you say you needed?" The soldier reached into his pocket for a handful of nuts and with a disingenuous grin offered some to Jusuf. Jusuf remained expressionless, and after a long pause, ever so slightly defiant, he slowly shook his head.

"Let's go, you fucking wiseass. I've had enough of your goddamn bullshit."

With his paint-spattered T-shirt clinging to his perspiring chest, Jusuf crossed the pavement but lost his footing on a fist-sized rock hidden by the curb. Normally he could catch himself with graceful ease, but unnerved as he was, he fell into the road. The soldier walked over and pointed the barrel at his groin, a smirk on his face.

"Well, this makes it even easier." Another gob of brown spit sailed through the air and smacked Jusuf's knee. "Get up, you fucking clown, and start moving." Jusuf stood and pointed his finger in a few directions, not sure which way to walk. The soldier raised his boxy cleft chin toward the town square.

After a few steps, Jusuf stole a glance through the darkness of his living room and into the bright glow of the kitchen. His tape deck, barely audible, was playing the last track of his favorite rock group out of Bihac, Mehmed and Boneface. As he began walking, he picked stone chips and glass splinters out of his trembling palms.

The neighborhood was oddly quiet for that time of day. No sounds of red roof tiles being hammered back in place or concrete block walls being stuccoed, no children playing in yards, no cars rumbling on the road, just a few old Zastavas sitting on their rotting tires. And, most curiously, no friends in conversation on stoops or porches. Why was it so deserted at this busy afternoon hour? he wondered. And why would so many shutters be closed on a sunny spring afternoon? Was there a party in town, after all, as the soldier claimed? He saw no cars but heard a commotion of large vehicle engines continuously revved in the center of town. A pistol shot fractured the silence, sending a mass of ravens exploding from nearby trees, their wings beating like leather gloves clapped in frenzied applause. Jusuf looked over his shoulder at the soldier, who was fidgeting with the sight of his rifle. Jusuf tried in vain to swallow the saliva pooled in his mouth. He leaned and spit in the gutter.

At a narrow cross street, there was a police barricade that Jusuf had not seen the previous day. Beyond the barricade, he saw one of his buddies, Elmir Umerovic, being shoved out of his house and down his front steps by someone wearing a ski mask but not dressed in military uniform. The friends eyed each other, arched their eyebrows, and hunched their shoulders to signal puzzlement and disbelief. Elmir was wearing only a red sweatshirt and his underpants. His black hair was mussed, and one side of his face was rosy and wrinkled from a nap.

The black ski mask was unnerving. This was not just another bit of intimidation by a Serbian thug wanting extra cash or looking to rough up a Muslim. Jusuf was now sure there was no party in town and certainly no rock concert. A block further on, two more shots rang out, followed by a scream. Moments later, he smelled a faint reek of gunpowder and then glanced over his shoulder to see if Elmir was close behind him. The road was empty.

"Keep walking, you damn *majmune jedan*. That was just a few firecrackers to get you Turks in the mood to party."

As they got closer to the town center, Jusuf looked into the windows of the few houses whose shutters had not been closed. He saw only women. Some faces he recognized; the mothers, sisters, and grandmothers of his friends. He wondered what they must be thinking, seeing him led away at gunpoint. The women wearing *maramas* tied at the neck had expressions of alarm. One woman wept. Jusuf wondered whether his own mother had by now awakened and was herself at a window looking out onto a similar scene. He grew alarmed, fearing the soldier would later return for her. From the high balcony of a nearby minaret where three loudspeakers were strapped to the ancient stone railing, the usual pre-recorded late afternoon call to prayer started to drone but was abruptly terminated mid-phrase with a jarring squawk similar to the feed-back honks that Jusuf winced at hearing at the start of weekend rock concerts in Sarajevo.

On the faces of the few women without headscarves, particularly the older Serbian women, there was a blank expression or, in the case of a few, a dagger-like stare. The mother of one of Jusuf's closest Serbian friends, who had always greeted him in a seemingly pleasant tone, now watched him with a look that seemed to be a troubling fusion of long-awaited satisfaction and contempt. Her look brought to mind his mother's comment as they sat at breakfast less than a week ago. "What about Dubrovnik?" she had asked. "That's not a barbecue going on over there. People are dying—the town's in flames."

"It's probably just a skirmish, Mom. I'll bet it's over in a week or two, like the others."

"If you'd read a paper once in a while and watch something on TV other than ball games and music, you might think differently. I saw an article two days ago about what's going on in Modrica and Bosanski Brod. That's not the other side of the Adriatic, Jusuf. It's right here in Bosnia."

Jusuf had chuckled at what he perceived to be her alarmist interpretation of recent events.

"You laugh," she said, "but we should really think about going somewhere, disappearing for a while if anything odd starts to happen around here. We could visit Adnan and Arijana in Munich or spend some time with Sasha's uncle in the country." With his youthful sense of invincibility, Jusuf had dismissed her worries with a gentle pat on her arthritic hand and flashed one of his disarmingly sweet smiles, his teeth as white as their folded napkins.

"Come on, Mom, you're always so serious. You're always certain the sky's about to fall in."

"Jusuf, if you ever saw a real war raging, like your dad and I saw, you might think differently. You've seen the barricades on the roads leading into town—what are they calling it—*the log revolution,* or something? And what about the soldiers patrolling the roads and standing on our street corners." Ismeta had removed a piece of food stuck between her teeth and looked out the window. "I keep seeing officers huddled in front of their military trucks, hands jabbing the air, arguments between them, then belly laughs, and when I come upon them talking about *Turks* and *unity*, I see them glancing up side streets toward who knows what. And what about those Serb flags going up on the rooftops? First one was on the police station. Then another went up on the town hall, and now the hotel. You don't see that as odd?"

"Oh, Mom, you're reading too much into things."

"To me, it's alarming."

The further from his house he got, the more he fretted about his mother's safety. He hoped he could somehow get word to Sasha, his closest Serbian friend, to look after her … find her a place to stay, perhaps in another town with some of Sasha's relatives, until things quieted down. Jusuf knew he could depend on Sasha because Sasha had once confided in Jusuf that he felt closer to Ismeta than to his own mother. Ismeta always greeted Sasha with a warm hug and a kiss, took an interest in his music, and was curious about his plans for the future. Jusuf sensed from an early age that his mom regarded both boys almost equally as her two sons.

As they turned a corner, Jusuf snuck a side glance and saw that the soldier was looking woozy from the *slivovitz*. Nevertheless, the recruit tossed another handful of peanuts into his mouth. A crisp flake of red husk must have fallen into his windpipe because he began to choke. He wheeled to the right and then left, coughing and gagging, his face first white and then purple. When he wobbled into the middle of the street, spitting nut-chips and gasping for air, Jusuf darted into a narrow alley, racing as if the old brick pavers were as hot as the embers in his stove.

He and Sasha often took this alley route to Sasha's house on their way back from town when they were kids. Halfway through the maze of interconnecting passages, they one night passed a window with the shade not fully drawn and saw a woman in her thirties parading half naked around her bedroom as she languidly applied lotion to her arms and bullet-shaped breasts. But today, Jusuf just flew by the window without even a side glance and sprinted down the snaking alley, his sneakers squealing as he navigated each bend. He jumped a fence and finally slipped behind a shed that was just a stone's throw from Sasha's house. After taking a few minutes to catch his breath, he cautiously peeked out from between two houses and readied himself for a dash to Sasha's front porch, but the soldier suddenly rounded a corner, obviously surprised by his own good luck. Their eyes met.

"Pasalic, you fuck! Don't move." He fired a warning shot, which splintered a piece of window trim over Jusuf's shoulder, causing Jusuf to spin on his heels and race back down the narrow alley, heart pounding. Jusuf hoped he could circle around and at the right instant steal silently down through Sasha's sloping metal basement door. He leapt over a pile of trash, causing a mass of flies to explode off the matted orange fur of a dead cat. He was about to drop to his knees and crawl under a delivery truck that had just stopped at the far end of the alley, motor still rumbling, when the soldier, now also in the alley, bellowed, "You're dead, motherfucker."

Jusuf froze. He slowly turned and raised his hands, struggling to gulp a breath of air as he watched the soldier approach him. The soldier squeezed down the alley, stiff jacket sleeves scratching noisily along the crudely mortared concrete block walls, his spiky, orange crown backlighted by the low spring sun. When he reached the pile of trash, the soldier stopped.

"You know what happens to stupid fucks like you?" He pointed to the barrel of his Kalashnikov and then turned his open palm facing skyward. Jusuf closed his eyes, expecting a bullet to tear through his chest before he could inhale his next breath.

The soldier yelled, "Catch!"

Jusuf's eyes snapped open, his hands instinctively flying forward to catch or deflect the missile hurtling through space, but the cat's hardened carcass smacked the side of his face, its inertia forcing a stream of maggots wriggling out of the half-eaten body. As a contingent of flies madly buzzed the stinking slime on Jusuf's cheek, the soldier exploded in laughter, raucous guffaws that bellowed through the narrow chasm. "I should blow your brains out right here, you little shit, but that'd be a gift I'm in no mood to give. The slow roast is what you deserve. Turn around and walk toward that lady hanging clothes. Keep your mouth shut. Then turn left."

At the end of the alley, Jusuf stole a glance toward Sasha's house, hoping his friend might be outside. He was sure Sasha would have intervened on his behalf. Three months older than Jusuf, and considerably taller, Sasha had stepped in on many occasions in the past, pretending to be Jusuf's older brother when a pack of rowdy Serbs came into town looking to beat up a few Turks.

Minutes later, Jusuf approached the cluster of three-story commercial buildings and apartment houses along Route 5 that comprised the center of Kljuc. It sounded like a large crowd had gathered for a public event with someone barking orders through a megaphone. As the soldier's muzzle poked against the right side of his lower back, Jusuf understood to turn the corner at Hasan's coffee shop. A huge assembly of Muslims stood in the main square. They hung about in huddles, many shivering from a fusion of cold and fear, their faces long and wan. The throng grew larger as men and boys were herded in at gunpoint through several cross streets. To Jusuf's right, three silver-haired Serbian men sitting on a bench appeared to be bemused by the unfolding spectacle. These were men Jusuf had seen in town many times before, men he had waved to and who had waved to him, men who had been friends with those whose plight they now found entertaining.

"So they got you, too, Shorty," one said.

"Do you know what's going on?" Jusuf asked.

"You'll see," one man said, opening a can of beer. "This party's been planned for many months. It's in your honor."

The soldier shoved Jusuf into the crowd and walked off. "Enjoy the festivities," he called over his shoulder. "They're sure to last well into the night."

CHAPTER TWO

Soldiers on the perimeter barked at the Muslims to move in closer to one another. A few voices from deep within the crowd called back in mild protest. Several older men, bent with age, were jostled and fell to the roadway.

A soldier in his fifties, an elegant man with a stylish haircut and an obvious air of self-confidence, walked toward Jusuf pushing a green wheelbarrow. The man was someone Jusuf remembered seeing a few times behind the desk in the town library. The soldier first nodded toward Jusuf in recognition that he had seen him before. Almost politely, he instructed Jusuf to give up his wristwatch, ring, sneakers, and leather vest. The soldier was courteous but firm, claiming that he would hold these items in safekeeping. Jusuf stood on one leg as he pulled off one sneaker and then the other. The road surface was cold. He tossed them into the wheelbarrow. "The rest, please." Jusuf had trouble twisting the ring off his paint-encrusted finger. The ring, which had been hammered to shape from a misfired brass cartridge casing, had been a deathbed gift from his father. Although Jusuf was never fond of the ring, he brought it to his lips before dropping it into the toe of one sneaker. Then he pressed down the tongue to form a compartment for safekeeping. Jusuf's bulky watch with its silver stretch-band landed on the heap of stuff before tumbling to the side of the barrow with a loud clink.

"Come on, now, my friend. That vest."

"But my …?"

"You have no choice."

Jusuf removed the vest, folded it carefully, and set it down as if placing it in a bureau drawer. His mother had given it to him several weeks earlier for his eighteenth birthday, and he barely had time to wear it. The cold wind now rippled his T-shirt, and his thin frame began to shiver.

The soldier turned to look at a crimson-faced man telling a guard that his wife was in the hospital, in surgery. He pleaded to leave. "Shut up and stay where you are." Jusuf saw this distraction as an opportunity to slip his beaded leather choker under the neckband of his well-worn Grateful Dead T-shirt. Without looking back, the soldier pushed the barrow and its heap of belongings toward a group of new arrivals being pressed into the crowd. Although Jusuf knew many of the men and boys surrounding him, he suddenly felt profoundly alone, as though sheets of thick glass had been lowered between him and those nearby.

Minutes later, Jusuf saw his friend, Elmir, shoved into the throng. Elmir was pale and shivering wildly and was clearly embarrassed to be standing in public in his underwear. A few feet behind Elmir stood the baker from Jusuf's neighborhood—his right hand shaking in palsied rage.

Then Jusuf noticed Suljo Begovic, his next-door neighbor, speaking softly with his two sons. Jusuf waved weakly. Suljo nodded gravely, but his eyes did not speak. A writer of long romantic poems whose message lay obscured within circuitous phrasing, Suljo was a man of even temper. He analyzed situations with an abiding sense of tolerance and goodwill. Those who had watched him in a courtroom said his skill as a lawyer was based as much on his out of the ordinary sensibilities as on the persuasion of his logic.

Jusuf whispered to a very tall man standing beside him, "Can you see what's going on?" The man was able to look above the heads of those nearby but didn't respond. He simply shook his head slowly as tears welled in his eyes. Perhaps he had not heard Jusuf's question, or maybe he chose not to hear it.

Jusuf looked back at Suljo, whose unfocused eyes created the impression that he was flowing back and forth between Bosnian history, which he liked to read, and events in the future, vaguely imagined—

between what had been and what could be. Friends of Begovic regarded this trait as a lack of emotional mooring, but others, particularly those who knew him from his skillful maneuverings in a courtroom, saw a lawyer empowered by uncommon perspectives and a deep sense of humanity.

A man on a balcony bellowed through a megaphone names from a sheet of paper with two typed columns. With fire in his eyes and an occasional smirk, he located particular individuals in the crowd and pointed at them until the person was spotted by a soldier and taken away. Was this for questioning? Jusuf wondered. Curiously, certain Muslims, after a brief exchange, were pushed back into the crowd. Jusuf couldn't figure out whether these were cases of mistaken identity—or did a bond of friendship, or family connections, embolden a soldier to disobey a command?

Jusuf knew the loudmouth on the balcony only by his first name. Slavco was a hotheaded, thin-lipped, muscular Serb with a ruddy complexion and thinning hair who ran a failing sawmill three and half kilometers north of Kljuc. Many of the names Slavco was calling out were familiar to Jusuf—local heroes and respected members of the community. Some names Jusuf recalled from newspaper articles his mother had read to him—judges, police officers, bankers, politicians, businessmen, and shopkeepers. He also recognized a few local sports heroes. All were Muslim; all were prominent in one way or another, many of them well-educated.

A gunshot near Slavco's balcony was followed quickly by another shot that came from just under the balcony. The captives nearby gasped, color draining from their faces. They turned in unison and tried to flee. Jusuf looked around for any pistol-wielding soldier heading his way, even though he was sure he was not the kind of Muslim the Serbs were looking for. How could he be? He was just a young man getting ready for college, an average student who happened to be handy with tools. Would the Serbs really be looking for a guy just five foot seven that his friends happened to regard as fearless on a soccer field? Probably not. But what if they knew he was deadly with a rifle? *The reluctant hunter*, his buddies called him. He once split a plum from sixty feet that Sasha sent swinging pendulum-style from a string tossed over a tree branch. But this skill with a rifle was not something Jusuf chose to speak about.

In fact, a few weeks after his father died, Jusuf told Sasha he would never hunt again.

The captives had quieted somewhat by the time several freshly painted military trucks roared into the square led by a jeep with a couple of young, tense Serbian recruits in the front seat honking the horn. Bouncing about on the rear seat was a boy that looked twelve, maybe thirteen, years old. He was trembling uncontrollably, his face streaked with tears. The boy looked around for someone who might recognize him and perhaps say something to those who had seized him. As the jeep screeched to a stop, a soldier jumped out and grabbed the crying boy by the collar and threw him in with the Muslims. Other soldiers jumped from their vehicles. There was a lot of Serbian-style saluting; three fingers extended in a self-conscious proclamation of newfound status and collusive camaraderie. Outfitted in still-stiff fatigues and carrying freshly oiled weapons, some of the recruits moved with a jerkiness that reflected the uncertainty they felt in being thrust into a war that, for many, seemed to materialize overnight. Some strutted with cocky arrogance, inflated by the power that a weapon and a uniform often impart, while others were anxiously unsure of specifically what they were expected to do.

Many of these soldiers had been friends with the Muslim men they were now rounding up. Days before, they all drank together, played, studied, smoked, danced and sang together. A few had been their *kum*, the best man at their wedding. There was an ethnic difference between them, yes, but for the most part not a palpable division. They were all Bosnians, seemingly united forever by the glue of common territory. Other Serbs, however, came from the mountains and freshly plowed fields, Serbian farmers and farmers' sons trucked in from outlying areas, boots caked with clods of ginger-colored mud. It was the farmers and farmers' sons, more than the others, who harbored feverish animosities passed down from the veterans of one war to the recruits of the next, from the Second World War and many wars before, to this one. It was on farms that life and death commingled, where slaughter and birth were frequent painful manifestations of the natural order.

Serbs dragged into this engagement by threats and intimidation, rather than by choice, drifted away from the center of the armed group. These men, brave in their own way, let their rifles droop slightly as a sign of resignation or mild defiance. Eyes lowered, they could not readily look at their fellow Serbs, and more poignantly, not at their Muslim friends who, in circumstances unimaginable a few weeks earlier, now had fallen into a strange new status that was neither friend nor enemy, but both. Jusuf felt like he had slipped into a surreal and unsettling dream—a dream in which the familiar everyday bonds connecting neighbors and friends had been severed and replaced with feelings that were so weirdly alien that the macadam beneath his feet felt sickeningly unstable, summer-soft and shifting direction one moment to the next.

Two young, edgy soldiers standing a few feet apart, facing in opposite directions, suddenly turned on their heels in response to the piercing trill of their commander's whistle and walked into each other. "Hey, man, are you fucking crazy?" the taller one said to the other, followed by a shove. The few Muslims, including Jusuf, who saw the collision, and some soldiers standing nearby, lowered their gaze in unison to conceal their momentary, silent, shoulder-shaking bemusement.

Sitting sidesaddle on rickety tricycles near a Serbian TV cameraman, three small boys also giggled at one another after witnessing the collision. The youngest had a plastic pistol poking out of his pocket; the oldest was crunching the last morsel of a chocolate ice-cream cone. Jusuf wondered whether for the boys, it was like a scene from an American movie they had seen on TV, similar to the movies he and Sasha went to see on the weekends. The boy with the pistol removed it from his pocket and pointed it at his friends. He pulled the trigger, making the sound of an explosion spitting forth from the tip of his tongue, and then beamed with pride.

A Serbian officer, with a bushy moustache and a cracked lower lip that stuck out and up toward his nose, waved a chrome-plated revolver and yelled orders through a red cardboard megaphone. "Load these fucking Turks in the trucks and get them moving north. Take the rest to the stadium." When the officer found himself near the Serbian TV camera crew, he spoke more slowly. His words sounded rehearsed, as if he were reading from a script. "These murderers and rapists must be punished. They can't remain on our streets any longer. They're destroying our country. They've got plans to take over Bosnia, to make it an Islamic state." He paused to straighten his jacket and then made sure the cameras were still rolling before he continued. "We've got to protect our people. We must unite. Bosnia must become a *Republika Srpska*. Act now to save us from this filth." When he saw the camera light click off, he exchanged winks with the cameraman.

A short, middle-aged man with a moth-eaten, diamond-patterned green sweater stretched over his hugely bulging belly strolled around the perimeter of the assembled Muslims. Jusuf had seen this fellow in town before. At parades and weddings, he would be seen sauntering on the perimeter, tolerated but privately ridiculed. He wore a pair of chinos that stopped well above his ankles, and his nearly bald head was covered by a cap flattened by the weight of many cheap badges and fake medals. In his puffy right hand, he carried a toy walkie-talkie, and nestled in the crook of the same arm was a kid's black, plastic rifle with a frayed red ribbon around the barrel. He had huge ears, and the left side of his face sagged like fresh dough. In his left hand, he waved a hand-painted banner that read Republika Srpska Forever! A few acquaintances hooted encouragement to him, so he began marching with exaggerated high steps like a youngster. "The day has *finally* come, and the spring of 1992 will never be forgotten. No Serbian blood will flow again." A reporter from the Belgrade daily, *Nasa Borba*, circled him, taking photographs, and pumped him for more inflammatory remarks. But he repeated the same sentences, almost word for word, no matter the changing nature of the questions.

More men appeared carrying placards reading: Bosnia is Serbia! They shouted slogans, drank beer, and swigged cognac. Suddenly they formed a circle and danced an impromptu *kola* with the walkie-talkie man in the middle. Their mascot for the day smiled and drooled, his mindless eyes twinkling, his plastic rifle now raised aloft. A stream of hoots and hollers from the men dancing around him egged him on to greater displays of foolishness. The dullard, today the focus of cheers and laughter, had been on most other days the focus of scorn and mockery. Jusuf tried to make sense of this merging of circus-like frivolity and serious military pursuit.

Suddenly the officer with the chrome-plated pistol ran over to the Muslims standing closest to the trucks and screamed through the megaphone: "Get in the fucking trucks. Come on, start moving!" Those near him scurried in opposite directions like panicked sheep. At first some turned toward the river, while others more hopeful turned toward the town hall.

"The trucks! Get in the damn trucks, you sons of bitches!" He raised his pistol and fired two shots that echoed in sharp claps between the facing rows of apartment buildings. Eventually the detainees began walking toward the vehicles. As the first man climbed aboard one of the trucks, the rest moved in his direction like rivulets of storm water passively flowing toward a drain. Jusuf, roughly in the middle of the pack, began to walk more slowly, finally falling back to the rear of the group. He watched Elmir and the baker climb into the last truck in the line. Elmir tilted his head as he often did on the soccer field when he hoped to get an indication as to what move, if any, Jusuf was about to make. He had also seen Jusuf streak through a tangle of basketball players and fly up to make a basket.

A soldier passed by dragging a Muslim woman by the arm. "Please don't," she cried. "I have children at home. Where are you taking me?"

"Shut your mouth, bitch."

Jusuf panicked with the thought of what would become of his own mother if he got in the truck. Did the pistol shots still popping in various parts of town mean that she had already been killed? Jusuf, gripped by terror for his mother's safety, stopped walking. A torrent of emotions surged through him as he stared into the eyes of the soldiers who had turned to look in his direction. He raced through his options and quickly concluded that if he ran, he'd be shot. If he stood his ground, they might beat him to death. He considered wrestling the rifle away from the soldier closest to him who looked momentarily preoccupied. But there was no way he could shoot his way out of such a dense pack of soldiers even though he was a superb shot. There was also the danger this action would pose to his fellow Muslims. Jusuf suddenly noticed a recruit that looked very much like Sasha standing toward the back of the huddle of soldiers that was closing in on him. For an instant, he thought by habit that Sasha had come to rescue him once again from a pack of Serbs hell-bent on kicking the ass of a defenseless, young Muslim. But no, this *was* Sasha in uniform and with a rifle.

Sasha's ever-present harmonica reclined at an angle in his breast pocket, the permanent insignia of the guy who had always dreamed of becoming Yugoslavia's answer to Bob Dylan. Sasha, a warrior? How absurd! Sasha stopped midstep when he realized the defiant Muslim in the center of the commotion was actually Jusuf. As their eyes met, it felt like a bar of hot steel had been driven between their skulls. Jusuf's eyes widened. Was this possible? Had someone forced Sasha to wear that outfit, grip that gun? There was no way Sasha would have volunteered! Sasha removed his left hand from his rifle, letting the weapon droop in what Jusuf, if circumstances had been different, would have interpreted as a gesture of shame. Sasha, looking like his attention had been directed elsewhere, slowly drifted back from the noose of soldiers tightening around his old friend.

Jusuf felt a penetrating sense of betrayal. His mind raced from one memory to another, searching for an answer as to how this could be taking place. He and Sasha had been best of friends their entire lives—a friendship marked by fort building, pissing contests standing on a rock high above the Sana River, excursions to Bihac for rafting tournaments, countless soccer games, double dates, even their most recent impassioned exchange about religion at Edo's bar last Saturday night. And what of their troubling hunting trips near Pounje and Plitvice with Jusuf's father and his friends? Sasha had always envied Jusuf's skill with a weapon, much as Jusuf envied Sasha's talent with a harmonica—not to mention Sasha's height and striking good looks. Sasha had said he would never tell anyone about Jusuf's firearm skills in order to help keep him out of the army, never tell anyone *anything* that could bring Jusuf any harm. Had all this been a lie? Had Sasha already informed the authorities about Jusuf's superior ability with a rifle?

The pieces did not fit together. Was Sasha his friend or his enemy? Hadn't Sasha pressed his case once again at Edo's bar for divine goodness and for faith in a benevolent God? What goodness? What benevolence? Jusuf suddenly felt a pistol jammed under his cheekbone. "In the truck or I'll blast your fucking head off. Run, shit head. Get your ass moving! C'mon! C'mon!"

Dazed but still empowered by a streak of controlled defiance, Jusuf took one last moment to stare back at the soldiers. He also glanced at Elmir, who appeared to be signaling Jusuf to give it up, let them have it. Finally, Jusuf turned and walked backward toward the truck, never abandoning eye contact. It was, for Jusuf, a test of wills to be resolved perhaps on another stage at another time. Jusuf thought for just an instant of his father and their own unending test of wills. He wondered how his father, a hunter of extraordinary skill, might have acted in this situation to protect his wife. Would his father have bolted?

Would he have tried to wrestle someone to the ground? Jusuf had observed his father hold his fire as a bear crashed through a thicket in his direction, waiting until just the right moment to pull the trigger. If Jusuf had learned anything studying his father in the wild, it was to know through sharply honed instinct *when* and *how*. Even the reluctant hunter knew clearly that this was not the time.

As Jusuf climbed into the truck, he looked back at the sea of faces. Some were smug, some sneering. And yet, among the swarm of mostly eager Serbian recruits, Jusuf saw two or three long and gentle faces burdened with sorrow. These soldiers were linked to a chain of events they knew was coming but were powerless to reverse.

CHAPTER THREE

Jusuf climbed into the dim interior of the canvas-roofed truck. A wooden bench ran the length of the truck on each side, supported by short, steel struts. He sat down in the last open spot on the right, next to the tailgate, figuring this location would be best if, when the truck slowed at a crossing, he decided to jump. Since Jusuf's truck was also the last in the caravan, there would be no one trailing to thwart his escape.

The truck's engine was suddenly gunned, and the vehicle lurched forward, sending both rows of seated Muslims swaying in unison. The convoy raced north, trailed by a tumbling coil of road dust and debris. It roared through the small mountain villages of Vrhpolje and Tomina, and then across a two-lane concrete bridge into the town of Sanski Most, where Jusuf's aunt and uncle lived. Dreary concrete apartment slabs constructed during the Communist era sat elbow to elbow with buildings from the Medieval, Ottoman, and Austro-Hungarian periods. Jusuf, the aspiring architect, much preferred the picturesque massing, colorful verge boards and Moorish-style door and window trim of the older buildings that had been a common sight until the Communists took power and introduced a more regimented, spare, and mud-colored aesthetic.

When the trucks reached the northwest corner of Sanski Most, Jusuf saw the seventeenth-century mosque where his Uncle Ibro went daily to pray. Its somber lead-sheathed dome and spike-shaped, ten-sided minaret always held him entranced as he sat on Aunt Naza's and Uncle Ibro's porch, fourteen feet above the street, his uncle often garbed only in his undershirt and running pants. Although religion meant little to Jusuf, he nevertheless always looked forward to the times Ibro asked him to walk with him to the mosque. Removed from the noise and activity of the outside world, Jusuf adored the mosque's interior, a place of quiet, solid refuge. When lonely, he knelt next to his uncle, enjoying the security of his warm, folded body that was aligned invariably, like a compass, with the holy city of Mecca. The warmth of Ibro's body was particularly welcomed in midwinter when frigid temperatures turned the mosque into a deep freeze. Often bored, Jusuf would stand and walk to the back of the mosque and either sketch architectural details, doze, or imagine the countless men whose whispered prayers had through the centuries been soaked up by the thick walls of this architectural vessel that sheltered their supplicant bodies. He had wondered as he filled out his college applications whether his interest in architecture had originated with these early visits to Ibro's mosque.

Jusuf looked around at the swaying bodies in the truck's darkening interior and at the nervous boy sitting next to him. When the boy turned his head to look out the back of the truck and was illuminated in the headlights of a car about to pass them, Jusuf realized that the youngster was the same crying child that had been yanked from the back of the jeep in Kljuc and thrown into the roundup. Jusuf watched the boy look up a few times and survey the faces of the men and boys surrounding him. Suddenly, as if gripped by some invisible threat, the boy drew two sharp breaths, one atop the other, followed by a sigh. It was then that Jusuf smelled the sweetly pungent odor of urine. He glanced down and saw that the boy had peed in his pants.

"Hey, friend, don't worry. This has to be just a big mix-up. You'll see—everything'll be all right. I'm *sure* somebody made a mistake or something." Jusuf looked over the boy's head at Amil, the neighborhood baker, who winked.

"Just stick with me. I'll see you get home safe," Jusuf said a bit too hastily, wondering himself how this could possibly be just a mix-up, a big mistake.

The boy's right hand started to tremble as he stared blankly at the truck's floorboards.

Jusuf spoke earnestly into the boy's ear. "Listen, I'm going to take care of you. You'll be okay, I promise. I won't let them hurt you." The boy moved a few inches to distance himself from Jusuf.

After a while and without turning his head, the boy whispered something back toward Jusuf. "There's a ..."

"Speak a little louder, kid. I didn't hear you."

"You ... you wouldn't understand."

Jusuf lowered his head. The boy kept staring at the floorboards, his right hand trembling in his lap.

"I can't ..."

"You can't *what*?" Jusuf asked gently. Amil also brought his head down closer to the boy and tapped his hearing aid.

"You know, with you ... with all of you." The boy looked up and glanced around the truck.

"You can't what?" Jusuf asked. "I don't understand what you're trying to tell me."

The boy fell silent, his small fingers opening and closing in tentative gestures as if he were trying to use his hands to explain the impossible. Tears fell onto his forearms. Finally, he blurted out, "I'm *Serb*."

The boy brought his hands up to cover his face. Then, through his fingers, he furtively looked around the truck once again as if to gauge the level of danger that resided among those he now surmised to be his enemy. His eyes returned to the floorboards and to the two rows of feet, some large, some small like his own, some with socks, some bare.

Jusuf looked at Amil and then down at the boy. "But why were you rounded up?" Jusuf asked. "How come they put you in the truck with *us*?"

The boy's head shook *no* to every explanation he was silently exploring. The truck suddenly shuddered as the tires thudded across three pipe-hard ridges in the macadam. "I live in the mountains. Way up above Kljuc. With my mother, in a little cabin." He kneaded his hands, studying them as if all the everyday pieces of his life were cupped there like a collection of paper-thin porcelain trinkets that could fracture with one wrong move.

"We got a goat ... and two chickens, and our dog, Tito."

"Tito, huh? He must be a good dog."

"Yea, Tito's a good pup. He runs in circles. Especially when my mother whistles or when the roof vent flaps a lot."

"But how'd you get in here, with us?"

"I was on the road. With some girls I know—they live down the hill from us. I was walking my bicycle." The boy paused.

"Yes, I'm listening."

"Sometimes one of the girls … you know, will help my mom in the house. They're … Turks … like you." The boy looked around, as if to see if it was safe to continue.

"It's okay, kid. Go on."

"So I had to go to town. Mom needed flour 'cause Uncle Dusko's coming from Belgrade for her birthday. All of a sudden, I saw some soldiers driving up the hill. They looked angry. None knew me, but it seemed one of them knew the girls, and he knew they were like you." The boy chewed his lip.

"Yes. I'm listening. It's okay."

Amil fingered his hearing aid again and bowed his head closer to the boy's head.

"They said bad things." He nervously clicked his front teeth. Jusuf assumed the boy was trying to decide how truthful he should be. "I can't … I can't tell you what they said. It would make all you guys really mad."

The boy paused again. Jusuf didn't hurry him.

"I started to walk away, to get on my bike, but one guy yelled at me to stop." The boy began to cry again and rubbed the back of his head.

"It's okay," Jusuf said. "I understand what you're saying. Trust me. I have a close friend myself. He's a Serb just like …" Jusuf paused to consider the currency of his friendship with Sasha.

"One soldier grabbed my arm really hard. He was angry … and cursing. Called me a little pig." The boy's whimpering confused his breathing. He coughed and wiped his eyes. "He asked me questions, but I was afraid. One guy kicked me in the leg, and another whacked me on the head."

"Did the girls say anything?"

"They ran off."

The boy tapped his knee with his fingers for a minute or so. "One guy got out his pistol and said something like, 'Let's finish this little prick right here. The rats will eat what's left.' Suddenly one guy picked me up by my belt, saying, 'We got orders,' and threw me in their jeep."

Jusuf looked over the boy's head at Amil and then at Suljo across from him. He wondered what Suljo's sons must be thinking.

"I thought someone I knew would see me ... another Serb ... and tell them to let me go." He spoke louder now. "I was so scared! They drove real fast toward Kljuc—the jeep was skidding in and out of ruts, bouncing around—and then, *boom*, they pushed me in with you guys. I was afraid to say I was Serb. I was afraid they wouldn't believe me. They'd think I was lying and could get real mad and hurt me. They had guns." He rubbed the bump on his head.

Suljo, who was sitting with his own two boys, reached over to pat the boy's head, but the boy recoiled and started to sob again. Very slowly, Amil placed his flour-coated palm on the boy's knee, but the sobbing continued. Finally, Jusuf placed his arm around the boy's shoulder, but the boy sat stiffly unresponsive. Then, slowly, he yielded to the gentle pressure as Jusuf drew him in against the side of his chest.

Evening fell fast. The canvas flaps at the back of the truck, tied to the sidebars like drapes, reminded Jusuf of the curtains in the tobacco-rank movie theater in Banja Luka. He and Sasha used to giggle and scream in the dark hall, munching popcorn, sucking candies, sitting in a state of terrified enchantment while watching the latest film out of Hollywood or Paris. When an English word they knew or could figure out was spoken, they repeated it. If by chance they repeated the same word simultaneously, they elbowed each other and howled, each claiming to have been the first to speak. From French movies, they borrowed short phrases they used as greetings for weeks thereafter, such as *monsieur* or *s'il vous plait*. Jusuf recalled these events with a trace of a smile until his reverie was erased by the image of Sasha standing with the other soldiers during the roundup in Kljuc.

How could Sasha have betrayed him and the other Muslims? When the two had been together at Edo's bar on Saturday night, Sasha suddenly had asked Jusuf to meet him on the second floor. He said he had to tell him something in private. Jusuf tried to recall if Sasha had said anything that night that would have been a clue. Any telltale sign that things would change? Those cigarettes! Sasha never smoked! And yet, there he was, chain smoking, and offering one to Jusuf, who Sasha knew only smoked when stressed.

Jusuf watched the countryside retreat into the distance—a huge faded tapestry rolling away toward the horizon. Houses, barns, mosques, and churches swept past him on either side, racing into the distance, shriveling into oblivion. Newly plowed fields, schools, and factories were dragged away on each side, slowing just before they vanished along the line where the land was stitched to the sky. Even the Sana River, a light copper color at sunset, appeared to slither away like the golden, blunt-nosed vipers he'd seen on hunting trips with his father.

Jusuf looked east, toward the border between Bosnia and Serbia. Flames licked the air, and plumes of smoke curled skyward. Was it possible all of Bosnia was in flames? To the west, the sun sank slowly behind the long, crab-leg expanse of Croatia.

After what felt like roughly an hour on the road, the sky had turned a deep blue and was without dimension. Those inside had descended into individual sinkholes of fear. Clenched fists pressed into sweating palms. Knuckles cracked. Lips were chewed. The psychic space of the truck descended into a jumble of threatening visions as the truck's gray-green canvas roof flapped incessantly, its steady beat accented at times when the stiff canvas suddenly popped angrily against the cage-like, U-shaped supports.

Someone spoke into the darkness. The voice sounded like it had risen from a grave. "Anyone know where we're headed?" No one answered, or at least no one had a guess they chose to reveal. Minutes later, there was a faint response from the forward section of the truck. "They better get us somewhere fast or I'm going to pee in my pants like that kid."

"Me, too!"

When the truck slowed around a curve, a teenager whose voice kept cracking said, "Maybe we could jump off when they stop for gas, or if they stop to eat."

The heavyset man next to him, whose rank armpit odor was permeating the interior, shot back, "Don't mention food, god damn it. I haven't eaten since breakfast."

Minutes later, another small voice floated out of the darkness. "Anybody got something to drink?"

"You got to be crazy, kid! You think they let us bring our beers on board?"

"Give the kid a break. He's just thirsty."

Silence returned for a half hour until Amil sneezed several times in quick succession, making his flour-dusted, blue apron stretch taut around his large, hard belly. The smell of flour permeated the truck, and although mouths watered, no one dared break the silence. Jusuf had known Amil Kapetanovic from childhood. Neither of them would say they were close friends, but Jusuf regarded the baker as a happy fixture in his life. Amil had watched Jusuf grow from the curly-haired tot squirming in his father's burly arms to the young man who had dated his opera-singing daughter for a few months last winter. When Jusuf kissed her—her finely shaped lips offered so willingly—he smelled the bakery in her auburn hair. And when he exuberantly said that he loved her singing, she took it as a shy boy's way of telling her something else. Several inches taller than Jusuf, Sabina herself was shy, but she had an explosive temper like her father. This was evident the night Jusuf confessed he didn't really love her. A month earlier, with her long eyelashes fluttering, she had agreed to sleep with him because she was sure this was a love that would last forever.

In his early teens, Jusuf enjoyed going to Amil's bakery. More often than not, he'd find Amil standing in front of the steaming loaves of bread piled across the length of the sagging plywood shelves. Amil always offered Jusuf a half slice of raisin bread when he arrived to buy a bag of steaming *lepinja* rolls or a loaf of whole wheat for his mom. Jusuf regularly studied Amil's habitual wink as the baker affectionately deposited a few pieces of change into the palm of each hand. In front of his bathroom mirror, Jusuf had taught himself to wink like Amil and to tap his ear the way Amil did when he thought his hearing aid was slipping out, or the sound was dimming. Amil doubled over in laughter when, for the first time, his own wink was met with Jusuf's first successful mirror image.

"Good *boy*! Now you've got it!"

"I'm really thirsty," the boy next to Jusuf whispered again into the darkness of the truck.

"Hold on a little longer," Jusuf said. "I'm sure they'll stop sometime soon." The caravan did stop at a crossing for a train to pass. Red lights flashed through the canvas, so all within could again see the faces of the others in the truck.

Jusuf leaned over and asked Amil, "What do you think they're going to do with us?"

"Not sure. Odd, it's only men they rounded up."

"Maybe we're headed for some kind of work detail."

"Perhaps. I just hope Vildana and Sabina are okay," Amil said.

"I've been fretting about my mom, too. I should have done something more to get back to her. Hopefully someone stepped in to help her. Since Dad died, she's never been alone except for those few times when Sasha and I went away for the weekend." The Serbian boy looked up at Jusuf but didn't speak.

A man with a croaky voice, sitting next to one of Suljo's sons, said, "Keep your mouths shut, will you. This whole fucking thing is driving me crazy."

"Take it easy," Suljo said. "We're in this together."

CHAPTER FOUR

WHENEVER THE CONVOY SLOWED to negotiate a sharp curve, clouds of exhaust filled the truck, throwing everyone into a spasm of coughing and cursing, hands waving across noses to catch a breath of fresh air. Later, when the convoy came to a complete stop, engines idling, tailpipe rattling, Jusuf thought about jumping to freedom, but two darting eyes appeared in a small window at the back of the cab. He remembered he also had made a commitment to protect the Serbian boy sitting next to him. A few truck doors up ahead opened and closed, and shortly thereafter, several soldiers could be heard talking on the shoulder of the road. At first, Jusuf figured there were two soldiers, then possibly three. As shadows cast by their heads and torsos slanted obliquely up the canvas wall, suggesting they were standing closer to the truck, some of what they said Jusuf clearly understood, but the sentences were sometimes choppy, certain words lost to the sound of truck exhausts.

"Glad this shit is finally started." The soldier spoke as if to no one in particular. "It's really been getting to me, the tension and all. I've had to tell a ton of damn lies, and I really stink at lying."

"What are you talking … man?"

"What shit? The Turks … fool. I'm happy we're moving … the hell out of here."

"You … all over the place."

"Things will be … when we clear every last one of these creeps the hell out of Bosnia."

"You ask me, we should … back to Turkey. A bunch of traitors as far as I'm concerned. And if a few of 'em die on the way, good riddance. They've had their own plans, ya know. All the way from Syria, or Iraq … or, wherever down there."

"I know what you mean. But …"

"Then it'll all be ours. Tell the truth, we should go in there right now and shoot the whole damn truckload of … and be done with it. I'm so tired of waiting. It's really been getting to … nerves shot and all."

Jusuf adjusted his arm around the Serbian boy's head to muffle the soldiers' remarks. Silence followed. Jusuf wasn't sure if the soldiers were still outside until the sound of gravel crunching under boot heels grew louder and eventually begat a new voice.

"I know what you're saying, but … seems a little extreme."

"What do ya mean, you don't know? Don't know what?"

"I got a … friends."

"So?"

"So I'd hate to see them get hurt."

"What the fuck … you talking …?"

"… guys I grew up with. We've been getting ready to head off to college, and … they're okay guys. That's the way I see it. Some … different, but they're okay. I just don't feel right about this whole thing. Too extreme, I … Besides, I got a cousin who's a Muslim. He's a good friend, know what I mean."

"Me too … my sister's been seeing this guy …"

"You guys are pussycats. Keep up that kind of talk and you'll end up rotting in the bottom of a pit. Along with all of *them*."

"What's eating you? I don't buy all the bullshit … the TV. Half of it's a pack of lies anyway … you ask me."

"Listen, fool. A friend of mine got the *shortcut* right in … of my eyes two days ago because he wouldn't join a firing squad."

Jusuf had turned his head slightly, and in the shadows sliding back and forth across the canvas sidewall, he caught sight of a soldier drawing the shadow of his fingers across his throat. When unexpectedly his truck engine stalled, Jusuf and the others could hear everything.

"I really don't understand you guys. These creeps are the worst scum in the world. Smell bad, look bad. Worthless, the whole lot of them. It's been too many damn years dealing with these lazy shits living off our land, taking our women. Milosevic and Karadzic are right." The air was still for a moment, and it felt to Jusuf as if everyone in the truck had stopped breathing. "We've needed to unite and get going with this for way too long. That's what I hear on TV, and goddamnit, that's what I'm ready to do. You've seen the reports. They're starting to kill *our* people, rape *our* women. It's them or us. Goddamn obvious to me."

The voices lowered to a whisper and then rose again.

"Somebody said you got a girlfriend lives up by the camps."

"How'd you know?"

"Word gets around. Is it that redhead with the long ears that's always at the pastry shop?"

"Her ears ain't that long. It's her head that's short."

The men guffawed. Jusuf smiled.

"Got to watch out for those short-headed ones. Saw one without a mouth once … and knowing what you like after midnight, that could be a big problem."

They laughed.

"What they got you doing up there, Mirko?"

"Fences. No other way to keep those suckers where they belong till somebody figures out what to do with them. And you? Still work the knife?"

Jusuf drew his arm more snugly around the boy's ears.

"I've done some butchering in my day. You do what you have to. Bothers me sometimes. I keep a bottle of *slivovitz* in my coat pocket. It'll be over soon. Tell you one thing for sure—rather their asses than mine."

The shadows of the men suddenly slid down the wall of canvas. Jusuf wasn't sure whether the soldiers had walked away or had stepped back momentarily from a cloud of drifting exhaust from the truck just ahead. He thought he heard one of them pissing on the gravel.

"Hey. Do you know whether we're headed for Prijedor or Omarska this time?"

"Don't know for sure. Asked around. Nobody knows for sure."

"Mirko. What time ya got?"

"Shit! Forgot my watch." The other two laughed. "I guess it's about seven-thirty, maybe eight."

"What time do you think we'll get up there?"

"Maybe nine, if we don't need to stop again ... ten, the latest."

"I should've eaten. My stomach's grumbling."

"You're always hungry. What do you eat—six meals a day?"

"For starters. But I burn it off fast as I take it in. You'd think I'd be fat like the butcher, here, with what I eat."

"Wait a few years. We'll have to push you around in a wheelbarrow. Here, take this candy bar. I've already had three. My teeth ache."

The piercing chirp of a whistle sounded up ahead.

"Catch you guys later."

"Hey, Mirko, stop by when this crap is over. Let's have a few beers, go for a drive or something. And maybe I can get you to swing a hammer for a few days. You know I've been trying to get that new garage finished. Give me a call."

The shadows crept up across the canvas again and then sank away in different directions as the crunch of boots across the gravel grew dim. The cab door of Jusuf's truck slammed shut, two eyes again peered through the little back window of the cab, the engine roared, and for a few moments it seemed to be gunned just for pleasure. The vehicle lurched forward. Jusuf lowered his arm from around the boy's ears and slipped it down onto the youngster's upper right arm. Jusuf wondered if the soldiers had been speaking that way just to frighten them. But their exchange had sounded too unrehearsed, too natural.

As the caravan passed through a small town, a line of overhead streetlights illuminated the truck's interior in pulsing flashes. Jusuf's eyes came to rest on Suljo's square, balding head and his bronze mustache that arched thickly above his upper lip and trailed a half-inch below the corners of his mouth. As he caught a whiff of Suljo's cigar breath, he recalled how he and Suljo used to chat across the vine-covered fence they had to prop up seasonally with angled braces and guy wires. They roared when one of them pulled too hard and a section of fence collapsed into Suljo's yard or Jusuf's.

As a troublesome destination became inevitably closer, Suljo began speaking to his sons, Zarif and Ahmet. Jusuf sensed that Suljo was trying to leave his deliberate, methodical cadence back in the courtroom, but it had become his spoken essence. "I have no idea where we're headed or what we're about to face, but I fear it isn't good. I want you to know that I will stay with you no matter what. I will do everything I can to protect you, but—now listen to me carefully—we must work like a team. Your eyes and your ears are as important as anything I might do to protect you. Keep your wits about you. Never act rashly."

The bodies of the two teenagers fell forward and sideways as the truck bumped along the road. As Suljo spoke, Zarif and Ahmet stared at the Serbian boy under Jusuf's arm.

"It's reasonable to assume," Suljo continued, "that some of the men who have rounded us up are plain evil—but others might not be. Some in fact may be good and are here against their will. You must learn to discriminate. You must do as you're told. Now is not the time to antagonize; now is not the time to protest. Do you hear me?"

They nodded mechanically, making every effort to conceal their fear. "We must always speak in whispers and eventually learn to speak also with our eyes and fingers. Above all, you must stay close to me. I promise you I will do everything in my power to get us through this together."

When Suljo finished speaking, the shivering boys began to sob and fell in upon his chest. In the chilly darkness, it was Suljo's sheltering arms and the indelible memory of his mighty hands that provided a fleeting sense of safety his words could not.

CHAPTER FIVE

FIFTEEN MINUTES LATER, THE trucks veered off the road and rumbled up a rutted trail into a desolate section of forest. The vehicles pulled up behind one another like a line of elephants directed to stand trunk-to-tail. Engines were left idling, the headlights of each truck illuminating clouds of exhaust puffing from the truck directly ahead. Following orders, the detainees climbed down stiffly into the frigid night air. At first, they stood in huddles, many bent over, and then melted into the semidarkness to pee. While some found a place to stand using the light of the trucks' headlights, others had to feel their way through pockets of darkness to the closest tree, bladders ready to burst, urine already leaking into the pant legs of the older men.

After Jusuf asked his guard, an edgy guy with a limp and a bony, unshaven face, if he could walk a few yards away to defecate, Jusuf got a grudging nod and ambled off into an area rendered quite dark by several closely spaced *krusina* bushes that were just coming into leaf. The guard's flickering flashlight beam held Jusuf in view until he dropped his jeans around his ankles and squatted. Alone in the darkness, Jusuf tried to recall the voices of the soldiers he had heard outside the truck. Was this the tolerant-sounding soldier or the one who sounded filled with venomous hatred? Suddenly, three gunshots sounded in rapid succession from near the lead truck. Jusuf's head swung to the right, but he saw nothing. Someone in the distance yelled, "Holy fuck, he shot him!"

With what appeared to be the guard's growing sense of panic that the mayhem might spread to his charges, he yelled for his group to return to the truck. He waved his flashlight beam across a scattering of alarmed, ashen faces. Suljo pulled Ahmet and Zarif close in behind him, keeping a cautious distance from the commotion.

As the detainees began moving back to the truck, the Serbian boy suddenly froze and began to wail for his mother. The guard waved his pistol at the boy and through clenched teeth snapped, "Shut the fuck up, you little shit." A few Muslim men took a cautious step forward and told the guard they would look after him and keep him quiet, but the guard pointed his flashlight and gun in their direction and motioned for them to step back.

The guard moved closer to the boy. "Cryin' for your momma, huh?" He pointed his beam straight into the boy's eyes. They were wide with terror, all retinal color drained into the night air. The boy cowered, tears streaming down his cheeks, his legs about to melt beneath him. He raised his hands toward his face, waving them as if to signal *okay, I promise not to cry, I promise.*

After the guard glanced around to make sure his charges weren't straying, he took one step closer to the boy, his flashlight beam jerking wildly. Panicking, the boy looked left and right for anyone who might come forward on his behalf, but the Muslims that had not yet reached the truck blended into a shadowy, undifferentiated mass. Jusuf considered yelling from his toilet-stall of bushes to say what the boy had told him in the truck, but he felt momentarily paralyzed as he struggled to process the swiftly unfolding mayhem.

If the boy claimed to be a Serb, Jusuf feared that the soldier would judge him a liar and crack him on the head with his pistol. Then, unexpectedly, the guard smiled. From Jusuf's vantage, it looked like he was about to calm the boy with a few pats on the head, but instead he brought his pistol to the boy's ear and fired. The shot hung in the air for what seemed minutes, like the verbal report of a horrific event that reverberates in one's mind long after the words of the event are spoken. Those nearby gasped as the boy's body buckled and fell to the forest floor. There was a rustle of leaves as his left arm twitched in several weakening spasms.

Unchained by his rage, Amil lunged at the guard in explosive fury. The guard beat him back with his flashlight, the beam flashing across Amil's flour-white hands, which appeared disconnected from the arms that waved them. "You fucking fool! He's one of yours, you idiot!" Flour dust puffed twice as two shots hit Amil in the belly. He sank to his knees, his apron drawn taut from where it was pinned under his knees to where it pulled against the tie-strings around his waist. He clutched his gut. There was a barely audible gushing as blood pulsed through his fingers. He groaned but summoned enough energy to again curse the guard and everything Serbian. The guard limped forward and pumped another shot into Amil's eye, sending a flare of glistening red strings gushing from the back of his skull along with a chip of something white. Amil's body dead-weighted into the leaves next to the body of the boy.

Silence fell as if thick blankets had been dropped from the trees to hush the scene. Suljo drew Zarif and Ahmet closer to him, and then as inconspicuously as possible, he guided them back even further from the circle of violence. The guard, still edgy but with a nervous smirk on one side of his mouth, instinctively kicked a few leaves over the bodies. Throat constricted, voice as tight and dissonant as an old gut string, he yelled for everyone to put their hands on their head and climb into the truck. As he uttered his final words, his voice cracked like that of a boy of fourteen.

He slashed his beam back and forth across the sluggish ribbon of captives queuing back to the truck. With the sound of leaves rustling and branches snapping, Jusuf dropped flat to the earth and wriggled deeper into the protective cluster of bushes, the smell of his own excrement pungent in his nostrils. He palmed a layer of leaves over his body seconds before a final sweep of the guard's light beam scissored the woods. As he looked up through the thin branches into a motionless cobalt sky, a tumult of electric currents raced through his body. After a minute or so, he breathed easier, but then he heard footsteps shuffling back through the woods. Jusuf remembered how wounded prey used to scurry into a place of hiding in a futile attempt to escape his father's final shot. He feared that the leaves tickling his naked thighs would make scratching them irrepressible. He anticipated the guard's *final shot* and wondered what it would be like to have a bullet zing through his brain or his heart.

"Where are you, you bastard? You're out here somewhere. I can smell you."

The soldier moved in Jusuf's direction. Crisp leaves sounded like shuffling parchments. A twig snapped. Jusuf feared that the thin layer of leaves on his chest was visible as it rose and subsided with the cadence of his constrained breathing. The flashlight beam suddenly snaked across the ground and up and over his chest. In midbreath, Jusuf stopped exhaling, certain that death was almost upon him. Acid terror raced through his veins. Just as the soldier cursed the prospect of losing a living captive, a whistle pierced the night air, followed by the gunning of engines. The soldier swept the woods one last time with his flashlight. "Shit!" he muttered and trotted back to the truck, but not before firing two shots at random into the forest floor. Jusuf's body jolted, but he did nothing to check if a bullet had hit him.

The trucks roared with a hellish effusion of diesel exhaust and surging headlights. As the vehicles started to move, Jusuf gasped for air, the black branches above him suddenly seeming to spin in wild loops. The convoy swung in a wide circle and headed back toward the access road, their jouncing lights torching the woods in a riotous fanfare of radiant clouds of exhaust. When the beams of the lead truck illuminated a path directly in line with his hideaway, Jusuf couldn't decide whether to roll to one side and risk being seen or hope that the truck tires would straddle him. Just ten meters away, the lead truck swerved to avoid a log or the cluster of tall bushes concealing Jusuf's prone body, and the other trucks followed the route. The trucks rocked madly in the ruts of the dirt trail and then almost without slowing turned right onto the highway.

The moan of tires eventually subsided, and all again was dark and almost quiet. With truck noises having roared in his ears for hours, the near silence of the forest was penetrating and strangely alive. Jusuf rose to his knees, wiped himself with a handful of leaves, patted his clothes for a sign of blood, and realized with a sense of miraculous deliverance that he hadn't been shot. He stood and pulled up his jeans. When he reached out to feel for the nearest tree, he barely saw his own hand at the end of his outstretched arm. Had he actually survived—or, he wondered, was this the living dream of a dead man?

Jusuf walked toward where he thought the access trail might be, his socks providing little cushioning against twigs and sharp stones.

He walked about ten paces and then stopped midstep, gripped with a sudden impulse to see if Amil or the boy, or both, had somehow survived. He looked around, but the moonless night rendered the woods frustratingly featureless. Fearing collision with a tree trunk, he walked more cautiously now, arms outstretched in front of him, feeling for the invisible. He headed toward where he thought he smelled blood and then cupped his ears to listen for a moan or a dying breath. He heard nothing but what had become a maddening chorus of insects searching for mates and staking out with their reverberating chorus of ratchet sounds the perimeter of their domains.

A car approached, smoke coughing from its rattling tailpipe, the driver-side headlight suffering from a palsied jiggle. It came down the road from the direction toward which the trucks had headed. As spears of light flashed between tree trunks, Jusuf darted behind a tree, circling the trunk to remain in its shifting shadow. Had someone come back for him? Should he run, or again drop to the ground and cover himself with leaves? Before he could decide, the car had passed and rumbled into the distance.

Jusuf saw the futility of searching for Amil and the boy without a light. He reluctantly turned and began to cautiously walk toward the main road, hoping to pick up the access trail somewhere along the way. He stumbled into what at first felt like a length of rotting tree trunk. Falling forward, his hands landed on Amil's apron-covered thigh and then snapped back as if they had touched an anvil baking near a fire. Troubled and embarrassed by his reaction, he felt for Amil's body again, palming the corpse like a blind man. He outlined the torso, the head, and limbs. A vision erupted in the darkness of Amil pacing back and forth in front of his shelves of steaming loaves, his face gleaming with a slick of sweat, his head bobbing like a parrot strutting in a cage. Jusuf thought he smelled his friend's bakery and imagined heat radiating from Amil's ovens. But the heat was from the baker himself, still smoldering with rage. Without thinking, Jusuf's body sank down next to Amil's body, drawn in part by the warmth of his corpse and in part by a lifelong affection.

Groping in the darkness, Jusuf's hand brushed the face of the boy only a foot from Amil's head. He patted and caressed both of them and began to sob. He smelled their blood and a faint trace of the boy's urine. The organic finality of their deaths fell upon him like a great weight. He doubled over like the men he'd seen praying in Uncle Ibro's mosque and thumped his forehead against the ground. In the coal-black nowhere of these godforsaken woods, Jusuf wondered whether he too had been deliberately removed from the realm of the living so that he could transport the two bodies to wherever the dead are believed to go.

He looked down and saw neither his body nor theirs, just blurry, barely visible patches of incandescence that he took to be hands and faces. He stretched his arms out over their torsos as if to make an incantation, and then lowered them until his palms and forearms lay across their bodies. Anger replaced his grief. He turned and hammered his fists into the forest floor. The thumb of his right hand brushed against something smooth and warm, like a snail shell that had been lying in a summer pond, a slippery film of something coating its warm surface. When it began to vibrate and buzz, Jusuf panicked and let the thing fall. It continued to hum until an image of the warm cavity from which it had fallen suddenly dawned on Jusuf and he quickly leaned forward to search for it in the leaves. He brought it to his cheek with affection at the same time that he envisioned Amil tapping it in his ear to subdue its annoying ring. The hearing aid was now just a pulsating remnant jettisoned by a corpse, an ear without a brain, a plastic fossil-turned-keepsake. He brought it to his own ear, thinking he might hear the voice of the man he had known, but it yielded only a faint infernal hum.

Jusuf tapped the nugget until it fell silent and then stashed it in his jeans. With despair and a dizzying fatigue borne of the day's torrent of intense emotions, his body finally wilted. He lay motionless, certain now that the trucks would never turn back to search for him. He could almost hear the soldier who had shot Amil and the Serbian youngster reporting with bravura that he had killed *three*, not just *two* fucking Muslims.

There was probably nothing Jusuf could have done to save Amil, but perhaps there was something he could have done to save the boy. If he had not needed to go off to relieve himself, he could have stayed with the boy, which might have prevented the youngster from crying. The others in the truck had heard him promise he would stay with him, that no harm would come his way. He had failed the boy and almost wished now that gravity would draw him into a grave for the living.

He tried to think of a prayer that would bring Amil and the

boy back to life, a cosmic appeal to defy the workings of nature, to reverse the direction of time. He wanted to sprinkle a few drops of a transformative potion over them and ask a mullah to recite several arcane prayers that would cause their eyes to flutter, their lips to move. He imagined their minds dancing again with feelings and ideas. He pictured their muscles tightening, returning their bodies to the upright in the jerky, paroxysmal gestures of a puppet. The two corpses now laughed away the talons of death that had been robbed of their catch. The three of them embraced, their tears washing the blood from their shirts. If this was a dream, he wished he would never be forced to awaken.

"He's a Serb! Don't shoot him. He's one of yours! Can't you even see one of your own? Are you blind? He's Serb! He's *Serb*!" The gunshot cracked once again and hung in the air. Why didn't he scream to save the boy's life? Had he been afraid? Was there no time? Why hadn't he asked Amil to keep an eye on the youngster while he stepped away? Jusuf had been seized by the same onslaught of ambiguities and vagaries that had paralyzed everyone else in those thirty-some seconds of unpredictable madness. Events had erupted in a deluge of flashes far too fast to process. But it had been Jusuf who had heard the boy's story most directly, most intimately, and it was he who had proclaimed himself the youth's guardian. He was the one who should have screamed to save him. He had been the one who said *it was all a big mistake*, that no harm would come. There should have been three corpses, Jusuf concluded, his among them. A beetle crawled under his T-shirt. He was about to jump up and shake it loose or pinch the life out of it, but, overcome as he was by his feelings of guilt, he allowed the creature to enjoy the warmth of his body, at least for a moment. It seemed this was the least he could do ... endure some mild discomfort to serve another creature's needs.

A cold breeze stirred the fine hairs on Jusuf's arms. Dizzy but reenergized, he lifted the back of his shirt and swept the beetle into his palm. It circled frantically, tickling Jusuf, before it crawled up his forearm. As it approached his armpit, he cupped it carefully and set it down in the leaves next to the boy and his old friend. The idea of having to leave them unburied, and in Amil's case—a Muslim corpse—unwashed and unwrapped, was a prospect that tortured him. He hated the idea of leaving them and recoiled at the image of them soon blanketed by a buzzing crust of flies and later to flatten into mounds of rag-covered bones. Again he put his hands on the stone-dead bodies and was overcome by a pervasive sense of impotence.

Reluctantly, Jusuf turned and began to feel his way, trunk by trunk, back to the road. He missed detecting a tree and bruised his forehead over his left eye. Headlights, this time from a huge, flatbed truck, once again blinked through the trees, but the vehicle did not slow. Minutes later, his feet were finally on a smoothly paved surface. The road home. He was free.

Far to his right, the convoy of Serbian trucks continued to head east. The headlights and taillights formed a string of tiny beads, red and white, worming through the darkness, slithering slowly through the hills. Although the air was cold, a lingering trace of heat from the macadam passed through his bloodstained socks. His head throbbed, and the muscles in the back of his neck and shoulders ached. He turned left and headed southwest, back toward home and his mother, away from the barely audible moan of truck tires echoing intermittently off the surrounding hills.

CHAPTER SIX

BASED ON HIS SCANT knowledge of the area above Sanski Most, and guessing about the number of hours he had been in the truck, Jusuf figured he was maybe fifty to seventy kilometers north and east of Kljuc. Getting back home might take three to ten days, walking at night, sleeping during the day, detouring where necessary, or waiting it out when the weather or his fatigue forced him to stay under roof. If he laid over in Sanski Most with his aunt and uncle to wash, borrow some clothes, and get a good night's sleep, he would have to add another day or two. He planned to call his mother from his uncle's house and arrange to take her to a safer location, maybe even back to Sanski Most.

Several hours after getting on the highway, Jusuf came to a road on his right leading into Rasavci. He had a vague sense this was primarily a Serbian enclave, so he kept walking toward Sanski Most. From time to time, weird objects ahead of him loomed suddenly out of the ink of night. At one point, he came upon a huddle of men talking on the other side of the road about five cars lengths ahead of him. He stopped, heart racing, and after a moment cupped his ear. What if they wanted to question him or tried to pick a fight? But after several minutes studying the threatening mass, he realized that the bush-shaped silhouette never moved much, never resolved itself into heads, legs, and hands, and in fact was simply a dense, irregular clump of three arbor vitae bushes roughly a head taller than he. Whatever had sounded like voices—perhaps wind strumming through the branches—instantly dissolved into the aural ambiguities of the night, and whatever had looked like people was the result of his mind playing its devilish game of self-propagated illusions.

On his left, a wall of forest extended for as far as he could see, and on his right was a more complex landscape, puzzling in the dim light of a just-risen sliver of moon. Scattered trees, bushes, rolling fields, and large angular forms that Jusuf assumed were buildings or farm equipment rose and fell from view as his perspective of land contours shifted. He crossed back and forth from one side of the road to the other, not sure which made him feel safer. He wondered what he might say if by chance he were to pass a woman walking alone. Would he pass her and then circle back to engage her in conversation? Would she pause and turn? Would he detect a glimmer of compassion, or would he detect fear, repulsion? He banished the idea as quickly as it arose, feeling stupid he was even considering such an absurd fantasy here in the frigid air, halfway between somewhere and nowhere. What was more pressing at this moment, than a plan to get home, or the fantasy of an encounter with a woman, was his craving for something to eat, a safe place to sleep—and more urgent still, something to drink.

About a half hour later, after exiting a short stretch of dense woods whose closely spaced trunks clamped the road like towering ebony bookends, he saw an old cottage on his right, sitting at the far end of a little garden. Two huge silver maples not yet in leaf stood near the road close by a shallow swale, the longest of their branches reaching almost to the front door. A table lamp glowed dimly in the kitchen. On the second floor, in an otherwise darkened room above the front door, the blue-gray phosphorescence of a TV screen pulsed in spasms, the brightest bursts flashing across the maple branches like lightning. It was an eerie but intimate light, private, excluding those who happened by in the night. Jusuf thought of knocking and asking for help. But how would he explain his bruised forehead, his bloody hands and socks, his smelly dungarees. Would they assume he had been in an auto accident? Would they offer to get him something to drink, a warm jacket to throw over his T-shirt? Would they freely identify themselves as Serb, or Croat, or Muslim?

Where are you from? Your socks are bloody. No shoes?

I must have dozed and driven off the road. No, there is no one to rescue. I was alone.

A man wearing a dark purple sweater appeared in the kitchen window. Jusuf watched him open wall cabinets and then a refrigerator. He stacked a tray with a few things, clicked off the table lamp, and then vanished. Minutes later, raucous laughter erupted from the room with the TV. Jusuf pictured the man and his wife sipping beer, munching pretzels, cuddling under a blanket, watching a comedy.

The roadway suddenly brightened. A truck rounded a bend a half-kilometer down the road. Jusuf dropped to his knees and then rolled flat into the swale at the base of the maples. The truck roared past. When his thumping heart quieted, he rose, palmed dust and debris off his hair and clothes, and walked nervously along the flagstone pathway to the front door. Figuring it could easily be several more kilometers before he encountered another house, a house that then might be locked for the night, he peeked through a narrow sidelight trying to assess his chances of being offered any help. He faced a steep, well-worn run of painted wooden stairs to the second floor. After trying to summon a pool of saliva to swish across his tongue, he looked back at the road and then at the TV light pulsing in the branches. He lightly tapped the sidelight pane. No one appeared. Minutes later, he rapped again, this time knocking the door with his knuckles.

"Who the hell could be out there at this hour?" It was a woman's voice.

A harsh hall light flashed on, and then off, and then on again. Huge, flat white feet appeared on the top tread, followed by short, square legs with no visible ankles but laced with a netting of varicose veins. Then came the man's baggy underpants, holes along the waistband, hems near his knees, and the purple sweater flecked with crumbs. When Jusuf saw the small black pistol, he jerked back, turned, and raced along the garden path, across the road, and crouched behind some boulders. A naked light bulb hanging on a chain over the front door flashed on. Two wide shadows from the massive tree trunks fell across the road in a shallow V. The front door opened. Seconds later, the man peered out, pointing his pistol around like a flashlight. In a graceless, rooster-like strut, he walked toward the maples and across a wide, flat ledge stone that bridged the swale. He walked up the road a few meters, looked into the forest across the road, stared for a moment at the boulders, and then walked back down the road in the other direction, a few meters past the maples. Before crossing back over the ledge stone, he tilted his balding head and peered up into the branches and then across his garden. His stanchion-like legs, almost hairless, splayed in knock-kneed disfigurement. The casement on the second floor squeaked open, and a middle-aged woman in a ratty nightgown looked out.

"Who the hell is it?" she asked in a high-pitched voice that sounded like it was used primarily for frequent complaint. Her fulsome breasts swayed forward as she craned her neck to locate her husband.

"Fuck if I know. I didn't see *anybody*." He looked up at the woman and scratched his ass through his underpants. "You heard that sound, didn't you? Must've been a falling branch or something. Don't see anything on the ground."

"Bring up an aspirin and a glass of water, will ya, and that bag of raisins. Think there's still a few left."

The man went back in the house and closed the door. As the bare bulb winked out, the tree trunks' shadows melted into the blackness of the macadam. Then the kitchen light went back on, and a cabinet door slammed. A few seconds later, the kitchen light went out again, followed by the stair light.

Jusuf was desperate for something to drink and decided, if the door had been left unlocked by chance, to slip into the kitchen. He crossed the road and tiptoed along the path and stood at the door. He was about to try the knob when he heard someone cranking open the casement again directly above his head. His heart beat wildly, his eyes wide with panic. He flattened himself against the door and tried to look up without fully tilting his head. Although it was dark, save for the light from the TV, Jusuf could see against the muted glow of the sky the man's right arm extended toward the trees and the pistol in his hand. A crimson flash burst from the muzzle. The bullet ricocheted off the boulders with a resounding *ping*. Jusuf held his breath and hoped the man would not look down. The pistol was lowered and fired again. This bullet hit one of the maples, sending a spray of bark chips sailing across the garden.

Jusuf took a breath but for several minutes did not move, could not move. He was paralyzed with a bone-deep sense of dread. Eventually, when the laughter resumed overhead, he turned the doorknob and quietly opened the door. A half-empty glass of water with greasy fingerprints sat on the counter, no more than four steps into the room. He tiptoed into the narrow stair hall and saw nothing but a dim glow of light at the top of the stairs. He stepped quickly into the kitchen, picked up the glass, winced at the stale taste of what was easily two-day-old water, and set the glass quietly on the counter. He swiped six almonds and a pretzel lying near a tin marked "flour" and was about to tiptoe out of the house when he noticed four potted plants on the kitchen windowsill. Some leaves had yellowed, and a few wilted philodendron leaves had fallen to the sill. He couldn't resist the urge to quickly press his index finger into the nearest pot. The soil was dry and hard. He considered adding some water to his glass but feared the faucet would squeal or the pipes would chatter. As he shifted his weight to lean forward and direct the few remaining drops from his glass across one uplifted root, a floorboard whined underfoot. He froze for a second and then quickly dashed out of the house, down the path, across the ledge stone, and within seconds was back on the road. While chewing the almonds, he looked back to see the door still open and the TV light pulsing like cannon fire.

About an hour down the road, his left foot snagged in a pothole in a low, wet section of the roadway. To avoid falling, he danced around with his arms flung into space. As he quickly regained balance, he heard a faint hissing sound, like water needling out of a pinhole in a hose. He searched for the source but could see nothing in the blackness of the night. Just as he was about to move on, he stubbed his toe on a short pipe poking up at the end of a driveway. He ran his fingers along the pipe and discovered with his fingertip an invisible thread of water that alternately gurgled and spritzed from a tiny crack. He lay down in the mud and brought his lips to the crack and sucked in the needle-thin stream, drawing the icy water blissfully across his tongue and down his throat. He drank deliriously and then washed his hands and cleaned the bruise that had swelled to a nut-sized lump on his forehead. Standing too quickly brought on a dizzy spell that sent him keeling over into the mud.

He resumed walking for what seemed like an hour, but time had become elastic, one hour easily having been at least thirty minutes more or less. His old, thin socks had begun to wear through in places to the soles of his feet. As he was about to hobble off the road and lie down in a field, he saw the dim, formless hulk of a barn. As he worked his way behind a tangle of farm equipment netted with cobwebs, a few cows lowed with curiosity and mild concern, shifting their weight in the half-light before dawn. He covered his shoulders with a half-rotted burlap sack that retained the smell of onions. Rodents scurried across timbers overhead as he fell asleep.

When dawn arrived, a cacophony of loud snorts arose as the cows were milked. Jusuf did not fully waken. When he did stir to the knock-clopping of hooves rapping and skidding on a slippery patch of cobblestones, he made sure he was well hidden. He tried to fall back asleep but was haunted by the fear that his mother had already been taken by now to a detention camp. It was impossible to erase a life-like chain of images of the pumpkin-head recruit walking back to his house after the roundup, his mother standing in a room with no walls, and the soldier spitting on the floor at the foot of her bed. The soldier then vanished and was replaced with an image of himself walking into the house as his mother was trying to scrub away the soldier's white boot smears on the floor. She rose stiffly to embrace him. He helped her pack a small suitcase she had stashed away in an upstairs closet. He tried to drive her to safety but encountered an endless string of obstacles—road blocks, packs of Serbian soldiers, one of them stepping forward with a pistol, barking his intention to … to do what, Jusuf wondered. Ismeta complained of chest pains. Unfamiliar with the roads, Jusuf got lost in the suburbs of a strange town, trying to reach a hospital. He turned to tell her he was sorry and realized in panic that she was no longer at his side. Panic, however, slowly yielded to exhaustion, which in turn gave way to slumber and then finally to a deep sleep.

As night fell, he returned to the dark road, groggy and ravenous. He passed quickly through the small, sleeping town of Alisici and was nearing Ostra Luka when he noticed several sheets of disintegrating newspaper snagged in the branches of a bush. He pulled them loose, crumpled them, and wadded them under his T-shirt, hoping they would insulate his chest against the cold. He did not anticipate the other advantage. The sound of the papers sliding one against the other as he walked produced an unexpected sense of companionship. He felt oddly comforted being wrapped in the news of the day, particularly knowing these stories must have been written before May 28, 1992, the day of the roundup in Kljuc. He imagined the writings of numerous reporters, their stories recounting everyday events in his peaceful homeland: marriages, buildings under construction, new businesses forming, successes on a soccer field, the planting of new crops. The sound of the papers shuffling under his shirt brought back memories of the times he was a toddler and used to curl up in his mother's lap as she read the news. He remembered the sound of her turning the pages, sometimes chuckling to herself. When she read of a friend's obituary, she clicked the tip of her tongue on the roof of her mouth and shook her head. Jusuf sometimes dozed against her breast, only to awaken to find her dozing with him. Once, he awoke and found himself ensconced in a cocoon of pearly light cast by the papers that had settled over his head, his mother snoring peacefully, her ample breast a cushion for his small head. When he changed position, his hand inadvertently fell across the front of her blouse. He slid his hand into her blouse and positioned it over her breastbone, which was smooth and straight, unlike his breastbone and his father's, both of which rippled like a washboard. Her heart beat softly, and he reveled in a sense of boundless peace and secure love inside his newspaper cocoon.

CHAPTER SEVEN

IT WAS EARLY DAWN when Jusuf spotted a cinderblock barn with a ramshackle wooden shed attached at the back, a good place to sleep through the day. He stole through a tangle of vine-laced saplings and pulled open a rotting door barely supported by two whining hinges. One corner of the shed's tilting roof was near collapse, holes in its curled and moss-covered cedar shingles offering a patchwork of light blue sky overhead. He breathed easier when he saw that an archway connected the decaying shed to the sturdier masonry barn. As he entered the barn's dark and frigid interior, a rat scrambled across a bench stacked with piles of moldy magazines, a few with ultra-nationalist Serbian slogans emblazoned on their covers. Unnerved by a sudden premonition that he would be shot while sleeping there, he considered returning to the road, but exhaustion won out. He looked for a concealed place in which to sink down and sleep.

A closet-like enclosure in a far corner made of rough planks caught his eye, perhaps a toilet stall never plumbed. He tried jiggling the latch and finally whacked it loose with the heel of his fist and then pried the tight door free with his fingertips. The stall was festooned with dusty cobwebs that hung from the handles of a few ancient tools. The barrel of a rusty shotgun leaned between two studs, and a faded tan and blue cap hung on a nail. As soon as he entered the closet, he grew lightheaded and sagged instantly to the floor. He struggled to lift his buttocks just long enough to reposition a heap of moldy clothes beneath him into a cushion for his bony backside.

Even though his eyelids were heavy and beginning to droop, he observed a bright ray of sunlight sneak through a gap in the exterior siding and fall upon an old, brown pant leg under his thigh. Inside a pocket of the pant leg, his hand wormed through a mass of flaking tissues encasing a wax-paper wrapped stick of gum. Saliva gushed from forgotten springs on the floor of his mouth as he removed the wrapping and gazed with expressionless delight upon the powder-coated stick. But when he brought it to his nose, he smelled nothing. He tried to fold the slab, but it snapped like chalk. Hands shaking, he put the two pieces into his mouth until a taste barely resembling spearmint, half-imagined, half-real, brought his taste buds to life. Except during Ramadan, there was always a handful of loose gum sticks in Ismeta's apron pocket, sweet-smelling cinnamon for her and Jusuf, edgy spearmint for his father.

As he chewed, a bark-colored spider the size of a bean descended from the ceiling toward his knee in quick, broken falls. The spider's acrobatics were spotlighted in several other blades of sunlight razoring through gaps in the sheathing. When the spider disappeared into a zone of darkness, Jusuf's eyelids slowly closed.

The first was a milky dream, incoherent and aromatic. He was trapped in a coffin that smelled richly organic but poisonous, like a silo recently emptied. He was folded in the coffin much like Ibro folded his body on the rugs of the mosque. That dream vanished, and in a flickering instant, he was leaning over next to his mother in her garden, helping her transplant seedlings and set out tomato plants. She liked white lilies and placed a few in a vase. Jusuf, now a bee, flew around the blossoms, intoxicated by their fragrance. Then in the next instant, he was in his house sitting by a roaring fire, cleaning rifles with his father, the one aesthetic ritual associated with hunting that Jusuf had always loved.

When he awoke many hours later, the closet was aglow in garnet light. For a moment, he thought he was looking through a spider web of blood vessels in his own eyelids, but outside the barn, the sun was setting and slivers of ruby light crisscrossed his hideaway. It was in that blood-red crystalline light that he noticed a single strand of spider silk improbably affixed to his thumbnail. He followed the sloping thread halfway up the closet as it intersected other angled strands and then detected the spider perched at the upper end of its web awaiting the telltale vibration of its next unsuspecting meal.

Jusuf marveled at the spider's patience, its corpse-like inaction. He studied the filaments in this strange scarlet light, their leisurely, weightless drift through space. His own faint breath caused the filament fixed to his nail to move toward him, and then away, then toward him again like the window curtain in his bedroom that he used to watch lazily drifting to and fro in a summer breeze. He was about to trouble the web hair by twitching his thumb, hoping to watch the spider scramble down its lattice trap, intending to paralyze its prize, but a pressing discomfort—a painfully full bladder—intensifying with each passing minute, interrupted his musings. As he began to unknot his body, a loud, coarse cough on the other side of the door froze every muscle in his exhausted frame.

"Where they got ya working, Mladen?" It was a woman's voice creaking faintly from the far end of the barn.

"This week? They got me up at Prijedor. Don't like it as much, though." He coughed again and spit. "Next week, commander said they'll need me over at Omarska. A lot of fucking Turks crammed up there *now*." The man's voice boomed as if he were actually standing in the closet next to Jusuf.

"How many they got?" The woman's voice grew louder as she approached.

"Got what, Mom?"

"Turks! How many up there?"

"Hundreds. Probably lots more by now. Coming in by the truckloads every day."

Jusuf, gripped by panic, wondered how he might quiet his bladder as he heard large tools pulled off a shelf. Suddenly the closet door banged like a post had hit it, rattling the latch. Jusuf recoiled and reached for the barrel of the old shotgun, realizing he'd have to use it simply as a club.

"Goddamn it!" the man yelled. "That was my funny bone."

"That'll hurt," she said. "So, you were saying ... truckloads every day."

"Yeah, and truckloads leaving by night. But those that are leaving, they're lying down on the way out. Can you picture it? Sardine-style. Oily and smelling just as bad. They're heading for the pit."

"The crevice, you mean. Isn't that what they've been calling it?" She laughed. "The long sleep."

"How do you know that stuff?"

"I know some things, damn it. You think I live on the moon? So they got you shooting them?"

"No. *Not me!* It's Rade. Crazy Rade ... with a gut-full of *slivovitz*. I told you he gets a kick seeing their brains fly against the fences. Laughs like a madman. Tell you the truth, it hurts my stomach."

Jusuf clenched his fists and pressed his knees together, simultaneously trying to keep from pissing and exploding in rage. There was a loud clank and then the angry screech of a tool dragged along the floor, a piercing retch of iron against concrete. As the two voices dimmed, Jusuf could no longer endure the pressure. A stream of urine flowed between his legs, saturating his pants. Fearing the two would see the stream flowing out from under the door and come after him, he grabbed the steel barrel and tried to stand up but hadn't the strength.

"You tell Rade," the old lady said, "I got two bottles of my best brandy for him if he can send me a couple of bodies. Big ones though, tell him. Pigs would love to chew on a few Turks. Pigs for pigs." The man laughed.

"I'm not kidding," she said. "You tell him the bottles are on the top shelf of my pantry with his name on them and ... if he's got an extra hour to spend with a ol' lady, you tell him I still got some energy to lay on him. He'll remember."

"Let's eat. I'm starved." The barn door screeched on its rusty overhead rollers until it smacked the iron catch and rang hard like a cracked church bell.

Breath burst from Jusuf's lungs, tearing a section of spider web loose from its moorings. Jusuf figured the spider had registered *prey*—its venom sacks readied—but the disturbance was too extreme. The creature changed course and scurried up the wall, compressing itself into the shadow of a crack. Jusuf pictured his rivulet of pee worming under the door, through bits of straw and chips of caked mud, and finally pooling around one of the legs of the bench that supported the stacks of magazines. Rage made his face feel as hot as a baker's oven, and his hands shook with the violence of an electrocution. When they closed into fists, he wished he saw in each a bloody dagger withdrawn from the throats of those whose echoing barn voices had just enflamed him. He lowered his head into his palms, his fingertips digging into the muscles of his forehead, his body shaking with a maddening fusion of impotence and fury.

Attached to the barn in which he slept the following night was a chicken coop. It took him several minutes to figure out how to work the home-rigged, strangely elaborate door latch, but soon he was in and looking for a meal. A chorus of low clucks questioned his permission to move among the birds while dozens of beady eyes spied on him sideways, heads tilted in dim-witted puzzlement. He found two eggs. One he cracked and ate immediately. Although he gagged for a moment just after it slid down his parched throat, he soon felt a pervasive sense of nourishment no doubt more imagined than real. The other egg he swaddled in a nest of damp wood shavings he found piled in a back corner under a bench. He worked the interior door latch in a fashion similar to his method to get in, but it wouldn't open. Panicking, he hammered it with the heel of his free hand; it wouldn't budge. After taking a calming breath, he studied the contraption and concluded it must have been fabricated by someone with a quirky sense of humor. Following a variety of failed combinations, he finally realized that a hazelnut fixed to a steel pin had to be turned and withdrawn at an angle ... not pulled or pushed at a right angle to the lock. In the time it would take for one of his chickens to lay an egg, he was back on the road.

Before dawn, he came upon another barn, rank from a recent fire. In a cardboard carton, he found a heap of work clothes, threadbare in places and stiff like an old hide, but wearable. He put on the shirt and bundled the rest, slinging the sack over his shoulder. The smell of wet smoke in the shirt was vaguely threatening but also appealing, somewhat like the welcoming odor of a long-unused fireplace damp from recent rain.

A day later, he found a heavy, waxed paper bag by the roadside near a stream where he stopped to drink. The bag contained a box of cereal, half empty, crawling with worms. There was also a candy bar, hard as wood, its foil wrapper still intact. The cereal flakes and worms that he didn't eat immediately he stowed back in the bag and later sprinkled on his tongue whenever his energy waned.

Two days later, he found a pair of leather boots, hard as rhino hide and two sizes too big for him. It was painful to pull on the first boot, but he quickly yanked off the other one to shake out a black beetle agitated over the invasion of its hideaway. Having walked barefoot for many days now, his feet were cracked, blistered, and raw. Nasty sores had formed between the areas of bloody flesh, and his right heel was inflamed. Whenever his mind wandered and he slipped back into his natural gait, it felt like an electric shock raced from that heel to his hip.

The morning after a particularly cold night, he thought he was getting a cold, but the draggy feeling was replaced with joy and a sense of well-being when he found an empty plastic seed bag. He tied it around his waist with a piece of string cut to length on the edge of a plough blade. The bag became something of a valise, and in it he tossed things he came upon in the dim light of dawn or dusk: a strip of white cloth he snatched from a fence post, storing it to bandage a possible future wound; a well-worn toothbrush he found lying crosswise in the middle of the road, which he hastened to use at a nearby stream; and a broken penknife poking out from under a moss-covered rock. He used the knife to cut clippings from airborne sheets of newspaper he snatched out of the feisty spring winds. He also pocketed a pencil stub with a half-eaten eraser. Pieces of discarded fruit were also tossed in the seed pouch for moments his hunger became intolerable, and he even pocketed a pack of moldy cigarettes hoping he'd find a dry match. He wondered whether he would start smoking again three years after he had quit.

From a German pornographic magazine spotted in a roadside trashcan, he tore out a picture of a naked woman. The dark-haired model's navel was almost completely closed like the eye of someone sleeping. Her navel reminded him of one of his lovers, two years back, a Serb he had screwed seventeen nights in a row. He nicknamed her Ingrid because she had Ingrid Bergman's sometimes teary, sorrowful eyes.

"My, you're quite a lover," she once said after both had climaxed numerous times through the night. "But you don't talk much, do you?"

She ran her fingers through his long, brown hair. "Don't have anything to say, Shorty, or am I just a bore who you just love to fuck?"

He remained silent, but a sly kind of smile softened his face.

"And I've been meaning to tell you, Shorty, you little devil, that you've got the whitest damn teeth I've ever seen. I swear they're brighter than that full moon. You must brush them ten times a day."

He looked away for a moment, pursed his lips, and then said, "They're not really mine, Ingrid. I broke out all the front ones, top and bottom, when I had a nasty fall last year at school." As he tapped them, he said in what seemed like a tone of deep embarrassment, "I drop them in a glass at night with detergent. That's why they glow so brightly. Here, let me show you." He opened his mouth as if to remove them for her to see. When he saw her horrified reaction, he guffawed.

"You fucking liar. Why am I always so gullible." She whacked his buttocks with her palm, and they began to wrestle, both laughing until their eyes filled with tears and he was erect again.

When they finally settled down, he said, "Talking and making love at the same time confuses me. I prefer to simply get lost in the sensations. They transport me." He stroked the narrow strip of beard on his chin. "I guess I'm just not big on talking."

"But a woman likes to know you're with her and not with someone else. She needs to feel connected."

"So who else have I even looked at for the last two weeks? I guess I need a bit more time, Ingrid … to open up with you, I mean." But their tryst ended as suddenly as it had begun, like an itch that had to be scratched until it subsided.

A Serb, she was! he now mused as he walked along the dark road. Her ethnicity had meant nothing to him at the time. Now he wished she were stretched out naked on a couch right at his feet, her sleeping navel winking at him, her limbs bathed in her various skin-softening creams. He craved to breathe in again the fragrance of her perspiration from their last night together. He remembered that her knees were knobby and she had a scar that ran along the inside of her left leg from below her knee to halfway up her thigh. It embarrassed her, and she tried to conceal it, but when Jusuf ran his ring finger with the wrinkled nail gently along its length, it both tickled and aroused her.

"Please don't touch me there. It embarrasses me."

"It's just a scar, Ingrid. Look at my ugly nail. Sooner or later, we all have scars in one place or another. Things happen. Life's not pure."

"Oh, how poetic! Then touch me again wherever you want."

If he were to see her again, he would ask her if it had been love—what they had shared—or simply the gravitational attraction of two bodies in need? Or had it been for her a sexual experiment with a man she knew would one day soon be her enemy? And what had she really meant when she called him *you little devil*?

Memories of her body began to arouse him, and he thought of masturbating, but his genitals were half-dormant from stress, fear, and exhaustion. He fantasized that he would find a woman in a nearby town who craved what he thought he wanted or needed. It would certainly not be love—not under these circumstances. What he felt he needed in this godforsaken stretch of no man's land was the simple pleasure of a woman's warm body tangled with his. He needed Ingrid again, as long as she didn't ask him to speak. He needed a woman with a scar.

Around what he presumed was close to midnight, a scream pierced the silence of the countryside. What at first sounded like someone clapping slats of hardwood were, he soon realized, pistol shots. A light blinked on in a small farmhouse not too far from the road. Doors banged, glass shattered. A woman began sobbing, and a child wailed.

"Don't touch me. Keep your hands away from me. Don't you see my daughter in the doorway? She can see what you're doing. Please don't touch me. Please don't!"

"Shut up, whore!"

"Leave us alone, *please*. I must go to my husband. I beg you. Can't you see he's going to bleed to death?"

"I don't give a shit about your damn husband."

"Please spare us. We've done nothing. I don't know why you're so angry. Why do you hate us so much?"

A light went on in another house. More shots. The commotion died away as quickly as it had erupted, except for the backfiring of a vehicle that sped off down a gravel lane and then took a fork and headed in Jusuf's direction.

Jusuf raced into the woods as quickly as his clunky boots would permit and followed a narrow stream that paralleled the road. As he tried to sort out what had just happened, he remembered his mother's words after she had read mention in the newspaper of what sounded like a rape. She whispered into her coffee cup that she would rather die than be taken against her will. "The dishonor," she sighed. "The dishonor would be worse than death."

"Worse than death, Mom? You can't mean that."

"I do mean that, Jusuf! Worse than death. Why does a Muslim woman saying that surprise you? You've become too modern."

CHAPTER EIGHT

Upon reaching the outskirts of Podbrezje at about five in the morning, Jusuf knew he was now only about three kilometers north of Sanski Most. Uncle Ibro had a good friend in Podbrezje, an accountant who also raised pigeons, and Jusuf sometimes had joined his uncle for a lunchtime visit. As he circled the village, passing through a hilly area where he and Ibro used to hike, he could have sworn he smelled beef and biscuits wafting his way from Naza's kitchen. His stomach rumbled, and he pushed even harder to quicken his hobbled gait. He couldn't wait to be swept up in the warm embrace of his Uncle Ib and see his uncle's early-hour, six-inch vertical spike of gray hair on his otherwise almost bald head. And he couldn't wait to be once again in the town he had come to regard as his second home.

Uncle Ibro was Jusuf's mother's older brother, a professor of astronomy who had taught for a while at the University of Sarajevo. A younger brother had died three years earlier in a rush-hour accident on the autobahn outside of Munich. Conscientious but not passionate about his teaching, Ibro was always ready with a joke or with a story that turned bizarre through an unexpected blossoming of improbable events. He spoke with a slight lisp, which Jusuf discovered at age ten that he could replicate, but only in his dreams.

It had been just four months after his father died back in 1987 that Jusuf began hitching rides to Sanski Most. His mother knew that

Jusuf enjoyed helping his Uncle Ibro with a bedroom addition Ibro had been building on the back of his house. Ibro was good at measurements but clumsy with tools, and for all his knowledge of cosmic forces, he had no innate sense of how building materials behaved under gravity, or how they responded to the horizontal forces of the wind. Working alongside his uncle, Jusuf discovered how much he had learned in the preceding years, first watching and then working at his father's side on various handyman jobs at home and in the neighborhood.

Ibro was delightfully surprised one hot summer day when they broke for lunch and Jusuf, in a teasing manner to conceal the depth of his affection, started calling his uncle "Papa Ib." Childless and out of love with his cold, know-it-all, humorless wife, Naza, Ibro happily welcomed his nephew's new nickname with a simple nod and a pat on Jusuf's thin shoulder.

As he reached the northwest suburbs of Sanski Most, Jusuf heard gunfire. From atop a low hill, he could see house fires reddening the underside of clouds hanging low in the sky. Then he saw men and boys being led at gunpoint through the streets toward a line of trucks, engines revving, tailpipes pumping smoky plumes of exhaust, a scene both familiar and distressing. Jusuf ducked behind a wall as he watched a soldier just one street away splash white Xs on certain houses after checking a list he stowed in his breast pocket. Jusuf's heart began to pound as he grew alarmed for the safety of his aunt and uncle.

A huge explosion rocked the main square. The minaret of Uncle Ibro's mosque appeared to sway like a shaft made of rubber, not stone. Then it broke into segments and collapsed into a mushroom of churning dust. Moments later, an even more thunderous explosion lifted the mosque's lead-sheathed dome from its delicate mooring of carved clerestory mullions. The blast wave thudded against Jusuf's chest as the dome rose several feet before falling like a giant, tilted clay saucer. Huge masonry fragments crashed down on thick supporting walls as lead roofing tiles creaked, their cleated seams splitting open in sounds that reminded Jusuf of human moans. Unable to watch this beloved sanctuary crumble to dust, Jusuf turned away and began to cry. He used to sit with a cup of hot coffee cradled in his palms on Ibro's porch, watching the sun crawl across the walls of the mosque, its minaret standing proud like a pointed rod of alabaster. He remembered the dust-filled shafts of sunlight slanting through the mountain of holy space within. Tears continued to roll down his cheeks as he realized he would never again see those awesome spears of sunlight fall solemnly through the ring of high windows just under the blue-tiled dome and land as a dazzle of jumping lights on the *mihrab*. His uncle's mosque, his home, his family, his friends, his entire world—everything dear—seemed to be disintegrating and falling away at a pace that was terrifyingly swift.

Jusuf turned and ran. When he reached the bottom of the hill, a convoy of trucks rounded a corner and headed down the road in his direction. A soldier in the lead truck stuck his arm out his window and fired several shots. Jusuf felt like a clown trying to sprint in his huge boots, bullets smacking the blacktop as he wove from side to side. As the first truck neared, he leapt into a roadside gully, sinking instantly up to his knees in a viscous pool of foul-smelling muck. The soldier slapped his knee and howled at the sight of the vagabond clown leaping into the trash-strewn swale. Jusuf hunkered down in a cluster of swaying reeds as the other trucks roared by.

A ribbon of terrified eyes stared out the backs of the trucks. Jusuf's heart sank when he thought he caught a glimpse of his uncle's blue sports pants and his sky-pointing tuft of hair, which Aunt Naza had not yet smoothed down with her usual *tch, tch*. Jusuf fought an impulse to slog out of the gulley and call to his uncle, to signal him with waving arms that he should jump off the truck *now*, no matter the consequence. It was just seconds between the time the impulse hit him to warn his uncle and the instant the absurdity of the idea registered. The convoy was already well down the road and disappearing around a bend.

A blanket of fumes hung over Jusuf's muddy refuge. He pictured the trucks pulling off the road into the same dark corner of the woods into which his convoy had driven a week before. He envisioned the captives climbing down out of the trucks, just as he and his comrades from Kljuc had been directed to do. He saw Uncle Ibro walking to a tree and beginning to pee and then heard a pistol shot ring out as if it had been fired on a street close by his muddy swale. Jusuf suddenly couldn't breathe. He reached up to finger his beaded necklace, the last tangible and dear possession that connected him with his life in Kljuc. He fingered it with affection and longing and desperation, as a Catholic fingers a rosary. Thinking of home, of Kljuc, of his mother, of Sasha, of his other friends, and his lovers, he had the unnerving sensation that these places, these people were now just characters and places he had read about ages ago in a fairytale. It felt like they had become only figments of his vivid imagination. He could no longer separate what was real from what his mind invented. This feeling of being unmoored, living in a world that had no tangible substance, terrified him. He felt dizzy and toppled into the stand of tall rustling reeds.

As the sky began to show a trace of light, Jusuf dragged himself out of the muck and clawed, crablike, up the slippery bank. He sat on the side of the road, pulled off his boots, and shook out cupfuls of goop. A few meters away, a small hand-painted sign atilt on a thin aluminum pole caught his eye. Peeling blue letters read: *Stari Majdan 6 kilometers*. He figured that a tiny village like Stari Majdan might be safer than a large town, particularly when the town he had been headed for hours earlier was now reduced to wide swaths of smoldering rubble. He stared at the sign, half-expecting in his cerebral numbness for it to speak to him about what might lay ahead if he followed its arrow. But the risk of being caught in Stari Majdan now that it was daylight was too great, so he trudged west into the foothills of what he thought might be Grmec Mountain and collapsed in the corner of an unplowed field.

He slept fitfully under a scant layer of leaves for a day and a half. The times he did awaken, and they were few, he hadn't the strength or the will or enough fear to get up and seek a safer location. Even in his state of stupor, he figured if danger did come his way, he would be able to deal with it better if he were rested and clear-headed. Late in the middle of the second afternoon, a hard rain began to fall. Shivering and weak, he walked further west, higher up into the mountain. Along the way, he picked shriveled blackberries and ate clumps of certain grasses his father had taught him were edible. When he later came upon a patch of plantain leaves, he ate four of them and then used the residue of pulp from his tongue to coat the lingering swelling on his forehead—another tip from his father on one of their last hunting trips together. Although Jusuf had been repulsed by how his father equated hunting with manhood, he now wished his father was walking alongside him, the two of them escaping together, now the *hunted*, no longer the *hunters*. He finally found shelter under a rock outcropping that formed the entrance to a shallow cave. He lay down next to two crushed beer cans and a stiff gray condom. Within minutes, he was once again asleep, the drumming rain a welcomed lullaby.

When he awoke, a rivulet of rainwater flowed from overhead and spiraled down an arm's length from his nose. He extended his hand and watched the stream pummel clean a disk the size of a large button on the back of his gray hand. Not having seen a patch of clear skin in weeks, his spirits lifted.

He ate a dry piece of carrot he had stowed in his plastic pouch until he heard a dog bark from somewhere down the hillside. A German shepherd came charging up the hill in his direction. Fearing his cave would be more of a trap than a refuge, he looked about for a stick big enough to battle the animal or to scare it off but saw nothing to use as a weapon. As the dog closed in on him, a woman appeared lower on the hill and called and whistled for the dog to return. The dog growled, circled Jusuf, bared its teeth, and then turned and loped back down the grassy slope toward a small stone and stucco house with a red tiled roof. Minutes later, after tying the dog to a short post, a door slammed, and there was silence.

Jusuf sat down to still his madly racing heart, but after ten minutes, the woman reappeared walking up the hillside without her dog. She waved. Halfway up the hill, she nodded, set down a basket, smiled, and returned to her house. Jusuf walked to the basket and removed a jar of water, a sandwich, and a cookie wrapped in a once-used scrap of foil. There was also a white flower stuck through a piece of notepaper. *Good Luck, I'm sorry for you.*

As Jusuf ate the sandwich and drank the water, he wondered what she meant by *sorry*. Most likely, it referred to her dog, but perhaps she knew he was on the run. If she was Serbian and sympathetic to their cause, it would be doubtful she would express sorrow, even if it had been in response to the dog's aggressive behavior. Jusuf returned the jar to the basket and placed the flower in his plastic carryall. Tentatively, he began to saunter down the hill, hoping she might reappear and perhaps even invite him in. He longed to speak with her, to hear a human voice, to speak with someone, with anyone. He imagined closing his eyes and just listening to her soothing voice until he was asleep, a voice he hoped had the power to calm him like his mother's voice often did when he was young and fretful. He imagined the inside of her house, the color of her bedspread, but his reverie ended abruptly when the dog growled and lunged, his rope drawn tight and vibrating like a cable. The woman pushed aside a curtain and waved. She then stepped out to quiet the dog and scold it with a gently wagging finger. Jusuf caught a glimpse of a frail old man through a window, coughing in a wheelchair, a cigarette dangling from his lips, his arms waving as if he were conducting an orchestra. Before returning to the cave, Jusuf thanked her with his customary bow and palms pressed together as if in prayer. When the drizzle subsided, he climbed still higher to the first of several ridges. As he stopped to polish his teeth with his treasured toothbrush, an armada of dark clouds scudded overhead toward the northern horizon where, from a sliver of blue sky, spears of sunlight slanted earthward in supernatural splendor.

When Jusuf reached the top of what was the final mountain ridge, a large city appeared below him, carpeting a broad valley floor extending out to the horizon. Was this a place of safety or danger? At least there were no current signs of warfare. A square stone tower rose in the foreground on the far side of a river surrounded by a sea of what looked like red-roofed, small shops and houses. In the distance, drab concrete apartment slabs, remnants of the Communist era, were aligned in rows, and forward of them sat what looked like a huddle of low office buildings adorned with garishly colored panels. Here and there were stone minarets that were much slimmer and taller than the few church steeples. Could this be Bihac, where he had visited on occasion with his mother? Whatever the city, it seemed peaceful.

Directly below him, the mountain flattened into fields covered with rows of feathery green sprouts. A road paralleled a river until it ended at a low bridge with blue-painted steel girders. The bridge spanned the river at a sharp angle and disappeared into the heart of the city. As he studied the road more carefully, one unpaved shoulder seemed alive, as if a long caterpillar, colorful and composed of many uncoordinated dots, was snaking along its edge. He rubbed his eyes to make sure he was not dreaming or hallucinating.

Jusuf worked his way down the slope, grasping bushes and occasional tree branches for support, but where there were stretches of sheer rock, he felt safest sliding on his rump and braking with his boot heels. Halfway down and now closer to the road, he was able to make out small trucks piled high with bundles of household belongings. A few noisy tractors pulled squeaky hay wagons loaded with children and old people, and here and there were smaller carts hitched to oxen. Most travelers, however, were on foot, just a few on horseback.

He paused to sit on a large, flat stone to catch his breath. Was he drawing closer to friend or foe? If the city they were headed for was in fact Bihac, those below him would probably be refugees like himself, escaping from or driven out of Muslim hamlets and heading for the safety of one of Bosnia's largest Muslim enclaves. Reasonably confident now that this was likely the case, he rose and moved further down the slope.

Young women with infants at their breasts trudged along the rain-slick roadway, dogs trotting at the heel. A man hobbling with a cane and wearing a faded red fez held a befuddled chicken under his arm. Bundles of clothing, sagging from the drizzle, sat precariously balanced on the heads of those on foot. Littering the shoulder between the road and the river were large books with gold lettering, huge ornately framed photos, and antique mirrors too heavy to lug any further. A lovely table had been jettisoned, its carved legs pointing skyward in a puddle of mud, reminding Jusuf of a dead cow. Most of the refugees wore white armbands, and a few carried white flags. The older women had *maramas* tied around their heads and wore the traditional baggy-legged *dimije* rather than slacks or a dress.

Jusuf worked his way down the rock-strewn slope toward what he now recognized as Put Avnoj-A, the two-lane road leading into Bihac. Though the terrain was still treacherous in places, he let gravity and his growing excitement pull him into a slow run. His oversized boots caused him to fall once, but he preserved his momentum by turning the fall, as his soccer buddies had frequently witnessed, into an impromptu somersault. His heart beat wildly, and his lungs pumped with a throbbing sense of anticipation as if a homecoming of some miraculous making was about to embrace him.

Closer to the road, Jusuf's eyes, which over the last several weeks had narrowed into cautious slits, began to relax. Because his eyeballs jounced in their sockets, the line of refugees appeared to worm about in an intoxicating blur of color. He felt joyous and wanted to laugh, but the desire failed to actuate the requisite face muscles. At the edge of the first planted field, his tears turned to threads that flowed into the creases at the corner of his eyes and then sideways around his face. A surge of sweet saliva welled up under his tongue as he hopped across sprouting rows of peas, radishes, and lettuce. Unable to restrain his eagerness, he started running as fast as he could, his arms outstretched in blissful relief. He hummed to himself and then sang a few words in a voice that had turned harshly coarse until a bullet suddenly sliced through the drizzle and whizzed past his ear. He fell to his knees and then dropped flat to the ground in one smooth motion, the side of his face sinking into a cushion of plowed earth. When he raised his head to see who had a gun, another shot was fired.

He couldn't believe that after such a treacherous odyssey and now so slow close to safety, his life would be taken because he was mistaken for he knew not what. After lying motionless for several minutes, he reached into his plastic pouch and felt for the strip of white cloth he had put away for the wound that had never occurred. Still prone in the plowed field, he raised his left arm and waved the cloth until he could see that the stalled knot of refugees had resumed their march. In a cautious progression of movements, he drew himself up to a kneeling position and then stood. Believing that a signal was required further confirming he was not a threat, he waved the cloth above his head and then brought his palms together, prayer-like, in front of his chest. When he felt that he was no longer viewed as a danger, he walked slowly toward the road, all the while scanning the queue for anyone else who thought a warning shot needed to be fired his way.

Jusuf blinked in disbelief and his heart thumped an extra beat when he saw his mother in a pool of sunlight walking arm-in-arm with what looked like one of her friends from Kljuc. He was relieved and excited and was about to call to her when the woman turned to watch a deer dart out of and then back into a stand of trees. As soon as he saw that the woman was wearing glasses, his smile withered. Further on, when he thought he saw Suljo walking arm-in-arm with his two sons, he was more guarded and realized he was seeing only what he wished to see. A heavyset man with a rifle over his shoulder, perhaps the one that had fired at him, reminded Jusuf of his father, but this beyond-the-grave impossibility erased with finality any hope of seeing loved ones.

Jusuf sloshed joyfully through an irrigation ditch that bordered the road. Those walking closest to him drew back with concern as if, Jusuf thought, they were seeing some prehistoric scavenger that had just stepped out of the Ice Age. Jusuf tried to imagine what they were seeing: filthy face and hands, tangle of long hair, a jumble of rags roped to his scarecrow-thin body, his plastic pouch with its collection of jingling oddments. He was hoping for a welcoming nod, an indication that he was viewed as one of them, that they understood he was escaping a plight like their own. But those nearby either stared in amazement or looked away fearfully and quickened their pace. He kept a distance for a while and continued walking on his side of the road rather than crossing over and trying to work his way into the line.

Two small boys turned to look back at the stranger who had come up somewhat near them. Their eyes were wide with fear and curiosity as they stole glances at his dark face, oily beard, and tattered clothing. When one of Jusuf's boots twisted on a stone, lurching him forward unexpectedly, the boys scampered off and tunneled under the arms of their parents. But twenty meters down the road, they turned and looked back. They giggled and hugged each other and then slowed their pace to get closer to Jusuf, eventually crossing the road before quickly running back with a squeal. The braver of the two finally waved to him.

Jusuf looked around to the adults nearby for a clue as to how to respond—hoping he'd see if any kind of response would be welcomed. Although he could not get his troubled eyes to fully soften, he worked the muscles around his lips with his fingers. He got his lips to part but was unable to bring forth any understandable utterance from vocal cords nearly immobilized from days upon days of disuse. But then one of Jusuf's irresistible smiles materialized to decorate his face. His glowing white teeth still had a remarkable if surrealistic shine, and the irrepressible dancer in him tapped something of a jig on the macadam. The older child laughed with surprise and said, *"Ciao."* Moments later, Jusuf noticed an opening that had formed in the line beside him.

CHAPTER NINE

SEVERAL FAMILIES JUST AHEAD of Jusuf reached Prekounje, a neighborhood on the eastern outskirts of Bihac, and peeled off to the right, heading presumably for the homes of friends or relatives. Jusuf yearned to follow them and be taken into someone's home or kitchen. He even imagined finding his mother sitting in conversation, sipping coffee. This, he realized, might be more probable in Bihac proper, where his mother used to take Sasha and him to see the Regatta when they were youngsters. Realizing his thoughts had turned to nonsensical fantasy, he looked around to assess his progress along the road. The main line of refugees stretched as far back as he could see, and those in front of him continued trudging into Bihac.

The two boys who had originally befriended Jusuf began tossing stones into the River Una, now only meters away from the road to their left. The boys looked back to see if the *brown man*, as they referred to him in loud whispers, was taking note of how high and far their stones had arched before falling with a barely audible *glup* into the turbulent surface of the rapids. When a tossed stone sailed particularly far, Jusuf gave the thrower a wink and a thumbs-up. This encouraged the boys to make still more energetic throws but with minimal gains in distance. Their joyful competitiveness reminded Jusuf of the hours he and Sasha had tossed stones, swam, and fished in the Sana River near Kljuc. Had those good times occurred in another lifetime, on another planet?

A quarter kilometer downstream, the road veered to the left and crossed that bridge angling across the river and into the city that he had seen from Grmec Mountain. Its girders, railing, and light posts were all painted a sickly powder blue. He remembered from his Regatta visits that locals called this main entry point into Bihac the Blue Bridge. As he got within several hundred feet of the bridge, calls to prayer were broadcast from several minarets. Conversations immediately started up around him and he even heard subdued laughter from two young men behind him who walked arm-in-arm with a somewhat older woman who tried to conceal her limp. One man was short, shorter than Jusuf, the other tall and top heavy. As an ensemble, the three looked like clowns from a circus as they hobbled along in dissonant gaits. Jusuf sorely wished to join them in conversation, but as was his nature, he chose only to listen to their talk about the proprietor of a bar where the three had met a few months ago. After sixty-four years as a bachelor, the proprietor was finally getting married.

It was clear from other conversations that the refugees were mostly from Bosanski Petrovac, a town roughly halfway between Bihac and Kljuc, where Jusuf had traveled often when he was sixteen to spend time with a new girlfriend. Nadiya loved soccer, and she and Jusuf often worked up a sweat kicking a ball on a field near her house, her breath turning somewhat sour as she pressed her competitive game, until they eventually tired and left for a less competitive activity in a remote section of nearby woods. After some months, however, Nadiya jilted Jusuf in favor of a wisecracking, muscular goalie on the high school soccer team with a trophy scar angled across his white forehead. Nadiya had awakened deep feelings in Jusuf, and he cried in his bedroom for hours the afternoon he got her short, matter-of-fact letter breaking off their romance.

Although relieved by the sense of being in the company of other Muslims who were also escaping the war, Jusuf nonetheless felt isolated, like a shunned family member, if for no other reason than his disheveled appearance and rank odor kept others at a distance. He wanted but could not bring himself to ask anyone for suggestions on where he might find shelter and a meal, certain that no one would want to share that kind of information with the likes of him. Finally, he stopped walking and summoned the courage to make inquiry of those near him, but the queue fanned out and circled around him, everyone casting an eye down on the roadway or looking out toward the river on their left or the suburb of Prekounje on their right.

Once on the bridge, the light drizzle tapered off. The air smelled clean, perfumed by spring growth. Objects both natural and manmade were veneered with a thin film of rainwater, the glistening effect most noticeable on the stone walls of the old Captain's Tower standing proud above the other buildings at the far end of the bridge.

As he stepped onto the bridge's pavement, a gust of wind whisked several candy wrappers and tissues into the air, sending them spiraling above the macadam like whirling dervishes. He followed their dancing whorls until he reached the middle of the bridge. Off to his right, a constellation of boat-shaped islands in the river looked like giant kayaks waiting for the start of the Regatta. On one bank of the river, the pencil-thin and sharply pointed minaret of the Fethija Mosque rose stark and white against a now deep blue sky. Jusuf recalled picnics near the cataracts where he and Sasha enjoyed likening the mosque's minaret to American and Russian rocket ships they had seen blasting into space on their TVs.

Standing at the railing, Jusuf looked down at the river racing north from under the bridge. It felt like a carpet being dragged away beneath his feet. The sensation of almost being toppled was unsettling, so he turned and crossed through the line of refugees to the railing on the left side of the bridge. Resting his elbows on the cold aluminum guard rail, he looked upstream at the line of refugees still slogging along the road toward the bridge. He wondered whether his mother might be in this line or in another line approaching a different city. Perhaps she was already in Bihac. He felt a powerful urge to hug her and kiss the leaf-shaped birthmark on her right cheek. In a day or two, he would telephone and tell her of his plan to borrow a car and bring her to safety.

At the end of the bridge on the left and some twenty feet above the river stood a building perched on a promontory. The one-story structure looked fanciful in every respect, like the gateway to an amusement park with a copper roof that sloped up dramatically to a decorative finial. Café tables and chairs were set out in a line close by a cast-iron railing. He recalled that this was where his mother brought him and Sasha for sodas after the Regatta. The boys used to hurl stones from the terrace, trying to get a stone to strike the uppermost rail. When one hit, it rang like a bell, creating the impression that the one who had thrown the stone had won a prize.

With a fresh coat of bright yellow paint over its stucco walls, the building seemed much livelier than Jusuf remembered from years past. Perhaps this was not the same café. But then he noticed an arabesque embellishment, like a large eyebrow, arched above a circular window, an eyebrow that had kept the two boys amused as they sipped their drinks. They had tried holding one eyebrow down with two fingers in order to raise their other eyebrow, but Jusuf's mother easily raised one eyebrow without a finger, and this made the boys laugh and encouraged them to spit out their half-swallowed sodas. Jusuf reached the building's entrance pergola at the side of the road, its hand-painted sign reading *Kafana Paviljon*. The refugees who had been walking next to him had already veered to the right and walked through a park and into the center of town. Jusuf, hungry and urgently in need of a toilet, walked toward the café's porch, boots crunching along the gravel terrace.

The porch was an odd structure, almost as large as the building itself, its roof supported on a geometrically intricate wood truss that sat on two widely spaced Doric columns. In front of the porch stood a small stone fountain. The rim of its petal-shaped basin came to just above Jusuf's waist, which surprised him because when he was a child, he could barely look over the scalloped rim to see the dancing jets of water. Jusuf ran one hand around the rim and then lowered it into the water, which quickly turned the color of stone. He began to feel safe, as if he had arrived at the home of an old friend he hadn't seen in years. He recalled that he and Sasha used to hug the columns, one on each side of the portly shaft, their arms reaching around its massive girth, trying in vain to get their fingertips to touch. They would peer around the column, each struggling to catch a glimpse of the other while at the same time trying to hide. The columns looked so much slimmer now as Jusuf slid his index finger up one of the smooth, concave flutes, half-expecting to see Sasha's face and golden curls darting out from the far side with his devilish grin.

Jusuf hesitated before peering through one of the four glass panes in the upper half of the door. The smoke-filled room was full of people eating and drinking, heads bobbing in conversation. A gray-haired bartender languidly stirred a drink for a patron standing at the bar. At a table near the door sat a young redheaded woman laughing with a man who looked about the same age. The woman glanced up, her eyes widening and also revealing a trace of fear or disbelief, or both. She turned back to her friend and lowered her head as if to share a confidence.

Jusuf steadied himself, took a long breath, turned the doorknob, and stepped across the threshold. As he stood darkly ominous in the open doorway, the din of conversations quickly fell away to a hush, the near silence broken only by the sound of coffee cups lowered into saucers and the tinkling of knives and forks set slowly across chipped white plates. From the TV behind the bar, the angry voices of three actors in a popular Spanish soap opera suddenly sounded very loud, startling a few unsuspecting patrons. The bartender reached up and lowered the volume as Jusuf looked around the room. All eyes were on him as he closed the door behind him, causing a small brass bell to ring.

He wondered for a moment if he had just walked unwittingly into a Serb hangout. Why had none of the other refugees stopped here? Or were some already seated and enjoying a drink or something to eat?

In the far right corner of the room was a small green sign. It had a white fist with an outstretched forefinger pointing down to the toilet room at the bottom of the stairs, a hand sign Jusuf and Sasha used to mimic when one of them needed to pee. For a moment, Jusuf felt like his boots were glued to the floor. Finally, he took one tentative step into the sea of tables and chairs in front of him. The patrons stared and remained silent. A few seconds later, he took two more steps toward the stairway as the metal, plastic, and glass oddments in his makeshift valise jingled around his midsection. What had been a relaxed array of knees, tote bags, and tennis sneakers along the route to the stairs were all drawn back under the tables in a continuous wave of concern as Jusuf walked toward the stairs. Some heads turned—a few in his direction through curiosity, others away in disgust as the air was fouled by his passage.

As he descended the concrete steps, he heard the café come alive again with hushed voices and a few derisive laughs. At the bottom of the stairs, even his own pungent stink failed to mask the stench of the toilet room. He fumbled urgently through layers of clothing until he peed with relief, his stream pummeling several un-flushed twirling cigarette butts that spun like pinwheels in the urinal that was so much lower than he remembered. When he looked up and saw the face of a stranger staring at him from a jagged remnant of mirror tilting precariously out of its bent metal frame, he was deeply shaken. A beard clotted with filth surrounded a gaunt face that looked back at him blankly, eyes sunk deep within dark-ringed sockets. When he moved, the stranger moved. He wanted to cry, but no tears flowed.

Using a paper-thin sliver of soap, he scrubbed away a layer of filth and then dragged his weary frame back up the steps and cautiously approached the bar.

CHAPTER TEN

JUSUF CHOSE THE CLOSEST of seven mismatched wooden barstools and hauled his exhausted body onto the seat. The bartender, a thin man with wire-rimmed glasses and eyes that sometimes rolled up out of view under heavily creased lids, finally shuffled over in scuffed, pumpkin-colored slippers, his steps audible as the slippers clung to tacky, rubber floor mats. He placed one nicotine-stained finger on the edge of the bar and then nodded his head once to signal his readiness for Jusuf's order.

"Just water, please." Jusuf spoke in a weak and raspy voice.

The bartender looked at him warily. "No coffee? No Beer? No food? You look like you could use a meal." Then, in a voice raised for his all of his patrons to hear, he added, "And you also look like you could use a week or two at Gata. The mineral baths would do you a world of good." When two young men at a nearby table laughed, the bartender looked over at them and winked. His parted lips revealed the rotting remains of five front teeth.

After sitting in silence for a moment, Jusuf finally admitted without emotion, "I have no money. But I *am* thirsty ... terribly thirsty."

The bartender stroked the stubble of his beard as he focused on Jusuf with obvious suspicion. "How do I know whose side you're on? I don't take to aiding the enemy."

"Whose side? I don't think I'm on anybody's *side*." Jusuf again considered the possibility he was in a Serb hangout, much like Edo's bar in Kljuc.

Seeing that neither the stranger nor the bartender had anything more to say to each other, the woman who had been sitting near the entrance stood up and strode with confidence to the bar. She was a tad taller than Jusuf with sparkling green eyes and hair the color of fanned embers.

"What can I get for you, Azra?" the bartender said.

"Give the guy a glass of water or something, Igor. In his state, he couldn't swat a gnat."

"He could be a spy. Don't let appearances fool you. You never know who's going to walk in here."

"Then give me a glass of water."

Igor tacked his way to the sink and filled a small glass with tap water. He set it in front of the woman, almost banging it on the bar top, and turned away. She slid it in front of Jusuf, who nodded his appreciation and followed with a barely audible, "Thanks."

Igor walked to the window and looked through the panes of the large, round window above the sink. Jusuf assumed the bartender was probably speaking for everyone in the bar when he asked, "Are you with them?" He pointed with a long, curving, arthritic finger toward the refugees. "Sure don't look it to me."

"Yes … and no," Jusuf whispered. "I joined them several kilometers up river."

"You know any of them?"

"Not a soul. We simply crossed the bridge together."

"And?"

"And they all looked like they needed to find someplace better than where they'd been. So did I."

"Know where they're from?" With this question, Igor looked directly at Jusuf and focused his suspicious gaze even more intently.

While Jusuf pondered the question, the woman with the red hair sat down a few stools beyond Jusuf, close to a tray of bottled condiments. She tried to conceal that she was leaning away from Jusuf to escape the stench.

Jusuf took a cautious sip of water before tilting his head back and emptying the glass. He closed his eyes in bliss as the water filtered down through his parched innards. He pictured a potted plant in its final hours, imprisoned in rock-hard, dry earth receiving a lifesaving cup of water. "I joined them somewhere north of Ripac. There was a sign in the village. The line kept going back in that direction as far as I could see." He paused for several minutes while he closed his eyes. "Guess they came up from somewhere around Bosanski Petrovac. I seem to recall hearing something to that effect but couldn't swear to it." Jusuf's gut produced some squeaks and rumbles. "Thought it best to keep to myself."

"Let me have another, Igor." Igor took his time, placed the glass in front of the woman, glanced to his left, and without letting it go, slid it in front of Jusuf, who nodded his thanks.

"You didn't speak to anybody?" the woman asked.

"Given the way I look, I figured I better keep my mouth shut."

"Where'd you say you're from?" Igor stared into Jusuf's half-closed eyes, which again closed fully as if he needed to rest a few seconds just to answer, or to remember where he had come from, which barn, which shed, which stretch of forest near what village.

"Me?" He thought for a minute as to what the idea of *me* even meant anymore. "Kljuc. I'm from Kljuc."

"How come you look different from them, dressed in those rags. Filthy and all?" The woman winced at Igor's insensitivity.

Jusuf wasn't sure how he should answer, so he tilted the glass and held it angled toward the ceiling even after its contents had drained. He worried that the wrong answer might result in his being arrested again and thrown in a truck and taken to who knows where. Figuring he had no choice but to answer honestly, he spoke in just above a whisper. "I escaped."

Jusuf stole a quick glance out toward the tables, but no one moved. "I escaped from a convoy of trucks that was taking a bunch of us to what I guess was a prison. Never actually saw it. I've been in the woods for a while. Some Ser ... some soldiers rounded a bunch of us up in Kljuc. They killed a baker I knew, and a Serbian kid who was on the truck with us." Igor drummed his fingertips on the bar, pursed his lips, and gnashed his teeth.

"Why'd they kill the kid?"

Jusuf dropped his head and went silent for half a minute. His whole body recoiled as he remembered what had happened in the woods and his failed promise to protect the boy. The woman motioned to Igor to refill Jusuf's glass again. Igor banged it down with such anger Jusuf jumped.

"They didn't know the boy," Jusuf said. "He started bawling for his mom. A guard shot him ... just like that. But like I said, he was Serb, just like them."

Igor slapped his palm on the bar top. Jusuf jerked again. "Nobody spoke up to save him?"

"Everything happened so fast. It was night. Both were dead within seconds. The soldier killed them both for no good reason."

"I don't follow you, kid."

By this time, several patrons were up out of their chairs and formed a circle around Jusuf, who sensed he was in for trouble but hadn't the energy to even plan an escape. "What soldiers you talking about? Serbian soldiers?"

"Yes."

Igor's eyes narrowed, but Jusuf couldn't make sense why the bartender was so agitated. "Go on," Igor demanded.

"These soldiers. Some of them were our friends. Had been our friends, I should say."

"Go on."

"I've been living in the forest for days ... probably several weeks now. Just trying to stay alive. Living off the land best I could."

"Where you say you're from again?"

"Kljuc." Jusuf thought he had already said that. "You know that area?"

"I sure as hell do know Kljuc. It's not *that* damn far away. Used to know some people over that way. Haven't seen them in years." Igor wiped the laminate bar top from one end to the other with a rag reeking from food, beer, and a foul-smelling disinfectant whose odor hung in the air for several minutes. He walked out from behind the bar and among the tables to collect some empty glasses and beer cans. As he returned, a newsbreak flashed on the TV. The reporter was claiming that Muslims were attacking Serbs and Croats in various parts of Bosnia. He cautioned that Serbs must be on the lookout and protect themselves.

"Bullshit!" Igor exclaimed, still on Jusuf's side of the bar. "Nothing but fucking lies on that tube." With his eyes still on the TV screen, Igor asked, "What's your name, kid?"

"Pasalic. Jusuf Pasalic."

"Pasalic, eh. Well I'll be damned! Ain't too many of you around these parts anymore, are there?" Igor was still watching the report.

"There are a few of us, but not too many."

Igor lit a cigar stub. "Pasalic, uh? Years ago, I used to hunt with a guy up round Kljuc named Pasalic. Must be six or seven years ago now, give or take a decade or two."

"Really?"

"Guy's dead now. Fucking good shot, he was. And I mean *good*."

Jusuf said nothing.

The soap opera returned to the screen, and Igor strolled behind the bar to the sink. "Been quite a few years … quite a few years." Igor's eyes rolled up behind his lids for a moment as his thoughts seemed to leave the room and travel to some place deep in a forest. "You're probably too young, but did you ever hear of a fellow up that way … name was Braco? Braco Pasalic? He used to do some farming now and then and fixed a thing or two. A handyman, guess you'd say."

Jusuf smiled weakly and sat up a bit. "Yes, sir. Actually I did know Braco. Knew him pretty well myself for a number of years. Braco was my dad."

Those already gathered around Jusuf came in closer and looked back and forth between Igor and Jusuf.

"Come on! You're bullshitting me." Igor looked like someone trying to work through the final pieces of a difficult puzzle.

"Listen, kid. I've been looking at you since you come in here, at those dark brown eyes, that reedy voice, how you rubbed your thumb over your trigger finger a few minutes back, making that sound like a creaky door. That was just like Braco used to do. A strong chin, too, and those eyes. Now I see it. He also spoke like you, too, deliberate-like." Igor reached for the pack of cigarettes someone had left near the tray of condiments. "Here, have one."

"Much appreciated. Don't usually smoke, but feel I need one just now." Jusuf reached for the cigarette and noticed that his fingernails were long and packed with grime. "God! Looks like I've been dead a month or more."

Igor struck a match. Jusuf took a deep drag, coughed once, and then spoke into a lazy cloud of smoke that hung around his face. "You know, sir, I actually remember this place. I used to come here with my mom when I was a kid. We came with … with a friend of mine." In his head, he repeated the phrase, *friend of mine*, wondering what that meant now. "Mom used to bring us here for the Regatta once in a while. We used to play right out there on your terrace, played tag and stuff, tossed stones to hit that railing."

"I think I remember your mom. Recall seeing her a few times when I picked up your dad. Does she have some sort of mark, maybe a scar, on her cheek?" He pointed into the stubble, wrinkled skin, and skin spots at his cheekbone.

"Yeah, a birthmark."

"Then I do remember her. Probably also saw her with you and your friend, but my memories are fading lately. Used to know her name."

"Ismeta."

"I'll be damned. Ismeta it is." He slapped the countertop and hooted. "Nice lady, she was." Jusuf wondered whether he should read something into Igor's use of the past tense.

Igor turned and filled a cup with coffee. He put two greasy *cevapcici* sausages with extra onions on a *lepinja* and set them in front of Jusuf with a wink. "On me, kid, cause I'm sure Braco is watching. We were friends till the end. Even gave me a gift just before he died. He wouldn't think well of me if I didn't give his boy something to eat."

"Thanks." *Friends till the end*—the phrase played in Jusuf's mind. That's what he always thought it would be with Sasha. *Friends till the end.*

Jusuf took a bite of the sandwich. "Thanks a lot. I'm truly grateful for your kindness. Know Dad would be too."

"Name's Igor. I'm sure, after all these years, Braco'd be happy to know you stopped in here. I used to hunt with your dad many years ago when I lived in Drinic. He and I would drive up to Pounje on his tractor or in my jalopy four or five times a year. Now that was great hunting! Deer, grouse, pheasant. Occasionally a wolf or wild goat. And damn good fishing up there as well."

Jusuf devoured the sandwich and gulped down the syrupy coffee, savoring the grains on his cracked tongue. "Dad did love to hunt. He taught me to shoot too."

"You still hunt?"

"No, not really. Hunting never appealed to me."

"Braco's son not a hunter? I don't believe it. That must've broke his heart."

"He wished otherwise. I know I let him down, but it really got to me. The killing and the blood and all. I just didn't have the stomach for it."

"Your dad never mentioned it to me. Couldn't face it maybe. But by then, I might have moved away. Never could keep track of time. Forgot he even had a son. No offense, mind you."

"I did like fishing though. Fished a lot with Dad. All I had to do was put a line in the water, jiggle it a little, and damn! A trout would fly out of the water like I was a long-lost relative. Dad always got a kick out of my good luck." Jusuf took another drag on the cigarette and let the smoke drift out slowly between his lips.

Igor's face melted into a relaxed smile. "I stood next to your dad once when he brought down the biggest damn brown bear I've ever seen in my life. Could have been the end of the rope for both of us. That son of a bitch was angry and hungry. Teeth big as my fingers and twice as thick. Stood tall as this room ... well, maybe not that tall. Lucky I was with your dad 'cause he had a sense of timing that was uncanny. What others required three shots to do, Braco pulled off with one. And it wasn't just his aim. I don't know how to say it ... he could get the whole sense of a place in a single glance, sum it up quick as lightning, and in a flash, *bang*, the beast would fall. He was a perfect hunter. Master of the moment." Jusuf had seen this himself many times, more times than he wished to remember.

Igor went on recalling old times as Jusuf's head began to droop. His hands began to tremble with fatigue as he sipped his coffee.

"You okay?"

Jusuf turned toward the question, saw Azra's concerned expression, and weakly nodded a tactful but not accurate yes.

"Sounds like you've been on the run for too long," she said. "We heard on the radio that some kind of fighting started over in Kljuc some weeks back, but who can you believe these days? The reports of what's been happening here in Bihac have been a joke, too."

Jusuf's body sagged, looking like he was about to topple off the stool. Azra moved closer with an outstretched hand in case it was needed. She looked around the room to see if others had noticed and might offer to help.

"Excuse me," she said. "What was your name, again? I think you mentioned it to Igor, but it didn't stick."

"Me?" He tried to bring her face into focus. "Jusuf. I'm Jusuf."

"Listen, Jusuf. I don't know if you have a place to sleep tonight, but if not, you could come back to my house to bathe and have a night's rest. I don't think my father would mind. Then you can be on your way in the morning."

"Thanks. But are you sure? I'm a filthy mess."

"Come on, I'll give you a hand." When he felt her hand on his shoulder, he dragged himself off the stool, staggered like a drunk for a few seconds, and then shifted his weight to find his balance. The man who had been sitting with her had already risen and was waiting for her at the door. He wore a yarmulke, a striped, threadbare prayer shawl, and several small gold earrings laddered up one ear. Even in Jusuf's wearied state, he felt a mild animal ill-will toward the man, but he was too tired to resist when the man put a shoulder under his left arm as Azra had done on his right side. "Thanks, Dado," Azra said.

The three walked silently over the small bridge that crossed the canal behind the coffee house and then through a small park. They made a right on Viteske Brigade Road and then a left a short distance on Alije Derzeleza Street to Azra's house. Jusuf hung limp between them and almost fell asleep. At the door, her message to Dado was clear that she could manage from here on. "Call me in a day or two. Or better yet, I'll call you when I see how things are going."

Jusuf looked up just as Dado wagged his finger at Azra and smiled.

"Oh, get out of here, you fool."

CHAPTER ELEVEN

Azra, arm outstretched, pushed Jusuf from behind as he trudged up the creaking stairs to the second floor. She pointed to the open door of the guest bedroom where he immediately collapsed onto a neatly made bed. She cringed when she saw his grimy clothes fall against the yellow bedspread and his face sink into her crisply ironed pillowcases. Jusuf mumbled into his beard something appreciative as she slipped off his mud-caked boots. She gagged when she saw the dried blood and rawness of his feet. His multiple odors suddenly overwhelmed her, and she rushed to open a window to prevent herself from puking. Before leaving the room, she unfolded a lightweight camphor-scented blanket over his body.

On her way down the stairs, she wondered what madness she had invited upon herself through this act of kindness. She was relieved, however, that her father would be around the house tomorrow morning, even though she knew he would remain, as usual, largely out of sight. Now she had two men to protect, two men to care for, and maybe another man to hide.

Around eight in the morning the following day, Azra began cleaning the house. When she got to the second floor, she heard nothing from Jusuf's room and decided to see if he was still asleep or, worse, had died from his deprivations. She tapped lightly on the door and after a few seconds turned the knob and peered in. He was lying on his back, mouth agape, the pillow beneath his head now dark gray and so greasy it had a sheen. Despite the open window, the room smelled of garbage, smoke, decay, and camphor. In the middle of the bed, the blanket sloped up like a very shallow tent supported by a candle-size spike. She stared for a moment, blushed, and quickly shut the door.

Azra thought her father might enjoy the cup of coffee she had made for Jusuf. She found him tending his pigeons in the large coop he had built at the back of the house behind the tool shed. As he cradled the hot cup in his palms, she mentioned with a note of humor that the fellow sleeping upstairs looked like a man who had come back from the dead. Her father sipped the coffee and flashed an appreciative smile at Azra until her words registered with him in a manner she had not intended. His eyes darted about fearfully for a moment, and then his expression withered. He moved to the rear of the coop, appearing to look for his broom.

Azra walked back to the kitchen, scolding herself for her oversight, but her regret was mixed as usual with frustration and a tinge of annoyance. Would her father ever forgive himself? Would he ever fully explain what had happened so many years ago that caused him such continuing grief and distress?

Jusuf was still sleeping two hours later when an artillery shell crashed into a group of industrial buildings about a kilometer and a half south of the house. The sound of the blast barely penetrated his slowly evaporating dreams. When he finally opened his eyes, he was sure he was still dreaming. Peach-colored walls met the ceiling in a border of wallpaper printed with gray-green leaves and vines sprinkled with purple grapes. Table lamps with decorative but inexpensive shades sat on night tables, and hanging on the walls were family photographs and a collection of faded ink drawings of old Bihac. The room made him think of Sasha's house—also nicely decorated and furnished—the grapevine wallpaper in Sasha's living room being almost identical to what now bordered his dream room.

In his stupor, Jusuf thought for a moment he had actually awakened in his old friend's house. Brought to mind were his many sleepovers when the boys were young, their frequent hilarious breakfasts together when the number of jam-filled *palatschinke* they had cooked was twice what they could eat, their days listening to popular music from Yugoslavia and around the world, and the endless hours when Jusuf had to endure Sasha learning to play his harmonica. Suddenly a vision of Sasha standing with the other soldiers in the roundup in Kljuc penetrated his sweeter memories of years long passed. Jusuf still couldn't reconcile seeing Sasha with a rifle and fatigues with the ideas Sasha had expressed in their conversation at Edo's bar a week before the roundup. It had been one of their usual arguments about religion, but Sasha had seemed so distracted. He kept repeating his usual themes, but that night his mantra sounded mechanical, even forced.

"C'mon, Jusuf, God *did* create a good world. But it's not his job to maintain it." Jusuf waited for Sasha's next thought, but it never came. Instead, Sasha stood and beckoned the bartender to bring another round of beers. As he sat down, his Eastern Orthodox gold cross slid back and forth like a tiny sailboat, seemingly overwhelmed by the high waves formed by his collarbones.

"Sasha, you pray to God for help, don't you?" Sasha seemed distracted. "Hey, Sasha, that was a question. You pray to God for help, don't you?"

"Yes, sometimes I do."

"Well, has he ever delivered what you prayed for? And I mean in a ratio that exceeds the law of averages? You could pray to me for what you want, and I could deliver it as well as he has over the years." Sasha forced a weak laugh. "You always say God is everywhere but where's the evidence? A good god—if god exists at all—should make a good world."

"But what of the order in life, Jusuf. Do you think all the order you see around you just popped up by chance?"

"Sure there's order. But I see just as much disorder. Take war, for instance. It seems to come around these parts as frequently as peace. Serbs, Muslims, Croats fighting each other century after century, not to mention what the Nazis did here. And it's usually in the name of one god or another. Or one lunatic or another."

Sasha glanced around the bar. There was a sudden hush at a few nearby tables. At the time, Jusuf remembered thinking that the comment may have sounded uncharacteristically poetic for a guy better known for his reticence.

"Yeah, there's order, Sasha, but there's also plenty of chaos."

"You sound like you're just repeating your damned uncle's cosmological theories."

Jusuf was momentarily embarrassed that the source of some of his comments was so obvious, but he forged ahead anyway. "Maybe. But just remember, Uncle Ib is a bloody believer like you, just of a different faith. If I were ever to really need help, I'd never pray to Allah, or your god, or anybody else's god. That's just plain old superstition. When there's a problem, gods take too long to answer the fucking phone. And when they do, you can't be sure they're responding to your call or someone else's."

A few of Sasha's friends at an adjoining table began to glare at him. He dropped his eyes and picked at the label on his beer bottle. The conversation was suddenly over, as if someone had thrown a switch. Jusuf figured it had ended abruptly because of the hour and the beer.

Jusuf eventually slumped in his chair. His eyes drooped. Sasha leaned across the table, his Marine Band harmonica falling forward in his breast pocket. With his lips barely moving, he whispered, "Jusuf. Wake up for a minute, you shit, and listen to me. I'm going upstairs to the bathroom. When I come out, I'm going to stay up there. No one's up there at this hour, and there's something I really have to tell you. Give me five minutes. When you hear me playing, look at your watch and then come up like you're looking for me."

Jusuf's reveries of the exchange at Edo's bar were erased by an urgent need to pee. He untangled himself from the blanket, turned stiffly to sit on the edge of the bed, stretched, and then stood up holding the side of the bed for balance. The pleasure of polished floorboards was all but blotted out by the pain of his sore feet. He looked out the window and saw a sunlit city, not a nighttime forest! As he turned back toward the room, a breeze from the window fluttered a piece of notepaper that had been taped to the foot of the bed. The handwriting framed within a printed border of small flowers was vibrant, with an energetic flourish.

You will find our bathroom at the end of the hall to your right. Use whatever you need. I'll fix breakfast … or lunch, or whatever you want when you come down.

He hobbled across two hooked rugs and a threadbare blue oriental in the hallway. In front of the bathroom mirror, he untied the various cords that encircled him and dropped his grimy clothes to the floor. He pushed aside the shower curtain and stepped into the tub. The shower pipes looked freshly soldered but fitted un-artfully. Jusuf had not been in a shower since he and Sasha and two girls jammed into a single room eight months earlier in a newly renovated low-end hotel in Dubrovnik. Almost no one had a shower in Kljuc.

Needles of hot water scoured his back with a welcomed vengeance. As he slid the soapy washcloth across his limbs, he took pleasure in watching a grayish-brown puddle accumulate on the tub floor. Once, hunting with his father, he watched a snake shed its skin while he and his father slowly ate their chunks of lamb and cheese. Skin and memories left behind on a forest floor; filth and nightmares washed away in a stranger's tub.

After drying himself with a large, soft, yellow towel, he looked in the mirror and was again shocked to see that stranger from the day before returning his gaze. The face was gaunt, eyes filled with tension, sadness, worry, and fatigue, a still-wet beard almost hiding the neck. He raised a pair of scissors to his beard, smiled at the stranger he was about to undo, and began to cut. He went at his beard in a frenzy, filling the sink with shiny, dark crescents. Using a razor Azra had left for him, he shaved his entire face except for his caterpillar-wide goatee, which, as it took shape, made him smile once again with a sense that the man he had been in Kljuc had not been lost forever. He turned his head from side to side, admiring the results, reacquainting himself with the person he remembered seeing in the wood-framed mirror above his sink at home. His cheekbones were prominent now, as if someone had slipped small, flat river stones beneath the skin. But his eyes still peered out from darkly ringed hollows. It was like seeing, and almost not recognizing, a friend who had been away for many years.

Using a length of toilet paper, Jusuf swept his hair clippings into a wad and dropped them in the wastebasket. He combed his hair, parting it in the middle, leaving dripping ringlets to fall on his bony shoulders. There was also a new toothbrush in its plastic wrapper. Jusuf brushed twice. As he was about to leave the bathroom, he realized he didn't remember the name or appearance of the person who had brought him here. All he could remember was a mass of bronze light around a woman's face and a vaguely unsettling image of a man in religious garb. Perhaps they had simply been characters in the strange dreams he had last night—flashes of crackling gunfire, creatures running in the night, dark birds screaming, prey falling to the earth, and a never-ending panorama of human madness spiraling out of control under a strangely peaceful canopy of motionless stars.

Ear to the door, Jusuf heard no one in the hall. He hobbled quickly to his room, carrying at arm's length the pile of chocolate-colored garments he had swept up off the floor. With an odd sense of loss, as if he had to say good-bye to friends who had helped him through a difficult time, he stuffed the rags into a white plastic grocery bag that had been left on the bureau. He held up his paint-spattered Grateful Dead T-shirt for a final inspection, oily flakes of perspiration-stained newspaper falling free at the hem. He thought of washing the shirt and saving it as a keepsake, but he quickly stuffed it into the bag and voiced a quiet good-bye. On a small chair next to the bureau was a pile of clean clothes with another note reading, "Hope they fit." Before dressing, he retied around his neck his freshly washed choker of beads.

He pocketed a few of the old keys he had found in his wanderings, keys to a home he would never enter, and a town and a life he would never see. Perhaps they had been a source of hope during his weeks in the forest that he would one day be able to open some door, someplace, or that someone would open a door for him. It struck him, perhaps for the first time, that the name of his hometown, Kljuc, actually meant key. It had always just been the sound of his town's name, with no conscious or abiding connection to the physicality of his own keys that hung near the photograph of Marshal Tito near his front door. At least for now he was in *someone's* home in a familiar town, but would he ever need a few keys again, to get back into Kljuc, to get back home, or perhaps to return from some remote and threatening place and back into the arms of loved ones? Finally, he slipped into the pocket of his new pants a keepsake from his odyssey out of hell, Amil's pink but now silent hearing aid.

CHAPTER TWELVE

Jusuf walked gingerly downstairs in his bare feet. As he glanced at more family photographs atilt on the walls and a few pieces of mail on a small table near the foot of the stairs, he relished the fact that he was truly in a *home*. It seemed to be a place of simple pleasures. Worn rugs on polished floors, old lamps mixed with cheap modern ones, a small TV with two fingerprints on the gray screen, and a brown wire tracing a catenary curve under the living room window on its route from TV to outlet. Books were stacked like medieval towers around two oversized upholstered chairs, and a well-worn shawl was draped over the back of a dark-green corduroy settee. On a narrow shelf above an ornate desk, where small souvenirs competed for space with bric-a-brac, a fly circled the sticky mouth of a near-empty beer bottle. There was an undeniable charm to it all; easy livability free of contrivance. Then he picked up the aroma still hanging in the air of a meal recently cooked. The only word that came to Jusuf's mind was *paradise*. He had been delivered.

As he walked through the living room, he wondered whether anyone was home until he heard water rushing through a pipe and the ring of a glass accidentally colliding with a dish. He saw a door slightly ajar and cautiously pushed it open. Brilliant sunlight pouring through a casement window lined with sad-looking, leggy houseplants made the stark white countertop gleam like an iceberg. Squinting into the blinding whiteness, he stepped into the kitchen. A redheaded woman, back to him, stood at the sink in jeans, socks, and an orange sweatshirt. Sunlight shined through the loose ends of her hair, producing a blaze of bronze filaments. As she finished washing a few dishes, she began to whistle softly, swaying from side to side. With one hand shading her eyes, she peered out the window into her backyard in the direction of a small ramshackle structure partly formed of wire mesh walls, where a man was puttering with his pigeons. Jusuf assumed this was the young woman who had offered to take him home. *Then again*, he thought, *it could be her mother*. He was about to clear his throat when she turned to put away a pot.

"Oh my god, I … I didn't expect … didn't expect you to …"

He backed up into the doorway to give her space and nodded deferentially. The pot she had picked up was shaking in her hand. She set it on the counter and took a deep breath. "Wow! What a difference." She tilted her head as if to see him at a different angle. "It's hard to believe you're the same man. You looked so much older." Jusuf looked around the room, slightly embarrassed by her comment. He stood barefoot on the patterned linoleum, looked everywhere except directly at her, and said nothing.

"Jusuf? It is Jusuf, isn't it? You look so different. I see you found my notes and the clothes. Did you sleep okay?"

"I slept just fine, thanks. And yes, it's Jusuf. You were very kind to let me sleep here last night."

"I'm happy you're here."

"It's very strange to hear someone say my name. It's been so long since I've spoken to anyone, heard another human voice."

"How long were you out there?"

"Several weeks. I lost count."

"You're a very lucky man."

"My father used to hunt. He taught me how to survive in the woods with little more than my wits."

"Someday you'll have to tell me what it was like out there for so long. Unless it's too painful to recount."

When Jusuf was silent for many minutes, Azra changed the subject.

"I have a cousin in Austria named Jusuf, so your name brings good memories to mind. I'm Azra, by the way. Do you even remember meeting me in the bar yesterday?"

"I'd like to say *yes*, but it's all rather fuzzy. I'm sorry. I was so exhausted I could barely sit up. But I guess, now ... yes, you do look more familiar, the red hair and all."

"No need to apologize."

"But you were very kind ... or I should say brave to take me in. Incidentally, my clothes are in that shopping bag you left. I'll bring it down later."

Azra appeared lost in thought.

"Uh, bring what down?" she asked.

"The bag, my clothes. I wasn't sure whether ..."

"Oh, sorry. I'll get them later. I hope you had a good night's sleep, or did I ask that already?" She turned to pick up a dishtowel to dry her hands.

"Yes, I did. I slept like a log."

"I noticed. I mean, I peeped in to see that you were all right ... you had been sleeping for thirteen hours, and I was getting worried that a man who looked so near death might actually have died."

"I so needed that sleep. And that shower—now that was a gift."

As his stomach growled, he patted his abdomen. "Sorry. My stomach's rather rude at the moment." He thought she was about to offer him something to eat when the kitchen door leading to the back of the house opened halfway. Then it was slowly pulled almost closed.

"Dad?" She paused a long minute before saying, "It's fine, Dad, you can come in." Her comment was spoken in a whisper, almost confidentially, and in a practiced tone that sounded gently reassuring and yet open to a variety of interpretations.

Jusuf, puzzled and uncomfortable, looked at the closed door, and then at Azra, and then back at the door. He waited for Azra or her father to speak. Certain that her father couldn't see her at that moment, Azra mouthed the words to Jusuf, *It's all right*, and patted the air in a gesture suggesting this was not unusual behavior and to act as natural as possible.

Azra stared at the worn oak threshold of the doorway as she chewed the inside of her lower lip. Her father slowly opened the door again before taking a cautious step up the one riser from the shadows of his tool shed. He stood not quite in the kitchen but no longer in the shed, halfway between seclusion and engagement. He was stooped and unshaven, the upper half of his short, round body slumped like a sack of grain. An errant gray pigeon feather wavered on his shoulder like an uncertain epaulet. Jusuf tried to read Azra's actions. It looked like she was trying to hold onto her bright mood, but it was seeping out of her like a sail robbed of its billowing profile by a fickle change in the wind. For roughly a minute, the three stood immobilized, points of a triangle waiting for the emotional geometry of the moment to shift.

Jusuf wondered how Azra's warm welcome moments earlier could have shifted so quickly into such awkward and confusing territory. At the very moment that Jusuf felt the need to break the silence with an utterance he had not yet composed, Azra stole a quick breath and said simply, "Dad, this is the man I told you about. The man I met at the Kafana Paviljon."

Her father didn't move but coughed several times—a nervous cough was Jusuf's impression.

"And, this is my father ... Suad." Jusuf turned to Azra for a clue as to what he should say, if anything. She looked like she was about to sink to her knees and cry. Instead, she sighed and waited.

"Dad, this is Jusuf." Rather than look directly at the man her daughter had brought home, Suad's lowered eyes wandered around the room, his eyes in the shadow of his jutting, knitted brow that Jusuf thought might be part of the permanent architecture of his face. Then her father steadied himself and shook his head slightly as if to throw off an unwanted thought, some passing consternation that was troubling him at the moment. "I'm sorry, young man. You reminded me of, of, of ... I'm sorry, very sorry."

Jusuf wanted to be helpful, or at least change the subject, so he asked with genuine puzzlement, "Do I hear a motor running?"

Azra turned her head to focus on the sound and then smiled. "Oh, those are Dad's pigeons in the lean-to. Come to think of it, they do sound a bit like little motors. They're out beyond the shed." Then she added, "That's Pop's retreat back there."

Suad's eyes seem to drift until he said, "Yes, my dear Azra has always called it my retreat. I'm out there a lot. Guess the word fits."

"Pigeons. Really?" Jusuf said. "My uncle's friend used to raise pigeons. Over by Sanski Most." Jusuf didn't feel comfortable discussing at just that moment the violence he had seen there.

Suad turned toward Jusuf, his expression now more relaxed. He rolled up his sleeves and idly stroked his forearms, the golden hairs thick as fur. Then he and Jusuf looked at each other and simultaneously said, *"Ciao."* Suad's mild stutter seemed to evaporate, at least for the moment. Though restrained in demeanor, they smiled at the timing. Jusuf caught Azra's eye. She smiled, her shoulders obviously more relaxed now.

As Suad closed the door behind him, the cooing and clucking of the birds abated. "They fit pretty well," Suad said, nodding his balding head in the direction of Jusuf's trousers. Jusuf looked down at the rumpled khakis that gathered in folds under his belt.

"A bit loose around the waist, but compared to ... Are they yours, sir?"

"Yes, but I haven't worn them in years. They look better on you than they ever did on me. Please call me, Suad. Suad Sabanovic."

"Thank you, Suad. I will. I hope it's okay with you, my staying here last night. I could move on later today if this is any kind of imposition. Maybe there's a hotel I can ..." Jusuf knew that was an empty offer, with no money to even place a phone call.

"Don't even consider it," Azra said. "I hope you'll stay at least until I get some flesh on those bones."

"Azra works at the hospital. She'll bring you back to health very soon."

"Oh, Dad."

"Well, it's true. You're a fine nurse, and soon it's on to med school in the fall."

"A doctor?" Jusuf asked. "I'm impressed."

"Don't spread the word until after I graduate. I'm not sure I have what it takes."

"She has what it takes and more so," Suad said with a beaming smile that showed his pride.

Azra fixed a bowl of hot-pot soup, a few pieces of *sudzuk*, and a piece of trout. "Dad pulled that from the Una just yesterday. He fishes there from time to time. He's got his favorite spot a few hundred meters below the Blue Bridge. I'll show you one day."

"Azra, this tastes great. You can cook!"

"I'm happy. What I know about cooking I learned from my mom; that's her secret soup recipe you're relishing." Before she finished the sentence, a shell whistled overhead and crashed into a building several blocks away. They all ducked. Azra looked at her father with alarm as the windowpanes in the kitchen rattled and Jusuf's soupspoon jangled in his bowl.

"We've already lost a few upstairs," Azra said. "The windows, I mean. We taped some plastic over them for now. We're lucky it's not winter."

"I noticed plastic sheeting in the hall. I can fix them for you. My dad was pretty good at carpentry and odd jobs. I used to help him."

"Well, Jusuf. That's quite interesting," Suad said. "I own a hardware and appliance store in town. Perhaps you could give me a hand with some things in the shop when you're a bit more settled."

"Sure. My pleasure."

After finishing his beer, Jusuf looked around the room and then back into the living room. He asked, "Is your mom at work?"

Azra shook her head no.

"Out shopping?"

Azra closed her eyes and then tapped her fingers lightly on the dining table. Her eyes welled with tears.

"We lost her to lung cancer," Suad said, taking Azra's hand in his. "Just five months ago." No one spoke for several minutes.

Seeing her father drifting away in his thoughts, she said, "That's her writing desk over there in the living room. She used to write lots of letters. She loved writing letters to her friends, even those she could have just as easily called on the telephone. That was Mom's art."

"That's so unusual," Jusuf said. "I mean the idea of writing letters ... as an art."

"She once dreamed of being a poet. She made excuses for writing and sometimes wrote when she should have been doing chores. Dad would get mad ... not *really* mad, just hungry. Dad is always hungry." Suad squeezed Azra's hand in a gentle entreaty not to go on.

There was a long silence, and Jusuf felt he was in a space he didn't belong, at least not this soon. "It's still hard," Azra continued. "She was such a quiet glow. Always there for us. Then, overnight the rooms went silent. I'd give anything to have her back. But you can't wish for the impossible."

"I lost my dad some years ago also."

"Then you know. But in certain ways, it's like she's still here ... her letters, her furniture, her drawings. And yet you know she's not here and never will be here again. We keep thinking we see her, Dad and I, in town, coming down the street. We hear a noise upstairs, and for a moment think she's up there folding clothes, making beds, leaving the bathroom. I thought we'd be over it by now, but …"

"I am so sorry. I just assumed …"

"It's okay. How could you have known? Even though it still hurts, it does kind of bring her back for a time when we think and talk about her." Azra stood and walked over to the front window in the living room. "Dad bought her this desk from Sarajevo before I was born. Didn't you, Dad?

"What you can remember always surprises me."

"Mom saw it in an antique shop and fell in love with it. Dad had slipped the shop owner twenty deutschmarks and winked as they were leaving. Every time he drove to Sarajevo for things for his shop, he gave the guy another installment. I was around six before Dad brought the desk home for their anniversary. Mom was stunned. She had completely forgotten about it."

Jusuf walked over to the desk to look at it closer. "Wow, that floral fretwork around the top edge. Can you imagine someone actually carving all that stuff and gluing in all those tiny ivory inlays on the legs? It really is stunning."

"Around ten in the morning, the sun streams through this window. Mom used to sit in what looked like a pool of celestial light. That's a 'mother-word,' *celestial*. Those were her happiest moments at this desk. I polish it twice a week now. You want to hold on to every memory."

When Azra turned to look at her father, she noticed Jusuf deep in thought with a troubled look in his eyes.

She took a step closer to him. "Are you okay?"

He looked up but said nothing. After a moment, he took a deep breath, smiled faintly, and pressed both his worries and his longing for his own mother into a place in his heart he would have to visit later when he was alone.

CHAPTER THIRTEEN

Later that night, Suad, Azra, and Jusuf had a few beers before dinner and watched news reports about fighting breaking out in cities throughout Bosnia. The language on the Serbian side was blatantly inflammatory with references to Turks and fundamentalists, and a changed way of life unless something was done immediately. The three watched in silence until Jusuf asked, "Was there much shelling here before I arrived?"

"Yes. Some cannon fire and mortars. I don't know what it was like for you in Kljuc," Azra said, "but the Serbs living around here had seemed perfectly content, or so we thought. Then on June 12, I think it was a Friday, they threw their belongings in trucks and cars, all of which we realized later had already been packed, and in some cases, they even left their meals on their plates, and drove out of town. They drove like they were trying to escape the end of the world. And, come to think of it, they were, but it was our world. What a weird afternoon that was—wasn't it, Dad?"

"If it were rewritten in a novel, no one would believe it."

"That's similar to what happened in Kljuc. It was like someone threw a switch. No one was expecting anything, but then when you stop to think back…"

"Yes, there were signs here, too," Azra said, "but for some crazy reason, we all dismissed them. The day they drove out of Bihac, they called to us out of their open windows saying they'd be back sometime soon. That was true for all the Serbs except for guys like Igor."

"Igor?"

"You met Igor yesterday at the bar. I think he said he was your dad's hunting partner or something—the bartender with the glasses who wouldn't give you that first glass of water."

"Yes, yes. I remember. So he's a Serb?"

"Yes. There are other Serbs, like Igor, who stayed with us, but not many." Jusuf thought immediately of Sasha and wondered if this could have been said of him. He took a swig of beer, placed the bottle on a nearby table, rotated the bottle until the Tuzlanski Pilsner label faced him straight on, and then pressed his palms together, his fingertips thrust under his goateed chin. He stared at the label for more than a few seconds, then his focus was somewhere else. Azra and her father glanced at each other, eyebrows raised.

"I'm so sorry," Jusuf said, "I was back in Kljuc there for a minute. Azra, you were saying …"

"Oh, just that at first there were some gunshots here and there and a few planes and helicopters overhead, but that was all. We waved good-bye because it all seemed so normal. I can't believe we did that! We were so startled and confused, and actually also so sad to see our friends leaving."

"Some had told us they had vacations planned," Suad added. "Others said they were off to see relatives, and a few acquaintances of mine said they were going on business trips. All this travel talk meant nothing to us at the time. Then everything dawned on us a day or two after they had left."

"It was like that in Kljuc, also. The Serbs being our friends, so we thought. I mean … well … most of them played the game."

"What's really strange," Azra said, "is that when they got a short distance outside of town, many of the vehicles stopped right in the middle of the road. Some of us were still waving good-bye and we thought, oh, this is just a big joke. Here they come back. But no! The military guys unhitched their cannons, turned them around, and started firing at us, right back into the heart of Bihac. Right into their own homes and right into *our* homes. It was like a nightmare that you knew for sure could never be happening. But it happened; it truly happened. It was so damn surreal it's still hard to fathom." Azra got up and turned off the TV.

Jusuf opened another beer. As he took his first sip, Azra asked, "What were you doing, when it started?"

"Sounds odd, but I was home painting our kitchen. My mom had been after me for weeks to get the job done, but I hate painting, particularly all the spackling and stuff. Out of nowhere, this thug shows up at the door looking for guns, takes some money off me, then marches me into town with a rifle in my back."

"Was your mother home?"

"She was. That was her nap time."

"Were you able to contact her while you were on the run?"

"It wasn't possible, although I worried about her constantly. I've been sick about what might have happened to her. I tried to get back to Kljuc through Sanski Most, but the town was in flames."

"Yes, we had seen that on TV," Suad said.

"So I tried to change my route and went up in the mountains. Actually I was lost."

"At the bar, you said you escaped. From where?"

"They were trucking us somewhere up near Prejidor I think. Not sure exactly where."

"You were lucky! Is there anyone to look after your mom?"

"I had a friend ... but that's a long story. He's a Serb, and last I saw him, he was on their side, dressed and armed for war. As I said, my dad died several years ago. So I've really been the only person looking after her. I've got to figure out how to get back and get her somewhere safe."

"Do you want to try to call her?"

"Yes. That would really mean a lot to me."

"The phone's by the stair behind you. I hope she's okay."

Suad and Azra watched Jusuf hobble toward the phone, and as he did, they went into the kitchen. "I'll find a pair of my soft slippers for him, Azra."

With his heart racing and his breathing in broken rhythm, Jusuf dialed. He expected to hear her voice after the first few rings, to hear her cries of relief learning that he was safe, but the phone kept ringing. He tried to imagine why she might not pick up the receiver or could not—shopping, but that was unlikely, in the bathroom perhaps, visiting friends, at the mosque, or working in the garden. He hoped with each new ring she'd pick up. But the rings continued. He felt that if he hung up the receiver, he would somehow betray her. Finally, he returned the handset to the cradle—gently, slowly—fearing she would hear a rude slam if she picked up just as he hung up. He hoped even at the last moment that he might hear the ringing stop and her say *Molim*.

Jusuf remained sitting next to the telephone table. He picked up a pencil and a notepad and idly drew a circle, and then another, one over the other, and then darkened the rest of the page as if he were sketching a disk of bright daylight seen from within a tunnel or a tube. He replaced the pencil and pad and rested his hands on top of his head, his mind racing through possibilities frightening even to consider.

He thought of calling Sasha to see if he might know something or to ask him if he could look in on her until he got back to Kljuc. What could be more absurd? Sasha was now with the enemy. Had their friendship been a fraud all along? Jusuf tried to think back to the end of his conversation with Sasha in Edo's bar. What had Sasha been trying to tell him? At the time, it made no sense, just a cascade of drunken nonsense, or so it seemed.

When Jusuf walked in from the living room, Azra and Suad saw his reddened eyes and knew he hadn't gotten through.

"No luck?"

"She didn't pick up. That could mean anything. But it's hard not knowing."

No one spoke for a long while until Jusuf said, "Do I hear your pigeons again, Suad?"

"Yes. You can sometimes hear them from inside the house on a quiet night until we turn off the lights. They go to sleep when we do."

Suad opened the back door and tilted his head for Jusuf to follow. "Come, I'll introduce you." The two walked through the dark tool shed and into the coop where Suad pulled a chain for the overhead bulb. Jusuf tailed Suad around the benches stacked with cages while the pigeons cooed and turned their heads, their red eyes darting here and there like little glass beads. Suad opened a cage and removed a pigeon. He stroked its head and its green iridescent neck feathers, and then fanned the feathers on one of its wings. The pigeon rubbed its head over the cracked nail on Suad's thumb. Suad handed the pigeon to Jusuf, who had held many a dead bird, shot by himself, Sasha, or his father, but never a live bird, not even when he joined his uncle to visit the pigeon fancier in Podbrezje. The bird pecked Jusuf's fingernail and fluttered to be free. "The smell of your coop brings back many memories."

Suad misunderstood Jusuf's comment. "I'm sure she's okay, Jusuf. Your mother, I mean. She could be anywhere. But call again whenever you wish. We understand your concern. It's a very difficult time."

"Thanks, Suad. You and Azra have truly been a godsend."

When Jusuf retired for the evening, he was pleased to see that Azra had changed the bedding and aired the room. As he sat on the edge of the bed, the furnishings and wallpaper once again reminded Jusuf of Sasha's house, and his thoughts returned to their conversation at Edo's bar.

Sasha had asked Jusuf to join him upstairs after a few minutes so they could speak privately. Jusuf responded with a half-interested nod and then closed his eyes. Minutes later, above the inflamed rabblement of voices and bursts of laughter, he heard a few faint strains from Sasha's harmonica coming from upstairs. Sasha usually played flawlessly, but this night, as he played Dylan's "Gates of Eden," the sound was sour. He glanced at his watch, tilted the beer can for the final few drops, and walked upstairs. On a landing halfway up, he paused and, through a thick cloud of cigarette smoke, looked down on a knot of Serbian men at the foot of the stairs, leaning forward toward the center of their table. They focused on a sheet of paper with two columns of names and pencil lines crisscrossing from one column to the other. Following a brief argument, the man holding the pencil leaned forward, his head angled to convey his skepticism, and then erased one line and drew a new one. He pounded the table with his fist to confirm his satisfaction, looked into the eyes of those around him, and smiled through narrowed eyes. The others roared with laughter and also pounded the table. In unison, they yelled, "Boom!"

Jusuf found Sasha sitting upstairs, looking pale and nervous. He was toying with his harmonica, repeatedly pressing the slide with his thumb and tapping out the spittle on his thigh. Seeing Jusuf, he dropped the instrument into his breast pocket, where a final drop of moisture seeped out and blossomed on his shirt. Sasha lit another cigarette, his hand trembling, and again offered one to Jusuf.

"I couldn't say too much down there."

"What are you talking about?"

Sasha took a drag and scratched his cheekbone, looking for a way to start, a place to begin. Smoke streamed from his nostrils. "Listen, Jusuf, I'm sure you know there's some fighting going on around the country. Between your people and mine. You *do* know what I mean."

Jusuf tilted his head, half-acknowledging the fact but placing little weight on its significance.

"I never have used those words before, 'your people and mine,' but it *is* what's happening. You've seen the clips on TV." Jusuf looked at Sasha, waiting for his point.

"Didn't you hear that shit about staying in your house for your own security? What did you think when your guys were told to turn over your weapons?"

"So? So things are a little hot right now. It comes and goes."

"But only Serbs have the arms now. And the Emergency Committee? Are you blind? Are you fucking deaf? And the fighting in Sarajevo? Don't think it can't happen here. We've got to do something about it soon."

"What do you mean *do something*? Nothing's happening around here. This isn't Sarajevo or Croatia. We're far away from all that stuff." He paused and considered Sasha's words. "Okay, so I see a few changes. Things are a little different, maybe. But why should *we* do something? Do you think we should go to war too, you and I, and the guys downstairs? And whose side should we fight on? You're drunk and crazy and making a big deal over nothing!"

Jusuf scratched his goatee with both hands, a gesture, perhaps unconscious, that his friends had come to understand was Jusuf's signal that he was growing impatient or annoyed.

A rotund fellow with a shiny head came upstairs and pushed through the double-hinged door into the hallway leading to the men's room. The door whacked and clicked back and forth before coming to rest at the jamb. Seconds later, a urinal flushed with a loud sucking gush. The man coughed and then, with his gut-hard pig's belly leading the way, thundered back out through the door again. He adjusted his balls as he glanced over at Jusuf and Sasha. They sat in silence, pretending to be wasted. To Jusuf, it looked like the man had found the scene strange, the two of them sitting with their eyes half-closed in a dim room save for the flickering fluorescent near the toilets. The man brought his lips up to his nose suggesting he had caught a whiff of something foul, and then turned and thumped down the stairs, the racket of his descent intending to say something to somebody.

"He likes us," Jusuf quipped.

Sasha leaned forward and whispered, "Do you remember that old building where we used to play when we were kids? The one with the bones and the beer bottles."

"I have no idea what you're talking about."

"That abandoned little schoolhouse near Veliki Radic, near where my aunt and uncle live, over toward Bihac? You must remember. We had plans a few years back to take what's-her-name up there for a little see-where-we-can-get."

"Yeah, I remember. And she said forget it. I never knew what you saw in her in the first place, except for her knockers and loose tongue."

"I think you and I should meet there tomorrow. I have a plan."

"Are you nuts? What are we going to do way up there? Make toy rifles? I don't even remember how to get there."

"Now listen, damn it! I'm going to get a calf from my uncle's farm. I already asked him. We'll slaughter it and bottle the pieces. If we add bacon fat, they'll last for a long time, three years even. Maybe the fighting will be over soon, a couple of months, but who knows. And maybe we'll never need the stuff. The meat is just for insurance. Maybe nothing will happen around here. But if it does, you and your mom will have … I mean, we'll all have something to live on."

"You're fucking drunk, Sasha! You offer me cigarettes, but you know I don't smoke anymore. Well, almost never. You want to slaughter a calf in an old building and preserve it with pork fat, but you know my mother and I never eat pig meat and the very idea of pig fat turns my stomach. And you're sweating like mad, and you look like you're about to faint, or puke, or both. You can't even play your damn harmonica. It sounded like a fucking door-hinge. It's late, Sasha, and you need sleep. So let's get out of here before you throw up on me. Come on, it's late."

Sasha had looked straight into Jusuf's eyes. He had stared into them for a long time and then stood up. With his hand on his friend's shoulder, he said in the gravest tone Jusuf could ever remember, "I just think we should do something. I think … *you* should do something soon. God damn it, do you hear me, Jusuf?"

Sasha had lowered his voice to a whisper again. "Your people are in danger. I can't tell you more than that." Jusuf thought Sasha's eyes were searching for how he could say more. Finally, Sasha simply squeezed Jusuf's shoulder once again and said, "Take care of yourself, will ya, you obstinate son of a bitch."

The following day, Jusuf kept mostly to himself. With the door to the living room open, Azra and Suad heard him on the telephone a few more times with the operator. "I'm trying to reach Ismeta Pasalic at 77-214-337. Can you check the line for me? Yes, ma'am. What? No problem with the line. Are you sure? Thanks, I'll try again later."

Jusuf moped around the house in an old pair of Suad's slippers. He had little appetite and tried to nap but couldn't hold back a flood of worrisome thoughts. Whenever he heard the calls to prayer from the minarets, he stopped what he was doing and stared into space. His thoughts kept returning to the day he was rounded up and wondered what he could have done to escape before being trucked out of Kljuc. He had promised his father on his deathbed that he would always protect Ismeta, see after her needs, do what was needed to assure her safety. But in fact, it had been he who had been cared for by his mother—she cooked his meals, did his laundry, cleaned the house, bought the groceries. He loved his mother but resisted seeing himself as her protector, and was only infrequently ready to give up his pleasures for her happiness. "You'll grow up one day," his mother once said when her anger had peaked. "I'll always love you, but you've got lots to learn before you become be a real man."

Later that day, Azra asked Jusuf if he wanted to take a short walk in the neighborhood. He said he appreciated her concern but preferred just to sit at the dining table. He apologized several times for being despondent. "I guess I just need a good night's sleep."

The following morning, he came downstairs early, smiling broadly, his teeth as white as the kitchen countertop. A yellow leaf fell from a wilting grape ivy potted on the windowsill. He reached over the sink and fingered the earth around the roots and then checked the other six pots. Azra handed him a pitcher and said, "Hey, go ahead. I hope you have better luck than me."

"You don't mind? I love to rescue houseplants when they look like they're on their last legs. I can't stand to see them die if there's any life left in them. When they come back, it makes me feel so good, like I heard a tiny voice pleading for help that no one else had heard."

"Well, I know they see me as their enemy. If they do well, they're yours forever."

CHAPTER FOURTEEN

AFTER HE FINALLY HEARD the ring above the drone of his electric drill, Dado ran to the phone from the small woodworking shop he had set up in a closet in his apartment. *"Molim."*
"Hi, Dado. It's Azra."
"Oh. I'm so disappointed. I was expecting a call from the queen."
"Which queen?"
"Elizabeth. I've been darning some knee socks for her."
"Should I hang up?"
"Don't you dare."
"I'm in town running some errands. Do you have time for a quick coffee at the Paviljon?"
"Sure."
"Five minutes too soon?"
"I'll be there in six."
When Azra arrived, Dado was already sitting at a table in their favorite corner near the door. Igor waved as she walked in to the ring of the bell above the door. She waved back and said, "Hi, Igor. Who is he today?"
"Given the beret and the paint-smeared smock, I think he's *l'artiste*."
"He's always been the artiste."
"How's your dad?"

"He's fine, thanks. I'll tell him you asked."

Azra gave Dado a peck on the cheek as she rotated his beret back and forth to cheerfully annoy him. As she was about to sit down, he pinched her behind. She swatted his hand with her shopping bag. "So how is Picasso? I hope you're not going to ask me to pose for you again because I've given up modeling. I caught too many colds in that refrigerator you call an apartment."

"Just my luck." He slid over the coffee he had ordered for her and took a sip of his own. "So how's the spy?"

"What?"

"That fellow you took home the other night."

"He's no spy. He's a perfectly nice young man."

"He must be more than just a perfectly nice man. You haven't called since he arrived. It's almost two weeks."

"Don't exaggerate."

"Have you set a date yet?"

"Oh, Dado. Don't be so damn jealous!"

"I've missed you."

"I've missed you, too. But now that he's settled in and starting to feel better, we can all go out together."

"So he *is* going to stay with you?"

"Where do you think he could go at this point? He doesn't have a single coin to his name, and he's not even sure he has a house in Kljuc to return to. He's tried to phone his mother a few times, and there's been no answer."

Igor looked up from stashing some beers in the refrigerator. He said nothing.

"So how long will you put him up?"

"I have no idea. He's been through a lot. He needs his health back first and some peace of mind."

"I'm jealous."

"You're a fool! He's just a guy who needs a roof over his head."

"He's a spy."

"No son of Braco Pasalic is a spy," Igor piped in loudly. "To that I can attest."

Dado turned to address Igor. "For all we know, you may be in the same network."

"One more remark like that and the next cup of coffee gets served on your head."

Azra leaned forward and whispered, "Why would you ever say that to Igor? That was stupid."

"I agree. It was."

"So grow up."

"Tell me, what was it like when he came downstairs?"

"I was shocked. I was in the kitchen and I turned and suddenly there he was, standing barefoot in the doorway. I had left some of Dad's clothes for him, and he had showered and shaved and looked quite presentable. Well, the clothes actually looked pretty funny."

"I can't quite picture what might have been under all those rags and filth and grease when he walked in here last week. So what's he like? What'd he say?"

"Well … he's rather quiet. I think it's going to take some time for him to feel really comfortable and open up with us. It's obvious he's been through hell. He seems like the type that doesn't say much but appears to take in everything very quickly. Seems to keep a lot inside. Who knows?"

"And …? Come on, tell me more."

"And, let's see … he's very thin. And he has a Roman nose maybe a tad too long for his face. And he shaved that beard and left a cute little strip of goatee running down his chin … and I think he has sideburns, but his hair is somewhat long, so I'm not really sure. I have to say, I had to hold back a chuckle a few times because his goatee looks like a smudged exclamation mark rising from his chin."

"And …?"

"And he's nice."

"Sounds like you looked him over quite carefully."

"Oh, Dado!"

"But what's he really like? Is he friendly? Is he stupid? Does he laugh? Does he read, does he sing? Does he shit?"

"Don't be so crude. He's normal, Dado … unlike you … and yes, he's friendly, but it's obvious he's very worried about his mother, so I guess he's somewhat subdued."

Azra noticed a faraway look in Dado's eyes. She'd seen it before through all the years he was growing up and knew where it came from. She decided to change the subject.

"And you? What's new in your life?"

"Not much. Trying to dodge the bullets and missiles like everyone else. Also been reframing some of my butterfly boards. The wings eventually dry and fall off. It doesn't help when the building starts shaking when there's a bombardment."

"It's getting really scary, isn't it?"

"Oh, and I've also been taking some photos of the damage through town. But I'm starting to get low on film."

"Hey ... sorry. I just remembered I have some ice cream in my bag. I better get home."

"You changed your hair."

"I did, actually. Got tired of the same old look."

"Did he notice?"

"D-a-d-o. He's a *stranger*. And more importantly, I asked you to marry me when I was six, and you told me I was too short and had a runny nose."

"Well you've grown an inch since then."

"Go home, you silly man, and paint a picture. Don't they need you anymore at the frame shop?" She kissed him good-bye and then raised one arm and waved her shopping bag toward the bar, gesturing a slightly embarrassed good-bye to Igor.

On her way back home, Dado's questions and her answers brought back those first moments seeing Jusuf in her kitchen. She recalled that his upper lip was thin and his lower lip was full and sensuous. His eyes were not large and not particularly soft, at least not that first day, but his look had been gently penetrating. On one occasion, she had held his gaze for a few seconds, almost as if it were a test of wills. But she also liked the way his eyes, sometimes appearing half asleep or slightly cautious, would soften and seem to quietly invite entry into a private realm of inner feelings.

What she would never have shared with Dado was that the overall impression of this stranger had been very appealing despite the dark rings around his eyes that only slightly distracted from their beguiling twinkle ... a twinkle that was hard to put out of her mind. And she would never have admitted that she liked looking at his shoulders and his hands. When he lifted a chair or helped Suad carry groceries back to the house, she took delight in glancing at his strong neck and the muscles in his forearms that rippled like ropes. When she washed his clothes, she did not immediately toss them into the machine but drew them to her face, particularly his shirts, to breathe in the fullness of his scent. And it was perhaps the accidental or unexpected touch in passing that produced the most electric, breath-halting charge. She had the feeling that he wanted to be near her, and for the last two nights had made some reasonably convincing excuses for them to stay up after Suad retired.

The day after she had taken him to her home, when he had said, "You were very kind to let me sleep here last night," she had felt there was something conditional and short-lived in his comment, as if his next words would be to ask for a suitcase so he could move on. His words—*last night*—had not implied he would be staying the next night or the following night, and she had felt slightly odd wishing it *had* implied something more.

It was roughly two weeks later that Jusuf sensed his welcome to stay was for as long as necessary. Nothing was actually said by Suad or Azra, but Jusuf began to feel, or was meant to feel, somewhat like a member of the family. Their use of the term *we* no longer gave him the feeling of being apart from them but seemed intended to give the clear impression that it included him. And yet nothing was said specifically. It was just one of those subtle, unspoken, relational shifts that over time becomes apparent.

About this time, Jusuf became aware that Azra was following him with her eyes as he walked through the house. Once, when he turned to look in her direction, he saw her looking at him, but she did not avert her eyes. He watched as she combed her fingers through the soft russet curls at the nape of her neck. When he smiled, she smiled back, but then after a moment, she looked away.

One afternoon as they sat in the kitchen having coffee, Jusuf said, "I've been meaning to ask you. Who was that guy at the Kafana Paviljon who helped you get me home that first night? I think he was wearing religious clothes, or something. Was he Jewish?"

"Jewish? I don't think I ever met a Jew. At least, not one that I knew was Jewish. Whom on earth are you referring to?"

"Didn't you say good-bye to some fellow wearing a skull cap and a striped shawl? He looked Jewish to me."

"Oh, you mean *Dado*!" Azra started to laugh. "He's such a character.

I'm so used to him in those oddball get-ups, I almost don't notice anymore."

"Is he an actor or something? He did look bizarre."

"I never thought of him like that before—as an actor, I mean—but I guess he is an actor in a way. Maybe more of a jokester. Not everyone likes him, but we're really good friends. Have been since kids. There's a serious side to Dado underneath it all, if you dig hard enough. As for being a Jew? Maybe there's a gene or two in there somewhere. Dado claims he's one part Serb, one part Muslim, one part Russian Jew, one part Italian Catholic, one part Rastafarian, one part Australian aborigine, and … he'll go on and on if you have the time. Who knows? He likes being from everywhere and nowhere. And he's always ready to dress the part."

"Sounds weird to me."

"He's got a new identity every week, but eventually you get used to him."

"You see much of him?"

"Yes and no. Sometimes we're inseparable, and sometimes he annoys the hell out of me and I tell him to get lost … but with a kiss, of course. Down deep, we're really good friends—much like brother and sister." Azra stood and got two beers from the refrigerator. "I think you'll like him. At least I hope so. Actually, I owe him a call."

Whether it was the description of Dado's odd ways or Dado's long-term friendship with Azra, Jusuf nevertheless felt a negative current, almost a magnetic repulsion like the ones he felt playing with magnets at his uncle's house. And he felt this invisible force even though he hadn't seen him since the day Dado and Azra rescued him at the Kafana Paviljon. He wondered whether Azra had seen him or had spoken to him on the telephone.

An hour before dinner, as a few low rumbles of distant thunder accompanied the sound of a heavy rain, Azra did a light dusting of her mother's desk. She stopped to read a draft of one of her mother's old letters while Jusuf, sprawled in one of the oversized upholstered chairs, paged through one of Suad's fishing magazines. "It's amazing, Jusuf, how Mom's words and her handwriting bring her back to life for me. I'm sure it'll be the same thirty years from now. I've always felt that handwriting and clothes are such vivid reflections of personality.

When I see one of her dresses, it's almost like she's come back to visit me. Jusuf?"

"Sorry, you were saying?

"Oh, I didn't know you were reading. Not really that important."

Azra put away the dust rag and then opened the refrigerator and stood in its dim light as blankets of cold fog cascaded down her legs, feathering away into a cool tickle on the top of her bare feet. She shuffled several containers, looking for a package of ground beef. The American Top 20 was on MTV, and she began humming along with Michael Jackson to "Man in the Mirror."

"Jusuf, are you interested in watching *Murphy Brown* later tonight or playing a game of Ban-Ban or Scrabble?"

"Possibly."

"Possibly what?"

"I'm possibly interested in doing something, but I need to eat before I decide."

"You're just like my dad."

Jusuf put down the magazine and walked to the refrigerator. He looked over Azra's shoulder for some juice and a piece of cheese. He casually placed his open hand on the gauzy fabric of her blouse, square in the middle of her back. He felt her breath draw in sharply and thought he had frightened her until he felt a shiver run down her spine. She neither turned nor moved. Jusuf was certain he felt a sudden rising heat where his hand was on her back. Her breathing had stopped. They turned to face each other. As Azra slid the back of her hand across his neck and then fingered the beads of his choker, Jusuf looked deep into her eyes and brushed her cheek with a kiss.

"I'm so very happy that you needed a place to stay. It's as if you always lived here."

"You and Suad have been very kind and generous. I don't know how I will ever repay you."

"Kissing me square on my lips might be a good beginning."

Jusuf looked into her eyes but did not rush to respond. When he did kiss her, it was slow and gentle. The profiles of their mouths caused their lips and teeth and tongues to fit perfectly, as if these intimate parts had been carved by a sculptor intent on achieving a seamless marriage of forms. The result was that their deep kissing was so natural and so effortless that neither wanted to pause but just to go on, and on, and on.

They stood for many minutes, lips parted, tongue tips touching, eyes closed, as the cold white fog fell down their bodies and disintegrated into little phantom fingers that brushed the top of their feet.

Two weeks later, when there was a break in the bombardments, Suad left the house around dusk to visit his sister on the other side of town. Azra was listening to music as she vacuumed the living room. She threw in a little awkward dance step from time to time as she moved barefoot around the room. The rising and falling groan of the vacuum eventually wakened Jusuf from a nap. He came downstairs unseen and watched Azra as she worked. Although the air was still cool, she was wearing shorts for the first time, and the smooth lines of her well-shaped legs held his gaze. Without her seeing him, he pulled the plug out of the socket. The vacuum fell silent. Azra thought the Serbs had cut the power again, but the music kept playing.

"Hey, wise guy, I'm trying to clean," she said, ever so slightly annoyed but smiling. She couldn't read his expression. He walked over to her, took the hose out of her hand, and let it slowly slide down his outstretched leg to the rug. Although she had wanted to be in his company more and more frequently, she felt a bit frightened just now to be alone with him in the house. He was, after all, still something of a stranger whose life before his arrival in Bihac was nothing more real than what he had told her and her father. She had dismissed Dado's idea that he was a spy, but from time to time, it briefly crossed her mind.

Jusuf looked at her with what seemed to her an oddly focused expression. Although guarded, she did not pull away even when he put his hands on her upper arms as if to restrain her. Her face was blank, and she had no idea whether panic or passion would be her next emotion. He leaned forward and kissed her flushed cheek, and then raised her left arm and stationed it in space, perpendicular to her torso, straight out like the limb of a tree. She recoiled slightly when he hooked his right arm around her and placed his palm between her shoulder blades as he had done at the refrigerator. As he drew her against him, she was both expectant and nervous and wondered whether her old angora sweater smelled of perspiration. He took her right hand in his left and stood there until the song that had been playing ended. When the next song started, she feared that her thumping heart might give him the wrong impression.

"I'm not a good dancer, Jusuf. Particularly for dancing close."

"Perhaps you never danced with the right man."

"You've been warned."

At first she resisted, her body stiff, her limbs frozen with uncertain anticipation. She didn't feel that he was forcing her to move immediately but rather that he was just holding her body against his. He did nothing but sway to the rhythm of an old Sinatra tune, "Young At Heart," a song her mother and father had played frequently. Finally, she let her body begin to sway in unison with his. Her smiles came and went in flickering, uncertain succession. There was a quiet well of power about this man, she felt, and it unnerved her.

"Okay. This much I can do," she said. "But if you make me take a real step, you'll know never to dance with me again."

"Hush. If you talk, you can't listen. The music should be the only piece of your world that's real right now. So close your eyes and relax. The music and I will teach you to dance."

"Well, you certainly have your share of self-confidence."

"At times. Eventually, you'll forget about thinking what comes next, Azra. That's what my dad used to say when he taught me to hunt. You want to be one with the moment, he'd say. Your mind and your body will fuse, and whatever should happen, will."

Jusuf took one small step ... but just one. She sensed it was a step taken to measure the speed of her response, the depth of her trust in him. He began to sway again, and she tried to sway with him. It surprised her that they were still not dancing. She felt as if he were secretly knitting their bodies together, dovetailing their breathing, and assessing her willingness to follow him. She had never felt this way before in a man's arms—moving, but not moving—fearful but secure—unable to predict the next moment but strangely comfortable with whatever might come next.

"Are we ever going to dance, Jusuf?"

He laughed. "We're almost ready. Now hush and let me and the music take you out on the river."

He took a few more small steps, very slowly. She was with him now and rested her head on his shoulder and leaned into him. Her body nestled into his, and she could smell the nervous sweetness of her own breath. Once when Jusuf twitched, she assumed her hair was tickling his neck. When she coughed and was forced to slightly alter the tempo of her footwork, she was impressed with how Jusuf seamlessly wove her misstep into the dance step that followed. She felt there was nothing showy about how he moved, like others she had danced with, like Dado.

At one point, his own dance step faltered, and he almost lost *his* balance. "My fault," he whispered. Whether this had been a deliberate move to make her feel more relaxed, she wasn't sure, but the effect was the same. By the time the second Sinatra song ended, the pace of her breathing had quickened, but she tried to conceal it.

Another slow song came on, and she waited for him to start. He took his right hand from behind her back and touched her neck. She again closed her eyes and kept them closed, hoping for a kiss, but he again began to lead her across the floor, drawing her snugly against his thin but muscular frame. Then, without warning, he gently but confidently maneuvered his right leg between her legs in unexpected counterpoint to the music. Confused, she tripped. "Sorry," he whispered. She felt that his leg, although intimately positioned between hers, was not placed there to arouse her. She followed him more easily now and gave him her delicate frame to move about to the music as he saw fit. Her small, well-formed breasts pressed against his chest, and from time to time, she tried to follow his lead by tentatively interleaving her right leg between his.

She had never made love with a man in her house before. That was her father's rule. But now she was thinking about where they would go if he made it clear that's what he wanted. Which room would it be, or would it be the basement, where she and Dado used to go as kids to touch each other. Would she be able to relax? She had been taking birth control pills, so that was not a concern. Would she be able to muffle her cries of pleasure? What would she say to her father if he came home while they were still alone together behind a closed door? Her mind spun madly like the red and white pinwheel she had saved from her ninth birthday party, her body sinking deeper into whatever it was he wanted to experience with her.

As Sinatra's wistful "You Go to My Head" ended on a long trailing note, Jusuf placed the knuckle of his forefinger under her chin and brought her lips to his. It was a long, easy kiss but not a passionate one, not the kind of kiss with abandon she wanted just then. And yet she felt she had to hold herself back even though she was ready to give him everything he wanted. An extraordinarily sweet smile blossomed on his face, and after soaking it in, she smiled back and closed her eyes. She wished she were naked, that her skin was against his. As he moved his hands slowly down her bare arms, tiny gold hairs on her forearms rose up, as did the long searching hairs on her old angora sweater, as if they, too, were wired to the electrical storm pulsing in her heart.

CHAPTER FIFTEEN

THE EXPECTATION THROUGHOUT BIHAC had been that the fighting would end just a few months after it had started, but no permanent ceasefire or truce ever emerged and air raid sirens began to wail day and night. The war was the topic of conversation one evening after Jusuf, Suad, and Azra shared a small, thin potato pie. "Since the mortars are still flying," Suad said, "we'd like you to stay with us as long as need be. And that means certainly until the war is over." Azra beamed. Jusuf returned the goodwill by offering to help Suad in his store and to do small jobs around the house.

In Suad's shop and on their walks to and from work, Jusuf was introduced to many locals and was instantly well liked. He often went out with Azra and her friends and began to join Azra and Dado for coffee at the Kafana Paviljon, preferring to be with them together than having her spend time with Dado alone. He felt on edge around Dado, never sure how Dado felt about him, ill at ease with Dado's strange attire, and uncertain as to what the nature of Azra's relationship with Dado had been through the years. Whenever Azra mentioned Dado's name, something in Jusuf's gut tightened. She frequently hugged her old friend, tickled him, and kissed him, but at the end of the night, she snuggled contentedly under Jusuf's arm for the walk back home.

Jusuf and Suad would usually wake around 7:00, eat, and then walk to the shop on Zavnobih-a Street in the center of town. They worked together for eight hours and then returned home in the evening for dinner with Azra. Initially, Jusuf made sure he worked hard enough to avoid any possibility that Suad would retract his invitation to have him stay with them. But Jusuf also knew that Suad was delighted that his presence made Azra happy, much happier than she had been since her mother's death. Jusuf didn't exactly calculate the advantage of his relationship with Azra, but the fact that it worked to his benefit had registered in some back-of-the-mind sort of way. It wasn't that he was *deliberately* calculating or was ever inclined to be deviously scheming, but if he could slip by on something that should be done so he could do things he liked, that was the course of least resistance he'd follow.

The model for shirking responsibility had been set years ago by his father, who had done odd jobs for people in the neighborhood. He did no more than was required in order to earn enough money to pay the basic bills. Jusuf saw and followed his father's example, doing no more than was necessary to get by. His mother had developed a strategy to counteract her son's and her husband's ways of getting by on doing little. She would stop cooking until she heard the sound of a hammer or saw the garden beds weeded. Jusuf routinely did the minimum requested so he could feel guiltless when he flew out of the house to play soccer with his buddies or sleep late after a night of heavy drinking with Sasha and their more than willing girlfriends.

After the first few weeks of showing off at Suad's shop and doing a number of odd jobs around the house, Jusuf's efforts began to slacken. He fell into his old habit, perfected at home in Kljuc, of starting a job but not finishing it, or worse, never getting to it in the first place, even after he spoke with great enthusiasm about what he planned to do. On one occasion, he even sketched construction details for a new closet in Azra's bedroom and produced a beguiling perspective to illustrate the stunning end result. But the sketch remained a sketch, tacked up on the ever-moaning refrigerator for all to admire. His excuses for avoiding work were subtle and inventive and delivered with great charm that was all the more seductive when his audience was distracted by his ingratiating smile and his flash of sparkling white teeth.

One morning when Jusuf was sleeping late, Azra and Suad decided to take a morning stroll in the warming spring weather and ended up having coffee and a plate of sweet white cheese on the terrace of the Kafana Paviljon. It was early, and there were few vehicles on the road and one lonely-looking kid throwing pinecones in the nearby park. An older man with a shock of fluttering white hair was walking across the Blue Bridge heading into town, tapping his cane somewhat rhythmically on the aluminum railing.

"I'm not sure what to say to him, Dad," Azra said as she sipped her coffee. "It's obvious he suffered through quite an ordeal after his escape, and I want him to feel at home with us, but I have to admit he really isn't chipping in. I realize it was I who invited him into our home, so I'll talk to him in the next day or two."

"It'll be easier for me to speak to him, Azra. I'll connect it to doing work at the store. I really don't want anything to come between the two of you. He is a nice fellow. Just a bit immature." Suad and Azra turned to watch a Red Crescent truck cross the bridge into Bihac.

"Are you sure? I don't want him to end up resenting you."

"I'll be tactful. On the positive side, I have to say that his charm is attracting some new customers to the shop. People like him. He's very patient with people, and he offers endless ideas about how to solve their construction problems. Sometimes though, he jokes too much, comes up with a withering list of solutions, and even sketches design ideas far out of proportion to the job at hand. They'll ask him, 'Are you serious?' He won't respond for several seconds. Then he'll look up, and when they see that smile and those twinkling eyes, they'll give him a complicit shove and burst into laughter."

"He's going to lose you more patrons than he attracts."

"I doubt it. There's a bit of the sweet devil in him at times, but things will be fine."

As spring became summer, what had been occasional bombardments of Bihac became a full-blown siege. Despite the deadly bombings, refugees from surrounding towns and hamlets continued to find their way into the city. Conversations with patrons in Suad's shop provided no new information about the situation in Kljuc, and those few who arrived from that general area had heard nothing directly or indirectly about Jusuf's mother other than someone's vague memory about having seen her with a suitcase and a bundle under her arm walking behind a soldier. But when pressed, the refugee, weary from the road, wasn't really sure that had been Jusuf's mother they had seen after all.

Jusuf tried to call home frequently, sometimes several times a day at different hours—that is, when the bombardments didn't interrupt service. When he did get through, the phone always kept ringing. One night, just before he went to bed early with an upset stomach, he decided to try again, even though, or perhaps because, he knew his mother retired early and would for sure be home at that hour. A man answered, his tone brusque. Jusuf's first thought or wish was that a neighbor had moved in to protect her, but the dialect was Serbian, not Bosnian.

"Who'd you say you're calling for?"

"Ismeta Pasalic?"

"Never heard of her."

"She's an older woman and—"

"There was some old lady living here some time ago, but she's gone. This is my house now."

"Do you know where she might be?"

"No idea—nor do I care."

"If you hear anything …"

The man chuckled and said, "Oh, I do remember something now." Jusuf's spirits lifted, and his body straightened. "A little bird told me she went out one day for a very long walk in the mountains, and no one's seen her since." Jusuf's eyes closed, and his torso slackened. "Don't ever call here again, you shit. This is my house now. And what's more, just remember that Kljuc is now owned by Republika Srpska." The receiver was slammed back into its cradle.

She was dead—he knew it now for sure. Jusuf felt like his heart was imploding. He went to his room, fell on the bed, pulled a pillow over his head, and sobbed. For several nights thereafter, he barely slept and ate small meals in his room alone. Azra and Suad respected Jusuf's clues that he would prefer to be left to himself. Only infrequently did he allow Azra to comfort him with a tentative embrace. He didn't want to speak; he didn't want questions asked or any continuing expressions of hope. He took to walking in circles around Suad's chicken coop or aimlessly through the garden. Finally, his guilt and sorrow poured forth when Azra came out to see if he wanted something to drink or eat.

"I should have done more to get back to Kljuc. I should have walked back through the woods as soon as I got back on my feet here in Bihac."

"Jusuf, you'd have committed suicide trying to get back. There are some things one can do and others that are just plain insane to try."

"If I was able to get here after several weeks on the run, then I know I could have gotten back home. I allowed her to be killed. I failed her. It's that simple. And now she's dead. It's no different than me shooting her myself. You're looking at a fool, an irresponsible idiot."

Azra followed him back into the kitchen.

"Jusuf. Be reasonable. There's a war going on. You'd have been shot for sure."

"I could have done it, Azra." Tears welled in his eyes. "At least I should have tried. I could have made it. I know it for sure. It was I who killed her. No one else."

"Jusuf! Never say those words again. Do you hear me? It's total nonsense, and you know it. I never want to hear those words again in this house."

Later that hot July night, Jusuf's thoughts returned to the deaths of Amil and the Serbian boy. He was sure that those deaths also could have been avoided if he had done something differently, if he had somehow interceded, yelled out on the boy's behalf, attacked the guard.

Jussie, you have a lot to learn before you grow up. Don't be like your father. Reach higher, Jussie. You have it within you. I've seen it in you. Think of others first, and you could be a real man. For more than a week, night after night, his mother's words both supported and countered his deep sense of shame and regret.

Finally, he returned to work and began to eat again with Azra and Suad at the kitchen table. His eyes were frequently red, and he often went to his room early after dinner. Azra's friends and relatives wrote condolence notes and slipped them through the mail slot. One came from Dado. His condolence note was scrawled on an old postcard of Bihac showing the Blue Bridge under construction. After words of simple compassion, it concluded with two sentences that Jusuf would long remember.

At least you had the pleasure of knowing your mother all the years you were growing up. My memories are ones I've had to make up.

Due to the escalating frequency of bombardments, Azra had to put her premed studies on hold. This was not for her a sacrifice entirely undesirable. Academics, although she excelled at them, did not hold her interest. She was not theory-oriented, as Jusuf observed on the few occasions when he tried to engage her in conversation about his ideas on cosmology or architecture. She welcomed the opportunity to begin working as a nurse in a nearby hospital, learning hospital practices and dealing directly with the men and few women that had been injured in combat. The hospital work provided experiences that satisfied her desire to be useful in her field immediately.

Perhaps it was because Jusuf saw Azra working at the hospital and also doing housework when she got home, that he began to see what had to be done in the house and at Suad's store and did it without fanfare or request. Suad one day noticed that Jusuf's sketch for Azra's closet had been removed from the refrigerator door and that Jusuf was spending more and more time in the basement with lumber and tools.

Azra returned one day from the hospital at the usual hour and smelled a chemical odor throughout the first floor. She sipped a half-finished beer in the refrigerator before going to her room to change. She was startled to see a new closet on the right side of her room. The joinery was refined, the design of the doors and the selection of the hardware quite compatible with the rest of the room, and the vertical grain fir was beautifully finished with a stain and lacquer that explained the odors filling the house. She opened the door and jumped back, startled.

"Jusuf! Damn it, you almost caused my heart to stop."

"Come *in*." Grinning with pride, he held out his hand, drew her inside, closed the door, and in almost total darkness, save for the band of light at the floor, stole a kiss like they were kids playing grownups in a closet and experimenting with what was permissible in the realm of intimate touching.

"You do good work, Jusuf."

"It's easy when one has such an appreciative customer. Now tell me, ma'am, what gets hung in a closet? What can we put on these soulfully empty hangers?"

"J-u-s-u-f," she said with a smile filled with suspicion.

"How about just our tops?"

"You love to play, you silly man."

"I do." He took off his sweatshirt and hung it up. "That, my dear, is what a closet is for. Now you."

"Okay, but just for a minute."

"Don't worry. Your dad is out looking all around town for birdseed. He told me his pigeons are about to expire."

They shifted position in the cramped space so Jusuf could help her out of her blouse, but he left on her brassiere.

"This is totally silly."

"True."

"Now what's on your mind?" she said as she reached back and unhooked her bra.

He placed a finger over her lips and then hugged her gently until her squirming signaled she was getting nervous about her father's return.

"Just a few more minutes," he pleaded.

"If he comes home, I'm going to be visiting you in one of those barns you slept in out near Sanski Most."

"Hush."

He placed the tips of his index fingers on her nipples, which hardened to the touch.

"Oh, Jusuf. You seem to know just what turns me on. That feels so good." With eyes closed and moaning quietly, she reached for his wrists and guided his fingertips in circular excursions around her nipples. "Oh, Jusuf, that feels so very good. Every inch of my body is awakening to your touch."

When Jusuf bent his knees so he could lower himself to kiss her breasts, he lost balance and fell against the door, which sprang open and sent him spilling on the floor next to Azra's bed.

Laughing and pounding her thighs, she said, "You clumsy fool." She threw him his sweatshirt and put on her bra and blouse. "Come lie with me on the bed for a few minutes before Dad comes home."

They positioned themselves so she could study the closet construction and he could study her. "It really is a beautiful design, Jusuf. What I like so much is that it looks like it's always been here. It's not screaming *look at me*, and so it complements the room and makes the room itself look better. You really are quite clever. You have such a good eye."

"It's so good to hear that from someone without a vested interest."

"Will you design a house for us when the war's over? We should begin to look for a small piece of land next time there's another ceasefire."

"That could be—" They both stared at each other with widened eyes when they heard the front door open.

"That's Dad," she said in a hushed voice. "Sneak into your room and make believe you're napping."

Azra quickly tucked in the spread and fluffed the pillows as she called, "Dad? Is that you? Come upstairs right away. I have a wonderful surprise for you."

Four months had passed since Jusuf had arrived in Bihac. Frequent artillery bombardments had leveled many buildings in the city, and sniper fire was escalating. With the siege now in full swing, Jusuf, Azra, and Suad often stayed in the basement, a small room with flaking stone walls and a single transom window facing the street. They sat in a huddle looking blankly at one another, a smoking candle turning their faces a smudgy gray. The low-ceilinged space reeked of mold and unwashed bodies, and the smell of sawdust, stain, and sealers still hung in the air. The arrival of summer added heat, humidity, and mosquitoes.

When there was an occasional pause in the bombardment, Bihac became as quiet as a mountain village. This was not because anyone thought the war was permanently winding down, as had been expected after the first few weeks of hostilities, but because only a handful of vehicles now had gasoline. Electric motors also fell silent without power. Everyday commerce thinned, except for the black market where it flourished. Only the bakery, the brewery, and the main hospital managed to remain operational, and even for them, it was sometimes iffy. Azra had taken to pulling out the flowers in their garden and planting vegetables.

The racket of people hammering furniture into firewood in order to cook was both a reassuring sign of life and a depressing confirmation of sustained imprisonment. So too for the sloshing of plastic jugs filled with drinking water carried in a half-run from the River Una or lugged home from a distant spring. When sniper fire erupted, it was followed immediately by the sound of sneakers or shoe leather smacking the pavement as people dashed for cover. Then came the screams of the wounded and the cries of pedestrians coming upon a wounded or dead acquaintance or relative. Most distressing were the animal-like howls scratching from the throats of people gone mad. When Azra heard these sounds from neighboring houses, she covered her ears and buried her face in her hands. Suad's and Jusuf's pats on her shoulder or strokes through her hair did little to comfort her.

Like most basement hideaways in Bihac, the stench in the Sabanovic cellar was as strong as a gymnasium toilet room. A curtain with a purple peace sign hung in one corner, creating what they all referred to as *the stall*. This was their toilet when it wasn't safe to go upstairs. Glass bottles of assorted sizes lined a makeshift shelf. Some were empty, some filled with body wastes. When there wasn't a roll of toilet paper, they used scraps of paper found on the road, or a fouled cloth.

It sounded like a voice from heaven coming through the basement transom window. "You guys down there?"

"Who's there?" Jusuf asked, seeing only a pair of combat boots but no legs.

"It's Frank Sinatra and my brother-in-law, Dr. Karadzic—that motherfucking son-of-a-bitch."

"Uh, oh. A crooner and his handsome insane shrink. The door's unlocked. Come on down and sing to us. We need a lift."

Dado was wearing red pajamas and a World War II era German helmet. His boots made a racket as he stomped down the wooden cellar stairs. He had three pink roses he had taken from a dead neighbor's garden and handed the first with a flourish to Azra, and then one to Suad, and the last to Jusuf. They all lowered their noses to the petals and closed their eyes as the perfumed fragrance filled their nostrils.

"Smells lovely down here. You guys out of soap?"

"Yes, you idiot. You only brought these roses to cover your own stink," Azra said with a grin. "You should have stopped by to see that creep in town who's starting a soap business in his house."

Jusuf extended his arm to Dado for a handshake. "Hey, how's it going?" Their friendship had warmed considerably over the last month, but after initial pleasantries, they oftentimes still related to each other as benign rivals. Jusuf continued to harbor a suspicion that Dado was trying to win back Azra as a lover. Whenever she spoke openly to Jusuf about her past relationship with Dado, she denied they had ever been lovers except in a playful, short-term, experimental way about the time they were both turning fifteen. She admitted there had been some touching when they were young kids and a lot of kissing when they got older, but from then on, it just evolved into a loving friendship. Both

Dado and Jusuf loved her and wanted her company. And so, out of necessity, their friendship had become, at least from Jusuf's perspective, one of begrudging but benign accommodation.

"What's up, guys?" Dado asked.

"We're in the midst of a séance," Azra said. "Isn't it obvious?"

"Well, the timing is perfect because you guys may have to contact *me* in the afterworld in a day or two."

"Did they call you up?" asked Jusuf with alarm. "The front lines?"

"Not yet—but maybe worse."

"What could be worse?"

"The bread lines," Dado said with a nervous smirk.

"No food?" asked Azra.

"No bread!"

"Come on, Dado. Talk straight, goddamn it." Azra punched him in the shoulder.

"Someone asked if I would use my truck and drive to a bakery in Banja Luka to get some yeast."

"Please, Dado. Stop playing with us. Maybe it's okay with Dad and Jusuf, but not me."

"No kidding. There's apparently a yeast factory in Banja Luka under Serb control. And the manager at Zitoprerada, down near where I live—a guy I know named Mesak—asked around for someone to go get some yeast. They're running really low. And no yeast, no bread. Someone knew I still had some gas in my truck."

Simultaneously Jusuf and Azra said, "Oh, shit!"

"Anyway, Mesak buttonholed me, and after he finished his pitch about how I must do my civic duty and how Habib lost his leg to a grenade last week delivering bread, I … I said I'd go. What could I say?"

"Oh, God. You in that crazy purple truck," Azra said. "You'll be the perfect target!"

"Well the facts are that we have tons of flour and wheat—plenty for a few months, that is, probably enough until this insanity is over. But no damn yeast. You chefs understand, of course. No yeast—no bread."

"I don't understand," Suad said. "Why on earth would a Serb

bakery turn over some yeast to you? Do they need deutschemarks that badly?"

"Mesak, the manager, somehow he made a deal with their bakery. After seeing a report on TV about the bakery there needing flour, Mesak got a message through to a Serb buddy of his in Banja Luka proposing that if he delivered a ton or two of flour to them, could they give us some yeast. So his buddy arranged for someone in the army to write a pass for one of us to drive there … and … well … I'm very happy to report that I'm … one of us."

"Oh, God, Dado. Don't go," Azra wailed. "They'll kill you for sure. You won't have a chance."

"How are we going to eat, Azra? We all need bread. It's the fucking front lines or the bread lines. What's the difference?"

Azra got up from the thin mat she was lying on and embraced Dado. Jusuf saw her eyes fill with tears. "You've got to paint it before you go!" she cried.

"Paint what?" Dado asked. "What on earth are you talking about?"

"Your damned truck. It's a fucking target for sure."

"When are you going?" Jusuf asked.

"In about an hour."

"I'll go with you."

"Jusuf. Are you crazy? I can't live without both …" Azra began.

"What do you think I should wear?" Dado blurted out to get Jusuf to drop the subject. "I need a special outfit that'll bring me good luck."

"Come on, Dado, this is no time for jokes. They'll kill you in a wink if you joke around with them."

There was silence. Dado looked at his watch.

"Listen, guys, I just wanted to stop by and say good-bye. Just wanted to let you know where I was going."

"Dado! Don't use that word, please. I hate good-byes."

"I'll be back. Don't worry. And with the yeast! And we'll all break bread together! And wind as well!"

"Oh, Dado, you're such a fool. Kiss me … and be safe."

"Promise me you'll be her shield," Dado said to Jusuf and Suad. "She's Bihac's crown jewel."

"And promise *me* you'll behave," Azra said. "Don't be a wise ass.

No jokes. Nothing goofy. They would just as soon slit your throat as play your stupid games. Promise? You'll behave?"

"For you, my dear, I promise the world. I will look like a banker and talk like the pope."

The men shook hands, and then Suad hugged Dado good-bye. "Don't take any chances. We'll all be praying for you."

Dado's left boot was on the first step when he felt Jusuf's hand on his shoulder. He turned. Jusuf looked at him, eyes swimming with tears of uncertainty and concern. Then he moved closer and opened his arms for a hug. "Don't play with them, you crazy shit. They wouldn't hesitate for a second."

Dado patted the back of Jusuf's head as they hugged. Then, after knocking his helmet with his knuckles, he threw a dramatic stage kiss to all three and bounded up the stairs. At the top step, he called back, "The word is already out. They know I'm not worth a single bullet."

CHAPTER SIXTEEN

WEARING A GREEN TOP hat and a red T-shirt emblazoned with the words *Porno Star*, Dado climbed into his truck, set a small paper bag with a few nuts, a wedge of pita bread, and a piece of fruit one day away from being trashed on the cracked plastic seat next to him, and drove to the Zitoprerada bakery. As he loaded his vehicle with sacks of flour and several baskets of hot bread, he filled his lungs with the mouth-watering aromas wafting out of the bakery's doors and from the brewery across the street. He took a moment to pray to the gods for good luck before turning the ignition key. As his truck rumbled through Bihac's glass-strewn streets, he checked three or four times to make sure that the pass he had been given for safe passage through Serbian check points was securely stowed behind the sun visor. His legs were shaking, his mouth was dry, and he half-wished he really did believe in God. Any god would do, he thought, any one of those inebriated characters that ruled over chance and luck. He skirted countless mortar craters and piles of refuse, breathing easier whenever he drove alongside a wall of sandbags.

"Oh, shit!" he yelled as a sniper's bullet whizzed through the back of the truck and lodged in one of the flour sacks. Suddenly he felt doomed. Purple truck or not, he was convinced there was no way he would survive. He wished he could drive the entire route to and from Banja Luka with his eyes closed. What was ironic, he thought, was driving into danger while inhaling the sweet and homey smells of just-baked loaves of bread.

Wasn't there a way he could turn back and explain to Mesak that this mission was just not for him? How about a flat tire? A spell of vomiting? Driving into a crater? Losing his mind? He remembered the story Hijro had once told of how he got excused from serving in the army in Croatia. During his interview, Hijro had rolled his eyes and clapped his thighs, all the while babbling incoherently about watering flowers in graveyards with goat's milk and working for the CIA in Afghanistan for two years. He had hooked his elbow around the arm of his chair, farted repeatedly, stuck his tongue far out like a yogi trying to clean his breath, and then sang "Amazing Grace" over and over again in English. The guards couldn't stop laughing, and finally when he peed in his pants, they threw him out of the interview and told him to get lost. There was no way they'd risk having this lunatic on the front lines. As the image of Hijro's antics flashed before Dado's eyes, a crooked smile crept across his face all the way to his earring-laden left ear. Then he went back to rehearsing the half-dozen excuses he would provide as to why they should get someone else to trade flour for yeast.

Dado sped across the Blue Bridge, through the southeastern outskirts of Bihac, and finally onto Put Avnoj-A, the road the Serbs had instructed him to take on his way to Banja Luka.

He drove south along the River Una and eventually began to relax, believing this might turn out to be a pleasant summer day after all. The high summer sun was bright, the mountains lush and green, and the aroma of the fresh loaves filled his nostrils with their intoxicating perfume. As he made a sharp turn in the road, the sun suddenly blinded him. He pulled down the visor. There was a flutter of something white, something folded flapping like a bird between his face and the windshield, and before he could swipe the air in front of him, the Serbian travel pass sailed in front of his nose and out the window. He thrust his head through the window into the rush of outside air and watched the pass sail into a small stream that fed the Una.

"Fuck! Fuck! Fuck!"

He slammed the brakes and screeched to a halt. Leaving the motor running, he leaned against the door until the hinge cried like a dying cat and then jumped out and searched for a stick long enough to retrieve the document. He ran along the bank, poking at the water, and finally plucked the document free of the current with the gasping sound of a fish needing air. The pass had wrapped itself around the stick, and the ink of the signature began to bleed. He peeled the page apart to carefully free it from the stick and then returned to the truck and spread the paper flat on the truck's scorching purple hood. As he leaned over, preparing to blow on the curling corners so that he could turn it over, a sniper's bullet struck one of his headlights. Glass exploded in a cone-shaped shower looking like a burst of tinsel. Sounding almost like an afterthought, a few final shards tinkled out of the reflector. A second shot ricocheted off a stone, sending a chip of rock bulleting the sole of his black sneaker. He ducked for cover.

Rather than continuing to look like a helpless target, he snatched the curling Serbian pass off the hood of his truck and waved it over his head. Convinced, however, the next bullet was seconds away and headed for his heart, he jumped into the truck and floored the accelerator. As he raced away, two more shots sailed through the back of the truck.

"This is *not* safe!" he screamed. He recalled Azra's concern about the color of his truck. He was now certain that the clothes he was wearing would be the clothes he'd be buried in.

Two kilometers down the road, his heart sank again as he approached the first roadblock. He came to a slow stop, wet palms slipping on the steering wheel, legs shaking, heart pounding. Two paramilitary gunmen walked over to his side of the truck. The taller of the two, an impatient man with a potbelly and a bad haircut, spoke first. "Get out!"

Knees weak, Dado climbed out of the vehicle and stood before them. Fearful that whatever might come out of his mouth would offend them, he made believe he was chewing gum.

"What are you doing here? Why are you on the road?"

"Bread."

The soldiers looked at him, his top hat, his T-shirt, and his truck. Then they looked at each other and started to howl.

The soldier who had not yet spoken was shorter than Dado. He had shoulder-length blond hair, which on a woman would have been strikingly attractive. Dado noticed the soldier's habit of pursing his lips. The blond walked to within inches of Dado and stared into his eyes. "Who the fuck are you, funnyman?"

Not wanting to identify himself as the enemy, but unable to think of an appropriate response, Dado hunched his shoulders and diffidently offered, "Nobody special." Dado thought this was a clever response and definitely accurate.

The soldiers eyed one another, clearly wondering whether they should rush him right then or play with this kooky bird a little longer before slitting his throat. Again, the blond guy pursed his lips, creating a slight kissing sound. Dado—the irrepressible actor, a man addicted to trying on the skin of others and habitually inclined to mimicry—fought back the urge to purse his own lips. Regrettably, habit won out. A little kissing sound slipped out of his mouth, but Dado quickly made it sound like he was sucking a piece of lunch from between his two front teeth. Then he turned to the side and spit. He repeated the kissing sound and spit again. The blond guard squinted, pursed his lips, and rolled his eyes.

Then suddenly sensing insult, the bellied one screamed, "Before I blow your brains out—tell me: who are you? What's your name, you asshole?" The soldier drew his pistol.

"My name is Dado ... I'm the ... bread man. And I should have told you guys, uh ... told you I got papers ... and I grew up in an orphanage. They told me my parents were Serbian, well, one of them." When Dado saw their foreheads furrow, he asked, "Can I get them?"

"Get what?"

Get the fuck out of here, he mouthed to himself. "No, just kidding ... I mean ... get the *papers*." Dado pointed to the cab of his truck. The pot-bellied soldier peered into the truck window and nodded okay.

"It's okay?" Dado asked.

"Get 'em, you dumb fuck."

Dado climbed into the cab, got the pass, and then leaned deeper into the truck to grab two loaves of bread. Dado's body jerked when a bullet whistled past his ear.

"What's back there? What the hell are you reaching for, you silly shit?"

Dado held up one of the loaves. "Bread. Just bread. You guys hungry?" He climbed out of the cab, gave the blond the bread, and the other soldier the limp pass.

"Hey, these are still pretty hot," the blond said as he broke off the pointed end of one loaf. He pursed his lips and stuffed his mouth.

"Porno Star, eh?" the taller one asked.

"You bet. I got lots of bread, and I know where to find lots of girls. Girls that dance naked. Big bouncing boobs. You like?" He winked.

"You better have two more hot loaves of bread and two hot broads for us on the return trip, or this piece of paper will be your death certificate. What'd you do, piss on it? I can't even read the signature."

"It blew into a stream back near Bihac. The wind blew it right out of the truck. I tried to—"

"Bihac? That town's filled with Turks. You a Turk, Breadman?"

Dado wasn't sure whether the question required an honest answer, so he stalled. "I told you I'd do what I can for you guys. But I won't be able to come back with much of anything without that pass."

"I *said* are you a Turk?"

"Some days."

"What the hell does that mean?"

"It's complicated."

"Bullshit! Nothing's complicated. Are you a Turk?"

"Yes and no."

The potbellied soldier threw the pass at him, but it sailed in a circle and flew back in his eye. "Get out of here. Where did you get that ridiculous truck? In a whorehouse? Goddamn stupidest thing I've ever seen."

"Whorehouse? Yeah, a whorehouse. We cater to *all* kinds."

Dado climbed up into the seat, nodded, and then kept nodding like a doll's head bobbing unendingly on a loosey-goosey spring. After driving off and certain they could no longer see his face, he pursed his lips and started kissing the air. "I just love you guys." Two kilometers down the road, he drew in a long, deep breath, held it for more than a minute, and then emptied his lungs with a sustained sigh of relief. "Shit!"

His Serbian pass worked more smoothly at stops further down the road. He encountered waving arms signaling him to slow down, followed by a few questions, a quick review of the document, quizzical looks at his attire and truck, and finally a barked order to *keep moving*. Around noontime, when he arrived in the large, gray industrial town of Banja Luka on the left bank of the Vrbas River, he drove around for more than an hour looking for the bakery. Mesak had said the bakery was near the Ferhadija Mosque, but Dado saw no sign of a bakery, just a lot of tobacco factories, wide boulevards, rail crossings, and modern buildings that several decades earlier had robbed the town of its centuries-old charm. He stopped to buy a beer and asked the sneezing proprietor with a soiled eye patch for directions. Following the route as best he remembered it, Dado drove around in what seemed like circles. Ten minutes later, he found himself several kilometers out of town and staring at the remains of a Roman bath. He made a U-turn, drove back into town, made a single left turn, and there was the bakery. A few employees were on break, smoking and swapping jokes on the front steps.

Three Serbian workers took little time to unload the sacks of flour, but it was a different matter when he asked for the yeast. All sorts of people had to be consulted regarding their side of the deal, and at one point, a bossy woman with oversized lavender eyeglasses encrusted with fake diamonds suggested that someone walk Dado over to the police station for questioning.

"Just give the kid the yeast!" an old man with a three-day-old beard demanded as he walked toward the woman with the glasses. His cigarette was down to the filter. "A deal's a deal. We got what we wanted. Now give him what we promised. Besides, we may need more. Plus, the guy looks like my nephew." The man pulled up his baggy pants, tightened his belt, held a thumb on one nostril, cleared the other in the gutter, and walked away.

A worker, who looked like he could have been a gymnast before the war started, trotted off on tiptoes to fetch the promised yeast. When the worker returned to say it might take an hour or so to bag the yeast, Dado, figuring there was more red tape or other forms of resistance to be overcome, decided to walk across the street and sit on a crate. He walked with energetic strides, smiling and tipping his top hat to several passersby as if he were the city's mute mayor.

A tall, young woman with a triangular face and a blade-like nose passed by him three times, each time in a different direction. Dado wondered whether she was performing surveillance for the Serb military. Her eyes were large and gentle. She took a cigarette out of her handbag and appeared to search unsuccessfully for a match.

"I'm sorry. Do you have a match?"

"I have a lighter in my truck over there. Can you wait?" She nodded, and Dado trotted to the truck and returned with a blue plastic lighter.

Their eyes met as he extended the flickering flame. Dado winked. After she drew in her first deep drag, she smiled.

"Thanks," she said as she slowly exhaled a fulsome cloud of smoke that clung to her face like a veil. "That's my favorite color."

"What's that?"

"Your truck. I love it."

"Then why aren't you wearing purple yourself?"

"But I am." Dado feigned embarrassment by tipping his hat over his eyes. "I'm so sorry," she said, "would you like a cigarette?"

"Thanks, I would."

"You here for a pick-up at the bakery?"

"I am. Here for some yeast." She looked puzzled. "It's a long story," he said, "for when you have more time."

"Are you from these parts? You don't look at all familiar, and that truck would be hard to forget."

"I'm actually from Bihac, but I grew up around here."

"Really. Where?"

"In an orphanage somewhere up this way."

"Well, there's only one, Rada Vranjesvic. I think that's what it was called. My aunt used to work there. In the office, before the place was closed down—guess that's about ten years ago now. It's just a shell of a place now."

Dado fell silent and studied the stone aggregate in the pavement around his shoes.

"You know where it is?" he asked, not looking up.

"It's about a ten-minute drive from here. Up in those hills. Want to see it?"

On the drive up, although he clowned and flirted, he realized his hands were getting clammy. When finally he saw the hulk of the place on the side of the hill, he felt hot and jittery. The place was almost roofless, moss blanketing the stone walls, a few rusting bed skeletons standing in a long hall, weeds growing up through cracks in the concrete floor. He extended his damp hand to help her over a fallen tree. She said her feet ached and asked if he'd mind if she sat on the vestiges of a wall while he wandered through the place. Did her feet truly ache, he wondered as he tried to orient himself, or was she giving him some time alone?

He walked away and soon entered a square room that was out of her line of sight. A good portion of its wooden roof was still intact. Dado's breathing quickened and fell out of rhythm as he lay down on a tangle of whining bedsprings, the bed frame still holding prisoner a peeling coat of its original forest green paint. He looked up into the rotting wood trusses. The nostril-stinging disinfectant smell of the place had long since taken flight, but the room still resonated for him with the cries of new children brought here for safekeeping. The lucky ones fit in immediately, happy to find a refuge, while the others barely ate and for weeks refused to play.

Dado remembered a muscular boy, a bully, older than him, who ran naked up and down the wide aisle that separated the rows of beds. He ran early in the morning as the others were just waking up. Unlike the other orphans that were nearer Dado's age, this boy had a large nest of black hair between his legs from which his cock swung like a club as he raced around hooting and banging on the bed frames a steel bar he kept hidden under his mattress. Dado still felt the threat and cringed at his sense of vulnerability.

The painful emptiness and longing when he was first brought to the institution by an uncle came back to him as if not a year had passed since then. He was five years old. As the months rolled on, he grew quiet and very lonely, and he no longer could remember his parents' faces. He was able to picture only vaguely his mother's sorry eyes and his father's crimson face on the numerous occasions when he slapped her cheeks with the back of his hand and kneed her in the groin.

As new volunteers came to work at the orphanage, Dado was certain that each was either his mother or his father in disguise. He was convinced that they had sworn never to reveal their identities. Young Dado began to daydream about the different countries his parents might have come from and about the dress and customs of those faraway places. He wondered whether his parents were Serb, or Croat, or Muslim. Were they from a faraway place where they spoke a language he would never understand? While Dado lay on the creaking bedsprings looking up into the dark trusses, a bird flew into the room, circled once, and then swooped through a rectangle of light where a window had once been. It cawed as it flew up into a tree.

The woman with the triangular face called, "Are you okay in there?" Then again, moments later, with a louder voice, "Hey, are you all right?"

"Sorry. I'm coming." Dado walked back but avoided looking at her to conceal his teary eyes. "Sorry, I got a little lost."

"Memories?" she asked quietly. Dado assumed she did not expect an answer, did not want one, but wished to let him know that she understood.

They drove back in silence, sharing a cigarette. He parked, and they got out of the truck. He was nervously eyeing the door to the bakery. She put her hand on his forearm and fumbled for words as she asked whether he wanted to join her for a drink later that night. She promised to ask no questions. He was tempted but asked instead for her telephone number and garbled something about a dinner plan.

"Do you know what a rumpled porcupine is?" she asked as she wrote her name and number on a scrap of paper.

"A what? I have no idea."

"Well then, it'll have to wait until you call." He tipped his hat and thought that that was a question he would have asked. She smiled and walked away.

With the yeast carefully stowed away, Jusuf passed through several roadblocks just outside Banja Luka. Soldiers who had heard about the delivery waved him through without a second look. Word had circulated quickly that the purple truck was not a threat, except to your sanity. Dado looked forward to seeing Jusuf, Azra, and Suad and having a cup of coffee, even if it had to be in their stinking basement. About twelve kilometers outside of Bihac, the roadway became dark as Dado entered a stretch of narrow road cutting through a glen where heavily wooded, steep mountain walls ended abruptly like palisades at the edge of the macadam. He fretted about still having to get through the roadblock where he was first stopped on his way out of Bihac. He was sure they would want him to deliver on his promise of hot bread and hot women.

He rehearsed what he would say, even laughing at his own jokes, when two men plunged out of the woods with rifles leveled at his windshield, their faces concealed behind stockings. They carried additional rifles over their shoulders and several pistols stuck in their belts. As they scuttled into the middle of the road, Dado found the scene almost comical. Their cartridge belts added so much weight to their momentum they had to bend their knees and almost crawl to slow down. They came to a stop on the other side of the road and had to double back awkwardly into the path of his vehicle. Dado hit the brakes and screeched to a halt.

"What the fuck are you doing?" demanded one of the soldiers.

Dado could not get his brain or his mouth to respond.

"I *said* what the fuck are you doing?"

"Driving yeast."

"Answer my question, wise guy."

"I did. Honest. I was fetching yeast for a bakery." He knew this was not a moment to joke.

"Kill him," the other soldier sputtered through his stocking, snot from a cold mucking the area around his mouth, making it even harder for Dado to understand him.

"Wait. Please wait. Read this first. The others did—the other soldiers read it—and let me go. I'm on a mission—a deal. Truly, it's legit."

Dado turned to fetch the pass. His heart sank when he did not see it on the seat next to him where he had placed it under his top hat. He picked up the hat, saw nothing, then peered into the black cave of the hat's interior. "Oh, shit," he said to himself. As he pulled down the visor, he heard a rifle cocked. "Shit," he said louder. "I know it's here somewhere. Please give me one more second. Please." Then he remembered he had stuffed it behind the other visor for fear of it blowing out the window again.

The soldier read the pass and spit. "This is bullshit. You're dead."

"It's bullshit? It's real, believe me. I'm returning from Banja Luka. I got a loaf of bread. Maybe you guys are hungry—honest, that's all I've got to give you."

"Bread! We need money, fuckhead!"

"I don't have a single deutschemark on me. Really. I haven't had any money at all for more than a month."

"Well, whoever you are, you're about to see your brains fly right the fuck out your ears. Get out of the damn truck and kiss my boot."

"Please wait. Wait, one more second. Will you let me go if I give you a bag of yeast?"

"A bag of yeast? You're fucking nuts! What are we supposed to do, bake a pie?" The soldier who had just spoken tried to scratch his face through the stocking. Frustrated, he bellowed, "I got to kill this crazy fucker, right now!"

"Think about it for a minute. Yeast is like gold these days. Take a bag and let me go. I'm not fighting anybody. You can read right in that piece of paper that your guys needed some flour and my guys needed yeast. I know it sounds unbelievable, but it's the truth. I'm just the driver. This isn't my goddamn war."

"You know, Blagoya, this clown's right. A bag of this shit might really be worth something. Like cocaine." The soldier's lips moved behind the tight stocking, looking like worms squirming in a cocoon.

"We'll take a bag. And then we'll let you go … directly to your maker."

"Come on, give me a break," Dado pleaded. "I only make porn movies, and they're not even that good. What harm could a guy like me do?"

"Grab a bag and let the damn kid go. He's right. This shit might be worth something. And Mr. Porno Star, if you try to drive through here again, we'll turn you into a chunk of Swiss cheese."

The gunman with the nose cold pointed his rifle at Dado's head and sneezed. Dado ducked. The other guy opened the back of the truck, dragged out a sack of yeast and the last loaf of bread. The soldiers said nothing more and began walking off into the darkness of the trees. Dado got back in the truck and floored the accelerator but seconds later hit the brakes. He leaned out the window.

"Hey, you guys. One more thought. I know a guy just down the road with some money who was looking to buy some rifles. You interested? You said you needed money."

There was no answer for a minute.

"Get the money and come back. We'll stay here."

"I know he won't give me the money without the guns. He's tough."

"What would he give for them?"

"Plenty. He's no cheapskate."

"How do we know you'll come back?"

"This guy's tough but honorable. His word is gold. I've known him a long time. Trust me."

"Wait. Why the hell should we trust *you*? You look like you walked out of some drunk's nightmare. Rings in your ear, clothes from a circus."

"You guys need money, right? Trust me. You've got a hell of a lot more to gain if I'm telling the truth than if you don't buy this deal."

"What can we lose?" the one with the nose cold said to his comrade. We need the loot."

The truck groaned and bucked like a stubborn mule as Dado backed up. The men opened the back of the truck, and the sick soldier put in two rifles. His buddy put in one rifle, two grenades, and the bandoleers but kept one pistol.

"If you don't come back with the money, we're going to radio ahead so they fuckin' blast you off the road." They slammed the back doors and yelled, "Now go, you shit, and if you're lying, god help you."

Dado drove a hundred meters and stopped. He jumped out of the truck, raised the hood, removed an envelope taped under the battery, extracted a pack of deutschemarks, and set them on a boulder beside the road. "I told you he didn't live too far down the road."

He got back in the truck and drove down the curving road until he was out of sight and then again braked to a stop. He opened the back doors of the truck, grabbed a steel bar, and tapped a plate that served as access to a hidden recess on the side of the truck. He placed the weapons, bullets, and grenades in the compartment and fit the plate back in place, and then rubbed it with a handful of dried dirt and flour.

The sun dropped lower in the sky to the west. Relieved that his mission was almost over, Dado raced toward Bihac. He laughed out loud and thought about going dancing with Azra and Jusuf if there wasn't much shelling. His sense of good fortune and the cooperation of the enemy gave him confidence that the war could be over in another month, certainly before the fall. He started to sing and whistle while tapping the steering wheel. Three kilometers short of the Blue Bridge as the road passed through an open field, a barrage of sniper fire erupted. A small anti-aircraft shell, shot from a nearby hillside, passed through the passenger window and crashed through the windshield. A shower of ice-pick-thin slivers of glass flew back into the cab. Before he could turn and shift his head to the side, a dozen splinters pierced his right cheek and temple. One lodged just above his eyelid. He struggled to keep the truck from swerving off the road. Steering with his left hand, he gingerly used the trembling fingers of his right hand to remove some of the tiny daggers that had not penetrated beneath his skin. One side of his face was a thin curtain of blood, too slippery for his thumb and index finger to tweezer out the closely spaced spines. Terrified that another shell would hit the truck rather than pass through it, and fearing that he might faint from a continued loss of blood, he began deeply inhaling the cool evening air to keep alert and calm. He wiped his sticky hand on his T-shirt and began driving with both hands. Would another shell do him in? He drove another kilometer on a winding stretch of road and finally figured that there was no way he could still be in that artilleryman's gun sights.

He still had to face the last obstacle, which was the first roadblock he had encountered on his way out of Bihac. He now had no bread, no women, and was clearly a wounded animal that could only attract the savagery of predatory soldiers. What explanation could he offer? Would they pity him and let him go, or pity him and finish him off? He decided he would take them by surprise by driving straight through the barricade, hoping he'd be going so fast they wouldn't have time to shoot. The turn in the road just before the roadblock was suddenly upon him. He pressed the accelerator to the floor and raced through the curve toward where he remembered the roadblock to have been. It would be ironic, he mused, to survive the earlier part of the trip only to be killed in sight of the Blue Bridge. He thought he was hallucinating when he saw the roadblock abandoned. Nothing was in the road, and there was no sign of soldiers. Thinking they might be hiding in the brush, he kept the accelerator floored. Minutes later, he was hitting the brakes to make the angled left onto the Blue Bridge. He drove straight through the crater-pocked center of Bihac tooting his horn and headed for the Zitoprerada bakery, one hand on the steering wheel, the other resuming the search for another stinging splinter.

"Yeast!" he screamed as he pulled up to the loading dock. Mimicking the Fresh Prince of Bel Air, one of his favorite TV personalities, he screamed out, "Yo, Baby, yo! I got the god damn fucking yeast."

CHAPTER SEVENTEEN

IN AUGUST, ON THE heels of yet another negotiated ceasefire and the institution of a no-fly zone, people throughout Bihac were more than ready to throw caution to the wind. Impromptu celebrations flowered on street corners and in parks. As Jusuf stood at the open living room window and looked out at the clear blue sky, he heard the gaiety, the laughter, and the relief in the voices of neighbors nearby. What he marveled at was how war can be down upon you one day and nowhere to be seen the next. It's kind of like love, he mused. One day your heart is about to burst with feelings of joy and affection, and the next morning you're furious at the one you loved the day before for something done you wished were otherwise. He remembered how he sometimes got angry at his mother for one thing or another, for silly things, even cursed her on occasion under his breath after his father died, and then loved when they sat together later in the day and talked about whatever came into their heads. But now neither anger nor love were feelings he could express to her ever again. He was left only with his memories.

He walked into the kitchen and found Azra at the table humming a tune. Two months earlier, her piano teacher had escaped to Germany to live with relatives, and with her went Azra's access to a piano. So she had cut finger-wide rectangles of black and white paper and fashioned herself a keyboard by taping the bands to a tabletop.

"What on earth are you doing?"
"Practicing."
"On paper?"
"Sure."
"Does it work?"
"I hear it in my head. Sounds just like real music. I'm playing Saint-Saens. Parts of his piano concerto number five, which I never quite mastered. How does it sound?" Her small, delicate fingers danced across the paper keys.

"I guess I'm getting somewhat hard of hearing like your dad. But I have to say you sure do work for what you want."

"Playing the piano, real or otherwise, isn't work. It's pure pleasure."

"When you're finished with Saint-Saens, how about going for a little walk with me? I'm sure we can find a safe place not too far away. There must be a hundred quiet spots that you and Dado used to sneak off to."

"Stop it, Jusuf! You're such a pain in the ass about Dado and me. I hate those allusions. Hate them. Grow up, will you."

"Sorry, Azra. I only say that now to play with you."

"You say it because you're jealous. And I keep telling you there's absolutely nothing between us that should make you jealous. Nothing. You drive me crazy. You mention Dado one more time, and I'm going to—"

"You didn't answer my question."

With Azra still fuming, Jusuf turned and looked out the window again. A bird landed on the sill, chirped, hopped in circles, and continued to chirp.

"Come on, sweetheart, let's pack some sandwiches and some beers and get out of here. We really should take advantage of the ceasefire and this perfectly gorgeous day. We could look for some land to build our dream house." He walked around behind her, kissed her neck, and ran his finger down her nose. Then he leaned around and kissed her lips. It was a long and promising kiss.

"Are you sure it's safe? They could start firing again at any time. Isn't it too risky?"

"I've got to get out of here. We've been cooped up so long I'm going loony. Look out the front window. There are lots of people on the street. They can't all be nuts. The sun is shining. Let's have a few hours of fun."

Azra resumed playing her paper piano.

"If you're not going, I'll go myself. I'm just dying for some fresh air."

"Okay, if you insist. We'll die together."

Jusuf didn't want to say anything that would make her change her mind, but he wished she hadn't uttered that last comment, which unnerved him. They packed small sandwiches and two beers that Jusuf had acquired a few days earlier from a fifteen-year-old kid with an invented name who survived through trading on the black market. Azra scribbled a short note to Suad, telling him not to worry, and off they headed through town toward the river.

They passed Dado's apartment house and noticed him under a tree fiddling with his camera and wearing a construction worker's orange hard-hat too large for his head. His face still looked like a ying-yang symbol—half of it normal skin, the other half raw and angry-red from the lacerations he received when his windshield was blown out. The night he returned from Banja Luka, Azra had used tweezers for the better part of two hours removing the last splinters of glass from his cheek. When she finished, he asked, "Ever hear of a rumpled porcupine?"

"A what?"

"Oh, nothing. That gal I met in Banja Luka. She mentioned a rumpled porcupine. Thought it might be code for something I should know."

"The only porcupine I've seen lately is the one that was on this side of your face. You had more glass quills than a—rumpled porcupine. Go back and ask her when the war's over."

"Exactly my plan. She did give me her number."

As Jusuf and Azra approached, Dado leapt forward assuming the pose of an overeager press photographer. He had already installed a roll of film he said he had stashed away in the back of his sock drawer before the war started, planning to use it for a weekend on the Dalmatian coast.

"Hey, I just got an assignment from *Oslobodjenje* to get some shots of the unforgettable times we're all having here in Bihac during this truly invigorating war. Hold that position. You look perfect."

Azra and Jusuf stopped in the middle of the road and struck several suggestive poses. Then they hugged as Dado circled around them looking for just the right angle. "How about something a little raunchier for the folks in Belgrade?"

"Get your mind out of the gutter, Dado," Azra said. Jusuf reached around from behind and made believe he was buttering her breasts with his palms. "Hey, Jusuf, stop that. You're getting as bad as Dado. You guys can be real creeps."

Dado noticed a neighbor walking out of her front door. He ran over, fell to his knees, and implored her with mock desperation to take the camera from him and assist in a life-or-death assignment. Then he ran back and kneeled in front of his friends.

"And so, Mr. Hard-Hat, where do you think you're going to get your film developed during the war? Going back to Banja Luka?" Jusuf asked.

"For sure. I really hate the asymmetry of my complexion lately. It's having a negative effect on my love life. Plus, the Serbs are finally getting to know me like that chick I met delivering the yeast. I almost got married. When this war's over, I'm going back to propose to her."

"You idiot," Azra said and kissed Dado on his scarred cheek before she and Jusuf waved good-bye and headed for the river.

They followed a trail downstream along the Una, north of the city, the August sun hot on their backs. For a while, they walked along the railroad tracks, but whenever possible, they angled off along one of the footpaths that snaked through the woods. They had heard that the Serbs had mined trails along the river, but last reports were that this had only occurred much further north, closer to the front lines around Croatia. Nevertheless, Jusuf kept an eye out for anything protruding from the trail that looked peculiar and also for spent shells or signs of encampment. His father had taught him to watch for the slightest clues that a creature—man or beast—might have left in its travels; broken branches, the smell of feces or urine, tracks in soft earth, the smell of a recent fire, or, more worrisome, a strange silence.

Whenever Jusuf's antennae sensed anything unusual, he quickened his pace and positioned himself between Azra and the spot that instinct told him could be a place of hiding. He tried to conceal his intent, but Azra patted his back in appreciation. He listened for cracking branches and hushed voices, and his sustained vigilance made him wonder whether it had been wise for him to cajole Azra into joining him. Azra had told Jusuf that since Dado's trip to Banja Luka, she could not get out of her mind the image of the shell flying through the window of Dados' truck and was now more scared than ever. Jusuf now felt like a damn fool suggesting they go so far out of town into such uncertain territory.

"We have to be careful," Azra warned. "You know it's during these ceasefires that things can happen. We all think we can just let down our guards and go out and have fun."

"What soldier would be stupid enough to lie in the brush around here and be eaten by mosquitoes while waiting for two young, emaciated Muslims to pass by?"

"Well, I'm just saying I'm scared, and I think we should turn back pretty soon. I'm nervous."

"We'll stop and have our sandwiches up ahead, and then we can go back. I'll keep an eye out for a picknicky kind of place."

There was no evidence that anyone had been along this trail in a long time. Leaves were undisturbed, no broken branches, no cigarette butts, just the mouth of a beer bottle here and there poking up out of layers of leaves. Then with no time to caution her, Jusuf thrust the picnic bag into Azra's hand and dashed off the trail. Azra stopped breathing, eyes darting about to see what Jusuf had seen. Something was moving in the leaves off to her left. Jusuf grabbed a fallen branch and began striking at whatever he had seen squirming out from under a bush.

"What is it, Jusuf? Tell me quickly." She was about to turn and run back when a meter-long, black viper slithered across the trail a body length in front of her and headed toward the river. She took quick steps in retreat without turning around. "Oh my god!" Jusuf followed the snake for a short distance to be sure it did not turn back.

"And this was supposed to be a pleasant walk in the woods. God damn it. I knew I should have stayed home."

"It's not all that poisonous. I was more worried it would scare you."

"Scare me? I'm terrified. I can't even breathe. I hate snakes and told you that when you found that fucking little garden snake in the basement last week."

He put his arms around her shoulders and brought her close to him.

"Try to relax and enjoy yourself. Nothing will get you, I promise." His expression changed as he remembered that those were words he had spoken before, and he had failed or been prevented from keeping his promise.

"I'm really so nervous, Jusuf."

"Try to collect yourself and maybe we can find a spot nearby to eat. Then we'll go back."

"Just hold me a few more minutes. Then I'll see how I feel."

When they reached a small cluster of wild apple trees with a view of the river, they stopped to listen to the whispering ripples of a low waterfall. Although a moss-covered picnic table under one of the trees appeared on the verge of collapse, Jusuf cautiously moved from bench to tabletop and picked two apples. He shined them and handed one to Azra. She took a bite and watched Jusuf squeeze his apple with all his might. He began to smile.

"What's so funny, and what on earth are you trying to do?"

"I was just thinking of my next-door neighbor in Kljuc. He had a little apple orchard and could squeeze juice out of an apple with his bare hands."

"Really?"

"Suljo ... his name was Suljo. He used to hang an apple from his door, and that was a sign for our little gang to show up for the ritual."

"Ritual?"

"Maybe that's not the right word. There were only four or five of us initially—my friend Sasha, a girl named Ludmilla, and Suljo's two boys."

"But what was the ritual?"

"We'd scream in the orchard until Suljo came out his back door pretending he never heard us, even when we broke into applause. After gathering a few apples, he'd walk toward us smoking a fat cigar with an ash that seemed to defy gravity. I was sure there was a wire inside because I never saw the ash fall off. When he lobbed an apple for one of us to catch, I was always the one to bolt first and catch it."

"Why does that not surprise me?" Azra finished her apple and threw it toward the river. Jusuf bit into his and smelled the flesh in a dreamy sort of way.

"When Suljo held an apple over his head, we all stared at his huge hand. It was big and thick like a textbook."

"Come *on*!"

"Really. I'm not kidding."

"He'd give the first apple to one of us to see if we could dimple it. I could barely make a dent. Then he'd open and close his hand a few times to get the blood circulating. I couldn't get over how the muscles in his forearm used to ripple like steel cables. Then he'd tighten his grip like a vise until the skin of the apple split open like this."

Jusuf smacked the tabletop. Azra jumped.

"Jusuf! I'm scared enough as it is. Please." Azra put her hand over her heart.

"I'm really sorry. I didn't think it would be that loud."

"So then …"

"Anyway, when juice dribbled out of that first apple, we'd all scream and break loose to try to be next in line. It was great fun. After my father died, I felt very attached to Suljo … but I have to say there was something about him that also scared me. I never feared for my safety, I always felt secure living next to him, but his huge hands and great strength made a lasting impression on me."

"I wish I had known you back then. It sounds like so much fun. Some days, I dream about what it would have been like to grow up with you. I would have loved being your buddy when I was a kid."

"I've thought about that too." Jusuf reached out and took both of Azra's hands in his and kissed them.

They stood up, Jusuf's arm around her waist. "So how's this place to build our dream house? We'd hear the waterfall day and night." When they kissed, Azra pressed her hips into Jusuf's. He responded with a low growl and ran his fingers through her hair. "Let's walk a little further," she said. "That snake has me spooked."

"Sure, let's go."

As they began to walk, Jusuf sighed. "He's probably still in one of those detention camps with his sons. I wonder if I'll ever see him again."

"I hope you will. It sounds like he was an important part of your life."

"He was. He stood for good things."

Further downstream, they came to a much larger clearing where the river spread out into something like a pond. With the sun high overhead, the clearing glowed like a white porcelain bowl. They waded across shin-high water to a cluster of large, flat boulders the size of backyard patios that created an appealing vantage from which to view the little rapids that swirled around the boulders. A stand of cedars, birch, and maples encircled the clearing and concealed it from artillery positions in the surrounding foothills. At the edge of the tree line, off to the east stood a shack with a red, terra cotta tile roof half-covered with moss. An old canoe with a jagged hole in its bottom leaned against one wall.

"What do you think?" Jusuf asked. "Does this suit you?"

"Your travel agent is to be rewarded."

"And what if I'm the agent?"

They sat on the boulders and ate their sandwiches, speaking appreciatively of Dado's trip to Baja Luka to fetch the yeast. Birds chirped, and the soothing sound of the rapids in every direction was like an aural cocoon. Jusuf lay back, lit a cigarette, and smoked it with his eyes closed. Seen through his eyelids, the sun was a bright, hazy button of light. He took off his damp boots, stood, stretched, and looked down into the rapids. Four or five rocks appeared to wobble and change shape in the rushing river, their polished granite surfaces reflecting the sunlight in a dazzle of splintered flashes. The sparkling stones brought to mind the glazed tiles in Uncle Ibro's mosque in Sanski Most, and for several seconds, he forgot the building no longer existed.

Jusuf stood and wandered around the perimeter of the boulders. He peered into the surrounding woods and then came back near Azra. He knelt behind her, breathing in the sweet aroma of her perspiration mixed with the drop of Slovenian *Shock* perfume she had saved for a time just like this. He nibbled the nape of her neck, put his arm around her shoulders, and kissed the top of her head. She slipped her hand into his and closed her eyes.

Azra ached to have him move both her hand and his to her breast, but she did not want to rush him or the moment. She pictured a small flotilla of river-soaked leaves rafting downstream, sliding limply over smooth rocks, tumbled this way and that by the currents of the Una, and then racing over the edge of a waterfall and falling into a dark pool. As she imagined water-diamonds splashing skyward in a fan of sparkling light, she shuddered with delight.

"This *is* a lovely spot, isn't it, Azra? Thank God the Serbs left a few parts of our world undisturbed."

She didn't want to respond, didn't want any words or thoughts of war to enter her mind at that moment. But the spell was broken. "Please don't mention the enemy again while we're here, Jusuf. It breaks the mood of this lovely place."

"You're right. I promise to say not another word."

For a time, they remained silent and just looked around at the surrounding beauty and listened to the insects, the twittering birds, and the rushing water.

"So my dear, Jusuf. Tell me a story. Take me someplace far away, someplace exotic. Take me to some romantic beach."

"I'm not a good storyteller, Azra. I'd put you right to sleep. But how about if I just tell you how much you've meant to me since I straggled into Bihac. You have made me feel so at home with you and your dad. It's meant the world to me."

"We've loved every second you've been with us, even though Dad was a bit cautious at first, and understandably so. But he is quite fond of you now. I told you he always wanted a son. He used to try to get me to play with tools and even bought me a workbench when I was ten, but I was hopelessly into dolls and then into music."

"I'm glad you resisted. If you'd been wearing a tool belt with a hammer hanging at your side, I'm not sure I would have accepted your offer to come home with you that night."

Jusuf walked back toward the edge of the boulder and tossed a few stones into the rapids. He thought of Sasha and the good times they had had playing along the Sana River in Kljuc, throwing stones, shining beams of light reflected from mirror fragments onto the fish. Azra rose and walked over and stood next to him.

"Jusuf, I've told you this before, but I want to say it again. I've never been with a man that accepts me like you do. Being with you is so easy, so pleasant, even when we hit the rough spots. I don't want to say that you're like a brother to me, because I never had a brother, except in the way that Dado has been that kind of friend to me. But I feel so comfortable with you, like it would be wonderful to have you live with Dad and me forever."

"If that's a proposal, here's my answer." They embraced, and Jusuf gently kissed her. They chewed each other's lips and toyed with each other's tongues.

"Is that how you used to kiss your girlfriends back in Kljuc?"

"You should know, once and forever, that I never kissed anyone in Kljuc the way I kiss you."

"I'll bet."

"Do you ever believe a word I say? And no one ever kissed me the way you do. The softness of your lips, the way our mouths fit together. It sounds like a line, but it was never like that with anyone else."

Jusuf took two beers out of the picnic bag, opened them, and handed one to Azra. Then he stepped back a few feet and reclined against a rock. He kept the two bottle caps in one hand, and between swigs, he scraped the caps' serrated edges together between his thumb and index finger. Then he held them like tiny castanets and slid their smooth but dented faces back and forth, one against the other, in a shuffling motion. He started to click the caps together and began to hum and then sing the end of a Dylan tune that Sasha used to play frequently.

Leave your stepping stones behind, something calls for you.
Forget the dead you've left, they will not follow you.
The vagabond who's rapping at your door
Is standing in the clothes that you once wore.
Strike another match, go start anew
And it's all over now, Baby Blue.

"You sing well, Jusuf."

"You have to be kidding."

"I'm not." As Azra closed her eyes to doze, Jusuf continued playing with the bottle caps, tossing them in the air and then catching them. At one point, the sun reflected sharply off the unpainted inner surface of one of the caps, causing him to squint. He was surprised by the strength of the reflection. He took one of the caps and focused a reflected light beam onto his palm, forming a white disc the size of his thumbnail. There was a barely discernible trace of heat. He and Sasha used to play with mirrors, standing on opposite sides of a stream, sending flashing messages to each other and later trying to blind the other, as if in a duel. They also directed their light beams into the water, illuminating the sides of fish as they smoothly darted by. One big, gray fish with a strange patch on its side the color of an overcooked beet seemed to like the shaft of light and kept swimming back into the area where the light beams speared the water. The boys chortled as they watched the fish circle and circle, each boy struggling to win over what they perceived to be the fish's attention.

One of the caps slipped off his finger and rolled into a crevice. He turned and reached back to retrieve it and found not only the bottle cap but a double-sided, silt-covered makeup mirror that must have fallen out of the backpack of a woman attending a Regatta or canoeing along the river. The mirror, about the size of Jusuf's palm, was encased in a blue-green plastic frame. One side had a square mirror with an eroded silver logo of a stylized R, the other side a round magnifying mirror, below which was embossed in tiny letters the word *China*. After dipping the mirror in the river to remove the silt, then drying it on the hem of his shirt, he directed a beam of sunlight into the woods, half-expecting and half-fearing it would flash across the face of a Serbian sniper looking back at him through his rifle scope. But the woods were peaceful. Then he waved the beam up and over the rocks, forming snaking ribbons of light that magically crawled across the hard contours. The beam inadvertently crossed over Azra's left calf. He toyed with the square of light, sliding it up and down, smiling in amusement, hoping she might feel something, but he got no reaction. When he turned the mirror around, the resulting focused button of light from the round magnifying side produced the desired effect. She swept her hand across the warm spot on her white, sensitive skin. He figured she had imagined that a butterfly or an insect had fluttered close by. Moments later, she shifted position to make herself more comfortable, parted her legs, and raised her skirt several inches to tan her legs. Taking this to be an invitation, Jusuf pointed the beam toward her inner thighs. The circle of light migrated from her knees to the point where her skirt eclipsed a view of where her legs met her torso.

"Jusuf? What are you doing?"

"A science experiment."

"Jusuf, come on, I feel something. Are you touching me with a feather?"

"How could I possibly reach you with a feather from where I'm sitting?"

"I feel something on my legs. What are you doing?" Repositioning herself, using the obvious pretense of better facing the sun, she drew her skirt still higher and allowed a view of the bottom few inches of her black cotton panties that remained shaded by her hem. Jusuf then withdrew his light beam and hid the mirror under his shirt.

"Jusuf?"

"Yes?"

"Nothing. You're such a devil."

The disc of light was again crossing over from one knee to the other. It moved higher up her thigh and then back toward her knees, and then higher still. Her breasts began to rise and fall beneath her blouse. The button of light moved across the heat-absorbing black cotton of her underwear until he aimed it steady on the apex of the black triangle of cloth. Azra whispered Jusuf's name and moments later whispered it again. As the circle of heat moved slowly side to side and sometimes up a thumb width and down a thumb width, Azra imagined his hands on her legs and his real thumb nuzzling her underpants. Her head fell back as if in surrender. Then she raised her head and located the source of the light beam of pleasure.

"Jusuf, you sneaky devil! An experiment, my ass. What have you been up to?"

"About as much as I could get away with?"

"You are *naughty*."

"Not naughty enough, perhaps, for the likes of you."

"You always love to tease me."

"Isn't that what turns you on?"

She didn't respond. Then with eyes closed again, she asked, "What about that shack behind you?"

"What about it?"

"Don't you hear a love song playing in there?"

No response.

"Jusuf. Didn't you hear me? I've had enough sun. I burn easily, and I am very hot now. Please come and help me up. I don't think I can stand by myself right now. And I'm a little nervous about going in there alone."

Jusuf pocketed the mirror and threw the bottle caps toward the river, but they fell short and clinked quietly into a shadowy crevice between two boulders. He walked over and ever so slowly pulled her to her feet. With his arm around her and her head resting on his shoulder, they walked to the cabin. It looked as though the deep forest green paint on the siding and the red trim had been applied in the early spring in anticipation of this year's Regatta. The knob turned easily, and surprisingly, the door opened without a creak. The interior was filled with stacks of kayaks, canoes, folded rubber rafts, and a small rowboat. A small critter scurried out through a knothole in the wall. As they stepped in, a floorboard creaked. There was a strange but not unpleasant smell of rubber, wood, canvas, and varnish—the aromas of sport. The central aisle was the only space wide enough for them to stand next to each other.

Azra said, "Do you think it's safe in here? Someone could walk in."

Jusuf kissed her neck and her ears, looked into her eyes, and heard her breath coming unevenly. Again, his lips went slowly to hers as she leaned forward to meet him. He pulled back and smiled.

"Don't torture me, Jusuf. Just kiss me and never stop. You love to torture me. I need your lips to stay on mine." She ran her finger down his goatee and toyed with the beads of his choker. He kissed her again but this time did not pull away. He parted her lips with his tongue, her saliva sweet and warm. His tongue found hers. She put her hands on his hips and pulled herself against him … her hips moving in slow circles, and then forward and back and forward again. She felt him rising and pressed harder. His repeating moans were deep and excited her.

As she played tenderly with the end of his nose, he worked the buttons of her blouse and then slid his hands out from the center of her chest and gently cupped her breasts. Her nipples were dark and erect.

"I'm so thin. Please don't stare at me."

"You look absolutely lovely to me. I love every inch and every curve and every tiny mole."

"Oh, Jusuf. I've wanted you so badly. Pull me close. Hug me as tight as you can."

Jusuf removed her blouse.

"I'm still nervous, Jusuf. What if someone wanders in?"

"No one is around here, and no one's coming in, but I'll …" A broken oar near the door caught his eye. He left her for a moment to prop it under the doorknob. As he looked back, he saw that she had crossed her arms across her chest, concealing her protruding ribs and breasts. "It's just us now, my dear. You can relax." She tentatively lowered one arm.

Before returning to her, he dropped his jeans and tugged off his T-shirt. A partially deflated raft sticking out from under a kayak caught his eye. He spread it on the floor in front of her. After removing her skirt, they sank into the raft's cushioned softness and giggled as the rubber squeaked and stuttered. They couldn't stop giggling and purring as they tried to get comfortable, but passion soon erased all sounds other than the other's breathing. When he slid off her panties, she purred but covered herself with one hand. Her other arm crossed over her small shapely breasts.

"I suppose my body is the only thing I'm shy about."

They were both emaciated, bones jutting out where before there had been an adequate cushion of flesh. Jusuf lowered himself next to her and stroked her right cheek and then her left. They kissed again and soon were touching each other. Her hand between his legs soon became too much for him too soon, and he nudged it over to his thigh.

"I do love you, Azra. I feel so complete, so whole with you like never before in my life."

She moaned again as he continued to caress her, stroking her shoulders, circling her abdomen, and then moving his fingers slowly down to her silky moistness. When she finally relaxed, he slowly moved above her, gently parting her legs with his. The bird sound that came from her throat when he entered her distracted him for a moment, but then he was with her and nowhere else.

"You will be careful, Jusuf. A child would be a disaster until the war is over. Please stop before it's too late. Can I trust you? You'll know when?"

"I will. I only wish we could still buy—"

"Hush. Please don't talk mechanics right now. Just come out when you need to. Promise me."

"I promise. Don't worry."

At first he moved slowly, wanting to savor the pleasure of her warm and slippery interior and wanting her to rise along with him. But passion was about to peak quickly for both of them, and although he withdrew in time, they climaxed nearly in unison, a wild frenzy of contracting muscles and throaty sounds of deep pleasure. His tears fell onto her cheeks and mixed with hers. They both were sure that this moment, although compromised by circumstance, was a bonding of their hearts that would last forever.

"Oh, Jusuf, you have no idea what you mean to me. Stay close. Don't move away. Promise that you'll never leave me."

"Nothing will ever come between us. I know that with the deepest certainty. I've never loved anyone even close to the way I love you. I know this will be forever."

CHAPTER EIGHTEEN

A WARM FALL SHIFTED quickly to a cold winter. High winds blew constantly, snow fell frequently, and the sky was perpetually gray. On this particular January day, no one seemed to have need of nails or felt like trekking with a broken appliance through the slushy streets, so Jusuf and Suad stretched out in the back room of the shop on pallets fashioned out of sheets of cardboard from year-old shipping cartons. Even though this kept them ever so slightly elevated above the cold concrete floor, they still had to wrap themselves in tarpaulins to keep their bodies from shivering.

They shared a cigarette Suad had received from a patron in lieu of cash and passed a can of beer back and forth as they told each other old dirty jokes with slightly altered wording to make them sound new. One joke involved an old geezer coincidentally named Dado who caught something in his zipper that should have fallen back into his pants. They both thought that would be something that Dado might do on those few occasions when he was actually wearing pants and not his all too familiar pajama bottoms.

"By the way, have you seen Dado lately? I've been concerned," Suad said.

"I saw him just two days ago."

"Glad to hear that. You're keeping an eye out for him, aren't you?"

"What do you mean? Dado's a survivor if there ever was one. He'll get through this nightmare just fine."

"Oh, it's just that he lives alone, and it's wartime. For years he's almost been a family member. And Azra's been so fond of him since they were kids."

"He seemed perfectly fine to me. His spirits were up as usual. Is there something I don't know about Dado? Something going on?"

Suad looked uncomfortable, his face flushed. He left the room and headed for the toilet stall. When he returned, his face was freshly washed, but his eyes looked a bit red.

"I'm sorry if I made you uncomfortable. I wasn't aware there was a problem," Jusuf said.

"There isn't really a problem in that sense. It's just that Azra and Dado have been very close through the years, and I wouldn't want Dado to feel pushed out, alone, particularly now, during the war. People can feel really isolated in these circumstances."

"What do you mean by pushed out?" Jusuf asked.

"I've worried he was feeling left out in the cold. Abandoned. You know he's adopted, don't you?"

"Yes, Azra told me that, but god, he's the furthest thing from a lonely guy I've ever known. But you said *pushed out*, Suad. What did you mean?"

"Well, I see how close you and Azra have become, and it's not that I'm unhappy about that at all. Quite the opposite. I'm delighted to see her happy again. It's just ... well, I wouldn't want Dado to feel excluded or rejected. Sometimes he seems so sad to me. I worry about him."

"Really? I haven't noticed that at all when I've been with him. Actually, it's been quite the opposite. I've become rather fond of Dado. The three of us have begun to hang out together quite a lot. More at his place lately, I suppose, so you wouldn't know. Sometimes I'm jealous like any man would be when you see your woman express deep affection for another man."

"I'm happy to hear that. Truly I am. It really eases my mind." Jusuf said nothing more but felt that Suad was holding something back.

Soon after Jusuf had started helping Suad at the store, he had found it curious that Suad came up with various reasons to attend to things in the back room—even a simple repair job sent Suad puttering with it for days in the back work area. Not that Suad was unfriendly, but he seemed to avoid eye contact and tried to conclude business quickly on the few occasions he was behind the counter. He often asked Jusuf to take over in the middle of a transaction, mentioning a paint job he needed to finish before the brush dried, or clamps that had to be applied before glue set. Although puzzled by Suad's behavior, Jusuf was reluctant to ask why he preferred him to work behind the counter.

Jusuf remembered that there was a customer that came into the shop soon after he started working there. The woman's sonorous voice brought Suad out from the back room. There followed a warm greeting and an inquiry as to how Suad was feeling, how he was holding up. Jusuf sensed that the questions went beyond the circumstances of war, that something else, a shared and private knowledge of some past event, was the confidential subject of their brief exchange. The friend had looked Suad in the eye and held his gaze. "Don't be so hard on yourself, my friend. We all make mistakes. We all know youth and youthful passions go hand in hand." Suad nodded with a vague expression of appreciation and a far-off look of regret.

On their way home, Suad asked another question that Jusuf found a bit odd, as if Suad had been storing up a huge box of concerns that he no longer could keep to himself.

"I've been meaning to ask you why you feel so certain your mother is dead."

"I told you what that guy said who had taken over our house. He couldn't have been any more clear about …" The thought was too painful for Jusuf to finish.

"Well. I've heard of several cases recently where people have moved out or been forced out of their homes by the Serbs but are living with relatives or friends. Maybe that's what happened to your mom."

"I guess it's a possibility. It's just that I had such a strong feeling in my gut that she couldn't have survived what happened in Kljuc after we were rounded up. You can sense things like that. I was all she had after my dad died. There's no way to know for sure, but keeping the hope alive was torturing me."

Suad backed off for a time as they trudged through the snowy mush. Nevertheless, Suad's comment started Jusuf wondering again.

"Do you think I should borrow Dado's truck and go back to try to find her?"

"Oh, god, no, Jusuf! Now's not the time! I'm sorry I even raised the question. Wait a few more months. I think they're getting closer to some sort of a UN deal or something. Azra would never forgive me if I let you go off and you never returned."

"I've heard about those peace deals countless times already. That's an example of holding out hope when you know things are hopeless. It'll destroy you. It had been eating me up inside. I just had to let it go."

Suad nodded tentatively to some patrons from his shop that had waved from the far side of the street.

"But have you thought about writing to her to see if you get a response? It couldn't hurt."

"Yes. I have thought about it. But who the hell's going to deliver a letter from one Muslim to another during the war?"

"It's possible. Remember my friend, Ivan? He's the Serb I met in the woods the day I tried to get us hooked up to the electric lines. He's the guy who sells me stuff from time to time. I thought I mentioned him before."

"You did, but I never understood how the whole thing works. Why would you give him, the enemy, your money … and why on earth would he want to help you? What's in it for either of you? We're at war with one another."

"Look," Suad said, "he has things we need, and we have the money he wants to help his side buy the arms to kill us. It's business. Wars make odd bedfellows. But of course, the deal will end when either we run out of money or there's no one left on this side for them to shoot. Remember the deal Dado made for the guns—his money, their guns—or the flour for the yeast deal? Both sides make do one way or another."

"That yeast deal was strange when it happened, and frankly it still seems strange to me."

"So, this guy, Ivan, and I used to be friends, and despite the war, we still are in a fashion. Never question what works, Jusuf. Wartime turns everything upside down. We want to survive—they want to destroy us."

"It's just hard imagining the enemy being a trading partner."

"When someone's in a trench on the front lines, or starving, or separated from a loved one—what's hard to imagine in other circumstances can become commonplace when the bullets are flying.

Even horrific events can sometimes be a blessing in disguise. War's got its own crazy logic."

They walked in silence for a few more blocks, circling around old mortar craters until Jusuf said, "You were suggesting back there that I write to my mother. Then you mentioned your friend Ivan. Did I miss something?"

"Ivan will do me a favor from time to time. Nothing big, but if you decide to write, I'll see if he can get the letter delivered."

"I'm not sure I can set myself up for another disappointment."

"I understand completely. But if you decide to write, put a Serbian name on the return address. Use your friend's name. Was it Sasha, or something? Use his name and his return address. Positively don't use Bihac in the return address."

A familiar whistle sounded as they approached the house.

"Hey, there's Azra," Suad said.

Steam was coming out of the door behind her, and they assumed she found ingredients to make soup. But as they walked through the door, they smelled the stinging odor of boiling wood ash and waste fat. Azra had been sterilizing the pinkish-gray rags she used for her periods when the near-useless, black-market pads were not available. Her hands were raw, the skin peeling from the caustic goop she had brewed on the stove. Jusuf recalled the rash Azra would get between her legs if she failed to rinse out enough soap. She was in no mood to talk. She waved off the start of Jusuf's hug and shook her head *no* to every expression of his concern.

Later that night lying in bed, Jusuf mulled over Suad's suggestion. If his mother were alive but no longer at their home, then it obviously made no sense to send a letter to what had been their house. He figured that if anyone, any Serb, would know where she was and might possibly do him a favor, it would be Sasha. So Jusuf decided to send an envelope to Sasha with a letter in it for his mother and use what he remembered of Sasha's uncle's farmhouse address for the return address. The next day, he mentioned his plan to Azra. She located some of her mother's stationery that she'd put aside as a keepsake and set it out on her mother's desk.

CHAPTER NINETEEN

Jusuf tried several times to start the letter but could not get out of his mind the idea he was writing to a woman who already had been dead for several months. Nothing he penned made sense. He even thought of phrasing his message as if she were able be read his words in her grave. Everything sounded artificial, contrived, *stupid*. Finally after three frustrating days and a heap of crumpled tries, he gave up. Azra did not encourage him anymore, but she also did not remove the writing paper and ballpoint pen from the desktop.

Several days later, she came downstairs wrapped in two blankets, bleary-eyed after a mostly sleepless night. Jusuf was sitting hunched over the desk, shafts from a low sun just beginning to slant through the window, bringing with it a barely detectable ray of warmth. Outside it was blustery and cold, plastic sheeting popping in the broken windows, the wind in gusts penetrating the un-insulated walls and loose window frames. Jusuf sat with his head buried in his hands, rocking in frustration.

"Am I crazy trying to write this letter, Azra? I know she's dead. I feel like a fool."

"Don't think *what if*, Jusuf. Just write. It can't hurt. Maybe she *is* alive somewhere. Who knows. Think of it as just one last try. And keep it short. That'll be easier. Allah has his ways." She regretted adding the last thought but then realized her Allah was also his mother's and maybe that would resonate with him. Perhaps it did. A circuit in his brain finally turned on, and thoughts began to flow.

Azra went to the kitchen and made two cups of coffee. She set the larger cup next to Jusuf's elbow and gently tapped his shoulder. Jusuf felt secure when she settled into a soft chair next to him.

Draga Mama,
I have been so worried about you. I hope, hope, hope you're safe somewhere. I tried so many times to call you since I escaped from the roundup in Kljuc and I tried to get back to you after I escaped, but I only got as far as Sanski Most. The town was in flames, the big mosque destroyed! Have you heard anything from Uncle Ibro and Aunt Naza? I hope they're okay.

I was lucky to escape. They were taking us up north somewhere, to a prison I think. I lived in the woods for several weeks, but it may even have been a month. I lost track. Well I'm alive here in Bihac, and I'm in one piece, although I must admit the piece is somewhat thinner than when you last saw me. It's December the 16th (I think) and I should probably add, 1992, because I have no idea whether this letter will still get to you before the year is out. Lots of damage here in Bihac, and there's little food. Sometimes no running water or electricity and only occasionally do I hear the muezzin's calls to prayer. But the air raid sirens blare day and night. Our house is still safe though—it seems so strange to refer to this place that way, and yet that's what it has become for me in the last half year. I hope you don't take that the wrong way. Our house, yours and mine, will always be my home, our home. I hope one day it will be that way again.

Mama, I am sad to tell you that Amil Kapetanovic was killed. What a nice guy. And they killed a Serb kid for no reason! What are these bloody lunatics trying to prove by killing everybody? Do they hate us that much? And for what? Suljo Begovic and his sons were rounded up with us—I don't know what happened to them. They're probably in one of those camps you hear about on the radio or see on CNN.

Who's taking care of you, Mom, and where are you living?

Actually don't tell me. That's a secret you must keep. Do as Suad told me: don't use your real return address. You must be thinking: who's Suad? He's Azra's father, and Azra is the most adorable woman you will ever lay eyes on. Wild red hair and a determined spirit. But very kind, truly thoughtful and caring. Like you, Mom! She took me into her house the day I straggled into Bihac. Oh, Mama—you won't believe this! Remember that coffee bar we used to stop at after the Regattas, the one at the end of the bridge into Bihac? It's called Kafana Paviljon, remember? Well the bartender there—Igor—was one of Dad's hunting buddies. Do you remember him? He said he remembers meeting you with Sasha and me. Small world, huh?

Oftentimes when I tried to telephone you, there was no answer. Finally some creep picked up the phone and said you didn't live there any longer. All sorts of crazy thoughts went through my head. I hope you're okay wherever you are.

Did you get a chance to withdraw your savings from the bank, and did you grab the coins from your jar? I used to laugh at your funny ways. Stupid me. What did Uncle Ib always say? "If youth but knew and age but could."

Jusuf stopped writing and made more coffee for Azra and himself. She smiled at him encouragingly as they warmed their hands on the hot mugs. He kept tilting his head and raising his eyebrows, wondering whether this was all in vain.

"I'm happy for you, Jusuf."

"First I couldn't write a word. Now I can't stop."

"Keep going. I think it will make you feel better just to write something, anything."

Mama, have you seen Sasha? He was with the soldiers who were rounding us up in the square. I still can't believe he is on their side fighting against us. My friend ... and your "son." What's happening to this world? If I saw Sasha today, I wouldn't know what to say. What was he thinking? Do you think they forced him? Sometimes I want to believe that they did, but I don't want to dupe myself. I'm looking for the truth, whatever it might be. You were right when you said bad things were going to happen. I was so stupid not to have seen it, or too foolish not to admit it to myself. What you don't want to see, you don't see.

I feel bad, Mama, about so many things now. I remember when I was embarrassed to say your name and Dad's name in class. Did you know I was embarrassed just to say Braco and Ismeta Pasalic because they would know I was a Muslim? I'm sorry to tell you that, but I guess it's no surprise. I feel terrible now ... about everything. I really feel that I failed you, Mom. I hope you can forgive me someday. When I get home, first thing I'm going to do is repaint the whole house for you, starting with the kitchen.

Let me tell you about Azra and Suad. Azra's a bundle of energy. Most often with a smile on her face that makes her cheeks puff up in little pink balls. She's quite slim (skinny now, actually, like the rest of us.) And she can dance the Kola just like you. I like it slow; she likes it fast. She's usually full of good spirit, but frankly I can see the war taking its toll. She doesn't smile as much lately, and she gets a little snappy at times. If they're successful in negotiating a real ceasefire, one that really sticks, I'm going to borrow someone's car, beg for some gasoline from the NATO troops, and drive her to Kljuc so you can meet her. You will love her; I know it. She can be the daughter you never had!

Suad owns a hardware store, and I help him there, but the shelves are nearly bare. And, Mama, he goes to the mosque like Uncle Ib ... well sometimes. That's what Azra told me, but frankly I only saw him go once. But he does like to wear his fez around the house. Azra stuck it on my head one day and couldn't stop laughing.

I've been rambling long enough. There is still so much to tell you, but first I'll wait to see if this letter gets through.

Take good care of yourself, Mama. I know you can be resourceful, but I also know you need a man around to help you. Do you remember you used to call me your "little man"? I promised Dad I would see after you, and that is my goal, much more so now than when we were together. You may *find me a little more responsible than before. Maybe it's being without you; maybe it's the war. Perhaps the thing I miss most about you through all these long months is your voice. It is so melodious and soft and gentle, and it was like a salve that always soothed me when I was upset, even when I was angry with you. When we are back together, I want to hear your voice even before I see you. Faces change. A voice is like a fingerprint.*

I hope nothing bad has crossed your path. I can't wait for the day that I can hug and kiss you again. And I'll do whatever you ask of me; I promise.

Volim te, tvoj sin, Jusuf.

He put down the pen, looked out the window for a long while, turned to Azra, and burst into tears.

"Oh, sweetheart. I can imagine how you feel ... but you never know. She might have been spared. At least you've tried. At least you've written."

CHAPTER TWENTY

ON NEW YEAR'S DAY, 1993, Suad and Jusuf went to the store to see if the front window was still in place after a night of heavy bombardment. There was a crack in the upper right corner, but it was otherwise intact. As usual, Suad preferred to fuss with things alone in the back room, leaving Jusuf to work in the front. There was little for Jusuf to do behind the counter because people had less and less money for purchases. There was also the problem of diminishing inventory. Batteries in particular were hard to come by, but they were in constant demand because electricity flowed erratically and only for short periods. So Jusuf either read books he brought to work or he passed the time sketching architectural designs. As a kid, his parents were amazed at how he was able to produce accurate sketches of buildings he had seen after the family returned from vacation in Slovenia. Having experienced firsthand the highly original work of Joze Plecnik, Jusuf tried to replicate in colored pencil studies Plecnik's construction details. Although the architect's work had fallen out of favor in Yugoslavia after World War II because of his classical vocabulary and devout Catholicism, Jusuf remained attracted to Plecnik's masterly compositions, rich textures, and memorable colors. Jusuf's dream of becoming an architect had, for reasons he himself did not understand, turned into something of a secret since the war started, a goal he felt he needed to keep private. After completing a fresh batch of sketches, he stowed them in a cardboard box high up on shelves with tagged but never claimed appliances.

Over the months, Jusuf had come to know many of Suad's customers. In the absence of newspapers and scant radio and TV broadcasts, these exchanges became a valuable source of information about the progress of the war. There were on-again, off-again reports of negotiated settlements and ceasefires. Even though it troubled Jusuf to think of infants being born into such a violent world, he began to contemplate a future life with Azra and one day having children. But, like his dreams of going to a university and of becoming an architect, all this would have to wait for a permanent peace.

Over time, Jusuf had begun to emulate the way Azra covered for her father, allowing Suad to disappear into his back room with no questions asked, particularly when Suad's hands began to tremble, or his stutter or nervous cough reappeared. Jusuf also realized that no matter the season, Suad was never without his sunglasses out on the street, and he always wore a hat with a wide overhanging brim, even at dusk. Suad walked just behind Jusuf or to one side, so he remained in Jusuf's shadow. His excuse was that his legs were stiff or his feet hurt. Though this fashion of walking to and from work was at times noticeably awkward, Jusuf said nothing. He never challenged Suad or questioned him, figuring Suad would speak to him when he was ready, if that time ever came.

At the end of the day, they locked up and headed for home. Halfway there, Jusuf noticed that Suad, standing on Jusuf's left, seemed to recognize an older couple walking toward them, both of them old enough to be his parents. The woman picked up her pace, causing Suad's hands to shake. He muttered something, which Jusuf couldn't understand. As the couple passed, the woman suddenly stepped around Jusuf and raised a fist and yelled into Suad's face. "Did you have to be so selfish? Boris was our only son." Mites of spittle flew out of her mouth as her rebuke continued. "You just kept pushing for what you wanted even though you knew they were almost engaged." Her eyes squinted, upper lip curled nose-ward in disgust, lower jaw thrust angrily forward. "He was such a good boy. You have no idea how we've suffered all these years. No idea the nights we cried."

"Dinka, Dinka," her husband said, "it was so long ago. Give the poor man some peace. People *do* things. Don't you know how to forgive? If you did, maybe you'd get a full night's sleep."

"Shut up, Galib." As the couple shambled on down the street, the woman continued to fume, first in seething mutters and then in a few short outbursts directed at Galib. "I'll *never* forgive him, and I'll *never* forgive you for forgiving him."

Suad ducked into an alley and vomited. After a few minutes, he returned, his face ashen. Jusuf wanted to comfort him, but his embarrassment at hearing the woman's accusation intersecting with what he assumed was Suad's embarrassment and presumable shame kept him from coming up with anything he deemed appropriate. A block from the house, Suad whispered into the back of Jusuf's jacket, "Please don't say anything to Azra. I beg you not to mention this."

As months passed, the siege of Bihac intensified. Serbian artillery positions in the mountains rendered few areas in the city safe. There would be several quiet days in a row, and then shells suddenly began raining in again. Those who heard the shells whistling had time to dive for cover. For those who didn't, death struck in an instant. Splinters of glass lay everywhere—on the streets and in almost every room of every building that had a window. Fuel was hard or impossible to acquire. This forced Azra, Suad, and Jusuf to return to the basement where the earth kept that zone somewhat warmer than the frigid rooms upstairs. Jusuf and Suad moved furniture and clothing from the back rooms of the house to the front, which faced away from the majority of Serbian artillery positions. Small utilitarian pieces of furniture were carried to the basement. Upstairs they placed bags filled with sand and gravel on windowsills to create a shield from flying glass and fragments of shrapnel. Earth would have worked to fill the bags, but the frozen ground had become the equivalent of bedrock.

Azra was forever biting her lower lip, and she began blinking nervously whenever she spoke. Suad and Jusuf noticed that she was also grinding her teeth when she slept, and she frequently complained of pains in her abdomen and worried aloud that they might be signs of cancer. Dado had once reported that the hair of some of his friends had turned white overnight, causing Azra, when she first heard the report, to run to a mirror to see if she too was going white. Cowering in the basement made them feel as though their own aging had accelerated—

as if calendar pages were ripped off not a day at a time, but a batch each day. Time seemed to be slowing down but the aging process speeding up.

As the weeks passed, Jusuf could not escape the idea of enlisting with the locals that were defending Bihac. Several soldiers had mentioned to him on more than one occasion that men were needed on the front lines. Jusuf knew he was capable with a firearm, more so than most of his neighbors who were defending the city, and he knew very well that that skill would be of immense value on the front lines, but emotionally he was not yet ready to sign up. And yet the thought was there every morning when he woke up to the echoing pops of sniper fire and then again when he retired and heard the spine-chilling whistles of shells overhead. Hunting for animals or choosing not to hunt for them could not be spoken of in the same breath as the call to fight in a war, to defend loved ones.

One day in late January, snow fell steadily and piled up in mountainous drifts. Suad, by chance, was behind the counter tinkering with an eggbeater that a Croatian woman on crutches had brought in the week before. The blades had been contorted by a ricocheting piece of shrapnel. Suad knew he would never be paid for the repair but agreed to look at it anyway, if for no better reason than to pass the time. Jusuf was in the back room opening a carton of paint cans that had been out of sight under a stair to a second-floor storeroom. The front door opened, and a volley of snowflakes blew into the shop. Suad looked up. A man and a boy stood on the threshold but did not enter. They looked like somber and eerie statues against a blurred white curtain of snow slanting out of a dishwater-gray sky. The snow was piled high on their long matted hair and bony shoulders, and their bodies were wrapped with a motley assortment of filthy rags and torn sheets of plastic bound together by pieces of string and vines. Their faces, marked by sores and smudged with filth, stretched tautly over protruding cheekbones. Barely any flesh was visible to soften the outlines of the skull, leaving their faces devoid of expression. Lower jaws hung limp, and faint ribbons of breath seeped from their lips. Mucous ran from their noses, and charcoal colored circles ringed their eye sockets.

"Are you looking for someone?" If one of them had answered, it was so weakly Suad hadn't heard. "Can I help you?" Suad asked again.

In a raised but tender voice, he repeated his question, "How can I help you?"

He tried to look into the boy's eyes, but the eyes drifted from side to side absent any focus, interest, or energy. The boy fell against the man who, unsteady himself, quickly raised one large, gray hand against the doorjamb to support the boy and himself.

"Please. Please come in. Come out of the snow."

In a voice barely audible and dry with disuse, the man whispered, "Have you any water or a little something to eat. Anything will do."

"Please come in and close the door. It's cold in here but a bit warmer than out there. Jusuf! Any water left in that jug back there?"

"A couple of swigs at best. You thirsty?"

"Bring it quickly. We have some—"

Before the ragged man had time to close the door, the sound of sniper fire echoed in the streets. The boy shuddered with fright and clutched the man's rags. "Papa! Move fast. They're still after us." The man closed the door, and the two walked toward the counter.

Suad fished around beneath the counter and found the hard end of a loaf of bread, mice-nibbled along its edges. He intended to break it in two equal pieces but inadvertently reduced most of it to crumbs. "Shit." He set the morsels on the counter as Jusuf entered the front of the shop.

"Here's the wa—oh my God, Suad! Where did *they* come from?"

Jusuf stared at the strangers who looked much like many other Muslim refugees who had been living in the mountains and were still trickling into the center of Bihac, dazed and famished. He tossed the sloshing plastic jug to Suad, raced back through the doorway, and quickly came back with two plastic crates, setting them down quickly behind the man and the boy. The two swayed as if they were standing in a windstorm and then slowly lowered themselves onto the makeshift seats as Jusuf tried to steady them so they didn't topple over. Once seated, the father looked up into Jusuf's gaunt and fully bearded face, nodded his thanks, and then closed his eyes.

Jusuf and Suad exchanged expressions of grave concern. The man took a long breath, looked at Jusuf for a moment, and then bent his head again and stared at the floor. Jusuf stepped back when he noticed their heads crawling with lice and hoped there was a vestige of gasoline or paint thinner to pour around the crates to kill the bugs before they migrated. The boy, who kept scratching his head, armpits, and groin, stared at Jusuf intently as Jusuf handed them the jug and then the breadcrumbs. When the boy couldn't remove the green cap on the jug, he handed the jug to his father. The man took the jug in his left hand, revealing the raw scars of a missing finger, and then wrapped his bony but powerful right fist around the cap. It yielded instantly. The man handed the jug back to his son, who took a swig before they sprinkled the breadcrumbs into their mouths, working them around on their tongues as if they were both nervously learning again how to swallow. Then the man took a swig of water.

"I wish we had more to offer you," Suad said apologetically.

After studying Jusuf's face for several minutes, the boy pointed tentatively at Jusuf and nudged his father. "Papa ... look. Look!"

The man raised his head and followed the direction of the boy's twig-like finger. The man drew in a tiny gasp of astonishment while wringing his hands as if in prayer and gratitude. The skin stretched taut across the man's forehead began to relax, and tears welled in his reddened eyes. Then his head fell into his palms. He whispered toward the floorboards as his shoulders trembled, "Allah be praised." Suad and Jusuf looked at each other bewildered as the man started to cry. "I was sure ... you were dead." The man spoke through little coughs. He raised his head and reached out his hand with the missing finger.

Jusuf looked at the man and the boy, totally confused, taking the man's hand in his. He had no idea who these skeletons might be and was reluctant to ask.

"You don't recognize us, Jusuf? We've been on the run for a month or so. We don't look familiar?"

Jusuf searched for a clue, turning from the man to the boy and back again, peering into their increasingly familiar-looking eyes, summoning a replay of their strained and broken voices, trying to connect the voices and the eyes to something from his past. He had the strong sense that he should know them, but he couldn't figure out why or how. Something was missing. They were like strangers looming in a murky dream, a dream of unconnected fragments, and then for a moment, a curious image of two candles in a three-cup candelabra flashed before Jusuf's eyes. Their names remained frustratingly close but beyond reach. He was certain he knew them somehow from somewhere.

"I thought we'd never make it, Jusuf. We were in the camps.

Escaped, dear God! Jusuf, damn it, it's us. You forget your neighbor, Suljo, so fast? You still don't recognize us?"

"Oh, god! You made it."

"Some guy waiting near the bridge at the edge of town asked me where I was from, and when I said Kljuc, he directed us over here. He said he thought someone from Kljuc was working here."

Jusuf kneeled before them. He stared intently into their eyes. Dumfounded and mute, he kept staring and listening to Suljo's voice. The man's long beard, caked with melting nuggets of ice and debris, was now mostly gray with a hint it once had been red.

"Oh my god! Suljo! It really is you?"

Turning to Suad with joy bursting forth in his smile, Jusuf said, "Suad, these are my neighbors from Kljuc, my next-door neighbors. I can't believe it!" His face was flushed and glistened with tears. "These are my very dear friends." Jusuf looked at the boy and after a moment said apologetically, "I am so sorry, but I can't tell whether you're Ahmet or Zarif. I am really embarrassed."

"I'm Ahmet. Looking in shop windows on the way over here, I also didn't recognize myself or Papa."

"But where's Zarif? I think I remember seeing him on the truck with both of you when we were taken from Kljuc. He was with you, wasn't he?"

Ahmet quickly covered his ears with his palms and closed his eyes. Suljo looked away and waved his hands to make the question go away. Then he brought his huge hand down on his thigh and patted it in a confusion of tenderness and anger. He shook his head from side to side as if to keep at bay a memory he wished desperately not to relive.

"You guys stay where you are. We'll be right back." Jusuf went to the end of the counter and motioned to Suad to follow him into the back room. He asked in a whisper whether Suad would allow Suljo and Ahmet to come back to the house to stay with them.

"Are you fucking crazy, Jusuf? We're living in two rooms now as it is," Suad whispered. "Where will they sleep? How will we feed them? Azra's near the edge of losing her mind as it is. It's not a hotel, Jusuf."

Jusuf knew he shouldn't push any further. There were limits to what anyone was able to offer at this time, and he was still a guest of sorts himself in Suad's house. He finally realized that excessive generosity during wartime could translate into suicide for all concerned. And yet he recalled what a lifesaving gift it was when Azra and Suad took *him* in. Perhaps his old friends could live in the shop? He hoped Suad would come to suggest that option on his own before they left the back room.

Before returning to the front of the shop, Suad beckoned Jusuf closer with a wave of his hand. He whispered in Jusuf's ear. "I can be a fool sometimes. Sure they can stay. We'll work it out somehow." Suad pointed to the stairs. "Maybe the storeroom will work out for them."

CHAPTER TWENTY-ONE

FIVE WEEKS PASSED SLOWLY from the time Jusuf's letter to Ismeta was given to Suad's friend Ivan. For the first couple of weeks, Jusuf awoke each day hoping that would be the day he would get a response. Suad explained that he only saw Ivan infrequently and couldn't really press him, particularly on a matter of no benefit to his friend. After a month of daily disappointments, Jusuf gave up hope and concluded once again that the letter was undeliverable or that his mother had not survived, or both.

Suad was nursing a lingering cold the day Igor stopped by to say that Ivan wanted to meet him in the usual spot. Though his head throbbed and his chest felt like it was wrapped in steel straps, Suad headed alone to their usual place of exchange. As he approached the familiar clearing, he saw a blocky man he had never seen before leaning against a tree smoking a cigarette. The man whose face was puffy and pink nodded but was otherwise without expression. Suad assumed a double-cross. He had no weapon and wondered why the man had one arm out of view behind his back. The landscape suddenly looked strange, even threatening, and Suad's heart began to pound, his congested lungs about to seize. A thin trail of steam caught his eye. It came from behind a large tree directly in front of him. Then he heard a faint hissing sound rising and falling. Suad was about to turn and run when Ivan stepped out from behind the tree zipping his fly.

"God, for a minute there, I was sure I was a goner. Who's your friend?"

"My uncle. He's gonna give me a hand with some plumbing when we get back to my place."

"That arm behind his back scared the hell out of me."

Ivan's uncle chuckled and brought a large monkey wrench into view. "Thought you might have considered it a weapon."

They laughed.

"So. Any luck?"

Ivan reached into his jacket. He held up a letter covered with several greasy fingerprints and black tire marks sloping across the front almost obliterating the mailing address. Ivan shrugged off the mess, "No idea." The return address was from a hamlet far outside of Kljuc, one that was no more than eleven kilometers southeast of Bihac.

"Hmm, that's odd," Suad said.

"Hope this is what he was expecting."

"I owe you one, Ivan. Good luck with the pipes, guys."

Jusuf and Suad saw each other at the same moment as they were both walking back to the house from opposite directions. Jusuf had an arm full of branches and twigs; Suad appeared empty handed.

"What got you out of bed, old man?"

As Jusuf deposited the firewood next to the stove, Suad removed the letter from his jacket pocket and said, "I'm not sure the news I have will be what you're looking for, but I got this from Ivan a half hour ago."

Jusuf looked at Azra. "Take it, Jusuf. Open it," she said, almost as excited as Jusuf.

Jusuf immediately recognized Sasha's large, scrawly handwriting. His hand shook as he took the letter from Suad. As he held it, he was bombarded with a jumble of warring sentiments—fear, anger, love, and hope. He stared at the fingerprints and tire marks and couldn't bring himself to break the seal. Azra moved closer and with a permission-seeking tilt of her head reached forward and gently took the envelope.

"I'll open it if you want me to, Jusuf." He looked up at the ceiling in terrified anticipation.

"Jusuf, did you hear me? I'll open it if you want me to. I think you should read it … whatever it says, and as painful as that might be. If you want me to, I'll read it to you." Jusuf padded around in a wavering circle like a caged animal and finally nodded okay. Suad sat down.

As Azra was about to rip open the envelope, Jusuf raised his hand for her to pause. He felt that the letter might, if his mother was dead, contain some form of embodiment of her spirit. He reached for the fake-ivory letter opener Azra's mother kept in a cracked ceramic jar along with some cooking utensils. Jusuf watched intently as Azra meticulously and respectfully sliced through the top fold and slipped the letter out of the envelope. When she began to unfold the single page, several photographs fell to the floor. One landed near Jusuf's shoe, image side up.

"Oh, god, I think she's alive! I think she's alive!" Although lightheaded, he bent over and picked up a small photograph of his mother wearing a broad smile, the small leaf-shaped birthmark on her right cheekbone wrinkled in her crow's feet. He brought it to his lips and kissed the birthmark as he did so frequently as a child.

"Look, Azra, this is my mom. She's in front of the mosque. God, she's wearing the same headscarf she wore the day I was trucked out of Kljuc. Look, Suad, look." Jusuf bent over to show Suad.

"I can imagine how happy you must be. She's a very attractive woman, I might add."

"Yeah, but she's always been embarrassed about that mark. Thought it marred her looks."

Azra handed the other two photographs to Jusuf. One was old, sepia-toned, and smaller than Azra's palm. It was cracked and patched with tape.

"Hey, look, this is my dad in a parade. He always wore his blue overalls with all the paint splatters, no matter the occasion. It's hard to make out, but that's his communist flag stapled to a broom handle." Jusuf could almost see his father's slight limp, right foot dragging a tad, left foot turning out to the left to compensate. "He looks shorter than I remember him. And he always wore that black beret except when he hunted."

Then Azra handed Jusuf a worn, matchbook-size photo of two boys, both around the age of ten, zigzagging with butterfly nets through a field of windswept wheat stalks looking like swirls of finger-paint. Jusuf remembered that day or at least remembered the photo of that day. "I feel I should hate him. And yet my heart aches to see him again."

"But, Jusuf, he's obviously done you a favor. Who knows what trouble he went to in finding your mom and getting these pictures."

"I hope he found her and not just these pictures." Remembering there was also a letter, he said, "Read it to me, please. Quickly. I'm too nervous."

With trembling hands, Azra carefully unfolded the single sheet. "It's signed 'Mama.'" She smiled at Jusuf through her tears, nodding her head and biting the inside of her lower lip. Her gestures seemed to indicate he had gotten the letter he was hoping for. The letter was dated January 22, 1993. Azra's voice cracked as she wiped her eyes and began to read.

> *Draga Jusuf,*
> *I can't tell you how relieved I was to receive your letter! Are you becoming a writer? That's not like the old you. It was always so hard to get you to speak, or write, or tell me anything about what you were doing. What's come over you?*
>
> *I worried about you until it made me sick, wondering if you were safe, wondering if you were even still alive. After I read your letter, I folded it and put it against my heart. That's where I keep it. It helps me fall asleep knowing you are close to me with your words. Then it goes right back in my bra first thing in the morning. But sometimes I must first reread it before my coffee.*
>
> *I was so pleased to learn you are living with a nice family. Azra and Suad sound so kind.*

Azra looked up and smiled at Jusuf and her father. Jusuf walked over and stood behind her to read over her shoulder. Seeing his mother's handwriting, the well-formed letters, even slightly childlike in their naive extension, he felt like Ismeta was in the room with him.

> *Jusuf, promise you won't get married until the war is over so I can bake the wedding cakes. Promise!*
> *Jusuf, dear, Kljuc is no more—at least as you (we) knew it. The Serbs have taken over our homes. They destroyed the mosque there, too. Blew it up and paved it over. I've heard it's just a parking lot for trucks now. Our way of life is nothing*

> more than a dream now, a memory. I knew bad things were going to happen! You laughed at me, you silly boy! You should listen to your Mama more often. You're hopeless, Jussie, just like your Papa.
>
> Sasha still calls me "Mom." So the whole world hasn't gone to hell, yet. I guess one "adopted" son nearby is better than no sons at all. By the way, Sasha is not living in Kljuc anymore, either. He and his family are living with a relative that you might know, but I better say no more. I can't tell you too much about him, but I do know Sasha **is** fighting in the war ... on their side. How can I blame him; everybody's caught up in this thing now, and our boys want to kill him and destroy what he's got, so what else can he do. Well ... I can't really say he's fighting! He goes off to the front lines, yes, but I don't think he shoots anybody, at least that's what he's told me. He still loves his Dylan. The harmonica goes everywhere with him. If he didn't attract so many women with his lovely blond curls, he'd probably marry the contraption.

Jusuf, Azra, and Suad all laughed. Azra reached back to touch Jusuf's face. His cheeks were wet.

> My impression is that he cooks for the soldiers or something like that; do you remember he worked at that bar, Poggy's, as a cook for a while. Last I heard, Poggy still hadn't come up with the 500 DM to tack up the other "g" in his sign. What an idiot! Once cheap, forever cheap.
>
> Sasha asked if I've heard from you. I know he wishes the war would end, like the rest of us. And I'm sure he would like to see you again. He had his twentieth birthday last week, and your big one is coming up soon. Twenty years old! My word, you're a man already, my little Jussie. Hopefully the war will be over and we can celebrate together in Kljuc or in Bihac.

Jusuf squeezed Azra's shoulder. "So maybe you *will* meet her," Jusuf whispered in Azra's ear.

I don't know what you meant about pigeons in your letter, but believe it or not, they've got pigeons here too. I even feed them myself sometimes. They're kind of cute ... but in the middle of a war, I've got to tell you even a snake would look cute.

"Your mom sure can turn a phrase," Suad observed.

Jusuf, my dear Jusuf. Remember that I love you with all my heart and soul. Please be safe, and practice what your dad taught you. One day you may find yourself with a gun in your hand. Just make sure it's not Sasha you're aiming at! Why did I even write that?

And lastly, young man, when this war finally ends and we go back to our house in Kljuc, you do have some painting to finish up. The idea of walking out on me with the kitchen half-painted! The things you learned from your father! Do you remember this picture of him? Your dad was a darling but impossible. Keep the pictures safe for me, sweetheart.

Remember that I cherish you above all else in the world. You are my heart and soul. Be safe, Jussie. And take care of Suad and your Azra. I have heard of so many awful things—murders, rapes ... and with such unspeakable shame brought to the families involved. You can tell something has happened to these poor girls. There is just a painful silence. To be so dishonored. The beasts should be taken out and shot. I'm sorry to end on such a sad note, but we live in a ghastly time.

Puno te voli, Mama.

For several days prior to the start of the Muslim religious holiday of Bairam, which Suad and Azra were celebrating in their own quiet way, Jusuf tried to imagine how his mother might celebrate—going to a mosque, placing flowers on Braco's grave, or just visiting relatives and enjoying a flaky slice of baklava. When Jusuf was a teenager, however, Ismeta's religious activities caused him unending embarrassment.

"Mom, do you need to be so open about everything?"

"It's what I believe, Jusuf. You choose not to believe, and I choose to believe."

"But do you have to wear the headscarf on the street and go to the mosque so frequently? Can't you just read the Qur'an at home?"

"Jusuf, do you love your friends more than you love your mother? Or does love have nothing to do with it? Is it all about what you feel your friends will think of you?"

"It embarrasses me, Mom. It's so old-fashioned. I want to fit in, but I feel like an outsider with the Serbs and Croats. I really wish you were more like Dad." It was at moments like this that Jusuf looked at Ismeta's birthmark and saw it not just as a misprint of nature, or in good times as a facial feature he adored, but as an unwanted disfigurement, a stain that should embarrass her as it sometimes did him. Depending upon his mood, the size of the mark would change, its color growing pale or intensifying.

"Damn it, Jusuf, have some respect for your mother. It's not all about you. Grow up. Most of what I pray for these days is you coming to your senses. Life's not just a big party. You have to get serious about what's important and what's expected of you … and the sooner the better."

These thoughts of his mother doing what tradition expected of her during Bairam eventually motivated Jusuf to consider joining one of the brigades defending Bihac. It had been evident for months that men were needed on the front lines and he was finally feeling ready, obliged even, to defend those with whom he was living and had come to love.

One morning on his way to the shop, he mentioned his intentions to Suad. As Suad put his key into the shop door, he suggested that Jusuf talk to his old friend, Malik, a bald-headed, frequently squinting truck driver with one clouded eye who used to supply Suad with merchandise picked up in Zagreb and Sarajevo. "I have a friend who's been serving on the front lines and might have some useful tips. I'll get in touch with him. Name's Malik."

Suad wasn't sure what he'd say to Malik, or what he'd ask of him. Nonetheless, Suad rushed to get in touch with Malik before Jusuf did.

"Do what you can, Malik. I'm not asking for any special favors; just try to keep an eye out for him."

"I'll do what I can for him, but it's rough out there. It's us or them. The conditions are from hell."

Middle-aged and mild-mannered, Malik welcomed Jusuf's offer to serve. He explained that his own bunker was large enough for three men, but at the moment he shared it only with a young Serb named Obrad. Obrad was a nervous, silky-haired fellow with a bad case of acne. Malik told Jusuf that Obrad would probably be happy to have someone in the bunker his own age but never mentioned that three weeks earlier a third soldier who had been with them for several months had taken a piece of shrapnel that blew off half of his face.

Jusuf and Azra were cleaning broken glass and other debris that was scattered around the kitchen from a night of bombardment when he decided to tell her his plan to go to the front lines. She burst into tears. "Did you need to do that just now? What happens if you get killed? Isn't there something you can do around *here* to help the cause instead of going out there?"

"Please don't make it any harder for me, Azra. You know I don't want to leave you and your dad, and I'm not eager to kill anybody or get shot myself. But I just can't keep watching other men go out there and lay down their lives to protect us. That's something I could never live with."

"But couldn't you go in a month or so, or in the spring when it'll be easier on both of us?"

Jusuf tried to console her with a hug, but she broke away.

"You think I want to go. I don't. I'm scared. I'm fucking terrified, if you really want to know the truth. I've had diarrhea every day since I made the decision. I need your support, Azra ... not your resistance."

"But, Jusuf, maybe in a few weeks the US will be able to do something, or the Security Council will force the peace they keep promising."

"Damn it, Azra. Face the facts. It's not their war, it's ours. The Americans won't get tough with the Serbs because they're busy wooing the Russians. Everybody's stymied. Politics is in the toilet. Get it into your head once and for all. No white knight is coming to our rescue. I've got to stand up and be counted or we'll all be dead."

Azra picked up a wooden spoon and threw it into the living room and then ran down the steps to the basement sobbing. Jusuf went after her, but she refused to listen to him.

"I don't want to lose you, Jusuf," she wailed.

"Azra, please. I have to go. I have to."

As the day approached, Jusuf could see that Azra was growing even more nervous and edgy. She complained of pains in her abdomen. "Are you going to leave me like this? It's not a good time to go. Can't you postpone it for another week or two?" Whenever Jusuf went to hug her, she refused to look into his eyes, and at one point she pummeled his chest and yelled in frustration, "This fucking stupid war! First my mother dies, now you. Then it'll be Dad."

Suad tried to console her by saying he was sure that Jusuf would do everything he could to protect himself. "He's not a lunatic, Azra." Her sobbing and constant clutching at his clothes the day he left the house stayed with Jusuf during his ride to the front lines.

He looked out the windshield of Malik's truck as the sky darkened, the rutted ice-covered road racing toward him like an avalanche. The only thing Malik said was that several men in the brigade might have to share the same rifle and that he should not be surprised to see some on our side armed only with kitchen knives and pitchforks. Jusuf's knees started to shake and he felt like he had to pee.

As they walked into camp, Malik pointed out a few women who had chosen to fight. "But they get no weapons. They cook or work in the hospital, if you can call that fucking tarpaper shack over there with the lantern a hospital. I tell you, Jusuf, don't end up there whatever happens to you 'cause the shelves are bare. Well I guess Azra already told you there's near to no medicine in Bihac, not even any goddamn Novocain to pull a tooth. I don't want to think about the poor women in town who had to give birth."

"Yes, Azra told me."

"Every guy out here knows there'll be no antibiotics or anesthesia to get him through the worst of it." As they approached the bunker, Malik added, "By the way, did I mention we got a Serb in our bunker, so be careful what you say."

The bunker was dark as a tunnel when they entered. "Hey, Obrad, got a friend here for you."

A weak voice rose out of the darkness. "How about food? Bring any back with you?"

"Be a gentleman, Obrad. Say hello to Jusuf."

"Hi, Jusuf. What did you guys bring back?"

Jusuf's first military duties had nothing to do with combat. Suad had mentioned to Malik that Jusuf was handy with tools, so Malik directed him to maintain the trenches and the bunkers. The trenches were only a few feet deep and about two feet wide. They required Jusuf to lie prone or crawl with his head tucked low. Protruding roots and rocks made passage difficult. Two soldiers moving past each other in opposite directions meant one soldier had to crawl over the other. They quickly learned that the one on top was the most vulnerable, so there were often squabbles and jokes with sexual innuendoes about negotiating the preferred position closer to the earth.

Keeping the trenches clear was critical because they were used constantly to patrol and monitor the enemy's position and movements. Jusuf had to shovel snow out of the trench while lying on his back. He cautiously raised the shovel over his head and then lowered it behind him to scoop a clump of snow. With a quick and vigorous shake, he dislodged the clump and sent it sailing out of the trench, making sure his hands and arms did not rise too far above grade.

One beautiful March day, Jusuf interrupted his trench-clearing efforts to look up into a cluster of bone white clouds dry-brushed across a velvety blue sky. Distracted by the view, he began to shake free a shovel-full of wet snow, which was in the air for a fraction of a second longer than usual, when a bullet caught the edge of the curved blade, producing a high-pitched ping. The handle whirled around like a drive shaft suddenly forced into gear. Before he could react, the handle wrenched his wrist. Tendons and muscles stretched with a pain so intense Jusuf could do nothing but let the shovel fall on him like a limb in a storm. The edge of the blade cut into his nose, just missing his left eye. He felt certain his nose was broken. He rolled onto his belly and crawled quickly back toward the bunker, leaving a thin trail of blood in the gray snow. When Malik caught sight of him, he assumed Jusuf had been hit in the eye. He ran out incautiously to help him back into the bunker, inviting in return a salvo of sniper fire. Malik wiped the blood from Jusuf's nose with a handful of snow and wrapped a rag around his head to stop the bleeding. The sprained wrist forced Jusuf to stay in the bunker for three days.

When Jusuf got back to Bihac for a short leave and walked through the front door, Azra screamed and ran to him in tears.

"Oh, god. What happened? Did they shoot out your eye? Dad, boil some water, quick."

"I'm okay, Azra, I'm okay. The bandage makes it look worse than it is. I dropped a shovel on my nose."

"You did what?" She started laughing, belly laughing, and Jusuf and Suad joined in. "A shovel on your *nose*! You clumsy idiot."

Reaching for Azra, Jusuf said, "Now give your hero a kiss, damn it. I missed you terribly." As they embraced, Suad turned to look for wood scraps to build a fire.

Jusuf's nose was swollen and very tender to the touch. Azra had seen much worse at the hospital. She expertly cleaned and dressed the wound, laughing sporadically at the thought of his being wounded by a shovel. "I'm telling no one in town how this happened. *My* Jusuf wounded by a *shovel*!"

When they started to make love that night, Azra paused and turned Jusuf's head slightly so that his un-bandaged nose was illuminated in a blade of moonlight. "That really doesn't look so good. I'm so afraid for you, Jusuf, for what the next more serious injury could mean."

"I could hurt myself right here in the house or walking through town. Keep it in perspective, sweetheart."

"But I ache inside for you. I ache for what I see, and I ache for what might be next. As much as I've wanted you since you were last here, I don't think I can keep thoughts of something really serious happening to you out of my mind right now. Maybe we can be together tomorrow night?"

Although disappointed, Jusuf backed off and just held her head gently against his chest. After a while, he began to whisper expressions of affection near her ear and ran his fingers through her hair until her desire for him ignited once again. They used their fingers and mouths to bring pleasure to each other. For Azra, the fear of pregnancy and then perhaps abortion kept him from penetrating her even though both craved that purest expression of true and exclusive love.

Rain in the trenches was more of a challenge than snow. When the rainwater wasn't frozen, it lay in the trenches like a stagnant stream and had to be bailed out, one awkward bucketful at a time. This turned out to be more dangerous than shoveling snow and impossible to do lying down, so Jusuf worked at night and tried to sleep in the bunker during the day.

The bunker was two meters deep, and two and half meters wide and high, cold as a freezer, and dark as a closet with the door closed. Blankets lined the walls to both keep the walls of earth from falling in and to keep the heat of their bodies from seeping out. The blankets required frequent adjustments to make sure they stayed properly positioned. Sometimes the buildup of humidity in the bunker saturated the blankets, and the freezing air outside froze them hard as plastic boards. If a frozen blanket was bumped, the ice-film cracked like glass.

One afternoon as they were repositioning the blankets, Obrad noticed that one of the roof timbers was rotten and another looked weak. "Hey, guys, I think we have a problem here." Jusuf began to take charge of the repair, but Obrad explained that he used to frame heavy timber structures.

All three cooperated to build a dense palisade of thick branches to work behind. Jusuf and Obrad looked for new logs no thinner than the distance from outstretched tip of thumb to tip of pinkie. After setting them—Jusuf deferring to Obrad for the cutting and fitting—they installed a layer of plastic sheeting over top to make the assembly as waterproof as possible. "Let's break for a few minutes. I'm exhausted," Obrad said.

They sipped water from small jars and cans and ate a few nuts and small hunks of rock-stale bread before shoveling six inches of soil and loose debris and a one-foot layer of small stones over the plastic. "Maybe we can start a construction company after the war's over," Malik said.

Jusuf laughed. "You've got to be kidding. I'm getting Azra and heading straight for a particular hotel in Dubrovnik when this shit ends." They topped off the bunker with more soil and a layer of branches, followed by sprayed handfuls of camouflaging leaves. That night, they all slept soundly. Not even Malik's snoring awakened the two younger men until morning.

The bunker was without a stove when Jusuf first arrived, so on his days off, he scrounged nuts, bolts, and scraps of sheet metal from the back room of Suad's shop, soon fashioning a makeshift stove for heating and cooking. They whooped and hollered like madmen when they finally installed it in the back of the bunker. As smoke poured up through the short flue, they felt as proud as if they had just launched a rocket. When they were able to find dry wood, they had a few hours of warmth and even a hot meal on occasion. But using the stove carried a danger; a corkscrew of smoke seen by the enemy was the equivalent of the bright red bull's eye in a target.

Every bunker had a small wooden panel that opened out toward the trenches. If the enemy was seen approaching on foot, soldiers in the trenches hollered *attack*, and those in the bunkers walloped open the panels, thrust their firearms through the openings, and took aim.

Since the time Jusuf first arrived on the front lines, there had been no attacks, just mortar fire, but Malik thought he heard branches cracking and hushed voices far off in the woods. When a contingent of Serbian soldiers actually loomed out of the mist two hundred meters away, the soldiers in the trenches yelled in panic for action. Although it was an hour before noon, Jusuf was snoozing in the bunker, and Obrad was whittling a wooden whistle, sitting in the doorway for some fresh air. Obrad quickly scurried into the bunker, closed the door, and tossed his whistle toward Jusuf's legs to waken him. Malik ran for his rifle, the only rifle in the bunker. His vision had been failing for years, and a small cataract clouded his good eye. With color draining from his face, he squinted and suddenly thrust his rifle into Jusuf's hands.

"What the fuck are you doing?" Jusuf said, rubbing his eyes and raking his hair side to side with his fingers to erase his stupor.

"I heard you speaking to Obrad a couple of days ago. You mentioned you're a pretty good shot."

Jusuf waved off Malik's order. "I said I *was* a good shot. Shit, it's been years since I hunted."

Jusuf finally accepted the weapon but tried to pass it directly to Obrad, who backed away crying, "I can't. Those are my people. I can't do that yet!"

There was commotion and lots of yelling outside. Shots were fired here and there, but it was impossible to know from which side.

"Keep it, Jusuf!" Malik ordered. "I'm a terrible shot. I got one lousy eye, and the other's not much better, and besides, Igor told me recently that your father was a hunter and taught you to shoot. Goddamn it, use it or we'll all be dead." Jusuf pulled back the bolt to see if it was loaded.

"I need a fucking bullet, Malik. Quick!"

Jusuf thrust the rifle through the open window. He looked through the barrel and saw it had not been cleaned.

"Good god! Malik … what's keeping you?"

Malik rummaged through his belongings looking for his chewing tobacco canister where he kept his dwindling supply of cartridges.

"Malik. Bullets. Quick."

"Here."

Jusuf loaded the rifle and looked out the window at the small paramilitary band approaching through the woods. They were still too far off to waste a bullet. He half-listened to the muffled exchanges coming from adjacent bunkers. He had hoped he could ease into the violent side of warfare, see some of his fellow soldiers with actual injuries in order to desensitize himself and make killing the enemy an act for which there was no alternative. He was repelled by the thought of taking a life, but worried that these thoughts would cost him his own life or his comrades.

His palms turned slick as his recollection of himself as a hunter suddenly became a blur. He had trouble focusing his eyes and heard nothing but his own blood pumping through his neck. As the band of soldiers charged up the hill, Jusuf couldn't recall a single specific his father had taught him on how to aim at multiple targets. No words were in his brain, no intuition as to what to do next. He remembered only that his father was a hunter, a superior shot, a master of the moment. Jusuf was spooked when he felt his father's hand on his shoulder, steadying him. Startled, Jusuf looked back. He saw only Malik's bald head. Malik's hand was on Jusuf's back offering support, or maybe getting it from him. The Serbs paused and appeared to be positioning themselves behind trees and rocks. Then there was an eerie silence.

A calm settled over Jusuf, as if his father were standing at his side. Trust your instincts, Jusuf. He knew that he had within him all the strength, all the presence of mind he needed to shoot to kill, that he had learned his father's lessons well and now he simply had to resurrect that moment of calm before he pulled the trigger. He felt his father directly behind him, even smelled his brandy breath. Jusuf's breathing slowed, and his thoughts focused sharply. He was ready. It was as if his father was now inside him. A few shots were fired from both sides. The crook of Jusuf's forefinger itched for action. The spirit of the father and the flesh of the son had fused.

"Easy, Jussie. Gather the loose ends. Close the gulf between your eye and your finger. Close it … close it … and stay calm, Jussie. Stay calm, boy. *You* control the moment. Time is ticking only within *you*. You'll know the moment. Just *close* the space, and the moment is yours."

Jusuf saw one of the soldiers toward the rear of the pack drop further back and focus on orders squawked over his mobile phone. Jusuf took aim. His finger traced the smooth curve of the ice-cold trigger as he brought the center of the man's chest square into his sight. He steadied his elbow on the wood frame of the portal. The man's wristwatch glittered, and the *kokarda* sewn on the soldier's cap was sharp like an etching, its double-headed eagle taking on the loathsome impression of a swastika. Jusuf's breath floated out the opening as time slowly ticked inside his head. Just as he was about to squeeze the trigger, the soldier lowered his phone and called to his brigade to hold up. Jusuf was poised but not eager. The scab on his nose began to itch wildly. Again the soldier brought the phone to his ear and seemed confused or frustrated. He coughed nervously and then pointed to the east, to a bridge down the hill that led to a small hamlet alive with flames and billowing smoke. The soldiers turned in unison and ran down the hill away from the bunkers, yelling *Sperska Republica!*

Jusuf turned, exhaled, and handed the rifle to Malik. "Another day, I guess." He returned to the opening and took a deep breath, watching the enemy as they swung to the right around a dense stand of trees and disappeared behind a low hill.

CHAPTER TWENTY-TWO

Jusuf's normal schedule on the front lines was five days on and then two days off, but for his twentieth birthday on March third, Malik told Jusuf, "It's okay to go home for a few days. But don't disappear. We need you here." When Azra got word he'd be home for his birthday, she scrounged around to make a special though meager meal for him and a few friends. She also used all her charm and powers of persuasion to acquire the necessary ingredients to make something that might look and taste like a birthday cake. She was delighted when Suad said he would trowel a week of waste from the now waterless toilets, dumping the contents behind his pigeon shed while holding his breath for longer than he ever thought possible. However, delight switched to deep disappointment when Suad said in mock formality, "I regret to inform the girlfriend of the returning warrior that I have failed to secure enough fresh water for a bath. There was just too much sniper fire around the spring for me to stay any length of time." What he didn't tell Azra was that in lugging just a single five-gallon container of drinking water back to the house, he felt drained of energy. Maneuvering the heavy plastic jug month after month through the sandbagged streets and racing for cover when sniper fire erupted had been taking its toll.

Suljo and Ahmet had observed Suad's declining strength and came around the house when they could to help him in return for his letting them sleep in the storeroom of his shop. Using tarpaulins as mattresses and wrapping towels around small coils of rope to make pillows, they turned the single-window storeroom into their bedroom, living room, and when food was available, their dining room. A circle of rocks in the small backyard with a doormat-sized piece of tin overhead served as their kitchen.

Azra was ready to bake her cake, but it meant finding firewood. The day before the party, Ahmet headed off into a relatively safe section of nearby woods and dragged back a huge bundle of sticks for which Azra rewarded him with a flood of kisses across his down-turned blushing face.

Despite Suad's words of caution, Azra slipped out of the house the evening before Jusuf was to arrive to fetch additional water so she could wash up before her lover's arrival. On her way back to the house, she stopped at the home of a guy that locals called *the chemist* to get a bar of his soap and a small plastic cup one-quarter-filled with shampoo.

The chemist had set up something of a laboratory in his cellar where he manufactured soap and shampoo out of ingredients he bought on the black market or begged for from merchants whose businesses had been shut down due to the war. Two months after the hostilities had started, the chemist sprung up out of nowhere like a patch of fast-growing mold on a damp wall. Few people in Bihac remembered even knowing him before the war started, and fewer people still knew his real name. Some thought he was a spy and kept a vigilant eye out whenever he left the house. The prices he charged varied according to each person's gender and presumed financial circumstances.

He looked like someone trying for the part of a weirdo in a horror movie—drooping bushy eyebrows, a perpetual smirk, smeary wire-rimmed glasses perched at the end of his nose, and long bony fingers always wrapped around a flask or jar of powder. His long tie made him look slightly professional, perhaps even respectable, even though it had a collection of stains down near his waist. As transactions were negotiated, patrons stood at arm's length because his breath smelled like his storeroom. He had no interest in accumulating wealth and seemed satisfied just being the center of attention and the focus of appreciation. Azra saw a hint of benign mischief in his cheery, darting eyes, but they also seemed a tad menacing when magnified through his farsighted lenses.

His patrons found the potency of his concoctions unpredictable.

Sometimes they cleaned the skin. Sometimes they removed the skin. Sometimes they left behind a nauseating petroleum-like fragrance and sometimes a rash. Azra hated going there because he always looked at her as if he were about to propose bathing her himself so he could test the efficacy of his products. She was sure he would never admit anything to anyone about his lascivious interests, but her skin crawled until she was out of his house, away from his noxious, nostril-stinging chemicals and back into the fresh air.

When a fire, started by a mortar, had destroyed almost everything in Igor's apartment, Azra had asked her next-door neighbor, Emina, a woman well into her seventies, if Igor could live with her and her twelve-year-old granddaughter, Zdenka. Zdenka was small, serious, and already heavy in the hips. Although her personality would bubble manically at times, as her black eyes sparkled, it was obvious she was still grieving over the loss of her parents. Azra had asked Emina, Zdenka, and Igor to come to the party to make it as festive as possible.

Azra was still at the stove when Jusuf marched through the door several hours before the party was to start. "This place smells like a Parisian restaurant!"

"Oh. You made it. I was so worried you wouldn't get a ride back to town or you'd be late. People will be coming very soon. There's just enough water for you to wash up a bit. You look like you did when you first straggled into Bihac. But first a huge and happy kiss."

Around seven in the evening, the door opened sluggishly under the weight of two wedge-shaped pieces of shrapnel that had lodged in the door's raised panels. Zdenka and Emina each carried a small bowl of rice and beans. Igor carried a long, narrow wooden box that smelled of smoke and some "coffee" he made out of wheat. He set the box on the floor near the entry without comment just as Suljo and Ahmet knocked to come in. Ahmet brought some feta cheese he had saved from an aid package he had picked up about a week before at a UN distribution post. Suljo had saved fifty deutschemarks he had earned doing a few odd jobs and bought a loaf of bread from an acquaintance with black-market connections.

Ten minutes later, Dado arrived with two candles, a few wooden matches, and two cans of Coke for all to share. "I'm here with your groceries, madam." Around his neck he wore a large, brass peace symbol on a fake gold chain. Tilting jauntily on his head was a cracked UN blue helmet that he found in the trash outside the Kafana Pavilion. He made the rounds and kissed everyone in the room except Zdenka, who flailed her hands like she was swatting off a swarm of mosquitoes.

Dado brought his camera with three shots left on a new roll of film given to him by a peacekeeping soldier-friend from Finland named Eero, but he feared there might not be enough energy in the battery to kick off the flash. A wild round of applause filled the room when Azra brought out the cake. Ahmet whistled piercingly through his fingers, which made Zdenka smile. Her black eyes glittered for a moment and then faded.

Later in the evening, the wind whipped up. Plastic sheeting flapped angrily in the windows. Dado had added his candles to Azra's cake, and all held their breath when the wind suddenly gusted and popped the plastic sheeting like a gunshot. "Oh, no!" everyone exclaimed as the flames on the candles leaned over parallel to the tabletop and almost went out.

Near-empty dishes were passed around as stomachs grumbled. With only the edge of his hunger dulled, Jusuf's thoughts turned to the last piece of fresh fruit he had eaten months earlier, and then to the more distant memory of an egg sizzling in a skillet.

Everyone had questions about what was happening on the front lines, which Jusuf answered with appropriate censorship to avoid turning the mood of the party from gaiety to gloom. After a pause, Igor, who had not once mentioned the box he had brought, stood and walked solemnly to the door and brought the long wooden box to the table. With one hand on the lid, he launched into a rambling speech about old friends and celebrations. No one was sure where his comments might be leading or even whether there was a gift in the box for Jusuf. In the semidarkness, no one worried about offending Igor with their raised eyebrows and muffled laughter. From time to time, Igor returned his hand to the box but did not lift the lid. When Igor's monologue finally seemed to wind to a close, he raised the fire-charred top. The sweet, musty smell of lubricating oil melded with the odor of smoke. Like a magician about to perform a trick, Igor rubbed his palms together before withdrawing a long, thin object wrapped in rags. He struggled somewhat to hoist it high over his head. It was as long as a broom handle and for most of its length, about as thick. It wavered above him, casting an ominous shadow that roamed drunkenly across the ceiling.

"Now, Jussie. This was a gift to me from your father ... just before he died. Your father told me that his father bought it in Banja Luka after the First World War. Fortunately, I was able to retrieve it from my apartment after that shelling last week. It's unharmed, save for the box."

Igor paused to scratch his head, adjust his glasses, and collect his thoughts.

"Now, my old friend Braco ... well, most of you know that's Jusuf's father ... so he and I used to share this handsome piece of craftsmanship when we hunted together. I say with authority that although it's old, it's remarkably accurate, which cannot be said for me."

"At least the man is honest," Emina added. Laughter erupted.

Igor cleared his throat. "Now since I can't see well enough to use the damn thing anymore, I think it's time I passed it along to the next generation. Braco, you old geezer, do you hear me? You're probably smiling up there in heaven, knowing that I am giving this to your son. Jussie's hands will now grip it where your hands once did."

Igor cleared his throat again and carefully removed the cloth as if he were unwrapping a mummy. Then he held the rifle close to the candle flames. All applauded except Jusuf. Igor ran his right hand up and down the barrel and over the polished butt. "Look here, Jusuf. Now come close, damn it. This is one fine hunting rifle, the best you'll find 'round these parts. And I'm happy to say that for your twentieth birthday, it's now yours."

Jusuf took a deep breath, just as Zdenka stood and began clapping wildly. She followed with a string of celebratory birdlike shrieks, her eyes glittering like fireworks. Everyone laughed and applauded with her. She suddenly blushed, sat down, and folded her hands.

"I promise you, Jusuf, it will do whatever you need it to do. And if you have an eye anything like ol' Braco's, God help the poor creature that wanders into your line of sight. Maybe this rifle will save your life or maybe it will fill your belly when your belly's rumbling for food. Maybe it will protect us all from those of my brothers who are fucking war-hungry idiots." He winked before saying, "Present company excluded, of course. Now, one thing's for sure though, those sons-of-bitches will run for the hills when they see you bring this cannon up to your shoulder."

Everyone cheered, and Dado and Ahmet whistled through their teeth, their thumbs raised to endorse the prediction. Zdenka squeezed her eyes shut and pressed her hands over her ears as Azra leaned over, kissed Jusuf's cheek, and squeezed his knee.

Jusuf, who was beset by an onslaught of conflicting feelings, took the firearm from Igor, smelled it, and rested the heel of the stock on the tabletop, muzzle pointing toward the ceiling.

"Damn, Igor, this thing is really heavy! I'll have to start lifting rocks just to have the strength to steady it. Did you and Dad have to jointly hold this thing in the air for one of you to shoot?"

"You should know your dad would never ask for any help."

Jusuf studied the barrel. "Wow, look at these engravings. Azra, your mother would have appreciated the work that went into this." Suad and Suljo leaned across from opposite sides of the table at the same time to get a look and bumped heads.

"You'll get used to it," Igor said. "Just keep your elbow tucked against the side of your chest and you'll be fine. I had no problem holding it up there after a while."

"You do now," Emina quipped. Everyone laughed except Zdenka, whose face remained puzzled.

"No family secrets, now, Emina," Suljo said, coming to Igor's defense.

"Your dad and I once challenged each other and a few friends to a shooting contest. We strung a bottle of slivovitz to a tree branch and set it swinging. We all took turns trying to hit the bottle. One guy nicked it and sent it spinning like a top, and we all hooted. Then it was your father's turn. Knowing how good he was, I told him to hold up before he shoots so I could send it swinging back and forth again, even faster. Long swings like a pendulum from left to right. I kept pushing him back a few more feet to even the odds. He raised the rifle to his shoulder, took aim, followed that bottle as if it were the gun controlling the bottle's motion, then damn if the son of a bitch didn't put a bullet right through the string. Not just the bottle, mind you, but through the fucking string. Excuse me, Zdenka, got carried away there. You'll learn to steady it, Jusuf. You've got the genes. So … happy birthday to you, my dear friend."

After everyone applauded, there was a long, awkward silence while guests waited for Jusuf to speak.

"First I want to thank my dear Azra for organizing this party and preparing the refreshments. Her determination, persistence, and ingenuity could win any war. And thanks to Zdenka and Emina for the rice and beans. Thanks to Suljo and Ahmet for the cheese and bread, and thanks to Dado for the candles and the Cokes." The room suddenly exploded with light as Dado's flash created a blinding flare. There was another round of applause. "And thank you, Igor, for this beautiful rifle. It brings back many, many memories. Almost all of you know my father taught me to shoot. I wasn't too bad. My dad—Igor knows this—was quite a hunter, an extraordinary hunter."

Igor nodded, removed his glasses, and wiped his moist eyes.

"It is truly the madness of war that results in one having to take such a work of fine craftsmanship to a battlefield. My greatest hope is that I'll never have to use it to take a life, but of course that is delusional. I only hope that the life taken is taken to save a more treasured life or to …"

Jusuf left the sentence unfinished, closed his eyes, and lowered his head. An air raid siren started to wail then wound down after a few seconds. After a moment, he resumed.

"I'll never be able to shoot like my dad. Never. He was the best. Before he gave up on me, he used to give me just one bullet each day and told me, 'Son, now make it count because one day you may find yourself in the woods with more than one animal in your line of sight and you must decide which to kill first, and you'll have to decide in that single fleeting instant. But trust me. You'll know. You've learned what you need to know, and you'll just know.'"

The morning after the party, Azra slept late. Jusuf walked to the store with Suad in silence. He was uneasy, his eyes avoiding the low sun, the cold wind knifing through his jacket. He felt he should express his appreciation for the party, but his thoughts kept ricocheting from one subject to another; life in Kljuc, the front lines, life after the war, Igor giving him his father's rifle. It was a torrent of ideas without a unifying theme. He had a nightmare the night before, perhaps triggered by Igor's gift. He was looking out from inside a tunnel, a disk of bright light at one end, a murky darkness all around. It dawned on him it was a view looking out from inside a gun barrel. The wind whipped up, and he raised his collar.

It was so strange to hold a weapon that his father had often held. It was strange to finger the fine-tooled engraving around the breech and feel the cold weight of its chamfered blue-black barrel. Strange after these many years to again hear the clicking movements of its exquisitely machined workings, run his palm along the scarred face of the polished mahogany stock, thinking that this might have been the same gun on which he himself had once or twice practiced as a young teenager, although its heft made this unlikely. And yet there was something comforting in knowing that the oils of Igor's and his father's hands were still locked in the open grain of the stock.

But in another respect, it troubled Jusuf to smell the same lubricating oils he remembered from his childhood and know that they contained traces of blood from the veins and viscera of animals that had been shot. He pictured a bullet needling through the whispering air toward the unsuspecting heart of the hunted. He imagined the stun of the collapsing animal as if he, Jusuf, were not only the hunter but also the prey. He recalled one particular night lying in bed, his nerves in wild confusion as he rehearsed what he would try to say to his father to inform him that hunting just wasn't for him, that he had no stomach for it.

"Dad, I know you love hunting … and we've had good times together in the woods, and you've taught me so much about nature and surviving in the wild … but why can't hunting be a sport you enjoy just with your friends but not with me? You know by now I don't really enjoy it the way you do."

"This is my son speaking? I never thought my own flesh would ever say he was afraid to hunt."

"I didn't say afraid, Dad. I'm just not cut out to kill things."

"You've always been a baby, Jusuf. All men hunt."

"That's not true."

"I said all *men*."

Tears welled in Jusuf's eyes.

"You're so quick to cry, Jusuf … just like a woman. Well, do you think I want a pussycat for a son? What'll my friends think? The neighbors?"

"Do you think they really care?"

"My family always hunted. Always."

"So? Traditions are sometimes broken."

"When did these feelings first start, Jussie?"

Jusuf's eyes searched for what to say in the fluid shapes embedded in the linoleum floor, shapes that seemed to start moving as he tried to collect his thoughts. He recalled the day when his father said *do it now, do it now*. Jusuf had wounded a fawn but hadn't killed it. His father had demanded he shoot it in the head to finish it off. Jusuf had never been able to shake the indelible image of that huge pleading eye, terrified, wondering what would come next. To shoot that creature in the head was the most painful thing he ever had to do. Seeing the blood flow out of the deer's mouth and that pleading eye now bulging out of the cranium and misaligned, Jusuf knew right then and forever that hunting was not for him ... and never would be. "I tried, Dad, truly I tried. You must know that."

"All I can say is *what a shame*. You're such a superb shot, Jussie, and you're a good boy. Plenty of hunters wish they were half the marksman you've become. Maybe someday you'll grow up and hunt with me again. I'd love that."

CHAPTER TWENTY-THREE

A FEW DAYS LATER, Jusuf was back on the front lines, leaving Azra and Suad to stare at each other in the dim light of a candle across an almost empty dinner table. They kept their fears to themselves, each unwilling or unable to voice any hope. Suad saw that Azra was worrying constantly about Jusuf, terrified that he would return seriously maimed or dead. Once, when Suad scraped the table for crumbs to take out to his pigeons, Azra's anger flared. "Damn it, Dad! Why are you still trying to feed those birds? Let them go. They'll survive. There must be stuff in the woods for them to eat."

"Azra!"

"This is idiotic. Turn them loose. Their cooing is driving me crazy."

"Azra, please. I've tended them for how many years now. You can see I don't give them anything we could eat. It's just crumbs. They'd die for sure if I turned them loose."

She wailed. "Do you hear me, Dad? They're driving me crazy! If you won't let them go, I will." She pounded the table in frustration and then grew quiet. When she raised her head, she noticed tears in her father's eyes

"Oh, god, Dad, I'm sorry. I'm so on edge. I'm just worried about everything. And now Jusuf's out there trying to save his ass with that stupid rifle. It may be accurate, but how is he going to hold it steady with near to nothing in his belly?"

"I'm sure he'll manage."

"But I haven't heard anything lately. Not knowing is driving me insane. I'm sorry I yelled at you. Truly I am. I'll scrounge around at the hospital for something to feed them."

"My pigeons, his plants."

"What? Oh, yes," she said. "I guess we each have something to keep us going. He's going to cry when he sees how many leaves have fallen, how many have died. But I promised him I'd do what I could to keep them alive until he gets back with his magic touch."

"To me, they look okay."

"He once told me the secret to his success is in pinching them. You should have heard him howl with laughter when I showed him what I was doing. "Pinch them *back*, Azra. You don't pinch them like you're pinching a baby's cheek.'"

Three weeks later, the Serbs launched an unrelenting attack. Thousands of shells a day came in from the hills, sparing no part of the city. Few people ventured into the streets. Most took refuge in their cellars or bomb shelters or in barricaded living rooms. When things finally quieted down around Azra's neighborhood and she felt it was safe enough to try to get to the hospital, she hugged her father good-bye and told him she would be very careful and stay close to the buildings along the route. "I just feel there are more people than ever that need my help."

Inside her ward, Azra found wounded people lying everywhere—in beds if they were fortunate, two to a bed if the victims were small, otherwise on the floor, in hallways, and storerooms. She found one woman moaning under a bank of sinks in one of the toilet rooms. A jagged shard of shrapnel had not yet been removed from the woman's thigh. Azra took some toilet paper, moistened it with water, and laid it on the woman's forehead. "I hope I can get someone soon for you. I *will* try."

Returning to the ward where she had been working, she passed a man with a bandaged head, his hand brushing her apron as she passed, hoping to get her attention. As she crossed an aisle, a boy with his leg torn off was rushed by her, sprawled on a springy piece of plywood, screaming for someone to stop the pain. But with no medicine or anesthesia, the wailing and screeching clawed at every vibrating and weary fiber of her caring nature. She did what she could with what little there was, but it was mostly only comforting words and her palm laid over a feverish head that she had to offer. She was able to get to and from the hospital for three days straight, returning each night to bear hugs and frightened tears from her father. But on the fourth day, she needed to stay at home, no longer able to face the misery, no longer able to endure the cries of anguish from the wounded and the cries of frustration and heartbreak from family members having a loved one die in their arms.

On the fifth day, she felt strong enough to return to the hospital, but she was unable to stay very long. She left feeling extremely weak from her period. A leaden sky threatened snow, and it was bitterly cold. She mounted her bicycle and headed home. Two blocks from the hospital, with sirens wailing throughout the city and an enemy helicopter gunship flying overhead, she passed a young woman lying in the street. She had been blown off her bicycle by a shell, its remains still smoking nearby. Azra was about to stop but saw that her belly had been torn open and her innards were lying next to her, white, pink, and steaming. She paused just long enough to confirm that she was dead. She was troubled by the thought of what she would have done or would have been unable to do if she had found the woman breathing. She pedaled on, her own abdomen in spasms, her mind wondering whether ultimately she would crack at the sights and sounds of this devastation or whether she would become hardened and detached from seeing all the waste and misery.

As mortars kept whistling in from the hills and crashing closer and closer to her, she worried that Suad might leave the house to come looking for her. She pedaled the last two kilometers bent over like a racer, flying over a little bridge that spanned the canal. For a split second, the back wheel lost traction on the ice and she anticipated a bad fall. Her heart stopped, but as she struggled to steer and regain control, the wheel encountered a ripple of ice that caused the bike to right itself. Adrenaline coursed through her as she raced home.

Just as she reached her neighborhood, another mortar whistled low overhead. She braked, skidded to a stop, and ducked for cover against a leaning wall of sandbags. The shell seemed to fall almost silently to the ground. Hearing nothing but a muffled boom and seeing no damage, she assumed it had plowed into someone's yard.

As she bounced her bike over the threshold, she called out, "Dad, I'm home!" Usually she would see him rising off the couch to give her a hug, but today there was only a pennant-shaped trail of smoke drifting in through the kitchen door that was slightly ajar. She noticed an odd odor as she hurried to look for him in the shed.

"Dad?" she called. "Are you out there? Please answer. You're scaring me!"

She pushed open the door and looked out onto a heap of smoking debris. "Oh, God, please don't do this to me! Don't do this."

She hurried through the tool shed and across a jumble of twisted, smoking cages and bloody pigeon parts. "Dad, I don't see you. Answer me! *Please* answer me if you're in here."

She looked up to see if he might be in Emina's house. Suddenly she saw a blackened hand and then a half-clothed body twisted like a wrung-out towel. It protruded from a heap of boards and pieces of glass and wire. She carefully toed away a charred board and dropped to her knees, cradling his bloody head in her lap, her vision murky from tears and smoke. His right eye opened and then closed, and opened again as if he were forcing himself to stay with her. The eyeball rolled slowly from side to side as if he wanted to ask her a question or say something but could not find her in his fading vision.

She couldn't look at him anymore, at his singed hair, the bloody gash on his skull, his searching eye. She brought her fingers to her lips and hoped her heart wouldn't stop beating. Suad's warm blood pooled in her lap. She wanted to lie down next to him and go where he was going.

A pigeon waddled across the debris, head bobbing, cooing weakly. It hobbled through the shattered, shifting remains of its shelter, one injured foot barely touching the hot, smoking floor of wreckage, and followed a crooked path toward Azra until it saw Suad's body. The head cocked, its neck contracted, and then it rested its injured foot for a moment on a charred board.

"Don't leave me, Papa, please don't leave me." She raised her arms to the sky. A few snowflakes fell and mixed with several gray feathers that floated without direction in the steaming ruins. She shook her fists and howled, "You fucking bastards, you goddamn fucking bastards!

You're killing everything ... and for what? I hope you all rot in hell, you *fucking* sons of bitches."

When Jusuf returned to Bihac two days later, he found Azra curled on the living room couch, limp, staring blankly. The house was rank with the odor of burned wood, singed feathers, and charred flesh.

"They got word to me last night, Azra. Malik drove me home. You have no idea how sad I am for you."

He sat down and put her hands in his. She didn't move, didn't squeeze back, did not look at him.

"You know I loved him like my own father, Azra. You know that." He began to cry. "I wish I had been here for you."

Azra began to tremble. Jusuf sensed she did not want to deal with questions or think about answers. Nor, he assumed, did she want an expression of love or affection or sympathy. It was hard for Jusuf to look into her eyes; the depth of her sadness was that raw, that crushing. Her lower lids sagged, the whites dry and crossed with scarlet webbing.

"Jusuf." Her voice was fluttery and desiccated. "Jusuf. I think I'm nearing the end. I can't deal with this anymore. I'm so tired, so sad, so lost. I'm at the end, Jusuf, really I am."

"Oh, god, don't say that. I can't bear to hear you say that. But I understand, I do understand."

"I feel like an empty shell. Nothing left inside." She angled her hand across her heart. "No energy, no hope. Nothing to live for anymore."

"Please, Azra."

"It's all closing in on me. Maybe we should just end it now. Join Dad out there. I'm truly ready to do that."

"Don't say that, sweetheart. I love you. You can't give up." He touched her cheek. She pulled back. "I need you when I'm out there, Azra. I need to know I'm fighting for you, for our future." Jusuf drew her close.

"What are those bastards trying to prove?" she asked. "Doesn't the world know what's happening here? Where the hell's the UN or the US? They keep talking peace deals and ceasefires and safe zones, and we're here dying. Have they no balls?" She hammered the side of the sofa with her fist. "It's another goddamn Holocaust. We'll all die from starvation or frostbite or go mad before someone stops them. I can't take it anymore."

"It's okay, sweetheart. I'm with you now. Just let me hold you. It'll be okay."

"I know I'm losing my mind. I can't even do the simplest things anymore. All I hear are bullets and shells and bombs and promises from high places, and more promises and more promises. I'm sick. Really sick ... in my body, in my mind, in my soul."

"It's okay. I understand. Truly I do. Now that I'm home, just try to sleep. Malik said it's okay to take some days off to be with you."

"And what'll we do with Dad? He's still lying out there frozen, like a black rock, with only a sheet over him. I tried, but I couldn't move him, couldn't even get enough men together to wash him. We can't just leave him there all winter. We need to bury him somehow."

"Azra, trust me, I'll figure something out. Try to sleep. You need to sleep first. Then we'll do something."

"I can't bear to think of him lying out there as if he were abandoned, as if we didn't love him, as if we were no longer here to protect him, to shield him. It's tearing me apart. I know it's stupid, but somehow I think he knows we left him in that mess, and it's killing me. It's ripping me up inside."

"Azra, listen to me. I'll take care of him. We'll bury him properly ... together. Please don't think about it now. I promise I'll do something, tomorrow."

"What's left for us? The house is a shambles, Dad is dead, we barely have heat, no electricity, no water, almost nothing to eat. How long can we last?"

She straightened slightly and then turned to Jusuf and collapsed against his chest. Jusuf, himself starving and exhausted and with little energy to collect his thoughts, held her close, rocking her, feeling like he too was nearing the edge of a precipice.

He whispered in her ear. "Listen to me ... listen carefully. I really think it's just going to be a little longer. You've got to hang on."

"I've had it. It's just too much!"

"Please. You must be strong, as strong as you possibly can. We can make it. I know we can make it if we stay together. Spring is weeks away. It'll be easier. We can make it, my love. I know we can."

Jusuf stayed the week. He scrounged for food, lugged water, found scraps of wood to warm the house, and asked Suljo, Ahmet, and Dado to help him wash and wrap Suad's body and move the corpse to a protected location near the river where Suad used to fish. They lowered the rock of his body from a wheeled cart onto the riverbank, and with a kitchen knife, Suljo scratched the outline of his body on the sandy beach and then lifted the corpse off to the side and set to work excavating a shallow grave. They hammered and chipped the near-frozen ground for two hours as Azra stood nearby shivering and crying.

Azra kept picturing the proper burial she had always imagined for her father, in a grave next to her mother in the old cemetery with the lovely tombstones. But the circumstances of war demanded that they simply inter a frozen hulk wrapped in an old blanket, the way she had buried her dog. Azra kept moving around, positioning herself between Suad's corpse and the occasional passerby. *But he's dead now*, she thought to herself. Whatever shame and guilt had plagued him all these years was now also being entombed in the riverbank with his remains. As the men threw clods of sand and chips of earth over the plaid blanket, Azra took a deep breath, held it for several seconds, and then slowly released it with a long awaited sense of relief.

The next day, Jusuf heated a pot of water and bathed Azra and then himself. He knew not to touch her in a way she might interpret as an expression of sexual interest, though his body ached for her. It was easier for him with his eyes open looking at her bony rib cage than with his eyes closed remembering how she looked that sunny picnic day by the River Una.

Toward the end of the week, Azra borrowed a little henna from Zdenka to color her hair. Jusuf thought possibly her spirits might be rising. She even smiled back at him when he handed her a cup of coffee. When he felt it would be okay to leave her alone in the house for a short while, he did some chores for a sick neighbor who raised chickens and was paid with a fresh egg. The following day, he gave the brown egg to Azra before telling her he had return to the front lines. Before leaving town, he asked Dado, Emina, and Igor to look in on her each day until he returned.

CHAPTER TWENTY-FOUR

THREE WEEKS AFTER SUAD's burial, Jusuf was on leave again and went to Dado's apartment with Azra. It was a Saturday night, and Dado, in honor of his new flame, Aida, was dressed in a stained and faded tux and wore two unmatched phosphorescent sneakers of contrasting colors. Cigarette smoke filled the apartment, and several crushed, black-market beer cans lay sprawled in crippled disfigurement on the makeshift coffee table. The cigarettes were gifts to Dado from UN soldiers who got a kick out of his clowning attire and capricious personality.

Jusuf always took a few minutes to study Dado's collection of butterflies that hung on his living room wall in shadowbox cases Dado had fabricated in the frame shop where he worked before the war started. As Jusuf slid his forefinger up and down one of the five polished cherry frames, his thoughts turned to the custom of preserving these delicate creatures in satin coffins with nickel-plated pins pressed through their once-soft bodies. Wings spread but no longer in flight, he mused. Beauty wrought by nature. Capture, and then pain, and then death imposed for the delight of the observer.

Jusuf likened butterfly collecting to hunting. The pleasure of the hunter, the pain of the prey. A trophy on a wall. Sightless eyes staring back upon the perpetrators, row upon row of colorful bodies to be passed down from one generation to another like a bear-head trophy above a mantel. Over time, wings disintegrate and collect like dust on the bottom of the case, or the fur from a bear's head falls out and collects behind the family photos.

Why had he raced after such lovely, innocent creatures with Sasha when they were kids? To rob them of their precious few moments floating on a gentle breeze? It dawned on him that he and Azra, and Dado and Aida were much like these butterflies, pinned under glass, captives in their own town, Serbs on one side, Croats on the other, the four of them pinned down and unable to fly. Jusuf blew some dust off the glass of one case and tapped its corner with his fingernail to set it plumb. He mumbled to himself, "Fucking madmen want our land, want to make neat rows out of society so everyone looks and thinks and dresses alike. Green butterflies in one case; crimson in another."

He recalled something his Uncle Ibro once said during one of their philosophical exchanges. "Aren't we all obsessed with order? Our minds and eyes programmed to see what's the same but just as importantly to see what's different. But unfortunately, we all fear what's different. That's human nature, too. What's different and what we deem dangerous are two sides of the same coin."

Dado crushed his last cigarette in an ashtray shaped like a turtle lying on its back. He stood, removed the tuxedo coat, raised his sweatshirt to expose his white belly, pulled his pants down to shake his even whiter ass at his friends, and screamed at the top of his lungs, "This fucking war is bad for our health!"

Jusuf turned as Azra and Aida stood in unison and applauded. Aida said, "We need a party. Who's up for heading over to the bomb shelter? I'm tired of being a prisoner."

"Good thinking," Jusuf said. "Let's get the hell out of here!" They all danced about the room like school kids, hooting and wiggling their hips, Azra more subdued than the others but trying her best to conceal her lingering sadness.

Before they raced down the stairs, Jusuf stepped into the bathroom, and as he did, Azra slipped a small envelope out of her blouse and motioned to Dado to hide it quickly. She whispered, "They're the photographs Jusuf's mom mailed to him last year. You said you wanted to frame them. Hurry, hide them."

As Dado slipped them into a drawer, he raised his voice to quip, "Hey, Jusuf, you take as much time in there as an old man? You need to get your plumbing repaired. C'mon, let's go."

They thundered down the stairs and ran through the snow, laughing with abandon in the cold night air as they dodged piles of trash in the dark streets. Dado led the pack, but when he turned a corner, he fell into a car-deep bomb crater that had not existed the night before. The others howled like children as he tried repeatedly to scale the icy slopes. He finally lay down and deliberately set himself spinning like a piece of Jell-O in a wet glass bowl.

Azra and Aida started to shiver after a while, so they linked themselves arm-in-arm with Jusuf, who positioned himself with one foot pressing the crater edge, using it like a fulcrum. His right arm, now a miniature crane, descended to grab Dado's hand. All four laughed again as Dado ran in place on the slippery banks but failed to gain traction.

"Hold on a minute," he said. "I've got an idea." He unzipped his fly and peed on the glazed bank, his soup-hot urine eroding the ice and creating a few ridges. "Let's try again."

The crane went back in operation, and the roughened ice provided the traction he needed. His phosphorescent sneakers flashed eerily as he scrambled up the bank. After sailing full speed across the rim of the crater, all four fell back on top of one another, tickling the body closest and giggling like kids on a playground.

Still puffing clouds of vapor into the frosty air of the basement bomb shelter, they burst into song and fell into chairs around a small round table. The shelter was outfitted with a motley assortment of furniture, looking more like a funky bar than the concrete storage room below an apartment house it had been before the war. Coming to the shelter was for some locals an act of defiance, for others an act of necessity to maintain their emotional balance.

Dado and Aida soon joined others on the floor, gyrating to the beat of someone banging on a pot below an array of flickering candles that hung from the ceiling on a contraption made of coat hangers. Jusuf remained at the table with Azra and deposited a few grains of salt from an inverted jar cap into the canister of oil sitting between them, the salt keeping the smoky flame from smudging her face.

"We need some real music!" someone yelled. "This pot banging is for the birds."

It wasn't long before Jusuf saw Dado leave Aida in the arms of another dancer, edge toward the door, and steal quietly out of the shelter. Certain that Dado was up to something wild, Jusuf smiled.

"What's so funny?" Azra asked.

"Oh, nothing."

"C'mon, what's going on? What's the smile? I know you well enough to know something's up."

"Truly, it's nothing. I just saw Dado slip out of here a minute ago, and he had that mischievous twinkle in his eye. I'm trying to guess what he's up to."

"That man is *mister invention*," Azra said as she wriggled her hand into the warmth between Jusuf's thighs. "Always something going on up his sleeve. I just love him." Six months ago, that comment would have unsettled Jusuf, renewing his fear that whatever had bonded Dado and Azra through the years might once again take on a new life, but tonight all he heard was a simple statement of fact.

Dado went to a room on the far side of the stair tower, lifted one of the bicycles, rotated it above the others with a quick twist of his wrist, and rode out into the darkness, his mop of dyed-scarlet hair flopping without rhythm as the bike thudded and slipped on ridges of hard rough snow. He pedaled fiendishly toward Aida's brother's house as shells exploded in distant parts of the town.

Forcing up the heavy hood of her brother's snow-covered car, he tinkered there a few minutes, exploring the compact jumble of engine parts. Then he searched along a stretch of fences and burned-out car hulks until he found a discarded canvas bag into which he placed the object he had come for. He raced back to the shelter, looking down with pride at the heavy trophy balanced on his handlebars.

He replaced the bike in the room near the stairs, tucked the heavy load under his arm, and danced back into the shelter, twirling around on his squeaking sneakers. He thrust the load high above his scarlet mop as if he were triumphantly displaying the severed head of the enemy. Twirling one time too many, he lost his balance and almost fell to the floor. His friends hooted and whistled, their eyes remaining riveted upon the canvas bag as he lowered it to the floor. After rubbing his hands together like a magician prior to pulling a dove from a sleeve, he wrestled the car battery out of the sack and then danced backward with a flourish to reveal his gift for all the partygoers to see. Jusuf rose in case Dado needed help. Cheers and foot stomping erupted as he and Jusuf feigned a connection to the terminals with their fluttering fingers while they spat streams of static through pools of saliva bubbling on their tongues. When they actually wired the battery to the tape player perched on a shaky stack of Coke cartons and got nothing but silence, a chorus of boos swept through the shelter.

"Mother fucker! You creeps got to go back to trade school. Physics 1 for both of you."

Then, as if in response to the profanity, a mortar shell slammed into a nearby building. The bomb shelter shook so violently that the wheat-spiked cold water they drank as if it were coffee splashed out of their cups. A second shell hit even closer, jarring everything in the place and causing everyone to duck for cover. No one saw the tape deck slip to the edge of the carton. But the jostling achieved the unexpected. The town's theme song, Bon Jovi's "Keep the Faith," roared through the concrete vault as shells continued to crash into nearby buildings. The shelter exploded in jubilation with couples swirling across the filthy concrete floor, tear-filled eyes searching tear-filled eyes, young breasts heaving against war-hardened torsos, and the legs of lovers weaving song-shaped patterns in the flickering light of the candles and oil lamps.

Although they were all there to enjoy simple pleasures, they were also there to forget. To forget their gnawing hunger. To forget their freezing, dark houses. To forget the bodies of their friends and relatives, and in some cases their own children, who lay barely covered by a few shovels-full of earth and snow. And forget, too, the enemy's bullets and shrapnel, and in some cases the enemy's sperm, locked within those frozen bodies.

For Azra, the pain was too fresh. As she danced slowly in Jusuf's arms, she couldn't hold back the memories of blood pumping from her father's head. Her tears covered Jusuf's shoulder. She dreaded the thought of Jusuf returning to the front lines. He was now all she had, all she lived for.

When the music stopped unexpectedly, a groan swept through the crowd, but everyone kept dancing in silence. Then someone began playing a Dylan tune on a harmonica, and for a moment, Jusuf's heart stopped. He looked around to see if Sasha had somehow come in to join the sad festivities.

The following morning, Jusuf awakened early and sat alone at the kitchen table writing another letter to his mother with a pencil stub so short his writing was barely legible.

> *Draga Mama,*
> *I hope this letter finds you in good health and perhaps even with a smile on your face. For us here, it is so hard to keep our hopes up, and I don't want to lie and tell you all is well. All is not well! Suad, Azra's father, was killed by a mortar some weeks ago. I hesitate to share that with you, but you're probably faced with death every day yourself, wherever you are. I was hoping the war would be over by now and this letter could be one of joyous anticipation of our reunion, but the fighting goes on and on.*
>   *I should have started this letter by telling you how overjoyed I was to receive your letter and the photos. To see your handwriting and hear your words made my heart almost burst with joy. I am so happy to know you are alive and haven't been swallowed up in this madness.*
>   *It was wonderful to see your face again. So many memories came rushing back. I can't tell you how much I ache to see you again and hug you. And it was so good to see that parade picture of Dad again. I was sure it had been lost. And that picture of Sasha and me. Wow! How the world has changed! I wonder what we would say to each other at this point. I do think of him a lot and wonder if we could ever be friends again when the war ends. Could I ever trust him? I want to think that I could; I hope I could. We were so close.*
>   *Azra and I are deeply in love, and although we have not spoken about marriage, I guess we both know that is in our future. The only good thing about this sickening war is how close it makes you feel to the person you are living with. Hard times bond people like glue. I feel sometimes as if we are one soul divided into two bodies.*
>   *I have this bad feeling that even if peace comes to Bosnia, the Serbs will turn elsewhere to gain territory and unleash their violence. I hate lumping them all together as if there weren't Serbs who hate this war as much as we do, but you*

start thinking of people as groups, and that is probably how we got into this mess in the first place.

I have made some wonderful friends here and can't wait for you to meet them. Last night, some of us went dancing together at a bomb shelter. It was nice to forget the war for a short time.

I see I'm not really in a good letter-writing mood, but I just wanted to say hi. I'll make this short and write again when my mood picks up. Stay safe, and if you see Sasha, I guess you can say hello to him for me. Perhaps we could still be friends. Who knows anything for certain these days.

Volim te, tvoj sin, Jussie

After signing the letter, it dawned on Jusuf that with Suad no longer living, his trusted means of getting the letter to his mother was also dead. How would he ever connect with the mysterious Ivan? He had no idea where Ivan lived or even his last name, but it occurred to Azra the following day that Igor also knew Ivan. She remembered it actually had been Igor who let her father know that Ivan wanted to meet with him in the forest.

CHAPTER TWENTY-FIVE

For several days, Bihac was no longer a city under siege. The Serbs had suspended their shelling, and electricity was restored. Suljo and Ahmet had been cooped up for weeks, during which Suljo came down with a persistent cough. He decided to take a stroll and breathe some fresh air. "To hell with the risk," he muttered to himself. As he walked through the city, he coughed a little less and began to feel somewhat energized. He passed battered buildings, dodged street craters, and waved to a few acquaintances as they ferried jugs of water and bundles of firewood back to their homes. With an inexplicable urge to see the vibrant waters of the River Una, he strolled through the park and over toward the Blue Bridge. When he got to the Kafana Paviljon, he leaned against the plaza railing and looked out toward the rapids. Strumming a stick along the railing's balusters, he circled around behind the coffee house to the slower moving waters of the canal, studying as he walked the disintegrating chalk line of a jet's vapor trail high overhead.

On the far side of the canal was an abandoned hydroelectric plant. During the Communist era, the plant fell into disuse and a skin of rust grew on every metal part, rendering the mechanisms permanently impotent. For those with eyes like Suljo's that could see past the obvious, the old plant had become a piece of industrial sculpture. He wished he had some paper and a pencil to write a short poem about the transformation of this structure from one that had radiated power to one that now lay mute and fallow.

A sniper's bullet hit the wall of the canal, spraying fragments of concrete and stone into the water. Suljo dashed back around the side of the coffee shop and peered anxiously through the round window that faced the bridge. Igor was standing in a pool of copper light, hunched over his ledger, a cigar stub dangling between two fingers, his glasses near the end of his nose. A thin vine of smoke rose from the ash in a long, open spiral that collected in a slowly rotating galaxy of haze just below the ceiling. Suljo tapped the windowpane with his square fingernail. When Igor looked up startled, Suljo opened his huge palms to the sky and then shaped one hand into a pistol. Igor's smile drew the corners of his mouth close to his ears, almost erasing any indication of a chin. He waved for Suljo to come around to the front door. Head bobbing in delight, he slippered stickily across the stone floor, his fingers twitching in readiness to turn the latch. "Hello, hello, hello," Igor chanted as Suljo walked into the bar to the tinkling of the overhead bell.

"I did hear a shot out there I think. Come sit down. You must be more careful. Hold on one minute while I finish these last few entries. I hate keeping records! Never was good in arithmetic and no longer have the patience in my old age to deal with this shit. Want to take over for me?"

"No way."

Without looking up, Igor asked, "Something to drink, Suljo? There's still a bit of warm coffee left. A reporter from the *Washington Post* gave me a bag of beans the other day and this magnificent cigar. I did tell him all that I knew, which wasn't much more than rumor. Should have dramatized it a bit to make a better story. Here, take a puff." Suljo took a long drag and handed it back.

"Coffee would be perfect, Igor. You're probably the luckiest guy in town at the moment—and the most popular."

Igor held his palm over the small cup to feel for heat, brought the cup to his nose to savor the aroma, and then set it in front of Suljo, who sipped the thick coffee and listened to the clock near the TV tick away the seconds as Suad scribbled in a few more entries.

Although it was getting dark outside, Suljo noticed a few refugees from who-knew-where crossing the bridge. As they neared the Paviljon, a lone, white UN armored vehicle roared past them in the opposite direction.

"What a nightmare," Suljo mumbled.

A minute passed, and then Igor looked up and asked, "You say something?"

"Not really. I was just watching those refugees dragging their tired asses across the bridge. They just keep coming, don't they? Trickling in, day after day. And to what? A *safe zone*? What a joke!"

The room was silent except for the loud ticking of the clock echoing against the window glass.

"Ethnic cleansing? Horseshit! This is fucking genocide. Nazi Germany all over again—but without the gas chambers. Just pistols and knives and mortars and bombs."

"A half-century ago," Igor said, "most of my family was wiped out by the Ustashe and the Germans." Igor stroked the stubble of his beard and picked at little raised spots on the top of his head. "Four hundred thousand of us Serbs slaughtered in Croatia and here in Bosnia."

"Yes, I've read those statistics somewhere. Tragic. Fighting and more fighting ... one century after another. Will it ever end?"

"I don't know the politics like you, Suljo. I'm not a school-learned person. I simply follow my heart—not some asshole in Belgrade or that bastard Karadzic and his bully henchman, Mladic. Why so many Serbs believe the shit these guys toss around is beyond me. I can tell you one thing for sure. This particular Serb is never going to take up arms against his friends no matter what religion they follow or what 'tribe' they belong to." Igor wiped the counter as if he were trying to wipe away the madness of the last few years.

"This room will be my tomb, I'm sure. It will read 'Igor Miloradovic died here serving coffee and *cevapcici*. He never killed a friend, never killed a neighbor.' I guess this place is good as any to die in. I'm sure many Serbs will call me traitor. Let them, goddamn it! I know what's right. *Right* isn't slitting the throats of your friends." Igor stared out the round window, but with the growing darkness, he saw a reflection of his own long face overlapping what he could still make out of the bridge.

Suljo remained silent and drifted off into a world of his own meandering thoughts. He stared at the clock and listened to the room fill with the sound of time passing in discrete clicks. The red second hand, oddly wide and long like the minute hand (the result of an imperfect repair when the war had just begun), moved from one thin line to the next with a spasmodic jerk. It seemed to mark time with an attitude of restrained anger. Suljo stared as the red bar beat its way from one second to the next, impatiently, determined. *Tock! Tock! Tock!* The tapping was magnified as his thoughts were replaced by memories.

The poet in him and the lawyer searching for a half-hidden clue caused him to scrutinize the motion of the red bar. He noticed that although the jerking from one second to the next appeared almost violent, Suljo's eye for detail observed that the stroke ended gently, as if a boxer, at the last fraction of second, felt a pang of sympathy for his opponent and pulled his punch, sparing his challenger what might have been a nose-breaking blow.

Agitated by something stirring at the back of his brain, Suljo fiddled with his cuticles and clenched his teeth. He rotated the coffee cup in its saucer counterclockwise as if he were turning back a timepiece. He tried to align the finger grip with a chip in the saucer, wondering whether a precise alignment would unlock whatever it was pressing at the back of his skull in some dark chamber of buried memories. Again he listened to the clock as if he were being drawn toward something as yet unrevealed. His eyes closed. He felt himself sliding backward to an earlier time.

He saw sticks on a raw and misty morning slicing through the heavy air. He watched men and boys marched down a road in groups of two. He saw boys forced to hit men, men forced to hit boys. He heard guards yelling, *harder, you fuckers, hit him harder.* From fathers who were forced to hit their sons with rough-hewn clubs and steel bars came muffled cries and whispered apologies. From sons who received the blows, there were cries of pain held hushed in the throat, or cries to the father pleading not to stop the attack in order to avoid the punishment that was certain to ensue.

Suljo's eyes welled with tears. He continued to rotate the cup, the curved finger grip circling counterclockwise against the normal flow of time. Suljo saw the sticks and bars in the hands of his Muslim comrades crash on the bodies of fathers, sons, brothers, uncles. He knew from the blows he too was receiving from his oldest son, Zarif, that each blow was being pulled at the last instant, the wrist twisted upward to cushion the full power of the strike, to spare his flesh and bones.

Suljo heard his son Zarif behind him, weeping and apologizing for the beating. Blood, near black in the low light of the morning, covered the heads and shoulders of his friends in front of him. Some collapsed in the muddy road, the agony too great to endure. He heard Zarif crying his love for his father in a tortured voice. Then he felt the blows stop. "I can't do it anymore, Papa. I'm making you bleed. I love you too much. I won't! They can't make me do it anymore, Papa." Suljo stopped turning the cup and rubbed his hands together, twisting them in anguish and then tightening them into fists.

"Do it, Zarif!" Suljo whispered down into the road behind him. "Do you hear, Zarif? You must do it. I don't feel the steel. I only feel your love." Suljo turned to see if his son was still there. "You *must* hit me, Zarif. For God's sake, do it now. It will all be forgotten in a day. I promise. I love you."

"I can't do it anymore, Papa. Too much—"

Several quail flapped out of a nearby bush as the bullet ripped through Zarif's skull. Suljo was still screaming in frustrated urgency. "Do it, Zarif! For God's sake, hit me!" Ahmet, allowed to sit on an earthen bank because of a badly twisted ankle, covered his eyes and ears after seeing Zarif's hand slide down his father's back. Suljo turned and saw Zarif's body collapse into the puddle Suljo had just walked through.

Overcome by rage, Suljo railed hopelessly at the clock, at its relentless second hand. He bellowed toward the ceiling above Igor's bar, "Do it, Zarif!"

Igor's head flew up, his eyes wide. Suljo's fingers fanned out, looking for a neck to wring, looking for a way to turn back time, to bring his firstborn son back to life. He raised the coffee cup over his head and slammed it down on the countertop. Fragments ripped into his palm. Coffee streaked his shirt and Igor's. This was not the first time Igor had witnessed an explosion of grief and anger firing from the other side of the counter. Fearing he might have said something that triggered Suljo's memories, Igor asked, "Did I babble something? I'm sorry. When I get buried in these goddamn numbers or have one too many beers, I can say anything. What did I say to hurt you, my friend?"

Suljo whispered, "No, Igor, you said nothing. I was suddenly back in the camp. It's still alive in me as if I never left the place."

"You never spoke of it before, Suljo. It must have been horrible."

"It was ghastly. The cruelty, the filth."

"I'm afraid to ask what happened that caused such pain and anger."

"They killed my son, Zarif—I guess Jusuf didn't tell you that I had two. Zarif, my other son, refused their commands to beat me, so they shot him. Those guards were fucking *animals*." Suljo slumped and cried unabashedly. Igor came around from behind the bar, tears welling in his eyes, and patted Suljo's shoulders. "It's a story from Hell, believe me. The absolute evil of it all. It's been eating at me—eating away my guts, burning my heart." He paused and shook his head. "I'm sorry, Igor. I really don't want to burden you with all this. Those Serbs are not *your* Serbs; they're not your people. You're cut from different cloth. That I know. These guys were downright sadistic animals."

Igor patted Suljo's hands, offered him his cigar stub, and then went to fill the coffee pot with water. When Igor brought his lighted match to the hissing jet of gas, the burner exploded like a bomb. "Whoa!" He returned to his friend. "You don't have to speak. Just sit. Fresh coffee will be up in a few minutes."

Suljo sat with his chin in his hands, staring at the plastic countertop whose geometric pattern was worn away in ovals to a lower level of just one dull gray-brown color. He fiddled with his butchered cuticles again. When his hand began to sting, he extracted several jagged chips of pottery from his wide palms and then walked to the sink for a rinse under cold water.

"Where did all this happen?"

"I'm not really sure. They trucked the boys and me and half of Kljuc somewhere up near Omarska. Jusuf and I were in the same truck. Jusuf was able to get away, but I just now realize I never asked him how he did it. At one point, I looked over and he wasn't across the aisle from me. I was sure he was dead. There had been a couple of murders on the ride up, and I assumed he must have been hit until I saw him here in Bihac."

"So was it a prison where they took you?"

"The place looked like it might have been an old mine. I never saw the whole place, whatever it was. I thought they'd finally feed us when we got up there, but they gave us nothing for three days. Not a fucking crumb. Just water. The boys cried every day. Even many men cried for something to eat. Two older guys collapsed and died."

"The bastards."

"So we slept on the floor of ... I guess it was a garage. After a bit, I found some oil-soaked cardboard, and the boys slept on that. We stank day and night like a gas station, our nostrils always stinging." Suljo swept his hand across the bar top as if he were sweeping away a film of old dust. "I thought they were trying to starve us to death, but then they said to line up for food. All four or five hundred of us hobbled to the door like fucking half-dead wolves."

"What'd they give you?"

"First, they screamed at us ... to divide into groups of twenty or so. Why, I couldn't tell you. The boys and I were lucky. We got a few crusts. But the food ran out, and some guys got nothing. They threw plastic jugs with water into the midst of us. Most of it spilled on the floor during the fights to get a sip. I couldn't bring myself to look at the guys who got nothing. I had this horrible feeling of guilt. Eventually, though, they gave us something to eat once a day. Maybe the US or the UN or the Red Crescent pressured them. Who knows."

"All they gave you was crusts? That's it?"

"Sometimes it was a few stinking beans, a leaf of cabbage, or a piece of bread as dry as a pancake of day-old vomit. But just a meal a day! On the floor. We had to gobble it down in three or four minutes. Guards lined the route, and if you made one move they didn't like, *whamo*, they'd beat you with electrical cables or clubs studded with nail heads."

"You know any of them?"

"I recognized a few."

"That reporter from the *Washington Post*—who gave me the coffee. He told me he heard some prisoners were tortured."

"Tortured? Ha! Torture was everywhere, every day. Brass knuckles, ax handles, broom sticks up your ass, electrical prods. Anything to get some information. In the shack next to mine, they forced a guy to bite off the balls of another prisoner. And for what?"

Suljo made a fist and punched his open palm.

"They said they were looking for snipers, thieves, arms-runners, anything they could use as an excuse to break your will or your body. They wouldn't hesitate to cut off your cock or pluck out your eyes or force another prisoner to slit your throat. And if he was a son, a father—all the better. If I read it in a newspaper, I'd never believe it. But it happened sure as I'm sitting here."

"Suljo, you have no idea how it pains me to hear this, to know that my people did this to you."

"Do you think I hold you responsible, Igor, because you're a Serb? What do you take me for?"

"I don't know, Suljo. It wouldn't surprise me if you drew a knife right this minute and—"

"Don't be a fool."

"But why not? It was my people. It could have been me. Saints become sinners. Ordinary people become evil." Igor turned and looked out the window toward the few remaining twinkling post lights of the Blue Bridge.

"I'm sure Muslims did the same to your people in some other war and probably in this one as well. Madmen motivate ordinary men. Add in some booze, threats, bribes, and ... look, they'll pay for it someday, one way or another. Jail, a firing squad, or a conscience they can't live with."

"How'd you ever get out of there? We saw pictures of the camps on CNN. The chain-link fences, the razor wire. I can't picture anyone escaping. Did you know somebody?"

"Yes, but not the way you might think. It would have been easier if I had never known him. It still haunts me, what I had to do."

"I don't have to know ..."

"Better I tell someone since it's all coming back to me. Better I get it out."

"Stop whenever."

"It was about two months after they killed Zarif. Ahmet and I were in the yard alone. It was evening, and everyone else was too weak to move. They were all huddled in a chicken coop where they had taken us after the garage. I noticed that the guard on duty was an old acquaintance of mine from Kljuc."

"Really?"

"Yeah, he had worked with me in the courts. Not a bad fellow. A clerk with a neck like a chicken. A rather likable guy, actually. When he was younger, he was the lead singer in a rock group that had become quite popular. We had spoken at the fence a few times before. Seemed apologetic. Occasionally slipped me a few nuts or a bar of chocolate, little things like that, that no one could see. He had to be careful, do it when no one else was around."

"So there was still some good in him."

"For sure. So, on one of my previous walks around the perimeter of the yard, I had noticed there was a hinged section of the fence, larger than a photograph, roughly at eye level. Outside that part of the fence, there was an abandoned piece of machinery. A big pipe or something must have gone through this part of the fence. When it got dark, I pretended I was holding onto the wires in this area to support myself, but in fact I worked back and forth the wires that held this little door in place until they were worn almost through but not broken.

"The guard, his name was Goran, saw me that evening and gave me a wink as I walked past him in the opposite direction. That was his way of signaling to me. Goran stopped and put a boot up on the rusting machinery and looked out toward the woods. Then he lit a cigarette. I wandered around to where he was standing, paused, and whispered *hello*. He didn't turn, kept looking out toward the forest, said, 'What's up?'

"Where is everybody tonight?" I asked. 'The place is empty. This is the first time I've ever been out here with just one guard on duty.'

"He told me there was a big party up at the house, naked dancers, lots of beer, endless porn. He said it was his luck to have to be down here. He reached into his jacket pocket and without turning, slipped me a big chocolate bar. I ripped it open and ate it immediately. Normally I would have eaten half and given the other half to Ahmet, but I kind of knew what I was about to do. I knew where that chocolate had to go."

Igor struck a match and relit his cigar.

"The sky was beginning to darken, and I could tell he was feeling relaxed. To make him feel like he could drop his defenses even further, I periodically walked away and then returned, telling him I didn't want to get him in trouble in case someone came down from the house. He said forget it, they had to force him to go stand guard. He lit another cigarette. I got Ahmet's attention and wiggled my left hand like I was trying to get feeling back into it. Ahmet knew it was a signal to be alert and stick with me. The chocolate soon gave me a kick of energy. I began to whistle loudly, and as I did, I quietly worked the wires that held shut the little access flap in the fence. Goran was halfway through his cigarette. He was looking off at the rising moon and probably listening to the music and raucous laughter drifting down from the big house."

Igor took another puff on his cigar and passed it to Suljo.

"He asked me how I came to practice law. I made up a dramatic story to hold his attention, and after his first nod, my hand was through the fence and around his scrawny neck. Although my hand is fairly large, it didn't reach all the way around his throat but far enough for my fingertips to just reach the sides of his Adam's apple. With my other hand, I quickly reached through the fence wires and looped two fingers through his belt so he couldn't turn or pull away. Somehow I willed his gift of chocolate directly into the muscles that locked tight the fingers and forearm of my right arm. His cigarette fell from his lips and bounced off his boot. I was worried for a moment I couldn't last, but he went limp, and I had to finally shake him free from my frozen grip."

Igor took a deep breath, filling his lungs until his shirt stretched tight around his chest. Suljo wondered whether Igor was picturing that that could have been his neck, his bar of chocolate, his cigarette falling to his boot.

"I felt terrible, Igor. More horrible than you could ever imagine. It still haunts me. But there was no way I would let them take Ahmet away from me also. One son was already too many. It was us, or him. An odd thing for a lawyer to say, but in war, justice becomes an abstract notion that gets twisted to suit the moment. Survival governs."

Igor cleared his throat and then swallowed nervously.

"Anyway, I was able to reach his keys. I waved for Ahmet to come over. We raced to the gate. It seemed like hours to find the right key, but it must have been only a few seconds. Finally the lock popped. A beautiful sound. I dream of it still. In a second, we were out."

Suljo stopped speaking, swallowed hard, and lowered his head. "This next part was difficult, Igor, impossibly difficult. I relocked the gate so that it would take longer before the guards discovered our absence. I cried as I dragged Goran's body into the woods, all the time looking back at the coop with the other guys still in there sleeping or too weak to stand."

Igor breathed heavy. "Wow."

"I said nothing to caution Ahmet as we fled, but I was constantly terrified one of us would step on a mine. We raced into the woods and kept running until we dropped."

The two men looked at each other almost blankly in the pool of copper light from the overhead fixture. As the smoke from Igor's cigar spiraled slowly to its resting place amid the paint curls on the ceiling, the thoughts of the two men roamed in benign secrecy to worlds that were worlds apart. They both listened to the steady ticking of the clock, its echo reverberating off the windows, while Suljo's gaze returned to the peculiar, red second hand as it clubbed its way, blow by blow, from one instant to the next.

CHAPTER TWENTY-SIX

"Jusuf! Just forget it. That's the last thing I have of my mother's. No! I won't let you do it."

"What do you want me to do? I can't let you freeze to death and don't want to come back here to a writing desk and another corpse."

"Don't do this to me." She coughed and blew her nose in a rag. "I'll go out tonight and look for branches. I know a place that Dado told me about."

"You're bullshitting me. The few trees still standing are just trunks. You'd need a chainsaw to cut them."

"Destroy that desk, and we're finished. I mean it. You'll kill me if you destroy it. And for what—just a few hours of heat."

"You won't make it through the first night after I leave tomorrow. I'll carry you in the other room so you don't watch or listen, but I need to do it. You're all I have."

"Oh, god, I can't bear this. Then take me outside. It's not much colder out there than it is in here."

Jusuf walked over and was about to confirm his appreciation with a kiss, but she turned her face to the wall and began to sob. He carried her outside, set her down on the stoop, and returned for the blanket, which she pulled from her shoulders and doubled over her head to further muffle the sounds.

He looked at the desk, wishing he could think of an alternative, some way to avoid bringing her such pain but doing what her survival required him to do. He placed his palm on the polished top, gritted his teeth, and with eyes closed, kicked the desk across the room. He grabbed an upturned leg, lifted the desk, and smashed it against the wall. The fretwork splintered first as he hammered it blindly against the plaster. A leg finally snapped off, and after a few more blows, it was a pile of pieces at his feet, except for a small drawer that apparently had been stuck in place for years. Jusuf sank down next to the fragments, and as he cradled a piece of inlaid fretwork in his hands, he wailed like a child.

Shivering uncontrollably and no longer hearing any sounds of destruction, Azra walked back in the house. They could not look at each other and did not speak. From the couch, she stared at the wall and the crisscrossed streaks of stain and furniture polish.

"You didn't have to do it. I have nothing left of her now." But then Azra noticed the drawer still intact near Jusuf's knee. She got up and carried it back to the couch, hugging it against her chest.

They slept huddled closely on the couch with her on the inside to preserve her heat. She woke first to pee. When she returned to the living room, the first light of dawn was just beginning to brighten the room. She picked up the drawer again and noticed a yellowed envelope, almost the color of the wood, taped neatly to the bottom panel. Her mother's name was written in one corner in her father's nearly illegible handwriting. She wondered before peeling it from the bottom of the drawer what message had needed to be secreted away for so long. She felt the same flood of mixed emotions that had thrilled and scared her a year earlier just before opening the first letter Jusuf received from his mother.

Draga Lejla,
You have no idea how bad I still feel about Boris, even after these many years. Whenever I cross the Blue Bridge on my way to Sarajevo, my heart sinks. Who could have guessed what he would do?
I feel again the deep need to apologize to you, even though I know apologizing will never bring him back. You say that it was not entirely my doing. That he would never have jumped if you had not fallen in love with me, or if you had let him

down more gently. Perhaps. But I sensed his instability, and yet I persisted. I know most everyone in Bihac believes that my blindness killed him or at least that my determination to make you mine caused him unbearable pain. In the final analysis, it was I that caused his demise.

For bringing you so much pain, for wanting you so badly, I will always live in shame and disgrace. I hope one day you will find a way to forgive me.

You were, (and still are) so lovely, so beautiful; you filled my every thought throughout the day and throughout the night—I could think of nothing else. My love for you became such an overwhelming passion, such an obsession, that I simply could not subdue it. I had to see you, had to be with you, had to make you mine. I don't know what more I can say to you other than I am so deeply sorry. Thank God you stayed with me.

Allah Akbar.
Your loving husband,
Suad

The name *Boris* and the date *1973* were written in Lejla's lovely script on the back of the envelope. Something else had been written in pencil but had been erased.

The following day, Jusuf received a message to meet Malik in town near the Fethija Mosque around five in the afternoon for the ride back to the front lines. Malik had been concerned about his dwindling petrol supplies and his near-bald tires, so he was doing everything he could to reduce how far he had to drive.

Azra and Jusuf both feared for the other's safety for different reasons and were in tears for hours before Jusuf finally left the house at four-thirty.

"I'll see you in a few days," Jusuf said. "Rest, and we'll be together soon."

"My love is with you always."

"Stay warm as best you can."

The sun was setting as he passed the Kafana Paviljon and headed directly for the mosque, but Malik's truck had not yet arrived at the appointed spot just outside the wall to the courtyard. He stood for a while, expecting the truck to appear at any moment.

To keep warm, he decided to walk in square circles around the interior of the courtyard where he could see Malik's truck when it pulled up. A few trucks went by, but not Malik's. Jusuf began to wonder whether someone had written the wrong day or the wrong hour or the wrong place. Three men Jusuf had never seen before stood in a shadow on the far side of the wall. From time to time, they looked in his direction and pointed, so he quickened his pace around the perimeter of the courtyard and almost walked into a small dog that had crossed his path. The dog began following Jusuf, whimpering as he trotted behind. Jusuf remembered a stale piece of bread in his pocket and broke off a corner and tossed it toward the dog. As the dog nosed the bread out of the snow, Jusuf saw headlights and then heard a few familiar beeps as Malik's truck skidded to a stop along the courtyard wall. Malik rolled down his window and apologized for the delay that involved his fixing a flat. He made a right turn toward the Blue Bridge and headed back into the mountains. Jusuf's legs shook wildly until the cab heat penetrated his clothes. Neither man spoke a word until Malik mentioned that the front lines for them had moved to a steep ravine. "They're right across from us now, Jusuf. When we're not shooting at them, we can invite them over for a game of cards."

"At least we'll have a change of scenery."

"I'm really sorry about the delay. You must have frozen out there."

"I kept walking to stay warm. Gave me time to think. The courtyard reminded me of my Uncle Ibro's mosque in Sanski Most."

"I got a sister lives out that way."

"Then you must know the mosque was destroyed."

"I do."

Neither man said anything for the next ten minutes until Jusuf confessed that he had started to get concerned about the men who seemed to be watching him in the courtyard.

"Did they say anything to you?"

"No. They just spooked me. It brought back memories of a somewhat similar time when I had just turned nine. For the very first time, my Uncle Ibro allowed me to play outside the mosque alone while he was inside. I thought about playing near the river, but I knew my uncle would not be happy to find a courtyard with me not in it."

"I can understand that."

"So I played on the front steps with a stray dog I had seen several times before. Each time the dog whined, I handed him a piece of cookie my aunt had baked earlier that morning. I was alone in the courtyard and didn't see these young guys approach. Then one of them starts strutting on top of the low wall that circled the courtyard. The guy was shirtless and tough looking. He was the first to toss his beer can in my direction. His buddies laughed. When the other three pitched their cans at me, I kind of knew I was in for some trouble. The dog ran off, tail tucked between its hind legs. I suddenly felt very alone and vulnerable."

"I can imagine. They say anything to you?" Malik rolled down his window for some fresh air, took a deep breath, toyed with nostril hairs he hadn't clipped in a few month, and then cranked the window back up.

"Yeah. The guy prancing on the wall said, 'What you up to, little Turk?' I didn't answer. Then he said, 'Hey, Turk! I said what the fuck are you doing here?'"

"Did you answer?"

"Yeah. I kind of whispered, 'Nothing.' Then he said, 'You goddamn Turks are always up to *nothing*. Why don't you get the hell out of here? You're nothing but the scum of the earth.'"

"A bunch of cowardly bullies if you ask me. Did they come after you?"

"They huddled and whispered something, so I backed up a few steps but tripped over the shoes lined up near the entrance doors. Then one guy who was missing two front teeth said, 'Don't you know this is Serb country? You shits don't belong around here!'"

"Damn, Jusuf. I think I would have crapped in my pants."

"I wished the men in the mosque would finish their prayers and come to protect me, but I wasn't so lucky. Then the guy with the teeth said, 'Wasn't that your mother that just ran off with her tail between her legs?' The others howled and twirled in circles. 'Why don't you go follow her? You look like a momma's boy, you little freak.'"

"You needed our brigade to back you up."

"I wanted to say something, or even scream at them, but then the shirtless guy yelled, 'Let's get the little twerp and fill his pockets with stones and take him to the river for a swim!'"

"Oh, shit!"

"You bet, because the next thing I know is they've turned on their heels and were running through the courtyard straight at me. I swung around, tripped over a few shoes again, then reached up and grabbed the huge door pulls. I tugged at them, but the humidity must have caused the wood to swell. I couldn't get either door to budge."

"Shit, so what did you …"

"So I jumped with all my might, positioned both feet high against the left door panel, and pulled the handle on the door to my right with everything I had in me. I heard their sneakers chirping on the stone paving and pictured their fists flying and almost felt their feet kicking me, when suddenly the door yielded."

"Thank God."

"I didn't even look back. I just slipped through the slot that had opened and into the cool vestibule. Their laughter was muffled as the door fell shut behind me. That thud was music to my ears."

"You were one lucky kid."

"I was. I just leaned against those big solid doors, cried, and waited for my heart to stop pounding. I could hardly breathe.

"Nothing but a bunch of goddamn fucking punks. Guys like that are probably half the reason we're in this blood-sucking war to begin with."

CHAPTER TWENTY-SEVEN

WHEN A BREAK IN the gunfire quieted both camps, Jusuf flattened the thin bed of leaves beneath him and lay back on the cold earth. Obrad had been hacking and sneezing in their new bunker, and Jusuf figured he would sleep better outside if he could find a protected location. Exhausted and hungry, he half-listened to some of his comrades discussing the day's gunfights as they cleaned their rifles and nervously fingered their dwindling supply of shells.

"Hey, where the fuck are the beans?" a soldier yelled. No one had come yet from Bihac with supplies. "The least they could do is get us some fucking food out here and some water."

Ten feet from Jusuf, a soldier stood and stretched. On his way to empty his bowels in a latrine dug behind a sycamore tree, he accidentally kicked one of the near-empty water cans that had been placed near the fire to prevent the water from freezing. The few remaining cupfuls of water sloshed thinly on the bottom when the can rolled against a rock. The bonging hollowness silenced the banter of those nearby.

From the far bank of the frozen stream that separated the warring parties, Jusuf heard what had now become a few vaguely familiar voices interspersed with the sound of forks scratching dinner out of small metal tins. The aroma of their rich coffee and the mouth-watering smell of their food, even the synthetic smells of the processed food, drove Jusuf and his comrades wild with envy. But today the aromas served the better function of masking the unusually strong stench of bloodied earth, piss and shit, infected cuts, and the foul odors of his own mouth and armpits.

Too hungry and thirsty to drop off to sleep, Jusuf watched several small birds chirping and darting about against a pink winter sky as the sun slipped below the hill behind the Serbian encampment. When he lowered his gaze to look at the sky reflected in the frozen stream, he noticed the loosened strip of underwear that held together the flapping parts of his left boot. Concerned that the fighting might resume after he fell asleep, he dragged his body up to a sitting position, pulled his knee to his chest, and retied the strip of cloth. Then he spat on the strip in mounting frustration.

Life in Bihac seemed a lifetime away as he looked up into the few stars just beginning to shine. His second letter to his mother, which he wished had been more loving and upbeat, was never answered, and although he tried again to write another letter, he resigned himself to the fact, given the number of months that had elapsed, that she had died or been killed. He did not understand why he was not grieving more than he was, why he felt only numbness and a pervasive disengagement from all that surrounded him. Perhaps he was too tired, too sick of life and death, too fed up with an endless war to feel anything anymore. Life and death had both become fictions. Those who had died still seemed alive, and those who might be alive were presumed dead. It was a maddening reverie from which he hoped he would one day awaken, but to what? Would the dead come back to life and the living be found dead, lying half-decomposed by the side of a trail?

As he dozed off, he slid effortlessly into a dream. Azra was sitting between his legs, sipping hot coffee, and nibbling a potato pie. They were together in the only intact wing of a big mansion that had become their nest. He was happy with the warmth of her body next to his, but as he stroked her hair, they both felt the ground begin to vibrate, and then came a roar like the tectonic shifting of an earthquake. The light of day dimmed as the specter of war approached their hideaway, a vast army of faceless soldiers appearing over a nearby hill. Suddenly something howled into the room—furious and colossal, part-animal, part-tornado. Their cups of coffee, the potato pie, and Azra's mother's antiques were swept up in a fierce whirlwind and flung about the room, the furniture dashed to splinters. The windstorm contracted into a huge bird-like creature that clawed the air with razor-sharp, stainless steel talons. Its eyeballs flashed fire. It flew back and forth and then attacked Jusuf's mother, who had materialized in front of them reclining on a sofa. She wore the same dark blue dress and the purple flowered scarf she wore when Jusuf last saw her in Kljuc.

The screaming bird swooped toward his mother, licks of flame darting from its eyes. Jusuf was about to attack the bird when an icicle-like spear materialized in his right hand, cold and sharp like crystal. Inexplicably the beast turned and passed through the side wall of the room and into an adjacent house from which came shrieks, sounds of flesh tearing, bones snapping like pieces of chalk.

The bird grew great and darkened the sky. Its leather wings, the size of clouds, flapped in awkward thrusts. It reappeared through the wall of their room. He and Azra dove behind the sofa, heads down, arms crossed protectively. Jusuf's mother cringed and begged for help. "Jusuf, please do something. I'm very afraid."

Jusuf sailed over the sofa and attacked the bird. Leather wings flapped wildly, flashing talons swatting the air. Jusuf's father's unerring instinct for the perfect kill ignited within him. He anticipated the beast's every move, dodged each swipe, and then darted between the creature's tall legs. He relentlessly pounded every limb and wrenched the creature's muscular legs until the brute lost balance and toppled. As candle-sized flames shooting from the bird's eyes dimmed and its wings thrashed in lumbering aimless sweeps, Jusuf tore into the creature in a final frenzy, using only his hands and teeth. After a final moan, the beast writhed and fell dead against the wall.

Azra sank in a corner sobbing. When Jusuf looked for his mother, he saw that she and the sofa had vanished. He wondered if she had fled in fear, or had the bird, in its last instant of life, swatted the air and struck his mother in the heart, carrying her with it into oblivion.

CHAPTER TWENTY-EIGHT

When Jusuf awoke hours later, light was just showing in the early morning sky. The birds he saw the evening before were again chirping and swooping through the predawn air. He was rested but hungry, and fresh scratches covered his hands. His jaw ached.

He knew it would be hours before the beans arrived from Bihac, if they did at all, so he chose to lay on his bed of leaves and listen to the soldiers in both camps slowly rise and begin attending to their morning chores. There was the usual rattling of pans and clinking of utensils, trails of smoke rising from campfires into snow-covered branches, the smell of food wafting over from the Serbian side, and farting contests erupting on one side of the stream or the other, and sometimes cross-stream, which brought explosions of tension-relieving laughter.

As rays of stark, early-morning sunlight sliced horizontally through the trees like polished sabers, the banter across the stream started to change tone. Insults and put-downs were hurled like stones from one bank across to the other. Inventive cursing became a language all its own.

Because the slopes of the ravine were extremely steep except for the occasional narrow level areas where the encampments were situated, it was difficult at times to determine where a particular voice was coming from. When the birds were quiet and the wind was still, utterances seemed to hang in the cold air and ring hard with the hint of an echo, leading to the unsettling illusion in both camps that the soldiers at times were cursing themselves. A volley of laughter might then explode with an attendant cackling echo giving the impression of an audience in the round. To someone stumbling by chance upon these mirrored enemy encampments with their back and forth banter, real and reverberated, the impression would be that the two warring sides had mysteriously merged into a single united and cohesive fighting force.

Malik once told Jusuf that soon after the war began, he and a handful of his fellow soldiers agreed to meet a small Serbian force in an open field midway between the front lines to drink coffee and share news from back home. The cautious camaraderie lasted somewhat more than an hour, and then the two sides nodded solemnly and returned to their former battle positions. It wasn't long before a single shot, perhaps fired at a squirrel or an owl, started the soldiers firing at one another again. Malik tried to explain that there had been brothers he knew of on opposing sides and that familial love or simple curiosity won out for a time over a conflict that most had loathed. Nevertheless, Jusuf had trouble believing that Malik's stories were anything other than the product of Malik's unfettered imagination or a dream he believed had actually happened.

As Jusuf continued to listen to fragments of conversation from both sides, he focused on one particular Serbian voice coming from about sixty meters downstream. It sounded vaguely familiar, but the soldier had a cough much like the one from which Obrad was suffering. Then the voice dimmed and melted away.

As Jusuf replayed the voice in his mind, he grew excited and uneasy because it sounded so much like his recollection of Sasha's voice. But that was improbable, he figured, because the ravine was too far from Kljuc. Then he wondered if Sasha was on the front lines at all. He could have been killed since the time he was involved in the delivery of the first letter to Jusuf's mother. If Sasha were dead, that would explain why Jusuf never received a response to his second letter. Unsure of Sasha's fate, Jusuf nevertheless had begun to look forward to the war's end and hopefully seeing his old friend once again. He wanted to know so many things about his old friend and assumed Sasha would be curious about him.

As the sun rose higher in the sky behind the Serbian encampment, Jusuf got up and headed for the latrine. As he positioned himself over the trench, joints aching, body stiff as old leather, he heard the sweet wailing of a harmonica. Someone was playing Dylan's "It's All Over Now, Baby Blue." The plaintive twang floated softly through the trees, melding with the smoke of the campfires. As he walked back toward the bunker, he cupped his ears and held his breath. Sasha had a very distinctive way of playing that tune—it had been his favorite—so it was either Sasha himself on the other side of the creek or someone who had heard Sasha perform the tune enough times to master it with that particular cadence, close to Dylan's but more wistful. The sound got stronger as the man strolled upstream until he seemed to be directly across from Jusuf, perhaps fifty meters away, but distance was so difficult to judge because the echoes seemed to amplify the volume of every utterance. The soldier stopped on the far side of a thicket of brambles almost directly across from Jusuf and was concealed either by accident or choice.

When the player paused, Jusuf formed a megaphone with his curled palms and whispered.

"Sasha?"

There was no response.

"Hey ... music man ... is that you?"

The man sucked in a quirky off-key squeak and resumed playing. Jusuf sang softly to himself as the tune ended, *"Strike another match, go start anew—And it's all over now, Baby Blue."*

Jusuf again called in a stage whisper, "Sasha! Damn it. Nobody plays Dylan like you. Answer me, you son of a bitch!"

When a ruckus broke out in the Serbian camp, the soldier directly across from Jusuf began another song and quickly walked back downstream to investigate.

Fifteen minutes later, Malik came by for a chat. Jusuf had been digging holes in the pine tree near him and installing four-inch long cigar-shaped sticks on both side of the trunk to steady the barrel of his rifle. He figured this was a good time to let Malik know that his supply of bullets was dangerously low. "I've got nothing to give you at the moment, so just make sure that old cannon of yours is clean and ready to fire. Every shot has got to count."

All the soldiers spent hours cleaning their weapons with whatever materials were at hand. Jusuf lubricated the octagonal barrel and other metal parts of his rifle with a thin film of oil he wiped from the pores of his nose and forehead and shined the mahogany butt with his shirttail moistened with saliva. After snapping up the sight mechanism from the top tang to make sure it was clean and undamaged, he paused again to marvel at the engravings on the side plates. Amid a garden of vines and flowers depicted on the left plate was a longhaired gentleman with a pointy beard, facing a lass wearing a wide-brimmed hat topped by a large and fulsome feather. She was holding his rifle behind her, keeping it out of his reach, teasing him. His finger was raised as if to say *don't play with me,* but he had a sly smile on his lips. The right plate's engraving presented a narrow-waisted damsel holding several beer mugs in each hand, her head gaily tilted to the side, and the corner of her apron lifted by the wind. This depiction reminded Jusuf of his own damsel, and if by chance she did not have a mug of beer to offer him, then at least there would be a warm cup of coffee and a tension-relieving hug.

Jusuf used thin, rigid twigs whittled to a point to scratch out dry mud that had caked into the shallow engravings. The activity reminded him of the cleaning ritual performed by his father. Jusuf wondered whether this rifle was one his father had favored and, if so, how many living creatures it might have brought down. He pictured his mom at her stove stirring a rabbit stew, steam rising and reddening her face. A feeling of family warmth came over him as if he were linked to both parents by a conjured umbilical cord that carried a steady stream of childhood memories. Jusuf even surrendered himself to the feeling that his father's fingertips were guiding his fingers as he finished cleaning the decorative plates. He was almost accepting his own romanticized vision that the weapon was being prepared not for another hunt, and certainly not for the madness of warfare, but simply for some benign test of his skill as a marksman, a test of his deepening respect for the needs of others. As Jusuf struggled to bring a gleam to the arabesque trigger guard, he noticed a soldier in fatigues on the far side of the stream drifting slowly away from his comrades and in his direction. The man who had Sasha's easy gait and relaxed posture climbed a low hill just beyond and above the cluster of brambles on the far side of the creek. Was this the same fellow with the harmonica who had strolled by earlier?

For a long while, there was silence. Then the soldier whispered softly in a stage voice, "Jusuf. Are you over there?"

Because of the raucous exchanges emanating from the center of both camps that were roughly 120 meters downstream, Jusuf felt comfortable that he could speak across the stream and not be overheard.

"You goddamn shit-eating motherfucker, Sasha. It *was* you!"

The soldier looked down the hill toward his comrades to see if Jusuf's outburst had been overheard.

"Yeah, it's me," he whispered. You're alive, huh?"

"Yeah, I'm alive. What brings *you* up this way?"

Sasha did not answer. Neither was quick to speak again.

"Sasha, you shit. You been okay?"

"Pretty much. It's not been easy on either side I guess." He paused and looked down the hill. "Listen, I'd say more, but …" Sasha turned to go back to his camp.

"Hey, Sasha, before you go back … I wrote my mom, twice. I guess you know that. I only got back one letter. I'm afraid to ask. Is she okay? Just tell me that."

"She's fine. I saw her … last week. She's fine."

Before Jusuf could speak again, Sasha pointed down the hill at something Jusuf could not see at the moment from his vantage point. He hastily waved good-bye. Several meters down the hill, he turned and said, "I'll try to swing by again another time."

Jusuf began thinking he was a fool to believe anything Sasha had said. He had been told by many of his comrades, particularly Malik, that encounters like this were a trick Serbs used to get information from their old Muslim friends. Jusuf had so wanted to trust Sasha, but when Sasha returned three days later, Jusuf could not contain his uncertainty.

"Damn it, are you fucking with me? When you said Mom was okay, you could be telling me anything."

"I could be, but when we were kids, was there ever a question about the truth between us? Do you think that my love for her—or you—ever changed because of this war?"

"I'm over here on this side, and you're over there, with my enemy. It's life or death for both sides now. I don't know what to believe anymore."

"Jusuf, listen. Since you're not sure what to believe, I could bring her down here for just a minute so you could see her for yourself. I could bring her just over the ridge back behind me just long enough for you to see her. Then you'd know for sure. But it would have to be for just a quick minute."

Jusuf's heart began racing wildly. His eyes were so awash with tears he momentarily lost track of Sasha's whereabouts.

"I'd be really careful! Remember, she was like a mom to me, too. I lived in your house more than I lived in my own. And I know she'd give anything to see you even for a second."

"You know I'm dying to see her … but forget it. It's way too risky!"

Several Serbian officers who had observed Sasha speaking to someone across the stream waved Sasha down the hill. At first, there was just light banter between them, followed by moments of easy laughter, but then one officer began yelling and stabbing his finger into Sasha's chest. Sasha pointed across the ravine, roughly toward where Jusuf had been standing.

"Yeah, he was a friend of mine, so what? That was before the war. He means nothing to me now. I'm surprised the creep is even alive. All I said was hello. Get off my back. In an hour from now, I'll be shooting at the guy."

Jusuf watched another officer walk over and put his arm around Sasha in a way that was both gentle and oppressive. He spoke in confidential tones. Sasha tried to pull away.

"No way!" Sasha said in a voice loud enough that he hoped Jusuf could hear.

Then the officer withdrew a huge, chrome-plated Scorpion from his holster, pushed his glasses back against the bridge of his nose, pointed the pistol at Sasha's throat, and uttered something between clenched teeth. Another soldier standing nearby began to laugh but stopped midbreath when the officer with the gun turned in his direction and cocked the trigger. Then the officer turned back to Sasha and said, "You fucking dog. You're no better than the scum on the other side of the creek. Get out of my fucking sight. If I see you up that way again, you're dead."

A few days later as the sun began to set behind the ridge on the Muslim side of the ravine, Jusuf was startled to see out of the corner of his eye a string of small brilliant flashes, edges ragged, all flickering with nervous life. It came from high up on the ridge on the far side of the creek.

When it flashed again directly into Jusuf's eyes, jiggling insistently, Jusuf realized the source was a handheld mirror.

Sasha pocketed his mirror, smiled, and then reached behind a huge sycamore, and like a circus clown performing a stunt, he gently tugged Ismeta into view. As soon as she saw Jusuf, she raised her hands to her face and began to sob. Sasha reached quickly to cover her mouth. She raised her hands to the sky and then brought them to her breast. Jusuf was sure she would have been praising Allah out loud if she had been elsewhere.

Jusuf peered down the hill to see if anyone in the Serbian camp was watching. He was so terrified they would be detected he found it difficult to show his pleasure in finally seeing his mother alive, though he was overwhelmed and deeply grateful. He wanted to prolong the visit, to soak in the sight of her, to savor the relief in seeing her this close but felt compelled to wave them both away with little hand gestures as if he were shooing away an insect. A Serbian soldier with binoculars caught sight of Jusuf's hand signal and elbowed an officer standing next to him. The soldier pointed, and the officer looked back up the hill over his shoulder to the ridge.

"Hey, Sasha, my boy. Good work! Now bring that bitch down here, will ya."

Sasha and Ismeta froze. After a few seconds, Ismeta stepped behind the tree.

"I said drag that Muslim bitch down here *now,* you dumb prick, or I'll run up there and blow your brains out ... and hers too." The officer's words, every terrifying syllable, resounded in Jusuf's ears and brought him to a state of feral panic. His heart pounded as Sasha and his mother angled their way down the steep snow-blanketed slope, his mother reaching from sapling to trunk to steady herself. When she slipped and tumbled sideways into the snow, Sasha gave her his hand and pulled her up. Then he looked across the stream at Jusuf, who reached for his father's rifle.

The officer stood in silence as Sasha and Jusuf's mother walked into the middle of the Serbian camp. Catcalls erupted, whistles, obscene gestures. Jusuf moved parallel to the stream to get closer to the center of the Serbian camp, closer to the mayhem, closer to a scene that was enflaming every nerve ending of his being, and closer to the tree outfitted with the projecting sticks to steady his rifle.

Short bursts of contorted laughter erupted from a huddle of Serb soldiers. Ismeta shook uncontrollably, her face white as the snow. She turned once to see if she could still see Jusuf across the stream, but he had changed position and was now indistinguishable from his fellow Muslim soldiers. She was so disoriented, so overcome by panic and terror, that she wasn't sure which way to turn now. Sasha said nothing, fearing that anything he might do or say would further incite his comrades.

"We need some cunt over here, Sasha," one man bellowed. There followed a roar of approval.

"Whaddaya think, guys," another yelled as he unzipped his fly.

Another soldier pulled down his pants and humped the air, "I need some ass—any kind of ass—but preferably some red-hot Muslim ass. Look at her begging for it." Another explosion of laughter.

"Lay off!" a few men from Jusuf's camp called out. A few of them nearby had overheard fragments of Jusuf's exchange with Sasha, and several had seen Sasha and Ismeta up on the ridge when they first arrived. Word had spread quickly from one recruit to another on both sides of the stream.

"You guys are nothing but fucking pigs!" Malik yelled. "She's a woman for god's sake." A bullet from the Serb side whizzed past Malik's ear.

Even Obrad was incensed and called across to his fellow Serbs in the dialect they identified as their own, "Have you no sense of decency, no respect for anything?"

The Muslims fell silent. Jusuf worried their comments would only serve to enflame the other side. He wanted to scream and cry and kill all at the same instant. His hands shook, and his breathing was wildly out of rhythm, his chest tight.

"You Muslim shits are a bunch of pussies. You and the Jews—you both get the ends cut off, and your manhood goes with it. Now we'll show you what real men can do."

A soldier danced a frolicking step over to Jusuf's mother and untied her scarf. He pulled the pins from her hair, which fell in sliding swags to her shoulders. Ismeta buried her face in her hands and trembled. "Save me, Allah. You must come and save me from this shame." Her words were like a dagger thrust straight into Jusuf's heart. A soldier raised her skirt and patted her backside. Another roar of laughter erupted.

"Leave the poor woman alone!" an older Serb called out, his plea drowned out by the escalating mayhem.

"Who said that?" the officer with the chrome-plated Scorpion demanded.

"I did," the older Serb said, walking forward. "Enough's enough! Let the poor woman go back to town or wherever she's from."

The officer walked over to the older Serb and shot him between the eyes. As the man fell to the ground, the officer fired another shot in the air and waved his arms for his men to clear a path so the Muslim camp had a clear view of Jusuf's mother. "Turn her around so they can see her from the front. Who's going first with this bitch?" he demanded.

As several men, naked from the waist down, closed in on his mother, Jusuf placed one of his last shells in the breech and positioned his barrel on one of his handmade wooden spokes. Feeling like he was about to explode with rage, he fought to stay controlled enough to aim.

"Think she's still got some juice left in her?" one man asked.

"She will soon!"

As the daylight waned, one man walked forward, unbuttoned her heavy woolen sweater and pulled it off. Next he removed her blouse, though she tried desperately to keep it around her. He slowly removed her brassiere. "Not bad," he said as he cupped her breasts. Her nipples responded to the cold, and she raised her trembling arms to hide her body. To Jusuf it looked like her lungs were almost unable to draw in another breath. "Boy, she's hot; look at her tits."

Another soldier stepped forward and again raised her skirt as another tugged down her panties. As she stood shaking and wailing, several soldiers, underpants bulging, circled in. With eyes tightly shut and her body beginning to sink under the pressure of intense shame, Ismeta called out, "Help me, Jusuf! Help me, Braco!"

A chorus erupted, "Fuck the bitch! Fuck the bitch!"

She murmured, "Please save me, Allah. Oh, Braco, dear, come back. I'm so ashamed. Jusuf, Sasha. One of you must help me. Dear God, one of you, please."

Fragments of last night's dream flashed before Jusuf's eyes. Again he saw the dark bird's leather wings darken the skies, flames shooting from its eyes. He raised his rifle, steadying his aim on the Serbian soldier closest to his mother—then he aimed at another soldier to her right who was moving toward her more quickly, and then he aimed at the officer. Which to bring down first? *You control the moment, Jussie. Just close the gulf, and the moment is yours.* His gun sight passed over his mother's breasts, embarrassing him, intensifying his rage. He suddenly realized her rape would be followed first by torture and then her murder. Her words and his from several years ago suddenly reverberated in his ears.

"*The dishonor would be worse than death, Jusuf.*"
"*Worse than death, Mom? You can't mean that.*"

As his weapon moved from left to right, waiting for the perfect moment and the perfect target, Sasha appeared in his sight, his face contorted by fear, fury, and disgust. Jusuf again steadied the barrel and when he felt a familiar guiding hand on his shoulder, took aim, and when the moment arrived, squeezed the trigger.

The bullet blasted a ragged hole through Ismeta's chest. Bloodied pieces of flesh, heart, and bone fragments spewed across the bodies and stunned faces of the soldiers who surrounded her. She collapsed into the dirty, boot-marked snow. Her head jerked once and then was still. Soldiers on both sides of the stream froze like hardened wax figures, except for Sasha who fell to his knees, frantically trying to cover Ismeta's body with the clothes that had fallen around her in the snow.

Jusuf dropped his father's rifle as if it were as hot as a blacksmith's tongs. With wild eyes glaring and a mouth twisted in anguish, his hands sprang open as if they, too, were on fire. "What have I done! What have I done!" He fell back over a fallen log, tried to regain balance, but sank into the snow and started retching. When he noticed his comrades approaching him, he waved them off. "No! No! Stay away."

For minutes, he remained dazed, staring into space, too stunned to cry. But then he again stood, and with a flood of tears coursing down his cheeks, he picked up the old rifle and smashed it against the log. Repeatedly, he hammered the gun against the log until the polished stock cracked and finally broke free of the barrel. He continued to beat the barrel against the log as he wailed "Oh, god. What have I done? I did what you wanted, Mom. 'Worse than death.' You said that, Mom. 'Worse than death.' Forgive me, Mom. Forgive me, please." Then, like an animal, bellowing a howl from the wildest depths of his being, he flung the gun barrel out over the frozen streambed in a looping curve that ended when the barrel vanished silently in a mound of snow. He kicked wildly at the snow and leaves around his feet as if he were trying to erase all sense of place, all awareness of what had just happened. He fell to the ground and pummeled the frozen earth with his fists as raw, wordless noises scratched their way out of his throat. Then his eyes rolled back in his head, and his body went limp.

Sasha shrieked into the treetops, "What the hell are we doing here? We're nothing but a bunch of senseless beasts!" His scream reverberated in the crypt-like ravine as if an ancient conscience had broken loose from its slopes and risen to admonish the soldiers on both sides of the conflict. "Do you want blood?" He withdrew his knife from its sheath. "Do you all want more fucking blood?" He slashed the blade down the right side of his face from his ear to his chin, and then slashed both palms and raised them for the warriors on both sides of the creek to see. "Is it more blood you idiots want to see?"

He ran along the creek bank as the sky darkened, zigzagging and pounding his fists and thumping his bloody head into tree trunks, howling with such force his voice kept breaking. Suddenly he stopped short and turned. He cried hoarsely across the creek, "Jusuf, can you hear me? I just wanted her to see you for a minute … so you'd know she's alive. We tried to protect her, Jusuf, truly we tried. She was up at the farm with us. Near the cave around Veliki Radic, where we used to play. Now look! Oh, my god, Jusuf, now look. *I* killed her. I killed our mom, Jusuf. Dear God, help me."

Sasha dashed across the frozen surface of the stream onto the Muslim side and tried to race up the icy bank looking for Jusuf. Two shots rang out. The shot fired by the officer with the Scorpion hit Sasha's left knee, spinning him, so that he fell sideways on his other leg. Another shot fired almost simultaneously by a Muslim downstream from Jusuf tore through Sasha's ear and the back of his head. He fell backward down the bank, his body tumbling like a bundle of old clothes until it came to rest on the ice bed of the stream. Blood flowed from his head, knee, and hands and spread out over the somber, iridescent grays and silvers of the frozen brook. His gold crucifix spiraled down its chain as if on a mission and clinked almost inaudibly on the ice. Then it rose for a moment on a swell of blood and disappeared. Seconds later, as if acting on its own volition, his stainless steel Marine Band harmonica, with its slightly worn, pear wood comb, slipped out of his jacket pocket and pursued a succession of mindless, silvery loops across the ice.

CHAPTER TWENTY-NINE

MALIK AND OBRAD MOVED Jusuf into the bunker and covered him with two thin blankets. Then Obrad stepped outside and spoke with several soldiers who had gathered nearby while Malik stayed with Jusuf.

"Good god, to shoot your own mother," Obrad whispered.

"Obrad, you have no idea what you'd have done if you saw what he saw," an older soldier replied.

"All I know is I would have shot that fucking officer first. That would have ended it all."

"You fool. Shoot the officer and all hell would've broken loose. They'd have raped and killed her for sure and then hacked her to pieces."

"Can you imagine what he'll be like when he wakes up? You and Malik best keep an eye on him so he doesn't kill himself."

"You think he knows his friend was shot?" Obrad asked.

"Not sure. I think he was smashing his rifle at the time and seemed deaf to the world. Did you see who shot him from our side?"

"I didn't. The guy must have been scared thinking he was after more blood."

"Can you imagine living with that nightmare for the rest of your life?"

"Do you think he really intended to shoot her? Maybe his mom stepped in the line of fire."

"Impossible. You could see she was terrified. She was frozen with fear," Obrad said, his voice rising.

"Maybe his sight got knocked out of alignment. I saw him cleaning his rifle earlier today."

"No way. If anyone knows weapons, it's Jusuf."

"Had it been me, I would have shot his friend. He was a fool to bring her up here."

The door to the bunker opened.

"Keep your voices down out there. Obrad, come here. We can't let him waken and see his mother and Sasha down there. Give me a hand. We're getting him out of here now and taking him home."

They gently woke Jusuf, who was limp and groggy. They walked him over the ridge behind them to Malik's truck.

"Hey. Wait," he said, his voice weak and shaky, his head bobbing. "Where we going?"

"We're going home, Jusuf. We're going to Azra."

Jusuf sat between them, mumbling incoherently and staring at the grimy windshield. From time to time, a sound came from his throat suggesting he was about to vomit. Otherwise, there was only the incessant drone of the engine and the intermittent thumping of tires on the frozen road. Once, when the engine backfired, Jusuf jerked wildly, his fingers fanning out in panic. Malik's right hand went to Jusuf's knee. Jusuf's head fell forward and wobbled as the truck shuddered in and out of icy ruts. Finally Malik reached the Blue Bridge by a back route, passed by the Kafana Paviljon, and stopped in front of Azra's house and left the motor running.

After several knocks, Azra came to the door wrapped in a blanket. She opened the door ever so slightly to see who might be there in the middle of the night. She panicked when she saw Malik's truck.

"Malik," she said with eyes wide with fright. Malik angled his index finger across his lips. "Something happened, didn't it?" she asked. "Is he dead, Malik? Just tell me, is he *dead*?"

Malik signaled by patting the air for Azra to lower her voice. He whispered, "He's not dead, Azra. He's not even been shot. But he needs to be home. His mother's been killed. And his friend is dead, too."

"Oh my god. How? Where? Who shot her?"

Malik didn't answer. Azra grabbed his arm and squeezed it with all her might.

"Malik, who killed her? Did Sasha kill her? Tell me, Malik. Who did it?"

Malik looked down and in a barely audible whisper confessed, "It was Jusuf."

"What? You're making no sense."

"We're still not sure how or why, whether it was an accident or whether—"

"Oh, dear god." She staggered backward, almost fainting, Malik catching her before she fell. "Is he in the truck?"

"Yes, but he's in really bad shape. You can imagine ..."

"Let's get him in here right away." She stepped out onto the stoop.

"Stay inside. It's freezing out here."

As Malik and Obrad eased Jusuf out of the truck, Azra opened the door wide and stood shivering, tears streaming down her sunken cheeks. They walked him to the sofa. Jusuf hid his face in his hands and began to shake violently as Azra gently placed her hand on his head. She felt him melt. He reached over and slowly pulled her closer. "Don't ask me anything. Please don't. Just stay near, but don't ask ..."

"Not a word, my dear. Not a word until you're ready."

Malik motioned for Azra to come to the door. They stepped outside. He whispered in her ear, "He doesn't know about his friend yet."

"Oh, my god. That will kill him for sure."

For several days, Jusuf did nothing but lie on the couch, staring at the ceiling. From time to time, he looked at his hands as if everything but his hands had been erased from a drawing.

Friends brought small gifts of food, and Azra urged him to eat even a little. No one tried to lift him out of his grief, out of his penetrating sense of self-hate and shame. When he heard a knock at the door, he retreated upstairs or ran down into the basement. Azra met visitors outside, explaining that his pain was too overwhelming. "I can't even get through to him myself yet."

Azra brought him coffee and crackers and feared leaving his side for too long.

"Speak a little to me, Jusuf. It might help. I know you're in such pain."

"I can't. Please, I have nothing to ..."

She wove her fingers through his hair, but he quieted her hand. The idea of anyone loving him was intolerable.

Nightmares of his mother's bare chest and the taunts of the soldiers closing in on her woke him screaming night after night. He would bolt upright, drenched in sweat, struggling to breathe, able to suck in only one truncated breath after another, unable to exhale. Finally, he breathed out but then immediately gasped for air after hearing Ismeta's pleas repeatedly echoing off the slopes of the ravine.

"It's okay. It's okay, sweetheart. It's Azra. I'm here with you."

After a few weeks, Dado began to visit. He tried to bring Jusuf back through a touch of occasional light humor, offered with tenderness—but nothing penetrated Jusuf's gloom and despair.

When Igor finished work at the coffee shop and headed home, he often stopped to sit on the front stoop outside of Azra's house. He never would knock because, as he told Azra, there was no way he could face Jusuf. He said he was sure that he would be the last person Jusuf would want to see.

"I gave him the rifle for Christ's sake. He'll never forgive me. And neither will Braco."

"Sure he will, Igor. Your gift was a gift of love."

"You know, I knew Ismeta also, not just Braco. I used to look forward to her annual summer outings for the Una Regatta when the boys were young. They always stopped at the bar. I used to flirt with her over a cup of coffee and—don't tell Jusuf—she shyly flirted back. Particularly when she was angry at Braco for not doing stuff around the house. Ismeta used to say, 'There are certain little secrets I can keep as long as you stay on that side of the counter.'"

"You're a devil, Igor," Azra said.

"You must never mention a word of this to Jusuf. There was never anything serious. We just joked around. Oh, god, why did I have to give him Braco's gun. Now I feel as though I betrayed all three of them—Braco, Jusuf, and Ismeta."

In the past, Azra smelled alcohol on Igor's breath only occasionally, but now it was every visit. She assumed he was washing away his remorse whenever the pain turned unbearable, which now was ceaseless.

Five weeks after Malik brought Jusuf back from the front lines, and for reasons no one could fathom, Azra and Dado began to see signs of improvement. She kept a little notebook about his progress and jotted down "12 March, 1994," as the day things seemed to be turning around. Jusuf started to eat somewhat regularly, although little food was available for anyone. He took short walks in the neighborhood but kept a distance from others, much like Suad used to do. He kept to the shadows and crossed the street whenever people approached.

Igor turned sixty on March 27 during an unusually early warm spell. Those who had attended Jusuf's twentieth birthday party were invited to Igor's celebration. Igor, Dado, and Aida carried a round table from the coffee shop, followed by Suljo and Ahmet, who each carried two chairs. Suljo had his now ever-present American news magazine stuffed in his back pocket, which Igor would save for him in neatly tied stacks—magazines left behind at the café by American soldiers. Suljo had been brushing up on his English, which he had studied for a semester in college. As he entered the house, he was greeted with a smile and a *hello* rather than the usual *ciao*.

There was no cake, just a bag of stale pretzels and cans of beer supplied by Igor, compliments of the Kafana Paviljon. Jusuf lasted thirty minutes before the conversation exhausted him. Azra saw his hands begin to tremble and helped him up from the table, at which point he excused himself and disappeared upstairs.

After the last pretzel was eaten, and as Ahmet and Dado shared the last beer, Suljo whispered to those assembled, "I'm amazed he's doing as well as he is. Killing your own mother is something few people can do and stay sane."

"*That's* what happened?" Zdenka exclaimed. "I thought—"

Emina put her hand over Zdenka's mouth, afraid that Jusuf would hear. "I'm sorry, everyone. I never told Zdenka exactly what happened. I thought I could spare her."

"How could he have done that?" Zdenka asked in an astonished whisper. "Why would anyone—how could anyone kill their own mother?"

Igor looked away, causing Azra to recall a phrase Igor had mentioned under his breath more than once: *my gift, her death.*

"Zdenka," Suljo began, "this is very difficult to explain to a young girl ... but war can bring out the worst in almost everyone, but sometimes also the best in just a few." He chewed his lip as he tried to figure out how to explain what Muslims almost never discussed. "I'm sure you know the word rape, Zdenka." Zdenka closed her eyes. "I think you know what that means?" She nodded and then blushed. Suljo whispered, "We don't speak of rape in this country, but it certainly happens here, whether we discuss it or not. You know how it brings deep shame to the person raped and to the family." Zdenka nodded again but showed no emotion. She kept her eyes locked on the tabletop. "Well, Serbian soldiers were about to rape Jusuf's mother. She pleaded for mercy. When Jusuf realized he couldn't kill all the soldiers who surrounded her but wanted to protect her ... well ... we figure he killed her to save her honor."

Zdenka could not swallow. She got up and buried herself in her grandmother's arms. Meanwhile, unnoticed, Jusuf now stood at the open door of an upstairs room, thinking that maybe he was feeling up to joining the group again.

After Zdenka calmed down and wiped her eyes, she turned to Suljo and said, "But I thought Jusuf has been so sad because his friend was killed."

"That's true, Zdenka," Azra said. "His friend *was* killed. The same day Jusuf shot his mother."

From the top of the steps, Jusuf screamed, "What did you say, Azra? Sasha's dead? When? Who killed him? I can't believe you didn't tell me!"

Azra hurried to the bottom of the stairs. "We were going to tell you eventually, Jusuf. Just not right away. We thought it would be too much for you all at once."

Suljo rose and walked to Azra's side. "I'd like to come up and speak with you for a minute. Azra was only trying to help."

Jusuf fell against the doorjamb and sank to the floor.

In the days following the birthday party, Azra became alarmed when Jusuf's utterances no longer hung together. His sentences ended unfinished, words were repeated three or four times in a row, and then there was silence. He slept much of the day, woke shaking, stopped going out, and cried for hours on end. His eyes were often blank, his hands trembled, and he rarely washed. Azra came into a room once and found him pricking his fingertips with a knife and sucking the drops of blood. His head rolled slowly from side to side as if he had fallen into a trance.

On the few occasions when they tried to make love, he was often limp. Azra's sigh of frustration caused Jusuf to curl in a ball and cry.

"I'm useless, Azra. Good for nothing anymore."

"Please, Jusuf. You've been through hell. I understand. Things will get better over time. We'll be patient."

Dado came to visit. Azra told him that she was growing increasingly concerned about what Jusuf was calling his *visions*. "He says he sees rivers of blood, heads of friends superimposed on the bodies of strangers. He said yesterday that he saw his mother lying lifeless in a bank of red snow, and when he looked at her birthmark, it suddenly multiplied across her face, turning her face black. And today he said he's hearing people speaking in languages he can't understand."

One night, a week later, when American jet fighters were roaring overhead against a full moon, and Azra had high hopes that the war might finally be coming to a close, Jusuf became rough with her as he lifted her legs high in the air before entering her. He slapped her thighs and buttocks, which was something she often enjoyed when he was gentle, but tonight there was a ferocity and disengagement in his actions that terrified her.

"Jusuf, you're hurting me. Please stop. Jusuf!"

Jusuf rolled off of her and began to wail and hammer the wall.

"I … I don't know what's taking hold of me, Azra. I feel like someone else has slipped inside my head, or some winged thing is flapping around and scratching at my brain. My thoughts are its thoughts, or her thoughts—not my thoughts."

Azra asked Dado and Suljo to stop by the house more frequently, fearing what Jusuf might do to her or to himself. One afternoon, Jusuf, Dado, and Azra were sitting together in the living room when a mouse crawled up the arm of the sofa that Jusuf was lying on. The mouse sniffed around and began nibbling at cracker crumbs on the pillow next to Jusuf's foot. Jusuf didn't move. The mouse, sensing no danger, climbed on Jusuf's pant leg and approached his waist. In a motion swifter than the snapping leap of a grasshopper, Jusuf swept the creature up in his palm, brought it close to his nose, and then made sweet peeping sounds with his lips. He petted the mouse's nose with the index finger of his other hand, but the mouse bit his fingertip.

"You fucker!"

He pitched the mouse full force across the room as Azra and Dado looked on in disbelief. The mouse flattened against the wall with a feeble squeak and then fell to the floor. It lay there stunned for a few seconds and then began pin-wheeling, its damaged leg unable to gain traction. After several minutes, it righted itself and vanished along a crippled path through a crack in the baseboard.

"I need to get back, Azra." Initially Azra wasn't sure whether he was referring to a place or a state of mind. But when he began speaking of digging trenches and needing to clean his rifle, she became alarmed.

Although they concealed their plan, Azra and Dado began guarding Jusuf like a prisoner to make sure he did not try to return to the ravine. He spoke of feeling crowded and caged. He walked the house at night and slept fitfully during the day. Azra found him again pricking his fingertips with a knife, and on another occasion standing in front of a closed door banging his head until it bled.

One snowy night while Azra was sleeping, Jusuf opened a window and slipped out of the house. He ran across the Blue Bridge, along the road out of Bihac, through the woods, and back in the direction of the ravine. A few days after he had returned to camp, which was a surprise to his comrades, he wandered off alone, telling Malik that he needed to think. After an hour of walking, he stopped to rest. The spring sun was intense, but it was still bitter cold. As he sat eating a few nuts that he had pocketed at home, he overheard four Serbian soldiers walking in his direction through the woods. They were laughing. One repeated the words *Muslim bitch* and bragged about how he had raped a young woman in her father's barn. When the soldiers reached a fork in the path, three of the soldiers waved good-bye to the fourth, who sat on a stump to keep watch until nightfall.

Jusuf began to rock back and forth, and when he stopped rocking, his head rolled erratically from side to side. His breathing quickened as he kept hearing *Muslim bitch, Muslim bitch* echo inside the shell of his skull. A leather-winged bird began to flap around in his brain, its talons scratching his brain, scrambling his thoughts. The fire in the bird's eyes became the fire in his.

Jusuf stood, unsheathed his knife, and ran at the soldier fast as a cougar. Surprised by the sudden ferocity of Jusuf's assault and the animal sounds scratching out of Jusuf's throat, the soldier rose and was ready to wrestle Jusuf to the ground, but his heel snagged in a root that was arching out of the snow. Jusuf fell upon him and plunged his knife into the soldier's belly. As the man grabbed for the wound, Jusuf slashed his throat. After freeing the knife's cross guard from the man's collar, Jusuf again slashed at the skin around the man's neck, cutting through muscles and tendons to the spinal cord.

Jusuf's hands kept slipping off the soldier's bloody head. In frustration, he grabbed his uniform and dragged the body to a nearby tree. He bashed the back of the soldier's neck against the trunk. The vertebrae finally snapped, allowing Jusuf to almost break off the head from the body. Using his teeth, he bit through the remaining cords and ligaments and then dropped the limp body to the ground. He stuck his thumb in the soldier's mouth and his fingers into the warm, blood-wet rags of flesh that had been the soldier's throat. After uttering a grunt, he set his arm spinning like someone about to pitch a ball. The head sailed in a high arch—a red rock with hair and eyes—sprung from a human catapult. Thin spirals of blood spun out like the nascent arms of a galaxy. The head landed with a muffled thud, the eyes staring witlessly into snow. As Jusuf stumbled away, ribbons of vapor trailed from the furnace of his skull.

Twenty minutes later, he fell to his knees. He rubbed his bloodied hands in the icy crust near his boots and then across his face as if he were washing. He rubbed with increasing ferocity. Weak and wavering, he stood up and screeched into the emptiness of the woods like an animal wounded by an inexperienced hunter. He turned in one direction, and then another, his wail returning to him in broken echoes. Bellowing until voiceless, until the spiritless void within him imploded, he finally collapsed, a sodden heap of steaming debris sprawled in the snow.

CHAPTER THIRTY

Hours later and still sprawled in the snow much like a corpse, Jusuf's right fist caked in blood slowly began to uncurl in a string of minute spasms. When he took his first deep waking breath, a crust of snow fractured and slid off of his back like two pieces of broken armor. He tried to swallow, but it felt like his tongue was forcing a mass of sand down his throat, and vapor seeping from his nostrils had formed a frozen clot of mustache hairs above his bloodied lips, making it difficult to breathe.

His hand mindlessly closed around a ball of snow as an owl landed in a nearby tree. Its head suddenly spun, yellow glass eyes focused on the rodent-sized object moving on the ground. As the owl's wings spread wide, the branch drooped, sending broken slats of snow slanting into the wind. The bird swooped into the air before contracting its wings to dive toward Jusuf's blackened hand, but suddenly seeing that the hand was connected to the body of a large creature just beginning to rise to its knees, the bird broke its dive and flew off through the trees.

Jusuf struggled to stand but felt faint. For several minutes, he swayed like a stalk in a wind gust. Eventually he extended one foot through the deep snow in a half step, and then he took a full step. He circled for a while without direction until the weight of his body yielded to the slope of the land and drew him downhill toward the River Una, three kilometers to the west.

As it grew dark, he slogged on over lumpy fields, through stands of closely spaced trees, and across frozen streams, which, like he, wound their way blindly toward lower ground. Blood coursed through his temples, sounding vaguely like an insistent pump. The fabric of his jacket and pants brushing back and forth lulled him with a relentless, hypnotic cadence, and when he crossed a treeless pasture, he realized he could keep his eyes closed for a few moments at a time and almost doze while he continued to walk.

He wandered into a cornfield. Snow-crusted stalks bent over in rows of broken arrows looked like a cemetery for fallen warriors. Several meters away, a pattern of golden lights danced like beads beneath his almost closed lids. When he walked into a fence and became snared in its wires, his eyes snapped open. He tried to step back, but the head of a rusted nail had lodged in a hole in his pants at the knee. After tugging his pants loose, he looked up and saw a building faced with curled pine shingles blackened with age. From the top of a crudely laid chimney of rounded stones, smoke and sparks whirled skyward. Five crimson rectangles a few feet above the ground glowed warmly like the eyes of a geometric campfire. As the radiating heat of the house feathered his cheeks, tiny drops of moisture began to fall from the mass of icicles that hung from his mustache.

Sounds of joy floated out of the house, and he thought he heard someone calling: *Jusuf. Jusuf.* The name sounded familiar. Jewel-like splashes of color flashed behind the curtained rectangles until he realized these were flouncy blouses and swirling dresses sailing past one window and then another. Bodies orbited a table decorated with candles and a plate piled high with sweets, and this sight brought a thread of saliva worming across Jusuf's tongue. He heard the sounds of a clarinet and a *gusle*. Women sang the Serbian folk melody that Sasha's mother often hummed. He thought he could make out her face through one of the windows. Did she have her friends over to dance the *kola* as she always did for the holidays? Stepping closer he saw a framed image of Christ hanging above a smoke-blackened fireplace and next to it, a small faded photograph of Tito in a walnut frame with something scribbled in the corner. Tito had been one of Jusuf's early heroes, but the face now held no more meaning than a family photo in the house of a stranger. Jusuf rubbed his eyes as the picture of Tito and the image of Christ began to slowly rotate and then spin wildly. He rubbed his eyes as the frames of both pictures disintegrated and flew off in different directions. The sound of splintering glass and falling frames was lost in the din of the *gusle*.

Jusuf looked into the clear night sky at a thousand pinpoints of light twinkling in silence. A cluster of stars drifted short distances away from one another until all the stars in the firmament were wandering the vast vault of Prussian blue emptiness. Growing dizzy, Jusuf spread his legs to keep from toppling over. Again he looked back through the golden rectangles and saw the women continuing to dance. He was startled when a head, laughing merrily, disengaged for an instant from the body to which it was attached. Then an arm, wrapped in a red *samija*, shifted vertically a few inches above the shoulder, and then slipped loose of the shawl and sailed across the heads of the other dancers. Jusuf blinked. Limbs floated free, some passing through the pine siding, others through windows panes. A bare arm dangled halfway between himself and the house. A wedding ring sparkled on a finger. Then a face framed with long, black braids—the one that had reminded him of Sasha's mother—froze with horror as the woman made eye contact with the darkened form standing outside the house. She too blinked, but then her face brightened, and she was carried off in a spiral of color. Jusuf looked out across the snowfield, which began moving as if it were a white blanket overlaying currents of untamed air. The blanket swirled in one direction and then another. Was it the hide of a huge white bear? He had to move, to be elsewhere, to find a place to sleep, a place to be anchored. He needed stillness—he needed to be far, far removed from this rocking house of maddening jubilation. He headed toward a stand of trees and the inviting darkness that lay beckoning beyond.

After walking for more than an hour, Jusuf saw the silhouette of a jagged pyramidal mass perched close to the edge of a cliff. He trudged through the snow, feeling as if he were dragging sacks of sand roped to his ankles. The pyramid was not the solid mass it at first appeared to be but rather the remains of two thick stonewalls set at a right angle to each other, the last remaining corner of what had once been a large hall in a fifteenth-century castle. As he approached, the truncated vestige of a stone tower loomed between him and the walls. He circled around the tower and ended in a wind-protected triangle of space that felt like a courtyard. From this vantage, he looked out and saw a river snaking through a valley far below him. He sensed he was a good distance from the enemy—and yet many kilometers from where he dimly sensed he needed to be.

Three low-lying American fighters roared overhead. Jusuf shuddered with some premonition, founded on he knew not what, that the world was about to split open. He stepped further forward into the V and collapsed onto a snow-covered pile of leaves where the two walls intersected. He burrowed into the leaves, sending two rats scurrying out of their urine-damp nest. Within minutes, he was asleep.

When the sun came up in a cloudless sky, holding promise of spring's thaw, Jusuf awoke, the nest of leaves now heaped around him clear to his neck. A brown paper bag rocked back and forth in a fickle wind on the spalling remains of a stone windowsill. The bag was folded several times as if someone had intended to return to finish a picnic. Head throbbing, Jusuf dragged himself out of the leaves, and with hands shaking uncontrollably, he incautiously ripped the bag open and sent a frozen piece of sandwich and a rock-hard hunk of pie into the snow. He dropped to his knees, recovered the remains with his blood-black hands, and tried to bite the cheese-welded crusts, but they were hard as wood. He held them under his jacket until they thawed enough to chew.

At the edge of the cliff, Jusuf looked down at a curving river that stretched to the horizon. In one of gravity's mysterious manifestations, Jusuf was lured over the edge of the cliff and drawn down in slow, cautious steps toward the river.

CHAPTER THIRTY-ONE

FOR SEVERAL WEEKS AFTER Jusuf left the house, Azra had remained confident he would soon return, healed by whatever communion he needed to take on the front lines and in the ravine where those so dear to him had perished. By mid-April, however, everyone in Bihac who had known Jusuf, including Azra and Dado, concluded he had either frozen to death, drowned, been killed, or had taken his own life. The report from the front lines that he had wandered off alone one afternoon, looking totally spiritless, supported these beliefs. Azra blamed herself for not having been more aggressive in keeping him from leaving the house in such a depressed and fragile state. She knew with certainty she would never see him again and succumbed to a pervasive hopelessness even though there were rumors that the actions of the UN, and the US, though late, were finally proving effective. The war was finally winding down.

When she watched TV in the Kafana Pavilion, whenever electricity was flowing, she saw Serbian forces withdrawing from certain areas of Bosnia and UN troops moving around with more authority. This news meant little to her. Peacetime without the man she loved was nothing but an empty quietness. She was so tired, so drained, so inured to loss, that when she thought of Jusuf and the few years they had lived together, she was no longer able to cry. The sound and sight of American jets was encouraging to many people in Bihac, but even this development failed to raise her spirits. The *blue helmets* did bring food and medicine, and those people who survived the war were out on the streets. Azra once heard Suljo say to Igor in a typically ironic observation that the situation in Bihac these days could be likened to a group of good Samaritans finally bringing to the bedside of a corpse the meal that could have saved a life had it come a day earlier.

Hoping to find food and a place to hide, Jusuf wandered back and forth along the banks of the River Una every night, looking for a place to cross and for whatever he felt might lie on the far bank. When the sun rose, he disappeared into the woods, the routine he had perfected several years earlier after his escape from the Serb truck convoy. Although his thoughts were disjointed, there remained a vestige of common sense, enough for him to know that he needed a permanent refuge of some sort, a cave perhaps that was close to people and yet separated enough to escape their questions, their judgments, and their offers of help.

At dusk one evening, he stopped behind a windowless abandoned shack by the side of a road and watched two men use a thick rope thrown over a branch to hoist the body of a goat to waist level. They stripped the hide and clove the carcass with a small hand ax and then sliced the pieces with a large butchering knife. When the body swayed and jumped in response to the assaults, it looked as if the pulsing life of the creature had not yet fully surrendered. The taut rope sang lowly at times until the men finally cut down what was left of the animal and carried off the cookable parts in blood-splattered, white plastic tubs. Jusuf, who had watched his father slaughter animals in their backyard, waited a good while until he was certain no one was watching and then darted across the road. Trembling with anticipation born from intense hunger, he scraped clusters of fat, blood, and slivers of viscera from the grass using the heel of his hands and smeared them on his tongue. The greasy clots tasted like a sweet and salty delicacy, so he kneeled again and scooped up another handful of pinkish slime off the grass. A door slammed. Jusuf quickly scurried off like a nocturnal animal, half-crouching, running sideways, his head tilted and rotating this way and that to see both in front of him and behind, sensing that the two butchers could readily circle around the house for another kill.

An hour before dawn the following day, he left the banks of the Una and walked across the Blue Bridge, its post lights still burning.

Following a dim instinct, he headed for the familiar-looking coffee house at the end of the bridge. After striding across the gravel terrace and realizing he was alone, he sat down at one of the café tables. He was sure he had crossed that bridge before, but his memories were as turbulent and fleeting as the waters that raced beneath the bridge's blue girders.

Akin to the force that had brought Suad's pigeons back to their roost, some internal magnet had brought Jusuf back to the threshold of the Kafana Paviljon. This spot had been his first refuge once before, but this time he expected nothing and wanted nothing. He looked over the railing at the river, at the boat-shaped islands downstream, at the water tumbling over half-submerged rocks. As the sky began to show a faint trace of daylight, Jusuf stood and walked to the fountain. He pressed a finger through the thin skin of ice and then lowered his face to drink. He looked through the windows under the porch and saw that all was dark inside except for a small red light on the TV.

On his way back to the chair, he saw it. The thing looked at first like a section of sewer pipe, nine feet long and about four feet in diameter. It was smooth and slightly darker than concrete. Five days earlier, UN forces had removed their supplies from the thick plastic container but had not yet returned to claim the tube. One end was rounded like a cigar tin; the other end, open like a culvert. A canvas tarpaulin was left just inside the opening, half-obscuring a view further in. When it started to drizzle, Jusuf pushed aside the tarp, crawled into the tube, repositioned the tarp, and crab-walked back to the concave end. He fell asleep, a pupa near dead in its own cocoon.

When he awoke, he heard a confusion of muffled voices through the thick plastic walls. Propped up as one would lie in bed reading, head raised, he peered over the top of the tarp and saw only boots and sneakers crunching by on the gravel. He also saw a tangle of café table legs and spindly chair legs. An hour later, the drizzle ended, and the sun began to shine with heat that radiated through the tube's thick gray wall.

Later the next day, Azra and Dado stopped by the Paviljon for a beer. They sat at one of the tables near the railing and spoke of times past. Dado knew to avoid any mention of Jusuf, particularly in public. It was pleasure enough for them to spend a few minutes together on this cool spring day without fear of sniper fire and artillery bombardments. UN vehicles roared across the bridge in both directions. There was also a reassuring trickle of civilian vehicles with horns beeping and a steady stream of small trucks with much-needed supplies.

From time to time, Dado looked over at the gray tube, wondering how long the thing would have to sit there. With life coming back to Bihac and businesses beginning to see activity once again, he felt the tube was too much a reminder of war and would hurt business. He was thoroughly tired of a devastating conflict that seemed to last a lifetime.

Jusuf stared at the painted letters he could see through the gray translucent plastic: *HiB cahiB* on one wall; and opposite it on the wall that faced the bridge, *NU enoZ efaS*. Not only were the words sequenced in reverse and in an unfamiliar language, but from the interior, the letters were also reversed. Although incapable of formulating the thought, he nevertheless sensed he had fallen into a psychological abyss so deep and muddled there was no way he could ever scale its slopes. The cryptic message on the curving walls of his new home confirmed he was so far removed from the world he had known that he could never return.

It was only late at night that Jusuf felt safe enough to push aside the heap of tarpaulin and crawl out of the tube. He immediately rushed with a stiff hobble to pee or defecate in the bushes. Then he poked through the trashcans behind the Paviljon looking for food scraps and sips of beer and soda remaining in countless crushed cans and sticky bottles. Occasionally he found a cigarette worth saving, but he had no matches. He stored the cigarettes in a small green tin that had been dropped near the bridge by a UN soldier. The name *Aeron* was printed on the top with a black marker. Jusuf kept the container in the nest he was building at the back of the tube, along with other things he found: bottles, newspapers, a pin, a ring, a picnic plate, a bundle of plastic bubble-wrap, a new brass key. These lost or discarded items provided a sense of domestic comfort for a few days until violent spring winds began to howl out of the north one morning and spun the tube on its bed of gravel. The feeling of being cut loose from his only mooring scared him and made him sob. Sometimes he clenched his teeth, closed his eyes, brought his knees up to his chin, and covered his ears, retreating into the caterwauling crackle of the bubble wrap that, if nothing else, muffled the maddening sound of the tube scraping the gravel as it rotated first in one direction and then another. In the middle of the night, when the city was asleep, he took to mumbling over and over: *s'il vous plait, s'il vous plait, s'il vous plait, s'il vous plait.* Sasha and he had heard the phrase in a French movie and uttered it for weeks thereafter whenever they greeted each other.

He kept food scraps in a large, white paper bag at the back of the tube. It wasn't long before his space was filled with the stench of garbage. This smell, mixed with Jusuf's body odor, seeped like some form of bait from the open end of the tube. Squirrels, pigeons, and mice by day, and rats by night, ran close by the container's foul-smelling mouth. Some creatures would stop and peer in when the tarp had flattened slightly. Initially, Jusuf just stared back and hissed. But after a few days, he came to look forward to these small silent visitors. Pigeon heads bobbed drunkenly as they peered dumbly toward the back of the tube, one eye staring at the thing at the far end while their feet scratched gravel for fallen food bits.

One morning, Jusuf crawled forward with a food morsel and left it just inside the mouth of the tube. It attracted an old squirrel that whipped and twitched its tail with fear and curiosity. This was followed by a clicking sound like a rod drawn across grooves in a gourd. Jusuf tried to imitate the clicks with his tongue. On Jusuf's fifth try, the squirrel took three small hops into the tube, whipped its tail again, surveyed the motionless heap of clothing, and picked up the morsel with its front feet. It nibbled for a moment and then scrambled out with the scrap between its teeth.

In the days that followed, Jusuf lured the squirrel deeper into the tube and eventually enticed it to eat out of his hand. During one visit, the squirrel anxiously rubbed its greasy cheeks on Jusuf's knuckles, perhaps to clean them, perhaps to reveal a level of trust. This became a habit with the squirrel, eating out of Jusuf's hand, wiping its cheeks on his cracked gray knuckles. It did not run off the day Jusuf ever so gently petted its silver head with the back of his index finger. After eating, the squirrel usually looked directly into Jusuf's eyes, and Jusuf looked back.

For several days, the Paviljon was closed to the public; its interior was finally receiving a coat of fresh paint. During this period, Jusuf could barely find scraps for himself and was left with nothing to share with the squirrel. When the squirrel realized the supply of treats had ended, it stopped coming. Jusuf's mood sank. He assumed the squirrel had been hit on the road, died of old age, or decided to nest elsewhere, where the food supply was more reliable. When the squirrel finally reappeared at the mouth of the tube, it seemed to be on a mission. It tentatively scampered back and forth, in and out of the tube, each time approaching Jusuf more closely, and then finally gathered the courage to sit next to Jusuf's thigh. It coughed a small nut from its cheek onto the floor of the tube. Jusuf turned the nut over in his fingers, and then brought it to his nose, and then to his lips. The squirrel watched him drop the nut on the tip of his tongue and crunch it between his teeth. The squirrel's tail curled and fussed.

Early one day in May, Jusuf went down to the river to relieve himself. He looked up when he heard numerous calls to prayer droning from nearby minarets, coarse but comforting sounds he hadn't heard in many, many months. Three girls were strolling arm-in-arm across the Blue Bridge. They giggled and waved to soldiers in UN vehicles that were appearing more frequently in and around Bihac. One of the girls noticed Jusuf climbing up the riverbank. She pointed in his direction and ran with the other girls to the railing to watch his ascent until he disappeared around the side of the Kafana Paviljon.

The next day, Igor, having heard about the girls' encounter with a dark and ragged stranger, pushed aside the tarp and peered into the tube. He wondered whether someone, a refugee perhaps, was hiding in the tube or even living there. It took a moment before Igor's eyes grew accustomed to the murky shadows. When Jusuf's hand came up in a gesture not of greeting but as a signal to proceed no further, Igor, mouth agape, exclaimed, "Oh my god. You're alive! Oh my dear god!" He turned and ran to tell Azra.

"Don't play with me, Igor. I know he's dead. Maybe the guy just looks like Jusuf. Maybe—"

"It is Jusuf. I'm certain."

"Are you *absolutely* sure? I can't take another …"

She broke off midsentence, tossed some food in a bag, and filled a jar with lukewarm coffee. She ran ahead of Igor, heart racing, hoping it was Jusuf but preparing herself once again for disappointment. When she stooped to look in the tube and saw him sprawled amid his mess of belongings, she thought back to the day she first saw him walk into the Kafana Paviljon. But today his eyes appeared to look through her, his posture in total surrender. Clearly he was looking not at her, the woman he had loved, but at a familiar-looking stranger. She hammered the rim of the tube with her fist and wept.

"Why is God doing this to me? Haven't I had enough?"

She sat at a table and stared at the tube. Igor arrived panting heavily and sat down next to her.

"He didn't see me! Or didn't want to see me. I think he's truly gone for good. He'll die in there for sure."

"I know you want him back with you right away, but the man has been through hell twice over. You have to give him time. Patience is what he needs ... and what you need as well."

"But I want him now, Igor. I so want him right now! And he needs me to look after him, to bring him back to life."

"Give him a little more time. Perhaps time and love will heal him. I have to hope it will."

Azra picked up her care package off the gravel and set it on the empty chair to her right. Igor said, "May I?" He walked to the tube and set the bag on top of the tarpaulin.

Every day thereafter, she, Dado, Igor, and their friends stopped by the tube to leave things for Jusuf. They had the good sense—and were advised likewise by a few of Azra's physician friends—not to speak to him, not to try to get him to speak. She cried every night, longing to have Jusuf back in her life, longing to feed him and bathe him and clothe him and touch him.

About ten days after Jusuf had first been discovered, a contingent of NATO vehicles arrived at the café with a crane and a flatbed truck. Soldiers milled around, sipping coffee and waiting for orders. One of them called into the open end of the container for Jusuf to come out. When the soldier stood, he swatted the air to clear his nostrils of the stench.

Word quickly spread through the neighborhood that the tube was about to be removed. Within minutes, Igor, Azra, Dado, Aida, and several other friends encircled the tube with locked arms. Igor yelled to the young soldier who had climbed up to operate the crane. "There's a guy in there that's been through hell like you can't imagine. He needs a few more days to pull himself together. Can't you guys come back next week?"

"Listen, buddy, I don't know what the hell you just said, and I don't care who the fuck is in that container. I got orders. The tube is coming with us—with him in it or not. Now all you folks stand back. This thing's got to get back to the depot."

Moments earlier, Suljo and Ahmet had arrived with a tray piled high with bread, fruit, coffee, nuts, cigarettes, and a few steaming *cicccici*. When Suljo saw what was about to happen, he handed the tray to Ahmet and walked briskly over to the soldiers, asking in his practiced but not yet fluent English to speak to the commanding officer.

"So, it looks like we've got a problem here."

"We do indeed," said the officer.

"I guess you know there's a man living in that thing."

"Yes, it was just brought to my attention."

"The guy that's in there has been through a lot. If he's alive at all, it's just barely. Any chance you could give us a few days to see if his situation improves?"

"My orders are to get the container back to base today."

"I appreciate your circumstances, but we've really got an unusual case here."

"Unusual? Can't you or one of his friends just drag the guy out of there? I'd hate for one of our guys to have to go in to do it."

"I'd like to ask a personal favor."

"I'm listening," the officer said as he sighed impatiently.

"Can we speak in private for a moment? I'd prefer not to share his history in earshot of everyone. How about that bench across the street?"

"I got ten minutes." The soldier glanced at his watch and motioned to the crane operator to idle the engine.

Azra said to Dado, "What'll we do if he doesn't convince him? This could get messy."

"If things look bad, I'll go in and try to get him out, and then we'll do what we did when the war was just starting. We'll walk him back to your house. We did it once; we can do it again."

The soldiers continued to mill around, sipping coffee, smoking, and following with their eyes the young women that were coming and going across the bridge. Laughter erupted from time to time. After five minutes, Suljo and the officer got up, their expressions serious. Suljo offered the officer a cigarette. He declined. Not a word was spoken on their way back to the tube. Then after pressing his lips together in serious thought, the officer pointed to the black stenciling on the side of the container. *Bihac – BiH ... Safe Zone – UN.*

"I guess when orders conflict, the decision becomes mine."

Suljo looked the officer in the eye and then reached out and shook his hand. "Thanks."

The officer turned on his heel and addressed the men in his unit. "We're coming back for this in a day or two. Let's move out."

Later that afternoon, Azra went back and kneeled just outside the tarpaulin. She knew she was wrong, even selfish, but she pleaded with Jusuf to look at her, to say something.

"I'm so alone, Jusuf. You have no idea. You *must* try to come back to me; I'll stay by your side forever. You can't imagine how deeply I miss you, how deeply I love you." Jusuf raised his hand but did not close his eyes. He squinted and tilted his head, and then his eyes closed.

"Do I mean nothing to you anymore? Do you not even see who I am? They're going to come back for this thing soon. Do you hear me?" Totally frustrated, she beat the top of the tube as tears rolled down her face. "Damn it, do you even hear me?"

She got up and ran to the middle of the Blue Bridge, hoping that one final burst of sniper fire from the hills would end her wait, end her loneliness, end her despair. She walked to the railing and looked down at the water rushing under the bridge.

"Please, God. Help me. I've had enough. You must make him listen. I want him back."

CHAPTER THIRTY-TWO

Two boys playing near the river wandered over to the tube and began stoning it and beating it with sticks. They had heard the story of the man holed up within.

"You killed your mother!" they taunted. "How could you kill your own mother? You're a dirty man. You're sick and bad."

Jusuf covered his ears and hummed loudly until the boys left.

Several days later, a bicycle skidded to a halt in front of the Kafana Pavilion. A pair of phosphorescent sneakers appeared just outside the mouth of the tube. Above the sneakers, green-striped pajama bottoms. Dado knelt, pushed aside the tarp, and slid a package wrapped in cardboard onto the floor of the tube. Without even a hello or a look into the rear of the tube, he rode away.

A day passed before Jusuf thought to open the package. He pulled off the rubber bands, peeled away the cardboard, and gazed at two objects that made his eyes twitch. There was a cherry-framed case with a glass front. The case was filled with butterflies looking like a collection of colorful jewels, all aligned in rows against a creamy silk background. Pinned in their exquisite tomb, the butterflies brought back to Jusuf a vague and fleeting memory. He remembered a wall of similar cases hanging in someone's home.

An envelope was taped to the glass. Jusuf opened the envelope and looked at a small photograph of a woman, smiling, a small leaf-shaped birthmark on her right cheekbone. An unfamiliar pulse coursed through his chest and his eyes felt heavy. Another photo was of the same woman with a headscarf standing in front of a mosque. Jusuf stared at the photographs and chewed the inside of his lip. Her eyes, which he sensed he had seen before, seemed to speak. The words were many, but not clear, as if they were being written on the surface of a flowing stream. And he thought he also heard a voice floating somewhere in uncertain space, a soothing voice that gave him a sense of peace.

There was also a photo of a man in faded brown overalls, striding proudly in a parade and carrying a tattered communist flag stapled to a broom handle. The man was short with gray hair. He too looked like someone Jusuf had known. There was also a photo of two small boys playing in a wheat field.

The last two photographs were larger. They were color prints and not at all faded. One was of several peopled huddled around a table facing a young man with a finger-wide beard on his chin. A strangely shaped cake with two candles sat on the table in front of him. Jusuf's chest tightened. The other photo was of a young man and a young woman, the man appearing to be the fellow in the previous photo. The woman had a blaze of bronze hair. They stood laughing and hugging by the side of a road. In front of them was a man their age wearing an orange plastic hat. Jusuf stared at the picture with the two men and the woman. His breathing fell out of rhythm. He slid his finger slowly across the woman's face and the face of the vaguely familiar stranger standing beside her. He had seen her face recently; it was a face he had seen before. She appeared to be looking out through the surface of the photograph directly into his eyes. He knew those eyes. If he waited long enough, he thought, those eyes also would eventually speak to him. He tilted his head as the muscles in his chest began to relax.

That evening, Azra walked back to the Kafana Pavilion alone. There was a mild breeze. In each hand, she held a potted plant, or rather the barely living residue of a plant—the one in her right hand consisted of a dry stem with a single leaf. The other plant had a few leaves, but they were small and curled. She set the plants down about a meter from the mouth of the tube and walked home.

The following day, Jusuf was awakened by a commotion coming from what sounded like the roof of the Kafana Pavilion. He duck-footed forward out of the tube and saw two crows fighting for a footing atop the finial that rose from the tip of the café's curving roof. Each pecked at the other's beak and tried to claim the perch with loud raspy caws. Both were determined to claim the finial. The bird that circled the one now astride the perch eventually tired and flew off. The triumphant bird elevated itself proudly on straightened legs, flapped its wings a few times, and then caught the wind and sailed off in a sweeping circle in search of its mate.

Jusuf walked to the railing and watched the crows fly above the treetops. They flew side by side in a line that followed the ridge of Grmec Mountain, and then they unexpectedly dove in unison, sweeping low just above the rapids of the River Una. They floated effortlessly on outstretched wings, the tips nearly touching. Like paired warplanes, they flew under the bridge's blue girders and then soared upward high into the sky in a glorious wide curve.

Jusuf watched the birds as they sailed off and then returned his gaze to the piers that supported the girders. The splashing river had glazed the smooth concrete piers, permitting a reflection of the riverbank a few meters downstream. In the reflection, Jusuf saw the place where he and the others had buried Suad. Suad appeared like a mirage, his torso materializing in the darkness under the roadbed. Jusuf remembered the first time he saw Suad coming from the darkness of his tool shed, poised on the threshold of the kitchen door, immobilized by whatever fears and shame kept him from entering the room. It seemed as if Suad, now hovering ghostlike under the bridge, was trying to come out of the shadows, trying to summon the courage to move into the light. Or was it that Suad was urging Jusuf to come into the light and not return to the shadows of the tube?

Jusuf walked back to the Kafana Paviljon and noticed the potted plants next to the plastic tube that had been his home. He walked over, squatted, and felt the soil. He found a plastic cup lying sideways on one of the tables and walked to the fountain. The water pouring over the hard, dry soil squeaked and softly whistled as it found thin threads of air through which the water percolated down through the wanting roots.

Then he rose and walked back to the fountain and its arching jets.

Using his forefinger, he touched the cold water and then lowered his palm into the basin, holding it just above the dancing surface. One of the wobbly jets washed across the back of his hand. At first, the layer of dirt—his second skin—did not yield. Then he brought the thumb of his other hand to the spot where the jet was splashing and rubbed it to see if the grime was everlasting. Like a stubborn smudge of graphite finally yielding to an eraser, the dirt began to wash away beneath the pulsing jet. In time, a round patch of clean skin was revealed, pallid, almost a sickly shade of white, but clean.

Acknowledgments

Some—maybe most—writers of fiction, work in isolation, sharing their story with no one until it's finished. That's not my style. From the very outset I was interested in people's reaction to the tale that I was searching to discover and trying to shape. Because I'm an architect-turned-writer, there was much I had to learn about writing fiction from both lay readers and professional advisors. There was also lots of information I had to obtain through email exchanges and phone calls with those in Bosnia (and elsewhere) who lived through the war or who worked in uniform to keep the peace. So while this is entirely my writing, its informational and emotional roots go deep through friends, acquaintances, and total strangers. Although this novel is positively not the product of writing-by-committee, I still wish to record as many names as I can remember of people who helped me in ways large and small. I apologize to those I've overlooked or forgotten over the sixteen years of giving birth to this story. For some people, I have only email tags or first names; I wish I had more. Importantly, my failings in this work are mine alone; but recognition for whatever success I achieved in forging a compelling read is to be shared with those noted below. Lastly, the views indirectly expressed in this novel are attributable only to me, but I hope they contribute to an appreciation of what we give up when violent conflict turns lives inside out or, more regrettably, takes them away forever.

Aaron Levinson
Aeron
Aida Pasalic
Alan Heffner
Alen M
Alen Pasalic
Alexis Barad
Alma Smajic Bico
A. M. Blumenthal
Amanda Lippert
Amir
Amra Sabic-El-Rayess
Amy Baker
Amy Quenzer
Andrew Glendinning
Ann Dubuisson
Arijana S
Azra Hromadzic
Barbara Westvig
Barry Dinerman
Bill Blades
Bill Clegg
Bill Kent
Bob Cohen
Bob Novick
Bruce Ditnes
Budo Keranovic
C. Allen
Carol Freundlich
Carol Isard
Carol Moore
Caroline Paul
Caryl Levinson
Chris Linn
Chuck Sudetic
Claudia Mathe
Craig Lord
Cynthia
David Gunter
David Kniffen
Deborah Krupp
Denis Ronca
Dinka Majanovic
Drew Glendinning

Elaine Simone
Elizabeth Day
Eric Simonoff
Francesco Salvi
George Nedeff
Gregory Welsh
Hajrudin Hromadzic
Henryk Hoffmann
Hugh Maher
Igor Ibradzic
Ingrid Harris
Irving Seldin
Ivan Kavalesky
Ivan Miloradovic
James Rahn
Janet Thomas
Jerry Roseman
Joan Adelman
Joan Farkas
Joel Shupack
John Todd
Josh Kramer
Julie Levinson
Kate Churi
Kathleen M.
Kathy Foley
Krista Zimmer
Kunal Joarder
Kyoko Makino
Laura Uffner
Lejla Ibrahimpasic
Lyne Harmon
Margaret McLean Daly
Marie
Marsha Kramer
Martin Lozanoff
Mary Smith
Matt Moresco
Merrill Furman
Michael Berlin
Michael Papa
Michael Sells
Miriam Camitta
Mirnes

Nadir
Nancy Ginter
Parisa Abdollahi
Pat Collins
Pat Ligouri
Pat Nestler
Paul Harmon
Phil Schulman
Ramesh Churi
Raphael Villamil
Richard Lyntton
Rick Homan
Rick Josiassen
Rita Shaughnessy
Rob Fleming
Robert Brasler
Russell Vanderboom
Sabina de Rochefort
Sal Salazar
Samir
Sanela Pecenkovic
Sara Celello
Sara Robbins
Sean O'Neill
Selma
Sheri-Ann Lebowitz
Steve Hershey
Steve Purcell
Stuart Calderwood
Susan Wortman
Suzanne Bryla
Suzanne Garland
Tim Marcuson
Tom Jenks
Traci Ginnona
Traci Law
Vicky Villamil
Vildana Dupanovic
Werner Thurau
Zlatko Pasalic

PRONUNCIATION GUIDE

Ahmet	Aah-met
Azra	Ahz-rah
Begovic	Beh-go-vich
Bihac	Bee-hahtch
Braco	Braht-so
Dado	Dah-do
Deutchemarks	Doytch-marks
Drinic	Drin-ich
Hijro	Hi-row
Ibro	Ee-bro
Igor	Ee-gor
Ismeta	Iz-meta
Jusuf	You-suf
Jussie	Yoo-see
Kafana Paviljon	Kah-fahn-a Pa-vil-yon
Kapetanovic	Kap-eh-ta-novich
Kljuc	Klootsch
Lejla	Lay-la
Miloradovic	Mil-or-ahh-do-vich
Mirko	Meer-ko
Mladen	Mlah-den
Nadiya	Naad-jah
Pasalic	Pah-shal-ich
Prekounje	Pre-koun-yea
Sabanovic	Sah-bahn-o-vich
Suad	Soo-ahd
Umerovic	U-mer-o-vich
Zarif	Zahr-if

THE RELUCTANT HUNTER
BY JOEL LEVINSON

BOOKMARK

The Reluctant Hunter is Joel Levinson's first novel. It is based in part on brief accounts of the Bosnian War described by his "adopted" Bosnian daughter, Aida, and her secular Muslim refugee friends who came to the United States from their hometown of Bihac through the auspices of *The Community of Bosnia*. Levinson is an architect-turned-author. He has written articles about design and related issues throughout his career; his designs, produced over a forty-year career, are preserved by the Architectural Archives of the University of Pennsylvania.